OUR
LITTLE
SECRET

Books by Lisa Jackson

Stand-Alones

SEE HOW SHE DIES
FINAL SCREAM
RUNNING SCARED
WHISPERS
TWICE KISSED
UNSPOKEN
DEEP FREEZE
FATAL BURN
MOST LIKELY TO DIE
WICKED GAME
WICKED LIES
SOMETHING WICKED
WICKED WAYS
WICKED DREAMS
SINISTER
WITHOUT MERCY
YOU DON'T WANT TO
   KNOW
CLOSE TO HOME
AFTER SHE'S GONE
REVENGE
YOU WILL PAY
OMINOUS
BACKLASH
RUTHLESS
ONE LAST BREATH
LIAR, LIAR
PARANOID
ENVIOUS
LAST GIRL STANDING
DISTRUST
ALL I WANT FROM SANTA
AFRAID
THE GIRL WHO SURVIVED
GETTING EVEN
DON'T BE SCARED
OUR LITTLE SECRET

Cahill Family Novels

IF SHE ONLY KNEW
ALMOST DEAD
YOU BETRAYED ME

**Rick Bentz/
Reuben Montoya Novels**

HOT BLOODED
COLD BLOODED
SHIVER
ABSOLUTE FEAR
LOST SOULS
MALICE
DEVIOUS
NEVER DIE ALONE
THE LAST SINNER

**Pierce Reed/
Nikki Gillette Novels**

THE NIGHT BEFORE
THE MORNING AFTER
TELL ME
THE THIRD GRAVE

**Selena Alvarez/
Regan Pescoli Novels**

LEFT TO DIE
CHOSEN TO DIE
BORN TO DIE
AFRAID TO DIE
READY TO DIE
DESERVES TO DIE
EXPECTING TO DIE
WILLING TO DIE

Published by Kensington Publishing Corp.

LISA JACKSON

OUR LITTLE SECRET

KENSINGTON
PUBLISHING CORP.

www.kensingtonbooks.com

KENSINGTON BOOKS are published by

Kensington Publishing Corp.
900 Third Avenue
New York, NY 10022

All Kensington titles, imprints, and distributed lines are available at special quantity discounts for bulk purchases for sales promotion, premiums, fundraising, educational, or institutional use.

Special book excerpts or customized printings can also be created to fit specific needs. For details, write or phone the office of the Kensington Special Sales Manager: Attn. Special Sales Department. Kensington Publishing Corp., 900 Third Avenue, New York, NY 10022. Phone: 1-800-221-2647.

The K with book logo Reg. U.S. Pat. & TM. Off.

Library of Congress Control Number: 2024932262

ISBN: 978-1-4967-3701-4

First Kensington Hardcover Edition: July 2024

ISBN: 978-1-4967-4918-5 (trade)
ISBN: 978-1-4967-3702-1 (ebook)

10 9 8 7 6 5 4 3 2 1

Printed in the United States of America

PART ONE

CHAPTER 1

Seattle, Washington
October 2022

"How far would you go?"

Gideon's words stopped Brooke short. She was already late and she felt the seconds ticking by. Turning in the small cabin of his sailboat, she found him where she'd left him, lying on his bed, his tanned body entangled in the sheets, dark hair falling over his forehead.

"What do you mean?"

He pushed himself upward, levering on an elbow, muscles visible beneath his tanned skin, gray eyes assessing. As if he knew. Outside a seagull cried, and she caught its image flying past masts of neighboring sailboats, then skimming over the gray waters of the bay.

Tell him. Get it over with. End this now!

"For something you wanted," he said, and he wasn't smiling. "How far would you go?"

"I don't know." She finger combed her tousled hair, then started for the short flight of stairs leading to the deck. "Pretty far, I guess." She glanced at her watch. "Look, I really have to go."

Tell him.

"Wait." He rolled off the bed, and she noticed his tattoo, a small octopus inked at his nape, barely visible when his hair grew long. He caught her wrist, spinning her back to face him. A little over six feet, he was lean and fit, his skin bronzed from hours in the sun. "Why don't you ask me?" he said and he leaned down to touch his forehead to hers. His fingertips moved against the inside of her wrist and his pupils darkened a bit. *Tell him!* that damned inner voice insisted. *Tell him now!*

"Ask you?"

"How far I'd go."

Her heart started beating a little quicker, his fingers so warm, the boat rocking slightly under her feet. "Okay," she said, and hated the whispery tone of her voice. "Okay. How far would you go?"

"For something I wanted? For the person I was supposed to be with?" His gaze locked with hers and the breath caught in the back of her throat. The walls of the boat's tiny cabin seemed to shrink, and for a heartbeat it was as if they were the only two people on earth. He leaned close and whispered in her ear, "I would do anything." She swallowed hard.

He repeated, "*Any*thing."

"Anything?" She couldn't keep the skepticism from her voice.

His gaze held hers. "If I had to, I would kill."

Seattle traffic was a nightmare.

And she was late.

Of course.

Not only had she chickened out and not told Gideon that what they'd shared for the past few months was over, she was running late. Again.

"Come on, come on," she said, as much to herself as to the other drivers in the snarl of vehicles clogging the streets. She drove her SUV through the knots of vehicles, slipping from one lane to another, then turning her Explorer onto a steep side street, hoping to avoid the crush heading to the freeway.

"Come on, come on," she muttered as she caught up with a huge red pickup that inched forward. She glanced at the clock on the dash. She was supposed to be at the school in five minutes. At this rate it would take an hour! She pounded on the horn just as they reached a construction site.

The pickup, laden with a load of cordwood, eased past the orange cones guarding a wide hole in the asphalt as a bearded construction worker held up a stop sign. Though his eyes were shielded by aviator sunglasses, he glared at her through the windshield, daring her to try to slip past.

She didn't. Waited. Impatiently drummed her fingers on the steering wheel while a monstrous backhoe, alarm beeping, backed into the street, then moved forward. It was a warm day for October in Seattle, sunlight streaming through her dusty windshield. And the backhoe seemed to inch its way across the street.

"Oh, come on!"

She wouldn't make it.

Especially now.

Great.

"Damn."

She picked up her cell phone and texted her daughter: **Running late. On my way.**

How many times had she typed in those exact words and sent them to Marilee? At least once a week, often times more. Especially recently.

Marilee, all of fourteen, no, wait, "almost fifteen," would be pissed.

So what else was new?

Spewing exhaust, the backhoe inched forward, a hefty driver working levers to scrape up huge chunks of concrete and asphalt. In what seemed like slow motion, he swung his bucket high into the air, then tilted it to pour his load into the box of a massive, idling dump truck.

The minutes ticked by before the backhoe started moving out of the street and into an alley.

"Finally."

Her cell phone rang. Startling her.

Then she realized it wasn't her cell, not the one registered on her family plan with Neal and Marilee but her other phone. The burner. Not connected to her Bluetooth. The secret phone no one knew about. No one but Gideon. She flipped open the console, scraped out the bottom of the small space, and found the burner. Yanking it from its hiding space, she glanced at the screen.

She didn't recognize the number.

"What the hell?"

She answered abruptly, her foot easing up on the brake. "Hello."

A pause.

Her SUV started rolling forward.

"Hello?" she said sharply again.

The street cleared and the flagger turned his sign from Stop to Slow.

A rough, whispered voice was barely audible over the rumble of engines and shouts of men on the work crew. "He's not who you think he is."

"What?" she said, straining to hear. "Who's not—who is this?"

The call disconnected.

Her heart sank. Someone knew! Oh God, she'd been found out.

She blinked, staving off a panic attack. No one was supposed to know. No one did. Of course no one did. The call had to be a mistake. Someone who had punched in the wrong numbers. That was it. Sweat began to moisten her fingers and she mentally kicked herself for not having the guts to break it off earlier. She hadn't even found the courage to tell him today.

"Chickenshit," she grumbled. "Coward."

The flagger was motioning her through, frantically waving his arm, but her mind was on the message. What if it wasn't a wrong number? What if someone knew? Oh God.

She stepped on the gas, her heart pounding, her pulse pounding in her ears.

This couldn't be happening—From the corner of her eye, she saw a blur of yellow, a sports car speeding around her, cutting her off.

"Jesus!" she cried, nearly standing on the brakes as the disgusted workman kept waving her through, though he gave the yellow car a shake of his head.

But the Porsche was already through the construction zone and caught at the next light. "Idiot!" she muttered under her breath, driving forward, hoping to make the light as it started to turn green.

The burner jangled again.

What the hell?

The same unknown number showed on the screen.

Oh. God.

She answered sharply. "I don't know who you are, but you've got the wrong number!"

A pause, and then the whispered voice: "I don't think so, Brooke."

The caller knew her name?

"Who is this?" she demanded, frantic. Oh no, no, no . . .

"He's not who you think he is." The voice—male? Female? Old? Young? She couldn't tell. "You'd better be careful—"

Bam!

The front end of her Explorer slammed into the back of the sports car with a horrendous crunch of metal and plastic.

Her body jerked.

The seat belt snapped hard.

"Shit!" She hit the brakes, dropped the phone, her pulse shooting to the stratosphere.

The Porsche screeched to a stop.

The car behind her—a white boat of a thing with an elderly man at the wheel, his wife beside him—stopped within an inch of plowing into her. The driver looked up, startled. In front of her, the guy in the damaged Porsche jumped out of his car and strode to her window.

"What the fuck?" he yelled, his face all kinds of red, his jeans and black T-shirt faded and worn over a large, burly frame.

As she rolled down her window a little further, he yanked the hat from his head and threw the Mariners cap onto the pavement. "You fuckin' hit my car!"

Her mind was racing, her breathing shallow. "You started to go, then stopped."

"So what? You're supposed to have control of your vehicle. You hit me, lady!" He jerked a hand toward the curb. "And if you'd been paying attention, you would have noticed, a kid—that kid—was playing with a ball near the curb!" He stabbed a finger at the boy—four or five years old from the looks of him—staring at them with wide, frightened eyes. "The ball rolled into the street," the driver explained and she peeked past his angry body to see a basketball still rolling slowly on the pavement in front of a stopped van in the opposite lane. "I thought the kid might run after it. Jesus, what are you? A fuckin' moron?"

There was no way to deny it. When she looked to the near side of the street, she saw an older woman dragging the kid into an apartment house.

"You're just damned lucky he didn't chase the fuckin' thing!" The driver was still ranting. "Cuz if he did? And I didn't hit him? You sure the hell would have."

Her heart knocked painfully. He was right. She'd been so distracted by the phone call, by Gideon, by all of her messed-up life that she hadn't been paying attention. At least not enough attention.

But it would be fine—just some twisted metal. Nothing more. Nothing life-threatening. Thank God.

She peered up at him. "Are you okay?"

"Do I look okay?" he demanded, his bald head glistening in the sunlight, wraparound sunglasses hiding his eyes. Beneath a two- or three-days' growth of beard, a muscle in his jaw was working overtime.

"I don't know."

"Well, I'm not. Thanks to you. And my car! Shit, I just got the temporary plates removed! Brand-new and now—Now? Fuck!" He stripped off his sunglasses and looked about to throw them as he had the cap, then thought better of it and pushed the mirrored shades back onto the bridge of his nose. "Do you know what this is?" he said, jabbing a finger at his car. "Do you?" Before she could answer, he filled her in. "It's a fuckin' Nine-eleven! Did you hear me? A fuckin' Nine-eleven."

"Got it!" she shot back, her temper spiking. She gritted her teeth and tried to remain calm, even though this jerkwad was punching all of her buttons and her nerves were frayed to the breaking point.

The man in the white behemoth of a sedan had stepped onto the street. "We saw the whole thing," he shouted from behind the open car door. "If anyone needs a witness. Aggie and I saw it all." He motioned toward his wife, sitting stiffly on the passenger side of his Buick.

"Are you all right?" Brooke asked, yelling out her open window as other cars eased past them. "And your wife?"

"Yeah, yeah, we're both fine," the old guy said, flapping a hand. *Thank God.*

To the angry driver, she said, "I think maybe we'd better pull over," noting the crowd that had gathered on the edge of the street. "Get each other's information."

"Fuckin' A," he said. "You're goddamned right we're going to do that! You're fuckin' gonna pay for this!" He motioned to his car before jabbing a finger at her face. "This is on you." Then he yanked his phone from his pocket, snapped a picture of her Explorer's license plate before motioning jerkily to the parking lot of a strip mall across the street. "Over there," he ordered.

He swiped his cap from the street and jammed it onto his head. As he climbed into his car, he shot her a look guaranteed to cut through steel.

"Ass," she said under her breath and watched as he rammed his sports car into gear before roaring across a lane of traffic to nearly bottom out as he hit a speed bump in the parking lot.

Served him right. Yeah, she was at fault, but the guy was being a jerk about it. She slid her Explorer into a parking slot in front of a FedEx and got out of her vehicle to survey the damage. The front bumper was destroyed, crumpled beyond repair, a headlight cracked, and who knew what else? But the Porsche had fared worse, a huge dent in the back end, paint scraped away, the hood creased.

"Jesus, would you look at that," the driver said, stalking to the back of his car and shaking his head at the dented metal, twisted to the point that she caught a glimpse of the engine. "I'm lucky I can still drive it. The engine's in the back, if you didn't know."

"I do know." From what she could see, the engine didn't appear to be damaged.

"Who taught you how to drive?" he asked.

Her temper flared hotter and her back stiffened. No way would she tell him she learned to drive a tractor at eleven, a truck for the fields of her uncle's farm at thirteen. None of his business. With an effort, she held her tongue. *Don't get into it with him. It's not worth it! You have other problems to deal with, bigger than this ass's car.* "Let's just exchange phone numbers and information," she suggested as evenly as possible.

"But it's all your fault. You rear-ended me."

"I get that," she shot back, her temper snapping. "Okay? I was there!"

"Good." He started back to his car.

"But you don't have to be a prick about it."

He whirled, his face contorted. "What did you say?"

"That you don't have to be a prick." She'd had it with the jerk. "Yeah, the car's a mess. Mine too, but what's done is done, so let's just get down to business."

"'A mess?' Do you have any idea how much this car costs?"

"A lot. Yeah, I know. But yelling at me about it won't help."

"'Yelling at me won't help,'" he singsonged back at her.

She bit back another hot retort, refused to be baited any further, and took a picture of her insurance card with the camera in her phone. Out of the corner of her eye, she saw people collecting on the curb. "I'll text this to you. What's your number? Oh, and send me yours."

Grudgingly, jaw set, he rattled off his cell number and she, ignoring the curious looks from cars and trucks driving slowly by, typed it in. "I'm Brooke Harmon."

"Jim Gustafson. But James. Legally. It's James."

"Got it."

"Good, so, you know, when you hear from my lawyer."

"Great. Your attorney can contact mine: Neal Harmon."

He stiffened slightly, obviously catching the connection.

She filled him in anyway. "My husband."

He frowned slightly and she felt a second's satisfaction, then she offered Jim—legally James—a cold smile and sent the text before glancing up from her phone again and spying her distorted image in the lenses of his sunglasses. "We'll let the insurance companies sort it out."

"Not much to sort. Remember, I got witnesses. I took pictures of the license plates of the cars that were nearby. And that old guy and his wife in the Buick? They saw it all." Gustafson's smile was smug. Proud of himself.

"Good. Then we're done here." She only hoped it was true as she caught a glimpse of the flashing blue and red lights of a police cruiser in her mirror.

CHAPTER 2

"I owe you," Brooke said an hour later via Bluetooth in her dented Explorer as she drove. She was still rattled, her nerves stretched from the accident and the disturbing call.

From the other end of the connection, Andrea said, "Don't worry about it! Seriously." Andrea, who had been her friend since Marilee and Andrea's daughter, Zuri, met in kindergarten. Now, once again, Brooke had asked her to come to the rescue this afternoon.

She had texted Andrea earlier, while still dealing with Gustafson, and asked her friend to pick up Marilee at the high school. Of course Andrea had stepped up, located Marilee at the school, and given her a ride to the athletic club where they had a membership. Brooke had texted her daughter as well, but Marilee hadn't responded.

No surprise there.

Now, Brooke maneuvered her dented car into the parking lot of the club and pulled into a spot with a view of the gym's tall windows. Beyond the glass, teenage girls were clustered around the gymnastic equipment. Brooke caught a glimpse of Marilee dressed in her leotard and shorts. "You're a lifesaver," she said to Andrea, then cut the engine.

"You'd do the same for me."

"In a heartbeat."

"So there you go. Don't give it another thought. Besides, you'll pay me back."

"Of course. Name the time."

"Oh well . . . maybe next week? Zuri's got piano again and I've got to take DJ to the pediatrician at the same time."

"Done." Brooke nodded as if Andrea could see her. "Just text me a reminder."

"Will do. Hey—I just got a call from Joanna Nelson; you know her, right? She's Kinsey's mother."

Kinsey, a redhead with freckles, was another student in Marilee's class. The two girls had been close in elementary school but drifted into different cliques in junior high. "Yeah, the girls used to hang out."

"She says there's a girl missing from the class. Allison Carelli. Two days now. The police have been called in. As you can expect, Alli's mother, Elyse, is freaking out. Has no idea where she is. Has called all the friends and hospitals and everywhere."

"And they can't find her," Brooke said, feeling a drip of dread. She knew Allison of course, a quiet, petite girl with curly black hair, blue eyes, and an attitude that bordered on sullen.

"Gone without a trace."

"Two days?" Brooke whispered, sick inside. She told herself that two days, forty-eight hours, wasn't all that long, but she knew better. If Marilee were missing two hours, she would be going out of her mind.

"The police think Allison might be a runaway, but Elyse doesn't buy it. Neither does Joanna, who knows the family pretty well. Alli's a good kid, you know. Average student, on the swim team, low key— shit, I hate this stuff. Scares the hell out of me."

"Dear God." Brooke bit her lip. "Maybe she'll turn up." She tried to sound hopeful despite the little drip of dread that was becoming a steady stream.

Two girls in two years.

"Maybe, but Penny Williams didn't," Andrea said, as if reading Brooke's thoughts. "And that's been what—like nearly a year?"

Brooke was nodding. Penelope Williams just hadn't come home from school last fall. Since then the girl, in the class above Marilee's, hadn't been located.

Brooke's gaze was still centered on the oversize windows, her thoughts taking a dark turn when she thought about the missing girl and the pain her mother must have been feeling. If anything happened to Marilee, she would lose it. Absolutely lose it.

"Well, everyone's freaking out. I even got a call from Austin Keller; you know him, right? The fireman?"

"Yes." She smiled. "I've known Austin since high school. A shame about his wife." Stacey was a classmate as well and had died a couple years ago in a biking accident.

"He called. Worried sick. Single dad. Only kid." She let out a sigh. "You know, he always asks about you."

"Really?"

"Mm."

"Weird. I had such a crush on him my freshman year." She caught movement from the corner of her eye. A low-riding Honda wheeled into the lot, taking a space three slots down, the thump of bass audible through the driver's open window. He, a boy of about eighteen, cut the engine and unfolded his lanky frame from the car before heading toward the glass doors.

From the other end of the connection, Andrea said, "Oh crap, look at the time! Sorry, I've gotta run. DJ can't seem to find his soccer cleats for the third time this week. But warn Marilee, okay? About Alli. We need to be super-vigilant. More than ever. Later!" And then she was gone.

Leaning back in the seat, Brooke bit her lip. New fears crowded through her mind as she continued to watch her daughter. Marilee, her near-black hair pulled back into a long ponytail, was currently going through her routine. Her face was set, her expression determined, her shoulder muscles straining as she spun around the upper bar, then swung to the lower bar while her coach, a fit woman pushing forty, stood nearby.

At fourteen, her daughter was a good if not stellar student and a dedicated if not naturally talented athlete. Also, in Brooke's opinion, Marilee seemed more mature than some of her friends, and, as an only child, more than a little self-centered. Then again, what teenager wasn't? And having a sibling didn't make everything all peaches and cream. Didn't Brooke know that from personal experience? It wasn't as if having a sister had helped smooth out the treacherous road of adolescence for her. In fact, it had only deepened the ruts.

And as for being self-centered?

Was Marilee any worse than Brooke? She had only to remember rear-ending the car in front of her to remind herself of her total self-absorption.

How had she missed the warning of the Porsche's glowing taillights? And how had she not seen the kid with the ball in the street ahead? The boy could have been seriously injured or even worse. And what about the older couple in the Buick behind her? They had appeared fragile and certainly could have sustained serious injuries. Maybe even had a stroke or a heart attack from the stress? Who knew? Not to mention the ass she'd rear-ended. More than his ego could have been bruised had her Explorer pushed his car into oncoming traffic.

Still, Gustafson was a prick. A major prick! And she'd hated that she had felt forced to play the my-husband-is-a-lawyer card, but the jerk had goaded her into it.

But what about the call she'd received? Who was behind the whispered warning?

He's not who you think he is.

The single sentence revolved through her mind in an endless loop.

Someone was aware of her affair with Gideon Ross. Someone who had her private phone number.

Who?

Until that call, she'd believed only she and Gideon knew of their involvement. Brooke had told no one. But what about Gideon? How did she know she could trust him to keep his lips sealed?

A sick feeling came over her.

What had she been thinking? Why had she gotten involved with him in the first place?

Before she allowed herself to go there, to get into her own psyche, she reminded herself that she was going to break it off with him anyway. Time to calm down. It wasn't a problem.

Yet.

And there were bigger issues to worry about with the girls missing from Allsworth High.

She picked up the burner phone, studied the Recent Call menu, but there had been no name attached to the warning call. Just "Unknown Caller" and a phone number. Without thinking twice, she hit the button to return the call. It rang, and she felt her whole body tense. She would demand answers.

Who are you?

What do you want?

What do you mean, "he's not who you think he is?"
What the hell do you think you know?

And, most importantly, she'd issue her own warning: *Don't ever call me again.*

But she never got the chance. The phone disconnected after the fifth—or was it the sixth—ring? No voicemail.

Her stomach roiled. This was no good. Her secret fling had been discreet and now short-lived, but someone knew. And they were calling.

Who? Her mind spun with possibilities and came up empty. She'd been careful.

But what about Gideon? How careful had he been?

Fingers trembling slightly, she tried to send a text to the number. That didn't work either.

"Awesome," she said to the empty car. "Just freakin' awesome." She'd given out the burner phone's number to no one but Gideon. But someone had it. Someone, she assumed, who knew it belonged to her.

Frustrated all over again, she leaned back in the driver's seat, the accidents ever-more horrifying what-if scenes playing through her mind. She was at fault for the accident with the Porsche. No doubt about it. And the whole situation could have ended up so much worse. As it was, no one was injured, unless she counted her own pride. That definitely took a hit and was bruised black and blue.

Maybe it was a sign, she thought, watching Marilee dismount and converse with her coach before approaching the balance beam.

Brooke told herself she didn't really believe in omens or curses or signs from a higher power, but sometimes she sensed there was more going on than met the eye. She and her sister were brought up in a strict Catholic household. Her grandmother was always reminding her that the devil was lurking just over her shoulder, that God was expecting her to sin and ready to mete out his painful punishment.

Their summer cabin on the island, passed for generations in Brooke's mother's family, had once been filled with Nana's religious artifacts. Jesus statues adorned the mantel. Candles, most decorated with the Sacred Heart of Jesus, were placed on the hearth. Pictures of the Madonna graced the walls. Rosaries were draped over bedposts and crucifixes were nailed over doorways, inside and out.

When Brooke was a kid the cabin was a shrine to Christ. Over the years, after Nana's passing, most of the candles, crucifixes, and rosaries were packed away.

Despite her own teenage rebellion, some of the beliefs and teachings of the Church had rubbed off on Brooke. Her grandmother had always looked for signs that God was talking to her. So maybe, today, He was turning his attention to Mary O'Hara's granddaughter. The accident a warning of her sins.

"Yeah right."

Either way, it was time to end the affair. She'd even thought about doing it earlier that afternoon when she'd been with Gideon but had lost her nerve.

She glanced at her watch. Marilee's lesson would be over in ten minutes. More than enough time. She glanced around and saw no one nearby, but she turned on the engine again, rolled up the window, and with the AC blasting dialed Gideon's number on her burner phone.

He picked up on the third ring. "Hey, babe."

His voice caused the breath to catch in her lungs. Jesus. Even though she hated him referring to her as "babe." Even though she was mad as hell at him.

"What's up?" he asked.

"Who did you give this number to?" she demanded, her voice edgy.

"What? No one."

"You're sure?"

He laughed. "Of course I'm sure. Why would I tell anyone? That's what makes it special, you and me, right? Just our little secret."

She plunged on. "So then why did I get this weird call, like some kind of warning? From an anonymous caller."

"A warning?"

"Yes."

"About what?" he demanded.

"Us—or, more specifically, about you."

"Me?" he said, the timbre of his voice changing slightly, the laughter having drained away.

"Yeah. They said, 'He's not who you think he is.'"

"And they were talking about me?"

"Who else?"

"Anyone. Neal, to begin with." He was getting defensive. "Who was it? Who called?"

"I told you, I don't know."

"You didn't recognize the voice?"

"No! That's what I've been trying to tell you." Her voice had elevated an octave and she held the phone in a death grip as she stared through the dusty windshield.

"So what? You think l told someone and they called you?"

"I don't know what to think, but *someone* knows."

A pause. "Maybe it's a prank."

"Oh right, what're the chances of that?" Was he being dense on purpose? Outside a crow flew onto a nearby tree.

"I don't know. I have no idea what you're talking about." Now he was just being obtuse.

Tell him. Tell him now!

She gathered the courage she hadn't found earlier. "So maybe we should cool it," she said, her heart racing.

"What?" he said, a cautionary note in his voice. "What're you talking about?"

She drew in a long breath, then plunged in. "I've been thinking for a while now. And I don't really know how to say this, because it's new territory for me, but I guess it's best to just come out with it. Gideon, I'm done."

"You're—?"

"What we had?" she cut in quickly. "It was great. Okay? But it's over."

She waited, the silence stretching long.

Ten seconds. Fifteen. Twenty. Then, finally, "You're kidding. Right?"

"No. Not kidding. Dead serious. I can't do this anymore."

Another achingly long pause, then, tentatively, "But . . . why?"

"Because it's wrong, Gideon. We both know it." She stared through the windshield but couldn't see Marilee in the glare. "I have a family. And I don't know what I was thinking to let this go so far, but I just can't go on with it. I won't. I'm a married woman, for God's sake. I've got a kid."

Yet another stunned silence. Then only, "Wow."

She waited.

As if he finally understood, he said, "I don't know what to say."

"You don't have to say anything."

"You were just here."

"I know." She didn't admit that she'd been too nervous to say what was on her mind to his face, that she'd planned to break it off for weeks. "It's been coming a long, long time."

"As I said, you were just here," he argued, his voice a little harsher.

She cringed as she eyed the half-drunk cup of iced coffee melting in the cup holder, the dry cleaning tossed into the back seat with her gym bag, all part of her alibi if she were asked what she'd done all afternoon.

Lies.

All lies.

Well, it was over.

But Gideon still was not believing her. He said, "You could have given me a heads-up. You know, when we were together. If it's been on your mind for so long, why didn't you say anything?"

"I wasn't sure."

"But you are now?" Skepticism tinged his voice.

"Yes." No hesitation. The time was right.

More seconds passed, and she watched a jet rising in the sky before he said in a low voice, "I think this is a mistake."

"Please, Gideon, don't go there. Okay?"

"So, I have no say in this?"

She didn't answer. Shouldn't have to. If either of them wanted out, it was unwritten, unspoken, that the other would acquiesce. That had been their deal from the start. If not said aloud, at least inferred.

"Goodbye, Gideon."

She cut the connection.

It was over.

At least for her.

All of the tension drained from her body and she rested her head on the steering wheel.

The burner phone rang in her hand and she saw his number flash onto the screen.

Ignored it. Adjusted the air-conditioning. Watched as the jet, leaving contrails, disappeared. The phone stopped ringing.

Less than a minute later another call came in, the disposable phone again ringing insistently, Gideon's number again visible.

Nope.

"Take a hint," she said as if he could hear her, then rolled down the window. As she switched off the engine, she heard the ding of a text coming through.

She glanced at the burner phone.

No message.

But her cell, mounted on the dash, was lighting up with a text.

We need to talk. In person. Face-to-face.

"Shit." He'd contacted her on the phone that was supposedly off-limits, the one connected to her family plan with her husband and daughter. Though the call came through marked "private caller," she knew who was on the other end of the connection.

Her heart froze.

Gideon was never supposed to contact her on that phone. Not ever. He knew that. It was one of their rules.

But you broke the rules first, didn't you? By breaking it off.

Nervously, she punched in his number from her burner phone. Waited. Counting the rings. *One. Two. Three. Four.* He wasn't picking up. "Come on. Come on." *Five. Six. Click!*

Fine. She'd leave him a blistering message and opened her mouth to speak, then decided against it and hung up.

A text message came through—on her cell: **Face. To. Face.**

"Crap!"

Once more she tried him on the burner phone and glanced through the windshield, squinting against the glare.

Marilee seemed to be completing her routine on the beam, working on her dismount. Marilee, who was on the cusp of womanhood. Emotional. Impressionable. Like Allison Carelli or Penelope Williams. Young girls gone missing. Her heart twisted. What if that happened to Marilee?

She swallowed hard, thinking about her daughter before her thoughts turned to Neal. A man who trusted that his wife of fifteen years had been faithful, even if they were considering a separation to "sort things out." Even if they'd separated before. Even if he hadn't been as loyal as she.

Stupidly, Brooke had risked it all, tumbling with full-fledged abandon into what was probably a midlife crisis.

What had the jerk she'd rear-ended, Gustafson, called her? A fuckin' moron?

Unfortunately, he'd been right on the money.

Another text came through on her regular phone, the message clear and imperative:

Now.

"No. I can't," she whispered, but the texts kept coming.

We meet now.

She had to stop this. She couldn't go home and just have text after text come in.

We meet now. Or else.

CHAPTER 3

Or else what?

She didn't want to think about it. Gideon did have a dangerous edge to him. Hadn't that been part of the original attraction? But she never thought . . .

Not for the first time, she realized she didn't know him.

Everything she'd learned about him was based on what he'd told her. He could have lied. Her cursory search on the Internet had brought up nothing, revealed very little. But how deep had she dived?

Not too deep.

Because, truth be told, she didn't want to know too much about him.

That had been part of the mystery. The intrigue.

She'd thought it would be safer that way.

Now, of course, she realized just the opposite was true.

Well, she'd have to set him straight.

No matter what.

"Idiot," she muttered under her breath. She clicked off both phones, then dropped them into her purse. Once she was home she'd hide the burner phone either beneath the console of her Explorer or in the niche of the laundry room, a little cubby covered by half-used bottles of bleach, detergent, and rags. For now, though, she zipped it into a pocket in her bag.

From her vantage point she saw that Marilee's lesson was wrapping up, her daughter with her backpack slung over one shoulder.

Brooke snagged her purse and headed inside, where the high-ceilinged room smelled of sweat, barely diffused by cleaning fluid. Marilee, towel around her neck, sweat on her face and darkening the neckline of the shirt she'd tossed over her leotard, shifted her backpack from one shoulder to the other. She barely glanced up at her mother when Brooke said, "Hey, I'm sorry I had to have Andrea pick you up and—"

"Let's just go." Marilee had already started for the door, her ponytail swinging across her shoulders. Once outside, Marilee squinted at the Explorer with its dents, scowled, and threw her backpack into the back seat. "Geez," she said under her breath as she slid glumly into the passenger seat.

Brooke started the SUV. "I just wanted to tell you why I was late—"

"I know *what* happened. You texted me. An accident. 'Fender bender,' right?" Over her air quotes, Marilee gave her mother a look of long suffering. "I saw the messed-up hood, okay?" Her lips pursed as she motioned through the windshield to the spot where the hood had buckled slightly with the impact. "I just want to go home." Then she slid her mother a look. "And you're okay, right?"

"Right." Brooke slid the Explorer into reverse.

The kid in the black Honda had collected what appeared to be a little sister and, with his music still cranked, sped around Brooke to roar out of the lot.

"Jerk," Marilee muttered under her breath.

"You know him?"

"Kinda. He's in my first period. Algebra II."

"What's his name?"

"Not important, Mom." Then she turned her head to stare out the side window as Brooke drove out of the lot and through the shaded side streets of the Queen Anne neighborhood.

"I just—"

"Just what?" Marilee's head spun around so fast her ponytail swung wildly. She glared at her mother. "Just want to tell me why you're always late? Why I'm the only one waiting for my mommy like a toddler or . . . or . . . a dork? Or why someone else's mom has to pick me up and drop me off?" Her lips were a flat line, anger snapping in her blue eyes.

"I'm sorry."

"Yeah, I know."

"It won't—"

"Happen again? Is that what you were going to say?"

"Marilee—"

"Don't, Mom. Just . . . don't." She held up a hand. "Just drive, okay?"

"Look, I said I'm sorry," Brooke said, determined not to be cut off. "And I am, but I'm not crazy about your attitude."

"And I'm not crazy about yours." Marilee let out a long, agonized groan as Brooke turned onto the narrow street and spied the house she'd called home for nearly fourteen years, almost all of Marilee's life.

Over a hundred years old, the house was built of shingles and stone. It was unique, with its rounded turret and arched front porch. From this angle the Victorian home appeared to be two stories, though there was a basement beneath the upper floors that housed the garage, with the laundry room halfway up the stairs. A second staircase ran up the back of the house. Narrow, dark, and not too steady, that staircase was never used. Neal called it the "fire escape" and always talked of repairing or replacing it "someday."

So far, it hadn't happened.

The rest of the house had been renovated over the years, modern conveniences added, along with a wide deck off the kitchen. There was a dishwasher and a gas stove, along with tile updates in the kitchen and bathrooms. The wood floors refinished and polished. But the house itself still held on to its pre-turn-of-the-last-century charm, evident in the carved banisters and claw-foot tubs fitted with a free-standing shower rod and fixtures.

Brooke and Neal had purchased the home over thirteen years earlier, when Marilee, in a yellow onesie, was strapped to Neal in a front pack.

From the moment Brooke crossed the threshold that very first time, she'd felt as if she were home. Finally home.

Buying the house had been a stretch, but both she and Neal had decided it was worth it. Who could resist the coved ceilings, wainscoting, and mullioned windows with views of the city lights? They'd walked through the arched doorways and fallen in love with the house and each other all over again.

Baby Marilee, of course, was unaware of the huge decision her parents were wrestling with.

And it had all worked out, for the most part.

Well, until recently.

She glanced at her daughter. "Let's not fight. Okay? I said I'm sorry."

Finally cooling off a bit, Marilee sighed and gave an exaggerated roll of her eyes. "Okay." A pause. "Okay, okay, apology accepted."

"Good." Brooke drove down the steep slope of the driveway and cranked on the steering wheel as she hit the remote to open the garage door. "We can try to be nice to each other." The door rolled open with a clang and a groan and she pulled inside, parking next to Neal's Range Rover.

Marilee sent her mother a pained look, then a small smile started to play across her lips. "I'll *try*."

"Me too."

Her daughter was reaching for the door handle.

Brooke caught her arm. "I heard that Allison Carelli is missing."

"Yeah, it was all over school."

"Does anyone know what happened?"

"No. She just didn't show up. I mean, I don't know. That's just what I heard."

"Was she with anyone? Did anyone see her leave?"

"I said I don't know, okay?" When she saw more questions in her mother's eyes, Marilee added, "I don't hang out with her. We're not really friends anymore. All I know is that yesterday my phone blew up about it."

"Do you have any idea what happened to her?"

"Geez, Mom, I already said, I don't know! No one does." And with that she was out of the car, opening the back door, and grabbing her bag before heading through the garage and up the stairs, past the laundry room to the main floor.

Disturbed, Brooke decided to let the subject drop. For now. Carrying the dry cleaning and her near-empty cup of the melted iced coffee, she followed.

She expected to be greeted by the scents of roasting chicken or the tang of spaghetti sauce because it was Neal's night to cook, but she was disappointed to find him staring at his laptop on the kitchen table, reading glasses on the end of his nose. A half-drunk glass of white wine sat nearby.

As she walked into the room, he nonchalantly closed the computer.

As if she wouldn't notice.

Shep, their mutt, who appeared to have some golden retriever mixed with a bit of German shepherd in him, had padded after Marilee into the hallway to the staircase but now came flying into the kitchen, toenails clicking wildly on the hardwood. The dog greeted Brooke as if he hadn't seen her in years. She leaned forward and scratched his ears as he wiggled at her feet. "No dinner?" she asked Neal, hearing Marilee's footsteps squeaking on the stairs to the upper floor.

"I thought we'd order pizza."

She hung the dry cleaning on a door hook near the stairs. "We had pizza on Saturday."

"But we discussed this," he said. "This morning."

Vaguely, she remembered him saying something about Alphonso's as she'd stepped out of the shower. But she'd been distracted, thinking of a call from Gideon late last night suggesting they meet. At the time she hadn't cared.

From the upper floor, Marilee called down, "I like pizza."

Neal glanced toward the hallway where the stairs curved upward. "Funny what she can hear and what she can't."

"I heard that!" their daughter called back.

"See?" he said to his wife, then, more loudly, "Pizza it is!" Neal smiled, one side of his mouth lifting in his beard-shadowed jaw. Pushing forty, he was still handsome, with the same jet-black hair and blue eyes he'd passed on to his daughter. His features were bolder than Marilee's, of course. Their daughter had inherited Brooke's oval face and slim nose. "You have a problem with that?" His eyebrows arched in question.

"Nope. But get a half-and-half, okay? Not all meat lover's. Add veggies to one side."

"She won't eat 'em."

"I know, but . . . try. And you're on for ordering and picking up."

"Or delivery. From Alphonso's? Let's see," he said and pulled his cell from the pocket of his jeans. "I'll get a salad too." He looked up at her before he punched in the preset number. For a second she remembered him as he was sixteen years earlier, handsome in a rugged sort of way, his jawline more defined, his physique slimmer, but the sparkle in his eyes just as mischievous. One side of his mouth tended to lift in a smile that was nearly conspiring, the are-you-thinking-what-I'm-thinking look she'd found so endearing.

"Or delivery," she agreed.

As Neal made the call, she walked to the refrigerator, found a half-drunk bottle of Chardonnay and retrieved it. Pouring herself a glass, she heard Neal call out, "Anchovies?"

"Fine," she said, loud enough for him to hear, then recorked the bottle.

"Ugh! No!" Marilee called from somewhere upstairs. "Yuck!"

Brooke stepped onto the back deck and drank a long swallow. She thought about sneaking a cigarette from her secret, only-for-the-worst-catastrophes pack hidden in the fake birdhouse on the rail, but decided against it even though today certainly qualified as a disaster. Still, it had been a few months since she'd lit up, and she winced when she thought of that moment.

The morning after her first tryst with Gideon, when she'd crossed the line from faithful wife to adulterer. At that thought she almost caved and scrabbled in the dusty birdhouse for her lighter and a Marlboro Light. She should never have given in to him; she'd been a fool. Yes, she and Neal had talked of divorce, and he'd moved out for a few weeks, but still . . . Marilee.

Her heart twisted for her daughter.

The divorce was on hold, or maybe even the back burner.

Neal had moved back home, they'd started marriage counseling, and had promised each other to make it work until Marilee was off to college or at least had graduated from high school.

But she hadn't tried to end it with Gideon earlier and today's effort, over the phone, hadn't seemed to work. She crossed her fingers that she was wrong, that he'd gotten the message, but she couldn't stop the queasy feeling in her stomach. She unlatched the top of the birdhouse and reached her fingers inside, scrabbling for her lighter, then shut it quickly when she heard Neal returning to the kitchen, his footsteps growing louder until the French doors opened. Both he and the dog stepped into the night. As Neal came up to stand by her, Shep hurried down the deck's steps to the lower patio.

"Pizza will be a while. They're backed up, I guess." Then, "What're you doing out here?" he asked, glancing around the deck to the dark yard and the fence beyond. The lawn sloped downward sharply, and over the slats of the fence and hedgerow of arborvitae, the lights of Seattle were visible, winking through wisps of fog starting to settle over the city.

"Thinking." She hadn't yet told him about her fender bender but figured this was as good a time as any. She mentioned being in a hurry to pick up Marilee, being distracted slightly, and rear-ending the guy in front of her. She left out the part about Gideon of course. Fingers crossed her husband would never find out about the man with whom she had her fling. After all, it was over. ". . . so you'll be hearing from Gustafson or his lawyer," she added, then finished her wine in a quick swallow.

"Shit happens," he said and placed an arm around her.

Oh, I know. It happens all the time. "And there's something more worrisome than the car, a lot more," she said and repeated her conversation with Andrea about Allison Carelli being missing, then told him about their daughter's reaction.

"Scary stuff."

"Amen."

"Isn't there someone in your firm who deals with criminal law? Maybe he could find out what the police are thinking."

"She," he corrected. "Jennifer deals with the cops. She used to work for the department as an assistant DA."

Brooke felt her insides wither at the mention of Jennifer Adkins.

"I'll see what she knows, but I doubt if it's anything." He brushed away a strand of hair that had blown across Brooke's cheeks. "Are you worried?"

"I'm always worried," she admitted as Shep, from the yard below, gave out a sharp, single "Woof."

"Well, don't be. Maybe this girl—Allison—will show up. It's only been a couple of days." But he was worried, the lines etching his forehead giving away his concern.

"We can hope," Brooke said, but it was just a platitude.

"I'll see what Jennifer can dig up."

He gave her shoulder a pat as Shep scrambled up the steps. "Let's go survey the damage." Neal was already walking into the house and down the short hallway to the stairwell leading to the garage.

She followed him, sickened by the sight of her SUV, complete with dented bumper, creased hood, and cracked window.

"Ooh." He sucked in his breath. "And the other guy was driving a Porsche?"

"I think he called it a 'fuckin' 911.' Yeah, that's what he said."

"Carrera?" Neal let out a low whistle.

"I guess."

"Well. I see. I take it he wasn't too pleased?"

"That's putting it mildly. He was . . . what's the phrase?" She pretended to think for a second, then snapped her fingers. "Oh, I've got it: beyond pissed. Waaaay beyond. The car's new."

"And it looks worse than this?" Neal asked, rubbing the back of his neck as he walked around her Explorer.

"Yeah." She nodded, remembering. "A lot worse."

"Hmm. Well, at least no one was hurt. Right?"

"Far as I know. As mad as he was, he probably got whiplash from doing a pretty damned good impression of a Tasmanian devil."

"We'll see. You filed a police report?"

"Yeah. The police showed up just after we exchanged insurance information."

"Okay. Good. Then let's put it behind us for the night." He pulled his phone from the back pocket of his jeans and glanced at the screen. "Besides, the pizza will be coming in a while. Anchovies and all."

"You didn't," she said as they walked inside, and Neal poured them each another glass of wine.

"Nah, but I wanted to, just to yank Mari's chain," he said.

"I think it's been yanked hard enough for one day. She wasn't exactly thrilled that I was late picking her up and Andrea had to drive her to the gym."

"She isn't exactly thrilled about anything right now," he said.

"Amen to that."

Nearly an hour later, after Brooke had been on the phone texting with other mothers at the school and scouring the Internet for stories and the community Facebook pages that offered up local news, she gave up. No one had new information about the missing girl.

Brooke was sick inside. "I can't imagine what those parents are going through. Dear God, if it was Marilee, I'd be going out of my mind."

"But it's not her. In fact, she's home tonight with parents who just don't understand her."

The doorbell chimed.

"Finally," Neal said as he spied Marilee in flannel pajamas, a towel twisted over her wet hair, phone to her ear, hurrying down the stairs. "Speak of the devil."

"Me? You're talking about me?" she guessed with a shake of her head. "Well, don't. Okay? Just . . . don't!" Into the phone, she said, "No, no, not you. My dad." She was dashing into the front hallway and opening the door. Neal and Brooke were a step behind.

The pizza deliverer stood in the porch light. His red baseball cap was pulled down low over his eyes, but Brooke recognized him instantly.

Her heart nose-dived.

Her stomach soured.

Gideon.

The delivery guy was—

No!

—on her doorstep! At her house!

"I put a tip on the bill," Neal said as Gideon handed the box to Marilee, giving her one of his killer smiles, though she might not have noticed as she was deep into her phone conversation as she grabbed the pizza on the run, dashing back inside.

Brooke's blood froze. He'd never come to her home before. Never. That was one of their unwritten rules.

Gideon turned his gaze to Brooke, who was standing woodenly in the entry. He handed her a paper bag. "You all have a nice night." He touched the brim of his cap, but his eyes followed Marilee's hasty path.

Brooke sucked in a sharp breath.

Her skin crawled. *No!*

"You too. Have a good one." Neal, seemingly oblivious, was already turning toward the kitchen, following Marilee. Numbly, Brooke stared at him. What was he doing here? Why was he looking at Marilee . . . oh God. She thought she might be sick. She started to close the door, but through the ever-narrowing space saw Gideon smile and whisper, "Face-to-face."

CHAPTER 4

"Something bothering you?" Neal asked the next morning as Brooke opened a bleary eye, then stretched on the bed.

Neal was already up and showered, his wet hair glistening as he adjusted his tie and caught her gaze in the mirror over the bureau.

"Just the usual," she said, and it wasn't a lie. She'd tossed and turned all night and it was because of Gideon. "I kept thinking about Allison Carelli and Penny Williams." That wasn't a lie, not entirely. She'd worried about the missing girls off and on, her thoughts interrupted by disjointed images of Gideon on the deck of his sailboat or riding his motorcycle. She'd been haunted by an image of him reading at a small table on the boat. Behind him, the door of a slim closet was ajar and hanging from a hook within, she'd seen the red cap he'd worn on her doorstep just last night.

Her stomach ground.

"Maybe Allison came home by now." Neal was still watching her in the mirror.

"Let's hope." She reached for her cell phone, scanned the messages, learned nothing new. The school had issued warnings via text and email, suggesting students stay in groups and parents be extra vigilant. The school administration was beefing up security. A group text from some of the moms was full of lots of worry and little information. "If Allison's been found, no one's let me know."

"They would have." He frowned. "I already texted Jennifer. She'd heard about it—has a nephew at the school—but she said he didn't know anything. She's looking into it."

Brooke didn't respond; didn't want to think about Jennifer Adkins.

Neal broke eye contact in the reflection and turned to face her. "This okay?" he asked, motioning to his shirt and tie.

Eyeing him, she scooted up on the mattress to lean against the padded headboard. She scrutinized his white shirt and gray slacks. His silk tie was a muted blue. "You look like a successful attorney."

"That bad, eh?"

Squinting as if really sizing him up, she lifted a shoulder. "Or maybe a CPA?"

"What?"

"Yeah, like maybe someone who's worked for the IRS for about fifty years."

He laughed and his eyes twinkled. "Flattery will get you nowhere." Then he cocked his head. "It's the tie, isn't it?" He untied the silk knot and reached into their shared closet. "Maybe this is better." He held up a navy-and-white-striped tie.

"No." She slipped off the bed, yawning as she did so, then padded to the closet. Pawing through his ever-growing collection of neckties, she finally pulled out a small floral print of muted grays, peach, and mint green. "Now *this* is a statement!"

"Yeah, that I'm an ex-hippie."

"It's not yellow and purple tie-dyed, for God's sake."

"I had one of those. My aunt handed it over when my uncle died."

"I know." She laughed. "But this one"—she fingered the smooth silk—"is sophisticated. It speaks of a man who knows his own mind and isn't afraid to thwart convention."

"Yeah sure. If you say so."

"I do. And Marilee gave it to you for Father's Day two years ago," she reminded him.

"Fine." He slid the tie around his neck, tucking it beneath his collar. "But seriously, last night you were restless."

"I know. As I said. Worries. The girls, the accident, and no job," she said.

"The job hunt not going well?"

"Not that great." She helped him with the tie. These days she and Neal were getting along better than they had in a couple of years.

Hence the divorce was on hold. Hence breaking it off with Gideon was a priority.

"You know, with everything else going on, I forgot to ask," he said, looking suddenly abashed. "You went to the doctor yesterday for a follow-up?"

"Oh. Yeah."

"And—?"

"It went fine," she lied. She hadn't been at the clinic; she'd been with Gideon, and she felt uncomfortable lying about it, but she'd already rescheduled with her oncologist. The doctor's office, Starbucks, the gym, and dry cleaners had all been part of her alibi.

"So how did you end up having the accident near Alaskan Way? Isn't that the opposite direction from the clinic in the University District?"

Her fingers froze on the tie for a second. He was right. Her trip to the marina had been out of the way. "Yeah, I know," she said, thinking quickly. "Potential job near the waterfront. Thought I'd check it out and then I was late to pick up Marilee, and the rest, as they say, is history."

"Oh." He glanced in the mirror again, tightening the knot a bit, and Brooke changed the subject. "Is Marilee up?"

He shot her a disbelieving look. "How old is she? Fourteen? What do you think?"

"Okay, okay, I get it. My job." She made her way down the hall and rapped on her daughter's door before poking her head into Marilee's darkened room. "Hey, time to get up."

A groan emerged from the mound on the bed, where only a top-knot of black hair was visible. "Nooo."

"Come on."

"I can't." An arm reached out for a pillow, then plopped it over her head.

"Sure you can. See you downstairs."

"Nooo," came the muffled reply. "Mom, I don't want to. Really . . ."

"Too bad," Brooke said and glanced around the room, where clothes were strewn on the floor. Her desk, pushed into the windows of the rounded turret, was obscured by her computer, gaming equipment, and iPad. Gone were the teddy bears and "blankies" and picture books, all replaced by video games and electronics and bottles of nail polish.

"See you downstairs."

"No!"

"Fifteen minutes!"

Brooke closed the door again, annoyed by the confrontation that seemed to be a part of their morning routine. Just once Brooke wished she could escape the role of predawn nag. But not today.

By the time Brooke was through with her shower and dressed in jeans and a sweater, Neal had Eggo waffles warming in the toaster. A fuzzy blanket wrapped around her body, Marilee was seated on one of the barstools at the kitchen island. Her hair was pulled into a messy bun, her face pinched as if she were a vampire coming face-to-face with the sun.

"Good morning," Brooke said as Neal slid a toasted waffle onto a plate and placed it in front of their daughter. Shep had gotten out of his bed and was beneath the bar, waiting patiently for any crumbs that might fall to the floor.

Neal prompted, "Your mother said, 'good morning.'"

"What's good about it?" Marilee was hunched over, her head resting on the counter while she twirled the plate in front of her nose.

Neal grinned. "Oh to be fourteen again. The joy of—"

"Dad! Stop!"

That was enough. Brooke said, "I think you meant to say, 'thank you,' as your father was good enough to make you breakfast."

Marilee's eyes were slits as she stared at her mother, but she did manage to mutter, "Thanks," as Neal deposited a glass of orange juice in front of her. "I just don't want to go to school."

"You have to." Neal was adamant as he turned to face her and bit into a bagel.

"There's cream cheese in the fridge," Brooke reminded him as she walked to the counter, where half a pot of coffee sat warming in the coffee maker.

"No time." He took another bite and washed it down with a big swallow of coffee. "Big meeting this morning." Taking a look at his watch, he grimaced. "Gotta run. Oh, by the way, Leah called while you were in the shower."

"Leah?" Brooke hadn't heard from her sister in eons.

"Mm-hmm. Said she'd phone you back."

"Why?" Brooke asked, suddenly edgy that her sister had called. "Is something wrong?" Leah never called unless she was in trouble and needed help, usually in the form of money.

"Don't know. She didn't say. But she didn't sound upset, if that's what you mean." Another bite. Another long swallow.

"But—"

"That's all I know."

"She never calls or texts or—"

"I know." He held up one hand, as if fending off an attack, and then tossed the remains of the bagel into the sink. "Look, you can call her back. Or if that's—I don't know, too personal or whatever— just shoot her a text. You've got her number." He cocked his head. "Don't you?" Then, added, "If you don't, I do." He whipped out his own phone. "Here, I'll text it to you." He typed quickly and a second later her phone dinged.

"Weird that you have her number," she pointed out, seeing the information and adding Leah to her contact list.

"Weird that you don't," he countered and she let it go. For now.

Brooke wanted to argue, but there was no point. How could she explain that Leah made her anxious, that theirs was a frail, distrustful relationship at best? That Leah could go from zero to sixty emotionally in a nanosecond, especially when triggered by her older sister. "Fine." Marilee, who resented being an only child, did not want to hear about the complications of sisterhood.

"Geez, Mom, so your sister called. So what? That's not a major problem, right?" Marilee frowned, but she had picked up her fork and was cutting into the waffle. She tossed a bit to Shep, who deftly caught it on the fly. "I don't know why you have to make such a big deal out of everything."

"I don't—" Brooke began to argue, then let the thought run out. Marilee was right. She did make mountains out of molehills, as her grandmother used to say. That was a new little chink in her personality, one that had come with her breast cancer scare a year earlier. "I'll call her."

"Big of you," her daughter mumbled, the words barely audible as she pronged a bit of waffle into her mouth.

"Good." Neal brushed some crumbs from his shirt, snagged his suit jacket from the back of a chair, and jangled his keys. "She"—he pointed at Marilee, pouring more syrup onto her waffle—"is all yours."

"Real cool, Dad." Marilee flung him a dark look.

He responded with a wide grin and a reminder: "Be nice."

She pursed her lips and continued to glower at him.

"Love you!" he called over his shoulder and headed to the stairs leading to the basement and the garage.

"Oh, wait!" Marilee suddenly yelled as the door shut behind him. She turned her big, horrified eyes to her mother as the light dawned. "You're not driving me."

"I'm not?" Brooke took a sip of her coffee as she heard the garage door roll up just as the Range Rover's engine caught.

"Oh God, I'm *not* going to school in your car!" Marilee insisted. "It's wrecked."

"And still drivable."

"Unfortunately." Miserably, Marilee took another bite of her now soggy waffle.

Brooke stared at her daughter. "You'd prefer my car was totaled?"

"No, but . . . urgh. It's just so embarrassing." She dropped her fork. It clattered against her plate.

Brooke didn't know which was more mortifying for her daughter—the Explorer with its crumpled hood or being seen with her mother. She decided not to ask. "Look, unless you want to walk, and oh—it's too late for that; I don't think you have much choice." Brooke glanced at the clock on the stove. "You already missed the bus. Now eat up and get a move on."

"You're impossible." Marilee scraped back her barstool.

"I guess it runs in the family."

With an exaggerated sigh, Marilee headed up the stairs and stomped to her room.

And Brooke slowly counted to ten. Because as cool as the exterior she displayed to her child was, she was inwardly churning. Not so much at Marilee's insolence, which only added to the stress but worry over the missing girls and the determined man who had shown up on her doorstep last night. She couldn't do anything about the teens who had vanished, but she sure as hell could deal with Gideon.

This morning in the locked bathroom, after retrieving both her phones, she'd turned them on while waiting for the water to heat so she could step into the shower. She'd prayed for news of Allison Carelli. Instead, she'd found texts on her burner phone:

We need to talk.

Face-to-face.

It's not over.

We are meant to be together.

Meet me. TODAY!

The messages had been repeated, every hour on the hour, throughout the wee morning hours.

"Dear God," she'd whispered, an edge of panic to her thoughts as she erased them. It was as if Gideon was losing his mind.

And she wasn't far behind.

How had he known that they'd ordered dinner from Alphonso's last night? What had tipped him off? She'd never mentioned the Italian restaurant to him. She'd tossed and turned all night, wondering.

It had been all she could do to appear "normal" this morning after reading the messages and stuffing both phones into her purse before heading downstairs. Everything seemed off a bit.

She was jarred back to reality when Marilee returned to the kitchen. "Ready?" she asked, setting down her coffee cup and grabbing her purse.

"I guess," her daughter said sullenly.

The drive to school was uneventful, rain clouds gathering as if Indian summer had disappeared overnight. As Brooke turned toward the side street running past the school, Marilee insisted on being dropped off two blocks before they reached the campus.

"It wouldn't kill you to be seen in a crumpled car with your mom," she said.

"No? Not sure about that." But Marilee managed to scare up a smile, and Brooke was reminded of the girl her daughter used to be, a sweet, funny, and imaginative kid. A girl who loved books and climbed trees and dabbled at the piano when she wasn't forever cartwheeling around the house.

But all of that had changed with the dawning of Marilee becoming a teenager, which just so happened to collide with Brooke's diagnosis and the subtle cracks in her marriage to Neal.

"So be careful today," she warned, thinking of the two girls who had gone missing. "Well, every day. Be careful every day."

"God, Mom, I *am*!"

"I'll be here to pick you up. Right after school."

Marilee rolled her eyes.

"And when you get home? We're going to have a serious talk about your attitude," Brooke said.

"*My* attitude?"

"Uh-huh." Brooke pulled onto a side street, where a parking space had opened up and leaves had piled near the curb. "It needs to improve. A lot."

"Yeah right." Marilee was out of her seat belt in a second. She started to close the door but thought better of it and managed a quick "Bye" before slamming the passenger door shut and jogging along the sidewalk toward the school.

Brooke watched for a moment, then pulled into the street and followed her daughter. In tattered jeans, a sloppy sweater, tennis shoes and her dark hair pulled into a ponytail, Marilee crossed the school lawn and wove through clumps of students.

Brooke nosed into a spot in front of the school. With her SUV idling, she waited until she saw her daughter actually walk through the glass doors and into the building. Safe for now.

Brooke pulled away from the curb and nosed into the flow of traffic.

Then, mentally girding her loins, she headed toward the dock where Gideon's sailboat was moored.

He wanted a face-to-face confrontation?

Fine.

He was damn well going to get one.

CHAPTER 5

Gideon was waiting for her. Standing at the bow of his sailboat, he leaned over the rail to watch her approach. Flint-colored clouds gathered overhead. The wind was up, whipping Gideon's open shirt away from his body to reveal his torso, one she knew all too well.

Sipping from a mug, he stared at her as she climbed out of her SUV and slammed the door shut.

You can do this!

She marched across the uneven lot, where only a smattering of vehicles were parked—pickups and vans mostly and, of course, Gideon's monster of a motorcycle. It was parked in its usual space, next to a shed where seagulls perched on the spine of the roof.

She held his gaze.

Her heart was pounding, her nerves tight as bow strings as she strode along the dock and up the gangway to his sailboat.

She was determined to end this. Now.

While driving to the marina she'd considered what she was going to say and had decided it best to get onto the boat, away from the eyes and ears of anyone who was hanging out on the docks. Now, seeing his hair catching in the breeze, she felt a clutch in her heart and reminded herself of the reason she was there.

A smile stretched over his jaw at her approach, and though his eyes were hidden by sunglasses, she saw the corners crinkle—a sincere smile. "Hey," he said and reached for her.

"Stop!" She held up a hand and took a step back, every muscle in her body tense. "What the hell were you doing delivering the pizza to my house last night?"

He chuckled. "I thought you'd appreciate that."

"Appreciate it? Are you insane? We had a deal," she reminded him, churning inside. "My house was off-limits. My family is off-limits. My *daughter* is definitely off-limits!"

"Your daughter?" he repeated, amused.

"Don't go there, Gideon," she warned, balancing against the rail as the boat gently rocked. "You tried to flirt with her."

"Oh, right. Come on, she's just a kid." He sounded dismissive. Shaded eyes continued to stare at her. "But you sound a little jealous."

Jealous? Was he kidding? She scoffed, "How did you know? About the pizza? How did you find out what we were doing and how . . . how on earth did you manage it?"

His lips twitched. "I have my ways."

"This is not a game!"

"Isn't it?"

"It's harassment."

"*Harassment?*" he spat out.

"I'm serious. Leave us the hell alone."

"Or you'll do what?" His smile faded. He tossed the dregs of his coffee over the side of the boat. "What could you possibly do to me?"

"Don't try me," she said between locked teeth.

Setting his empty cup on a small folding chair, he said, "You reneged."

"I reneged?" she repeated. "No—"

"You left here yesterday and everything was fine. And then, not even a couple of hours later, you called with a message that I assumed was a joke."

"No joke."

"So you're serious?"

"As serious as I've ever been in my life." The wind blew a strand of hair over her eyes and she pushed it aside and glared at him. "It's over, Gideon, just like I said."

"Why?"

"It doesn't matter."

"Like hell."

"I'm going to make it work with Neal, if I can."

"You're not in love with him," he charged and she noticed a muscle work in his jaw.

"That's where you're wrong."

"That's what you told me."

"No," she countered, remembering the conversation that had occurred on this very deck. "I told you I wasn't *in* love with him anymore and that's true. But I still love him and I love my daughter. I want us to be a family. And maybe I'll fall in love with him again."

"Oh, sure. That's the way it works," he mocked. "And maybe he'll show up on a white steed and whisk you off to his castle and you'll live happily ever after."

"Maybe," she said, refusing to take the bait, refusing to get into a fight. "So that's it. You wanted a face-to-face and you got it. It's over, Gideon."

"Jesus, Brooke." His cocky smile faded as he finally realized she wasn't playing games. "You can't do that. Turn it off and on at will."

"I told you, it's been coming for a long time."

"You were just here yesterday." He jammed a finger downward, past the decking and toward the cabin below. "With me. In my bed."

"It was a mistake."

"It didn't seem like a mistake to me. Not then, not all the other times." Undaunted, he leaned back against the rail again. "You're telling me it was a mistake when you wrapped your arms around me as I steered the boat. Remember that? Or when we drank champagne right over there?" He hitched his shoulder toward the stern. "Or when we took off in your damned Explorer—that SUV?" Motioning toward her vehicle, he ranted on, "We spent that weekend away in your grandmother's cabin. Hell, we even took your damned dog with us. You're telling me you don't recall that?" He scoffed in disbelief. "What about that?" Anger cut through his words, the muscle in his jaw working overtime. "And how about all the times you were in my bed? Begging me to fuck you? Remember those?"

She did. Vividly. Even the dirty talk in the throes of passion. She remembered the feel of his fingers running down the length of her spine, the desire that always burned when she was around him, the heat that dissipated quickly as her guilt took over and she came to her senses.

"Well, maybe it wasn't your mistake," she said. "But it was mine. I'm the one who's married, the one who has a daughter. We both agreed when this started that either one of us could call it off at any time. And that's what I'm doing."

"You wouldn't dare." She noticed the cords visibly pulsing in his neck. Didn't care.

"Wouldn't I?" Tension seemed to crackle in the air.

His eyes narrowed. "I can make your life a living hell, you know."

"And you'd do that?" She lifted up her chin, goading him. "Because that's how much you 'love' me?"

His lips flattened. "I just want us to be together. We belong together."

"No, Gideon. We don't. And don't make the mistake of threatening me. It won't work." She held her ground. "If I have to, I'll come clean with Neal."

"And your daughter?"

Her insides twisted. Oh dear God, Marilee would hate her forever. As bad as their relationship was now, it would only get worse. Much worse. She steeled herself and silently prayed he was bluffing. He was, wasn't he? He wouldn't dare try to ruin her life.

He prodded, "What would pretty little petulant Marilee say?"

He knew about her daughter's attitude? It curdled her blood to hear her child's name on his lips. She remembered the intense look he'd sent Marilee's way on the porch last night. The flirtatious wink. Nausea roiled her stomach. "She would understand."

"Oh, sure." He laughed harshly. "You're going to tell her how you've spent your afternoons and weekends away and the reason you're always late to pick her up from school?" His skin was stretched tight over his features, his eyes dangerous.

"If I have to." Her voice was surprisingly even, though her heart was galloping and every instinct told her to run. "So, now we're clear," she said, taking one step backward. "Don't call or text me, okay? And for God's sake, stay away from my family. Don't show up on my doorstep again. Whatever we had, whatever this was, it's over. Just let it go."

She turned for the gangway.

He caught her wrist. "No."

"What?" She tried to snatch back her hand, but he spun her around to face him. So close. Too close. His face was just inches from hers. She tried to yank away her arm, but his grip only tightened. "Let me go, Gideon."

"I love you." There it was. The words he'd whispered to her time and time again. The three simple words she'd never uttered back. Because she'd known. Deep down, she'd realized what they had would never last.

The boat rocked on the water, the masts creaked with the wind, and she was hit by the scent of the sea, but she didn't take her eyes from his.

His grip tightened. "I want you."

Did a part of her long to be with him? To forget the complications and stresses of her daily life?

She swallowed hard, the silence stretching between them.

"You want me too. You know, Brooke, that we're meant to be together. Forever." As if he sensed her wavering, he pulled her even closer. "We could go away. Just the two of us. Right now. Leave everything behind." Was there a desperation to his words, a rending of his soul?

Her own heartbeat was pounding in her eardrums.

She thought of Marilee. And Neal. And the life she had with them, the life she'd worked so hard for, the life she loved despite the stress of a husband with a wandering eye and a teenager who was outwardly rebelling, a job hunt and health issues and . . . "No." She shook her head, the brief temptation withering away. She peeled his fingers from her wrist. "No. I can't do this anymore and I don't want to."

"I can't let you go."

"I'm not yours to lose." She angled up her chin and said, "This was a mistake. I know it now."

His face twisted, pain and anger wrenching his features. "I said, 'I love you.'"

"And I'm saying goodbye."

"Don't, Brooke."

But she was done, and this time she made it to the gangway before he leaped forward, caught her in both hands, and yanked her against him. "No."

"Let go of me."

But his grip only grew stronger and she felt the length of his body pressed against her back and, worse yet, through her jeans and his, the hardness of his erection.

Oh God, really? This turned him on? She was suddenly disgusted.

She struggled and he whispered into her hair, "We should be together. You feel it. I know you feel it."

"You're wrong. Let go of me!"

"I love you," he repeated.

"You don't." And then she understood. His form of "love" was total control. She'd realized that too late. When he tried to pull her even closer and leaned around to kiss her, she twisted her head, bared her teeth, and bit.

He shrieked, releasing her, blood spurting. "What the fuck?"

"Just leave me the hell alone."

"That's not what you want." He was dabbing at his lip with his sleeve. "You're crazy!" His face twisted, and if her gaze could have pierced his dark lenses, she guessed she would have witnessed fury. Maybe pain as well, and an intense, dark rage. But she didn't wait, just turned on her heel and headed for the dock.

"You can't just leave me."

Oh no? Just watch. She kept walking, heard a rush of footsteps, and when she turned he was already leaping at her, his body slamming into hers. Her knees buckled and her ankle twisted painfully. As she fell, her head crashed against the deck, chin bouncing, cheek scraping.

Bam! Her head cracked against the deck.

"Ooh," she moaned, feeling blood bloom on her cheek. Pain radiated from the back of her skull.

Then she blinked, tears springing. Burning. Eyes closed, she retreated. Darkness. Escape. The world spinning out of control. She was falling . . .

"Brooke!"

Her eyes flew open.

Gideon was on top of her, gunmetal-gray clouds whirling above his head, blood trickling down his chin, mirrored glasses reflecting the horror in her face as the world came back into razor-sharp focus.

"Get off me," she ordered. Was he really going to rape her? *Oh, Jesus. No way!* She struggled, fighting. He was on top of her, breathing hard, his weight pinning her down, his hands pulling her wrists over her head.

What?

"Gideon, stop!" She was frantic, kicking and trying to roll away. "Get off me. You can't . . . get the fuck off me!"

"You love it."

"Are you insane?"

"Brooke!"

"Get. The Fuck. Off. Me." She was panting, her pulse thundering in her brain, but she fought. "This is assault! I'll go to the police!"

"Like hell you will." A small, cruel smile crawled across his lips. "So this is how it's gonna be, huh? A little rough. You like that?" His voice was a growl.

Bile rose up her throat. "I *hate* this!"

"Do you?" He mocked, blood dripping onto her sweater.

"I swear, Gideon, if you don't get off me this second—"

"You'll do what?" He leaned closer and she reacted, biting his lower lip again. Harder, as she swung up one leg. Her knee connected with his crotch.

He squealed. "Whaaa—?" He fell to the side.

She scrambled backward as his body convulsed, his legs bending, his body curling, his grip slightly loosened. She didn't wait but gave him another swift kick to the nuts with her boot.

"Ooowoow." Recoiling, he howled in agony.

She rolled swiftly away.

"You goddamned bitch!" he hissed, spittle flying.

Staggering to her feet, she took off.

"This isn't over!" he yelled after her, gasping as he rose up on his knees. "It will never be over!"

She tore down the ramp, mindful of the older guy with the ring of red hair. He'd been washing his boat and had stopped, sponge in hand, soap dripping onto the dock, as she raced by.

"Hey—hey, are you okay?"

She didn't answer, just kept running, her feet pounding down the long dock, fear propelling her, pain radiating up one leg. She kept going, across the small bridge spanning the water between the shore and the boats and into the parking lot.

She heard the man call out, "What the hell's going on?"

She didn't turn around. Didn't look. Just ran. She ran as if her life depended on it. Pain screamed up one leg. She ignored it. Clenching her jaw, limping, her mind racing, she ran. The flock of gulls took off from the roof of the shed in a thunder of wings and caws.

Still she ran, past his damned bike, over the potholes, tears blinding her, her fingers fumbling in her pocket for her key chain.

At the Explorer she hit the remote. The lock clicked. She threw herself inside and yanked the door closed. "Oh God, oh God, oh God," she murmured, her insides shredding as she caught a glimpse of Gideon through the passenger window. He was crouching, gasping for breath, his face red, his eyes fixed on her.

She rammed her SUV into reverse and gunned it.

"Hey!" a throaty, panicked voice yelled.

She stood on the brakes.

The Explorer screeched to a stop. A teenager on a skateboard flew past the driver's side, narrowly missing her side-view mirror. "Why don't you watch where the fuck you're going?"

"What?" Her heart was pounding so fast she could barely breathe.

Blond hair flying around an acne-riddled face, the kid cut around the front of her SUV, the wheels of his skateboard scraping against the uneven asphalt. She flopped back against the seat, adrenaline scorching through her bloodstream at the close call. Through the windshield, she watched him sail across the parking lot, flipping her off with a long, angry finger and turning to look over his shoulder one last time to scream a last epithet: "Fuckin' bitch!"

She let out a shaky breath, her heart hammering wildly.

She could have hit him. Hurt him. Maybe *killed* him. She hadn't even known he was in the parking lot. All because she wasn't paying attention, because she was freaked out, her mind still swirling with images of Gideon's attack.

She took in deep gulps of air and looked back at the sailboat.

No Gideon.

Her heart bucked.

Frantically, she looked around, at the boat, at the dock, in the lot, between the parked cars . . . Where the hell—?

Go! Just get out of here!

She threw the Ford into Drive.

Glanced at the rearview.

Oh shit!

He was right there! Hunched over and running through the trucks, trailers, and parked cars, he loomed, racing toward the passenger door, only a few steps away.

He sprang.

His hand appeared on the window.

She hit the gas.

Her Explorer shot forward.

Just as the scratch of fingernails scraped down the passenger door and it flew open. She cranked hard on the wheel and he flew off.

She heard a sickening thud, and in the side-view mirror she saw him on the pavement, on all fours, staring after her, breathing hard. She slowed at the entrance and pulled the passenger door shut.

Then she punched it again, her tires squealing as she drove through the marina's entrance.

Gideon was climbing to his feet.

She hit the automatic locks, gunned it, and didn't look back.

CHAPTER 6

Later and for once, Brooke managed to pick up Marilee on time. She saw her daughter in front of the school beneath the branches of a sapling planted near the front door, branches nearly bare, dry leaves strewn over the lawn, a fine drizzle falling from the sky. A security officer was posted near the door, a police car parked in the lot not far from the line of buses idling in the pickup lane, where dozens of cars waited, more than usual, as anxious parents waited for their children to appear.

Marilee was with a group of kids but broke away from the pack the second she noticed her mother driving into the pickup lane.

She slipped into the passenger seat.

"Hi—sorry I'm—"

"Can we just go?" Marilee said, buckling her seat belt but slumping down.

"Sure." Brooke drove to the street, waited for several buses to pass, then melded into traffic.

"What happened to you?"

"What?" Brooke glanced over at her daughter.

"Your face. It's all messed up." Marilee's expression was a mixture of worry and revulsion.

"Oh." Brooke caught a glimpse of her visage in the mirror. Saw the cut on her chin and the raspberry on her cheek that makeup failed to completely hide. "I fell down."

"You fell down?" Marilee repeated and turned on the radio, already set to her favorite station.

"Yeah, I was running and didn't see a curb, tripped, and down I went."

"Really?" Marilee asked skeptically as she turned up the volume. Taylor Swift's most recent hit was playing.

"Really."

"You have to be careful."

"I know."

Marilee's eyebrows drew together. "So—are you okay?"

"You mean other than my pride being wounded?" She flashed a smile she didn't feel as she turned on the windshield wipers. "I'll live."

"Geez, Mom, maybe you're too old to be jogging."

"Seriously? I'm thirty-four. Prime of my life!"

"Yeah, but didn't Grandma die at like thirty?"

"Thirty-eight." Brooke hated to think about it, how the cancer had come quickly, barely diagnosed and then Carole Fletcher was gone. Brooke had been a little younger than Marilee when she lost her mother. Even now, her heart twisted with that particular pain reserved for the loss of a parent. And despite her bravado, it wasn't lost on her that she would soon reach the age when her mother had passed.

"And her mom?"

"No, no." Brooke shook her head. "Nana made it to fifty-eight." Cancer too had taken Mary O'Hara quickly because she relied on faith, didn't believe in "popping pills for everything that ails you," and had ignored the symptoms. By the time she'd been diagnosed, it was too late to save her.

"So she was *really* old."

Brooke slid her daughter a glance. "I suppose at fourteen you'd think anyone in their fifties was ancient, but no, it's not all that old."

"So she didn't get sick when she was younger? I mean like you?"

"No."

Brooke had been lucky. Last year's lumpectomy had been a success and she was seemingly cancer-free.

So far.

She had the urge to cross her fingers but didn't.

"So, if you're not too old to jog, you need to be more careful,"

Marilee repeated, and some of her ever-present petulance seemed to have dissipated. When she turned to Brooke her eyes showed genuine concern.

"I'll try to remember that." Brooke turned the wheel and steered the Explorer onto the tree-lined street they called home. Their house came into view. Eyeing the Victorian situated across the street from a park, she remembered those happier days and tried not to think what their lives had become. What was it Nana had said? "For every problem there's a solution. You just have to look for it and pray. God will show you the way."

She hoped so.

Dear Lord, she hoped so.

"So, is there any news about Allison?"

"Don't know." But Marilee was shaking her head. "I—I haven't heard anything. Just weird rumors."

"What kind of rumors?" A commercial was playing, so Brooke turned off the radio.

"I don't know. Some people thought her dad came and got her and he, like, wasn't supposed to, I guess. Her parents are divorced, or separated or something, and involved in this custody fight."

"But," Brooke said, reading her daughter's expression, "you don't think that's true?" She pulled into the driveway.

"No, pretty sure not. That's what everyone thought at first. But it can't be right. Marty Unger, he's a junior in my algebra class and lives down the street from Alli? Anyway, he says Alli's dad is back at the house, and he and the mom have been knocking door-to-door, looking for her. So I guess the dad taking her was just a rumor." She threw a glance at her mother. "You know how that goes."

"Yeah." Brooke nodded. Gossip traveled faster than wildfire and, in high school, even more quickly, as if gasoline was poured onto the flames. "So what else did you hear?"

Marilee lifted a shoulder. "Just stupid stuff, like she hitchhiked out of town and joined a cult or something. Other people, though, they think worse."

"Worse?"

"Like maybe she was kidnapped or murdered."

Brooke's blood turned to ice as she eased the Explorer into the garage. "But there's no evidence of that."

"How would I know?" Marilee asked. "But the cops were at the school. Questioning everybody. Especially Mrs. Cooper, the school counselor. I guess Alli was checking in with her a lot."

"About what?"

"God, Mom, I don't know," Marilee snapped, suddenly angry. "Isn't that, like, confidential or something?" She was already reaching for the door handle. "It's just what I heard. Rumors. Why do you think I would know anything?"

"I'm just asking."

"Well, you can quit asking," Marilee said, climbing out of the car. "I already told you everything I know, so stop with the interrogation!" She let out an angry breath. "God, I shouldn't have said anything!" She flung open the door and was out of the Ford in an instant.

Once again, just like that, she and her teenage daughter were at odds.

"Wow. That's got to hurt," Neal said. He was examining the cut on Brooke's chin. "Maybe you need a stitch or two?"

"I'm fine," she said. She was seated on the bathroom counter, back to the mirror, her husband frowning, his eyebrows pulled together as he surveyed the damage. He'd gotten home late, after Marilee and she had eaten a quick, silent dinner of salad and tuna melts. "And you got this jogging?"

"Stupid, I know. Just took a misstep on the curb, my ankle twisted, and I went down." The lie came easily. Too easily. "It happens."

"Never to you."

"Marilee accused me of being too old to run. She practically called me 'elderly' or 'ancient' or something."

He laughed. "I bet you loved that."

"Mm." But Neal was right. Brooke was sure-footed and so far had been lucky, always able to catch herself or escape injury. "It happens to everyone. Now move."

As he took a step away from the counter, she hopped down, felt a sharp pain in her ankle, and winced slightly as she turned toward the mirror. "I might have to take a day or two off from the exercise routine."

"I'm thinking weeks, but that's up to you." They'd already discussed her ankle, and the fact that she didn't think she needed to seek medical attention. Neal rubbed his chin as he watched her. "Just be careful."

"I will," she said, meeting his eyes in the reflection before peeling the backing off a Band-Aid and applying it to her chin. The wound had stopped bleeding, but this was insurance, at least for the night, that she wouldn't reopen it. The scrape on her cheek was minor, just a graze on the surface, and she didn't have a lump on the back of her skull. She'd already probed it with her fingers, moving around her hair, a red-blond tangle, and using a hand mirror angled at the mirror over the sink to survey the damage.

Even her ankle wasn't too bad, definitely not broken, and if it was sprained, not all that bad. Nothing a little ice wouldn't help cure.

She'd lucked out.

This time.

But she'd had to lie to her daughter and her husband to keep her secret.

Despite her bravado with Gideon during the attack, she wanted to keep the truth from them. So far, so good, she thought as she walked into the bedroom she shared with Neal and plopped down at the end of the bed. "I'm glad you're okay." He eyed the scrape on her cheek and, to her surprise, leaned down and kissed it.

"Oh! Ick!" Marilee said.

They hadn't heard her, but there she was, just on the other side of the open bedroom door. In pajamas, her hair pulled back in a loose bun, she physically recoiled. "Are you like a vampire?" she asked her father.

Neal laughed. "It was just a little kiss."

"But . . . gross!" Her face was a mask of revulsion.

Even Brooke chuckled at her exaggerated response. Neal's phone beeped in his pocket. He pulled it out, glanced at the screen, then back at his wife. "You're sure you're okay?"

"Fine," Brooke assured him, though again, she was hiding the truth. She was anything but fine.

"Okay." He took the call. "Neal Harmon." Passing Marilee still lingering in the doorway, he headed downstairs.

"A vampire?" Brooke teased, pushing herself up to rest against the headboard. "Really?"

Marilee lifted a shoulder and hesitated.

"What's up?" Brooke asked.

For once Marilee seemed nervous. She bit at her lower lip, played with the end of her ponytail.

"Something wrong?"

"No."

"Then out with it." Brooke patted the edge of the mattress, indicating her daughter should join her on the bed.

Marilee didn't budge. "Uh—I was asked to go to the dance this weekend," she said in a rush and a blush crawled up the back of her neck to tinge her cheeks. "Tomorrow night."

Marilee was embarrassed?

Unusual.

Marilee was alternately combative, arrogant, determined, or a combination of all three. Sometimes she could be pensive but rarely abashed.

"So, of course you can go. Who asked you?"

"Nick."

"Nick Paszek? As in Tammi's older brother?" Brooke asked. Tamara Paszek was one of Marilee's friends, a girl she'd known from junior high, and Brooke wasn't familiar with any other kid named Nick.

"Yeah."

"Isn't he . . . what, nineteen?"

Marilee let out a disgusted breath. "He's a senior."

"Who is old for his class." Brooke remembered the kid, who had dropped Tammi off when the girls had a school project together. Tall. Good-looking. Almost a man. "And you're not quite fifteen. Young for your class."

"So?" Marilee's lips tightened defiantly. "Are you saying no?' "

"I thought we agreed that you couldn't officially date until you were fifteen."

"Ooh, Mom, that's like forever. And you always say that I'm wiser than my years."

"Do I?" Brooke couldn't remember using that phrase in front of Marilee, though she had said something about her being an old soul in a young body just the other day when she was on the phone to Andrea. Her daughter was now throwing Brooke's words back at her.

Finally, Marilee stepped into the room and plopped onto the bed next to Brooke.

"Come on, Mom," she wheedled.

Brooke said, "Wait a sec. When did you and Nick start seeing each other?"

"We haven't yet. That's why this is so important!" Marilee flung herself back on the mattress and stared up at the ceiling. "I can go, right?"

"Of course you can go to the dance. You can meet him there, sure."

"He's going to pick me up."

"So it's a real date? Marilee, I don't think it's a great idea—"

"Why not? Geez, Mom, it's not like it's nineteen eighty!"

"I know, but—"

"What do you think's going to happen?" Marilee demanded, turning her head on the duvet so she could stare at her mother. "Don't you trust me?"

Here we go. The age-old argument.

"Of course I trust you."

"Then you don't trust Nick, or that . . . that I can't handle myself around him."

That was it precisely, but Brooke didn't know how to say it. "It's not that," she said. "But since Allison has gone missing—"

"So?" She sat up and pinned her mother in her glare. "You think Nick had something to do with that?"

"No, of course not."

"Hey—what's going on?" Neal's footsteps were loud as he turned the corner and saw the ongoing battle. "Uh-oh. Girl talk."

Marilee gave a little puff of disgust. "Mom won't let me go to the dance with Nick. She thinks he's, like, some serial killer or something."

"What?" Neal looked confused.

Brooke clarified. "Nick Paszek. And I *don't* think he's a serial killer."

"Tammi's brother?" Neal was catching up as he walked into the room and took a seat on the edge of a chair near the closet.

Brooke nodded. "Yes."

"Isn't he in college?" Neal asked.

Brooke said, "Not yet."

"He's a senior!" Marilee cut in. "He goes to my school!"

"He wants to drive her," Brooke explained. "That's the issue here. Not the going-to-the-dance part. Of course she can go to the dance."

Neal said, "I thought we settled this, about dating, I mean."

"I'm almost fifteen," Marilee countered.

"In what? Three months?" Neal was amused.

"That's, like, nothing!" Marilee said.

"A few minutes ago you said it was 'forever,'" Brooke pointed out. She was rewarded with an angry scowl from her daughter.

Neal wasn't deterred. Standing, he cracked his back, then walked to the bureau and leaned against it. "Look, why don't you meet him there?"

"Ooh! That's what Mom said! Like I'm still in junior high. All of my friends get to date! *Their* parents trust them."

"It's not a matter of—" Neal started, then caught the tiny warning shake of Brooke's head.

"You"—Marilee swept her gaze from one parent to the other—"you just don't understand!" With that, she stomped through the door, down the short hallway toward her room.

Neal warned, "Don't slam the—"

Too late. The door to her room closed with a timber-rattling thud.

"—door."

Brooke let out the breath she'd been holding. "Was it my imagination or did the whole house shake?"

He smiled. "I think our whole lives just shook. She's growing up."

"I know, but she just sprang this on me today, a few minutes ago, and the dance is tomorrow night!"

"Maybe he just asked her today."

"Maybe," she admitted, frowning, a headache threatening. "I don't know."

"Fun times," Neal pointed out. "Teenage rebellion."

"I know. And we—the parents—we're so clueless."

"Trying to make her life a living hell," he remarked, scratching at his chin and grinning.

Brooke nodded as she got to her feet. "As if we haven't been there ourselves."

"Oh God, yes. Sally Matthews." He sighed and looked up at the ceiling. "She was the one I would have killed for when I was what—?"

His eyes narrowed as he calculated. "Maybe seventeen. Thereabouts." He wiggled his hand, as if it didn't matter how old he was. "All I could think about was getting her alone and into her pants. That seemed to be my primary goal in life."

"That and basketball."

"Well, yeah." He smiled and shook his head. "But man, was I horny."

"I know." Brooke shared a conspiring look with her husband. "I remember." Theirs had been a fiery, hot, guilt-ridden romance, though Neal was twenty-six and she barely eighteen at the time. Neal had been her first boyfriend since Keith Turnquist, and Neal was off-limits. Taboo. Which had made her want him all the more, caused her to find him incredibly hot. Now, remembering it, she felt cold inside. Their mercurial relationship, fueled by raw sex and teen angst and deception, had been an emotional roller coaster that had cost them both. And yet they were still together despite the obvious holes in their relationship. Deep abysses, in reality.

Brooke only hoped she could help Marilee avoid the same pitfalls.

Neal slid her a glance. "How long has this—this thing with Nick been going on?"

"She says it's not a thing, not yet anyway. But she's interested." Brooke thought for a second. "You know, she's been hanging out with Tammi more, going over to their house for about three months, maybe four. She and Tammi have gotten tighter recently."

"Maybe because of Nick?"

"What do you think?"

"Right." He nodded. "I'll talk to her . . . in a few minutes. Give her time to calm down."

"And—?"

"I think we should stick to our guns. She can meet him at the dance or ride with him and Tammi or some other kids."

"More teenagers in a car is better?" she asked.

"Probably not. But I'll negotiate with her." He grinned. "That's what I do all day long, right? Negotiate settlements for my clients."

"Somehow I think this one might be a little rougher."

"O, ye of little faith."

"Restore it," she suggested. "Restore my faith in your abilities."

She caught a glimpse of light dance in his blue eyes. If nothing else, Neal loved a challenge.

She remembered that too.

Well, he'd certainly get one in Marilee.

"And remind her that we have to be doubly cautious with Allison Carelli gone missing." The headache she was hoping to keep at bay pressed forward. She was still hoping it was really over with Gideon, though that last horrible fight, the vestiges of it obvious, still lingered. Thoughts of him only ramped up her other concerns. She was worried sick about the missing girls, her stomach in knots. "God, I hope Alli's okay," she said fervently. "And Penny Williams too, wherever she is." Brooke's voice had lowered to a whisper, an added thought because it had been so long since Penelope had vanished and hope was fading.

"Me too," he said grimly. "I checked the news. So far, nothing."

"I know."

"And Jennifer is still working on it, but . . . it's up to the police really." As if to change the subject, Neal said, "I'll talk to Marilee about the dance." He was already walking out of the room. "No time like the present."

"You're a brave man, Neal Harmon."

He laughed and she adjusted the ice pack, then picked up the remote for the television and found a local news channel, hoping to hear something about Allison. Instead, she got the weather—a storm rolling in—and politics about an upcoming mayoral race.

Just as she was about to turn off the TV, her phone buzzed.

Gideon!

Her heart leaped to her throat.

But no. The person on the other end of the call was Leah, her recently added name and number showing on the small screen. Brooke considered not answering, gave herself a quick mental lashing, and clicked on. "Hey," she said, walking out of the room and downstairs. "I was about to call you."

"Liar," Leah charged.

"No, really."

"Fine." Obviously, Leah didn't have time to argue. "Look, I heard you fell down while running today, so I thought maybe I'd fly up to Seattle to, you know, take care of you."

"You heard? That I tripped?" Brooke said. "How?"

"Well, you know, I follow Marilee on Instagram and, well, whatever." She said it as if Brooke were thick.

"She posted something there?"

"It wasn't really about you," Leah said, quickly backpedaling. "More like old people shouldn't jog or something."

"Great."

"She didn't use your name."

"It wouldn't take a genius to figure that out." Brooke was irritated at her daughter but tried to keep her mind on the conversation. "It's not that bad. A few scrapes, a twisted ankle, and a bruised ego," she lied. The last thing she needed to deal with right then was Leah and her drama.

"Whatever. It's a good time for me to come up anyway," she said.

"A good time . . . for you?" For the life of her, Brooke couldn't imagine why the middle of October was anything special.

"I just think it's time we got together. I haven't seen you in ages and when I see pictures of Marilee online I hardly recognize her. She is my only niece."

That much was true, but with everything else going on, Brooke wasn't ready to entertain her sister. "Well, yeah. How about Christmas, then?" Brooke suggested, still wary. Right now she didn't need Leah nosing around, not until she was certain Gideon was completely eradicated from her life. She had only to touch her chin or look in the mirror to remember how determined he'd been not to let her go.

Maybe he'd gotten the message.

But Brooke wasn't depending on it.

Not yet.

"Christmas is what? Eight? Oh no, more like ten weeks away," Leah said, her voice shrouded in disappointment.

"But time flies at this time of year," Brooke insisted, trying to find some enthusiasm. "It'll be fun. Maybe we can even go down to the island. Like we used to." The second the words passed her lips she regretted them. Her last quick trip to Piper Island had been with Gideon just a few months earlier. They'd driven down in her SUV, the windows down, the sunroof open. Her heart was pounding with the thrill of it all as they tore down the twisting coast highway, cliffs on one side of the road, the ever-restless Pacific Ocean on the other. Her gut tightened. She didn't need any reminders of her time with him. Not the good and certainly not the bad.

"Huh," Leah said. "The island? I haven't been out there since . . . oh, good Lord, maybe just after college? I can't even remember. Oh. Wait. Now I do. Because I had Ryan with me. It was just after we were married. . . ."

Her voice trailed off, and Brooke didn't want to traipse down that particular, dark memory lane with her sister. Leah's first husband, Ryan Connolly, was a narcissistic prick, in Brooke's estimation. That marriage was doomed before it started, fizzling out after a couple of years. The same was true of Leah's second marriage. That union had been to a stuffy older man named Harrison Bell, and Leah had run herself ragged trying to make him happy. It hadn't worked. Another mistake.

Then, of course, there was the guy who had left her days before they planned to marry. What was his name? Robert Something-or-other? Currently, Leah was certain the man she was married to for several years, Sean Moore, a flashy thirty-five-year-old who liked fast cars and had a penchant for online gambling, was "the one." That was the way it was with Leah. When she fell she fell hard, and always with blinders securely fastened.

She never anticipated the down side of a relationship.

And hadn't that been the reason that Leah's first serious relationship failed? Well, there was more to it than that, Brooke thought guiltily. A lot. But still . . .

From the other end of the connection her sister sighed, and Brooke remembered Leah as she had once been, a gawky preteen, all long legs and wild imagination, her pale hair sleek from her love affair with a flat iron that had tamed her natural, wild curls.

Now Brooke imagined her sister blowing her bangs from her eyes as she had then, before their relationship developed a schism that seemed impossible to bridge.

But to her credit, Leah was trying.

Once more.

It was Brooke who had to step up. Ignore her reservations and give her little sister another chance.

"I think it would be good if I come now," Leah was saying. "I'm kinda between jobs and I know you are too."

"I'm looking, but how did you know that . . . don't tell me. TikTok."

"X, I think. Doesn't matter."

But it did matter. Brooke didn't like her daughter sharing anything personal on social media.

"Anyway, don't argue," Leah insisted. "I'm coming to visit. I'll be there Friday!"

"*This* Friday?" Brooke was dumbfounded.

"Yeah. I already have my ticket and you don't have to worry about picking me up. I can Uber or Lyft or whatever."

"So . . . wait. You already planned this?"

"Yeah," she admitted, then added a little more soberly, "I really need to see you."

And that was the end of any argument.

"Okay, look, I'll pick you up," Brooke said, accepting the fact that she needed to deal with Leah again. "Don't bother with an Uber."

"If you're sure . . ."

"I am. Text me your flight information."

"Okay."

And that was that.

With everything else going on, the last thing Brooke needed now was Leah, with all of her drama and problems, but, for the meantime, she was stuck with her younger sister.

What had Nana called her two granddaughters? Irish twins? Because they'd been born about a year apart?

"You girls should be close," Nana had scolded when they'd been fighting over licking the beaters covered in cookie dough. She'd scraped off the thick, sugary paste that smelled of vanilla and cinnamon and handed each girl a beater, then took off her smudged glasses and wiped the lenses on the hem of her apron. "It wouldn't kill you two to get along, you know," she reprimanded softly as she settled the glasses back onto the bridge of her nose and looked pointedly at Brooke. "You only have one sister."

CHAPTER 7

The day had been long and emotional. After Marilee stormed out of their bedroom and Neal headed to his office, Brooke finally stripped and stepped into the shower.

Leaning against the wet tiles, she closed her eyes and let needles of hot water drive into her back, soaking muscles that were starting to ache from her struggle with Gideon. What had she been thinking? Why had she even gone to meet him? How had she let this go so far?

She'd been a fool to get involved with him. *Idiot*, she chided herself.

She remembered the first time she saw him that day early last June, before summer had really taken hold, at Pike Place Market. It was innocent, totally not intended, and she'd literally bumped into him near the stall for a vendor of handmade jewelry. Well, if she was honest, she'd admit that she'd been distracted and angry. She'd recently lost her job and Neal had just moved out. Their last fight, when she'd accused him of seeing another woman, was still ringing in her ears. It seemed as if their rapidly fraying marriage had finally snapped apart.

In the crowded market she'd been fingering a braided bracelet with a few glass beads that reminded her of garnets, Marilee's birthstone. Brooke had been thinking her daughter might like the bracelet, as Marilee too was despondent about the breakup. Would the bracelet cheer her up?

Brooke had stepped back and held up the piece of jewelry so that the beads would catch the light. At that moment someone had tried to get around her. Instead, he'd bumped into her, and the coffee he'd been carrying splashed, dousing both of them. She'd dropped the bracelet.

"Oh God, I'm so sorry," Brooke had cried, horrified, as she spied the stain blooming on his Mariners T-shirt.

He'd held up both hands, one still surrounding the now nearly empty cup. "No worries."

"But your shirt—"

"But *your* shirt," he'd said.

That was when she realized coffee had sloshed and dripped over her blouse, even splattering onto the lapel of her jacket. "No worries," she repeated and he smiled, a crooked grin in two-days' growth of beard that showed off slightly uneven white teeth.

"Tell ya what, you buy me another coffee and we'll call it square." He leaned down, picked up the bracelet, and handed it to her.

She arched a brow. "So you do think it was my fault?"

"Totally." He nodded, sandy hair shifting over his eyes.

"Okay. Fair enough." She returned the bracelet to its stand, then they walked through the booths and around the customers and tourists who clustered around everything from displays of fresh fruits and vegetables and local wines to flowers and exotic fish. Near a counter filled with baked goods, a woman pushing a stroller nearly cut her off, and this man—whose name she didn't yet know—caught her fingers in his to help her through the throng, then dropped her hand as they reached the coffee shop.

They found a booth near large, curved windows that looked over the street. "I'll have a coffee. Large. Black," he said. His gray eyes seemed to touch hers. "I'm Gideon. Gideon Ross."

"Brooke Harmon."

He smiled again, and she felt her pulse jump stupidly. What was wrong with her?

She said, "Time to pay my debt. One black coffee coming right up." She left him at the table to order and as she picked up his coffee and her latte, she noticed that the barista had decorated her drink with a foam heart.

Oh sure.

Back at the table, she handed him his cup, then sat down and quickly took a sip before he could see the artwork in her cup. Too late, his eyes had followed her movements. She felt herself blush and quickly looked away, returning her change to her wallet before dropping it into her purse.

When he looked up his gaze lingered on hers for a second too long. Breaking it off, he leaned back in the booth. "So, what're you doing down here at the market?"

"Shopping," she said evasively. She wasn't about to confide in him that she'd just been let go from her job, that the start-up tech company she'd given her all to for the past two years had failed. That she, as of this very afternoon, was unemployed. A male coworker's last words still rang in her ears: "Don't let the door hit your pretty ass on the way out." Max Wyckoff was such a sanctimonious jerk.

Worse yet, the nest egg she'd invested in the company was gone.

She had yet to tell her husband and didn't look forward to Neal's reaction.

"You're married," Gideon said, pointing at her wedding ring.

"Yeah."

"Kids?"

"A daughter. Teenager. You?"

"Married? Nah." He shook his head. "Got close a couple of times but never quite made it to tying the knot or . . . pulling the trigger, depending on what you think about 'holy matrimony.'" He made air quotes, even using the fingers of his hand surrounding the cup. "As for kids?" Again the crooked grin. "None that I know of."

She pulled a face.

"Sorry, bad joke. But no. No kids." His eyebrows raised. "That I regret." He leaned back in the booth. "So, this is the middle of the day. And you're here. No job?"

"No. Yes, I mean, no, I don't have a job anymore." Another sip. "I did until today. A good job. Selling software to hospitals, but . . . ." She shrugged. "Competition, I guess. The company's struggling and they had to cut back. So—" She set down her cup. "Anyway, I just found out today."

"Oh. Sorry." He stared at her over the rim of his cup. "You sad about it?"

"Sad?" She thought about it. She was worried. Angry. Upset. But sad? "No. Not really. But it's a problem."

"So, losing the job could be a release."

"What?"

"You know. Maybe now you're free." Gray eyes studied her. "Come on. The truth. Did you love it? Look forward to going to hospitals and trying to convince some budget-conscious administrator or manager how great the latest version of your software was, how they absolutely needed it?"

She lifted a shoulder. "It was a job."

"There are other jobs. Maybe there's something out there more exciting? Something you'll really be passionate about."

"I, uh—I invested," she admitted, then wished she could take the words back.

"And you got burned."

She was nodding, thinking she was divulging far too much to this perfect stranger.

He shrugged. "Happens all the time."

"Easy to say, but when it happens to you it's different."

"I suppose." He finished his coffee. "You know what you need?"

"No, what?" She eyed him skeptically.

"A ride on a sailboat."

"Oh right!" With all of her problems, the last thing she needed to do was throw caution to the wind and go sailing. Shaking her head, she got to her feet. "That is definitely not what I need." He was still seated, long, jean-clad legs stretched out. "You don't know me."

"You're right," he agreed. "I don't. But if you change your mind, I've got a boat down at the marina. The *Medusa*."

"You named your boat after Medusa? From mythology? The gorgon, or goddess, or whatever she was, with the head filled with snakes?"

He stood then and said, "You know, Brooke, things aren't always what they seem."

"Then what are they?"

He laughed and checked his watch. "Uh-oh. Gotta run." He smiled, his gaze finding hers again. "Thanks for the coffee."

Before she could say another word, he walked out of the coffee shop.

Two days later she received a package in the mail with no return address. Inside was the very bracelet she'd been fingering at the market just before she'd run into Gideon Ross.

As she'd plucked it from the tiny tissue-lined box, she'd seen the bloodred beads glitter in the sunlight from the lowering sun. And there was more. A tiny charm attached to it, a sailboat engraved with a date, the very date she and Gideon had literally run into each other at Pike Place Market.

That was the start of something that should never have begun.

Now, shoving the memory aside, she turned off the water, toweled off, and swiped away the condensation that had collected on the mirror's surface. Standing naked, she saw one bruise forming on her arm and another over her ribs, and then there was her face. The scrape on her cheek would heal, but the cut on her chin might scar.

Physical reminders of her fight with Gideon.

Great.

Her ankle was a little sore, but she'd survive.

She eyed her breasts and remembered how he'd loved touching them, but she wasn't about to go there, so she slipped on her robe and cinched it around her waist. She had to stop thinking about him.

Walking into the bedroom, she tried to concentrate on other things in her life. Her husband and the way they'd grown apart. Her daughter trying to grow up too fast and pull away from her. And two missing girls. Then there was her nonexistent job, her wrecked Explorer, and now her sister coming to visit.

"Perfect," she said, wincing a bit as she sat on the bed and turned on the TV. This time, after the local baseball and football scores, there was a report on Allison Carelli, a picture of the girl coming onto the screen along with the number for the police on a banner running across the bottom. The reporter, a thin man wearing a jacket with the logo of the station and a grim expression, stood in front of Allsworth High School. He recounted what Brooke already knew and asked anyone with information to call the police at the number in the chyron.

She clicked off the set and moved a little too quickly, the pain in her leg reminding her again of the fight. She'd never been in a physical fight, unless you counted the few times she and Leah got into spats as kids.

She made her way to the bureau, found her nightshirt and tossed it on, then opened her underwear drawer and stopped short.

She stared at the rows of panties inside.

Something was wrong.

She kept her panties rolled up neatly, which they were, but they weren't stuffed in as tightly as usual. The drawer wasn't nearly as full. Odd, she thought, touching the bits of lace and silk. Hadn't she done the laundry two days earlier? Shouldn't there be more pairs?

A feeling of apprehension, like the whisper of spider legs crawling up her spine, swept through her.

Slowly, she took stock. Several pairs were missing: the lavender lace and the pink silk and the pale yellow pair with lacy inserts . . . Oh. God.

Her stomach turned over as she opened her bra drawer and discovered that the matching pieces were missing, all lingerie she'd worn when she was with Gideon. Her sports bras were untouched, the plain panties neatly rolled where she'd placed them. Only the sexy items were missing, the scraps of lace and silk she'd worn with him.

No, no, no! She grabbed the edge of the bureau for support.

Telling herself that she was mistaken, she searched again, riffling through the other drawers. She slipped on a pair of cotton panties and hobbled down the stairs and through the kitchen to the laundry room.

She tore through the laundry basket, frantically tossing aside Marilee's leotards and shorts, Neal's T-shirts, and her own sweatshirts and jeans.

Her stomach dropped like a stone.

She threw open the lid to the washer, thinking maybe she'd forgotten that she'd put them in the tub.

Nope.

Of course not!

The old Maytag was empty.

She crouched to look through the glass door of the dryer, where she saw a tangle of towels, wrinkled from being left unattended.

"Shit!" Rocking back on her heels, she held her head in her hands and felt totally violated.

Somehow, some way, he'd stolen her lingerie.

She knew it in the darkest part of her soul.

Leaning against the washer, she remembered his teeth on the clasp of her lavender bra, a push-up with a clasp in the front. He'd glanced up at her, his hot tongue on her skin, his eyes searching upward as he opened the flimsy piece with his mouth.

Now the scenario repulsed her. "Son of a—"

"Mom?" Marilee's voice startled Brooke and she looked up sharply. "What're you doing?"

Her daughter was standing in the doorway half a floor above, backlit by the hall light, the dog at her side.

"I, um, just realized I left a load of towels in the dryer by mistake," she lied, straightening quickly. "Still damp." She turned the knob and pushed a button. The ancient dryer, on its last legs, clicked on and began noisily tumbling, towels of various colors flipping past the clear door.

Marilee eyed her. "You—you looked like something was wrong."

"Well, there is," she admitted, knowing she couldn't say differently. "I'm out of work, rear-ended an ass in a Porsche, tripped while running, and I'm worried sick about girls that I know who are missing." Then she added, "Oh, and on top of all that, my daughter thinks I'm totally out of it, an ogre of a mother."

"Not an ogre," Marilee argued. "Just super overprotective. You don't trust me."

Brooke disagreed. "I trust you, but . . ." She waggled her head back and forth before admitting, "I'm not too sure about Nick."

"You don't even know him!" Crossing her arms around her slim chest, Marilee angled her chin up defensively.

"You're right. I don't." She was making a mess of this.

"But you're judging him anyway."

"Okay, okay, so that wasn't fair. I'm sorry."

Mollified slightly, Marilee arched an eyebrow and asked, "So I can go?"

"To the dance? Where you can meet him? Yes, of course, as I said, but it wouldn't hurt if your dad and I met him. Didn't Dad talk to you about this already?"

"Yeah, but I thought maybe . . . ooh, never mind!" She was shaking her head, her face turning red with fury as she spun on her heel and stormed off.

Shep was left standing at the top of the stairs, his tail wagging slowly.

"I know. Teenagers, eh?" Then Brooke managed a smile. "I guess it's just you and me," she said as the dryer bleated and she realized she'd engaged the timer for five minutes instead of fifteen. Another stupid mistake. "Story of my life," she told the dog and gave the knob another angry twist.

CHAPTER 8

Brooke let out a soft moan.

Gideon was lying on top of her. Naked. Sweating and whispering that he wanted to make love to her, his hard body undulating against hers. She felt the rapture of his touch, wanted him desperately, ached for him there, on the island, with the sound of the surf seeping through the windows. She sighed as his fingers surrounded her nape, tangling in her hair, pulling her close. But in the distance, over the cry of seagulls, she heard another voice . . . a girl's voice, calling for help.

"We have to go," she told him, trying to push him away, but he was strong and wouldn't release her. As she stared into his eyes, she saw evil lurking in their gray depths.

"Brooke," he whispered, shaking her, "I'll never let you go . . . Brooke . . ."

"Brooke?" Neal's voice. Loud. Worried.

Her eyes flew open.

She was in bed, yes, but in Seattle, not on the island.

And with her husband, not Gideon Ross.

Thank God.

"Are you okay?" Warm fingers touched her shoulder.

She rolled over to find Neal beside her in the familiar room lit only by the clock's digital display and the city lights visible through the window. "You were whimpering."

Oh. God. "Was I?"

"And restless, rolling around." The twisted sheets were a testament to his words.

"Bad dream," she said. "Nightmare."

"About?"

"Marilee," she said quickly. "I can't remember the details, but she was in some kind of trouble." A quick lie as the particulars of her dream were fresh. Imprinted. And scared her to her bones.

"The only trouble she's in is that her mother won't let her go on a date with an older boy."

"And her father would?"

"No. We settled this." He levered himself up on one elbow and his face was more visible in the weakest of light from the window. The dim glow exaggerated his bold features, making his deep-set eyes appear more guarded, his nose more prominent, his beard shadow darker. "But I like it that you're the bad guy."

If you only knew, she thought. "Nice of you."

He tugged at the covers; she'd wound herself in the bedclothes. "Not nice, but practical." Once the sheets were straightened over both of them, he snuggled up against her, his long body spooning hers as she faced the window again. "Better?"

"Yes," she said, grateful for his strength. Theirs had been a far-from-perfect marriage, but she did care for him. And a once-passionate marriage that had seeped into indifference, even infidelity—was that so unusual? They'd weathered a lot of storms right from the get-go, but they were still together, if tentatively, the tether of matrimony that bound them frayed but not severed.

Yet.

She nestled into his warmth and felt his arms surround her, his big hands cupping her breasts, pulling her tight to hug against him. This was right, she told herself, noticing how her knees bent perfectly inside his. As she sighed, she sensed his arousal, felt his erection against her buttocks, noticed that he was fingering her nipples until they responded, which they did.

She closed her eyes.

For the first time in a long while, she welcomed him.

An hour after their lovemaking, Brooke was still restless. Neal, as always after sex, was sleeping soundly, snoring a bit, dead to the world, while she was keyed up, her nerve endings afire. She slid from beneath the covers and moved quietly down the stairs, her ankle aching a bit. Without switching on any lights, she padded to the kitchen and the French doors leading to the deck.

The dead bolt hadn't been turned.

So the house was unlocked.

Anyone could climb up the stairs from the backyard and walk into the kitchen and . . . She bit her lip. Was this how Gideon had gotten inside? This was the way they all let the dog out, and during the day it was usually unlocked.

Well, no more. She'd keep the house locked tight day in, day out. Now, still bothered, she stepped quietly onto the deck. This time she didn't hesitate but found her pack of cigarettes and lit up. Years ago, she and Neal had shared a cigarette after lovemaking. Now they never did. Neal was a holier-than-thou ex-smoker, and the phrase her grandmother always used, "There's nothing so self-righteous as an ex-sinner," came to mind as she took a deep drag. The cigarette was stale but hit the spot. She leaned over the rail to stare at the distant city lights, seeming to float in the darkness of the early morning. She heard a scratching and turned to see Shep on the other side of the glass door. "Oh man, did I wake you?" she asked, opening the door. The dog stepped out, paused for a quick pat, then made his way to the steps leading down to the backyard, waddled down them, and disappeared.

Brooke rotated her stiff neck. Her body ached from the accident with the jerk in the Porsche—Gustafson—and, of course, from her scuffle with Gideon.

Scuffle?

More like a fight to the finish.

And that worried her.

Was it the finish? Was it over? Now that she suspected Gideon had invaded her house and taken her private things, she had a deeper look into his obsession. How far would he go? The question, one he'd posed earlier, rang through her mind. Her physical injuries were evidence of how disturbed he was.

Gideon had been quiet ever since the struggle on the sailboat, but she wondered how long it would last. If it would.

And when had he been in her house—when had he been in her bedroom? Before she'd broken it off with him? Maybe because he'd sensed it was coming. No matter how gobsmacked he'd acted when she'd called and then gone to his sailboat for their confrontation, she'd hinted before in the last few weeks when he'd wanted to make plans, and many times she'd made excuses. Maybe he'd had access all along and had taken the items one at a time so she wouldn't notice.

Was it possible?

He'd had the nerve to show up on her doorstep, facing her and her family, so why wouldn't he sneak around?

Once more she mentally kicked herself for not vetting him before getting involved with him. She'd been such a moron!

She should have done a lot more research on him and wondered why she hadn't. Probably because she didn't really want to know.

After receiving the package with the bracelet and charm she'd done a little digging on the Internet, doing a perfunctory google search and scraping the surface of social media. Nothing there. Then she searched the registrations at local marinas for a boat named the *Medusa*.

As luck would have it, she discovered the location of the boat, the owner registered as Gideon Ross.

That matched.

So she checked it out by driving to the marina.

From the parking lot on that gray April day she caught sight of the craft, a gleaming white sailboat with the name *Medusa* scripted on the transom. She decided to get a closer look, to actually climb out of her Explorer and walk onto the dock so she could see the boat more closely. The artwork curving around the side of the sailboat was an artist's rendering of Medusa's serpent-infested head captured in the arms of a jellyfish. The snakes and tentacles were wound together, caught in what appeared to be a death struggle.

"Wow," she'd said under her breath, studying the disturbing scenario. "Dark."

This was his boat?

Sure enough. Because as she looked past the weird art to the deck above, she saw him stretching to clean the windows of the cabin, the hem of his sweatshirt rising over the waistband of faded, torn jeans.

She felt awkward being there but told herself she had a mission.

So, with one eye on the threatening sky, she made her way along the dock to the boat.

"Hey!" she yelled, standing close to the sailboat as it undulated with the dark water of the sound. "Hey, Gideon!"

He kept washing the windows, seemingly unaware of her.

"Gideon!"

"He can't hear you."

She turned and spied an older guy on the deck of his own boat, a smaller vessel moored on the other side of the dock.

His bald pate was rimmed with red hair turning gray and he was hauling buckets of bait. He set down one bucket on the deck of his boat and pointed to one of his ears. "He's got those ear thingies in. Always."

"Earbuds."

"Whatever they're called." He picked up his bucket again, and she caught sight of the shiny scales of some dead fish as water sloshed over the pail's rim. "He can't hear a goddamned thing." He shook his head. "Washing windows on a day like today. Waste of goddamned time, if you ask me."

She headed up the gangway and stepped onto the boat. Gideon's face was etched in concentration, lips flat, eyes narrowed as he rubbed at a spot on the window with a towel. Then, as if he'd sensed her presence, he looked over his shoulder and noticed her, his hair catching in the salty breeze. Slowly, a smile crept across his jaw. "You found me."

"Yeah."

Straightening, he nodded. "I wondered." He dropped the towel into a pail on the deck.

"What?"

The lift of one shoulder. "If you'd bother."

"I had to."

One eyebrow raised, encouraging her as the wind kicked up and her hair blew over her face.

"Because—because I wanted to return this." She brushed her hair from her eyes, then dug into her purse, came up with the tiny package containing the bracelet. She handed it to him. "I can't take it."

"Why not?"

"It's—it's not appropriate."

"If you say so."

"I do. I don't know you. And I'm . . . I'm . . ."

"What?" he asked, seemingly amused at her discomfiture.

"Well—"

"Let me guess. Because you're married," he guessed.

Nodding, she said, "Yeah, I guess that's it."

"And he would be—what? Offended? Or . . . jealous? He'd get angry?"

She thought about Neal and wondered if he'd even care. These days Neal's interest in her had waned. Big-time.

"Would he hurt you?" Gideon asked, his smile fading, his expression changing to concern as the first drops of rain began to fall.

Neal? "No! Never." She shook her head vehemently. Neal was a lot of things, but violent? No.

"But he wouldn't like it," Gideon guessed, glancing at the sky.

"Uh—maybe not. But more likely he wouldn't notice," she admitted, then regretted the words. She shouldn't confide anything to this man, this stranger.

"Oh." He nodded, as if agreeing with himself as the dark clouds scudded in the sky. "So then why bring it back?" he asked as the rain continued, the wind picking up.

"It seemed like the right thing to do."

"It doesn't seem right to me. It's a gift. And I can't return it. It's engraved." He held it out, the tiny charm dangling, but she took a step back, rain starting to fall in earnest, pummeling the deck. She felt the cold drops hit the top of her head and flipped up the hood of her jacket.

"Then you keep it. Seriously. I can't take it."

"Look." He held up his hands, the box still gripped between his fingers of one hand, the bracelet twined in the other. "It's not a big deal. Nothing all that significant, okay? It's just that I saw you looking at it just before we—you know."

"Bumped into each other."

"Collided," he corrected, shouting over the wind.

"Okay, collided." She too raised her voice.

"Hey!" He glanced at the sky. "It's really coming down. We should go inside."

"No. I have to go." She took a step toward the gangplank, then looked over her shoulder. "How did you know my address?"

Again the flash of a grin, the corners of his eyes crinkling. "I saw it when your wallet was open. Your driver's license."

"And you remembered it?"

"Yeah." The boat was rocking. "Come on." He didn't wait for her to argue but grabbed her hand and led her down a short flight of stairs to a small cabin. Though she told herself she was crossing some invisible threshold to a point of no return, she followed. Inside was a tiny suite of wood-paneled rooms, a salon with a galley nearby, and a bathroom, or head, beneath the stairs. Through an open partition she caught sight of the foot of a bed, the head of which, she guessed, was tucked into the prow.

"Coffee? Or tea?"

"Oh no, I don't think—"

"Wine, then, or a beer?" He cocked an eyebrow.

"Definitely not. I just came by to drop off the bracelet."

His glance told her that was a lie. "And you were curious."

"No, I—well, maybe a little." It seemed unreasonable to avoid the truth.

He walked to the small galley, found coffee in a carafe, and poured two mugs.

She wanted to protest but didn't. "Sit," he said, nodding to the built-in couch near a foldout table. She did. After setting the cups on the table, he said, "You can take off your jacket."

"I'm not staying."

"Still—it's wet."

"Fine." She slid out of the rain jacket and he hooked a finger under the collar and hung it on a peg near the stairs, next to a scuba-diving suit. He yanked off his sweatshirt and put it on a nearby hook and she saw his bare torso, flat abdomen, and muscular shoulders, the way his jeans hung low. She forced her nose into her cup but couldn't force herself to look away as he snagged a black T-shirt from the row of hooks and slid it over his head.

She felt a flush climb up her neck and did finally turn her attention to a porthole but caught his reflection as he forced his arms through a flannel shirt that he didn't bother buttoning.

Once more she tried not to stare and instead wrapped her fingers around the warm cup and pretended interest in anything but him. On a little hook she spied a necklace, beads, and what looked like a hook made out of bone. "What's this?" she asked, and he glanced at her, saw her fingers touching the hook, and for just a heartbeat seemed to tense. "Something I picked up in Polynesia," he said dismissively.

"You sailed there?"

"A long time ago."

Before she could ask more about it, he swung the desk chair around, the one piece of furniture not currently bolted down, and straddled it. "Tell me about yourself," he suggested, picking up his mug.

"Not much to tell."

"No? So indulge me." He cast a look to the windows. "Until the storm passes."

"I can't stay long."

"It'll be over in half an hour."

"And you know this—how?"

"Years at sea and," he yanked a phone from his pocket, "a handy weather app."

"Isn't that cheating?"

His gray eyes twinkled. "And what would I know about cheating? For that matter, what would you?"

She felt heat climb up the back of her neck. "Probably too much," she admitted, thinking of Neal and his attraction to his coworker, their rumored affair. A woman new to the firm and younger than his wife. And then, of course, there was what had happened years before.

He was intrigued. "Tell me."

"I don't think so." She set her cup on the table. "Look, I really need to go. I just came by to drop off the bracelet. Thank you for it. Very thoughtful of you, but I just don't want to give anyone the wrong idea."

"Meaning me?"

"Meaning anyone," she said and stood. She swept her purse from the floor and reached for her jacket. She started for the stairs. When she was on the first step he caught her hand and spun her around. She found herself staring at him at eye level. Her heart fluttered and she gasped as he leaned forward and brushed his lips against her cheek. "That's for taking the time to find me."

She gulped. "No problem." And then she raced up the remaining steps and out into the windswept, wet day. The clouds were parting and the rain had slowed to a steady drizzle. She felt the urge to pause and look over her shoulder, but she knew it would be a mistake. She kept walking until she reached her SUV. Once in the interior she stared through the rain-spattered window to see him on the deck of his sailboat, legs braced and parted, the tail of his flannel shirt flapping in the breeze. He found her gaze and grinned, that knowing, almost cocky grin she found far too sexy.

Stop it, she told herself, not liking the turn of her thoughts.

She switched on the ignition and rammed the Explorer into gear, nearly peeling out as she raced away from the marina. Her fingers were tight over the steering wheel, her pulse pounding in her brain.

What are you doing, Brooke? Whatever it is, stop it now!

She drove home, her mind spinning.

She shouldn't be thinking about him. Should *not!*

But she did.

A lot.

Late that night, after searching him out and spending time with him on the boat during the rainstorm, she'd been too keyed up to sleep. Just as she'd done tonight, she'd sneaked downstairs and out the back door to the deck in search of a cigarette. That time the lighter she kept with her pack in the birdhouse refused to ignite. Frustrated, she'd gone inside to search for her purse for a backup. There, she'd discovered the package she'd thought she'd left on the boat with Gideon.

Sure enough, within the package was the bracelet.

She'd been stunned at the time.

And slightly, silently thrilled.

Without thinking, she'd clasped the links over her wrist. Even in the half light from a moon peering from behind gauzy clouds, the bloodred stones had winked and glittered, portending a future she couldn't possibly have foreseen.

CHAPTER 9

Now, as she once again stood on the back deck, the tip of her cigarette glowing in the October night, she found herself caught in memories of Gideon and what they'd shared—the glee, the sex, the guilt. All of it.

From the moment she'd clicked the bracelet over her wrist, she'd found herself fantasizing about him. Gideon had brought some much-needed excitement into her otherwise drab life. Marilee had begun to pull away from her as she entered high school, becoming more independent. It was natural—a positive development—but it left an emotional hole. Neal had been wrapped up in his career as a corporate attorney, working long hours. When he did have time off, he was out of the house for his Wednesday poker nights and Saturday morning golf games, expanding his life beyond their small family. Well, some of that had been a lie. He'd been spending time with someone else, she'd learned, which was the reason they'd split.

Neither her husband nor her daughter needed her as much any longer, nor did the start-up company that had let her go after taking most of her retirement funds.

When Gideon came along she was feeling alone and useless, as if her life was spiraling into a dull, black hole.

"No excuse," she whispered into the night as Shep reappeared and looked up at her. "Promise," she added, as if the dog could understand her.

Over the past few months she'd done a little research online, trying to find more information about Gideon as her obsession grew. At first pass she'd found he had no serious social media presence. No google info. There were many entries under the name of Gideon Ross of course, but none seemed to match the intriguing man with the sailboat. Finding no information, she'd let it go and hadn't dug any deeper.

Not knowing more about him had added an edge to him, an aura of mystery that she hadn't been eager to puncture.

She'd been a fool. A stupid, gullible fool! That much was more than apparent now.

Brooke drew on her filter tip once more, then jabbed out the half-smoked cigarette on the underside of the deck's rail. She would wrap the butt in an old bit of trash and take the bag out to the bin outside the garage to hide it from Neal and Marilee. No reason to start a fight or give her daughter any ideas.

She thought again about the bracelet, which she'd hidden in the birdhouse with her cigarettes. She wasn't going to go through the melodrama of returning it to him again, no. She would give it away. Donate it anonymously and be done with it. She made a mental note to add it to her ever-expanding to-do list, then glanced once more at the sloping backyard and the city beyond it. As she turned to go inside, she looked up at the window of the master bedroom, still dark, only the faintest of light seeping through the window near the bump out for the old staircase, the "fire escape" that crawled up from the laundry room to the attic. At least she hadn't woken Neal.

Shep followed her inside and she secured the door, turning the dead bolt and double-checking the lock. She opened the cupboard for the garbage, then shoved the butt of her cigarette deep into the coffee grounds she'd tossed out earlier. Satisfied she'd destroyed the evidence and feeling foolish that she'd gone to such lengths, she swept up the sack from the wastebasket under the sink and carried it through an alcove off the living area. The door was locked thankfully, and she took the trash outside and along the path to the spot where they kept the large recycling and trash bins.

Before she went inside she heard a noise: the scrape of leather against concrete. A footstep? At this time of night? Standing on tiptoe, straining her ankle, she peered over the gate and stared at the deserted street at the front of the house. Watery blue light from a single lamppost illuminated the wide entrance to the park.

Was there someone moving between the trees? Brooke squinted, the hairs at the back of her neck rising. It wasn't unusual for people to be inside the community's wrought-iron barricade; the gates were never closed and the city had its share of people out at night.

She caught a movement, a shadow that seemed to dart between the thickets of pine and fir.

So what?

But it wasn't the quicksilver umbra of a nocturnal animal as it moved silently through the trees that bothered her. It was a primal sense, something deep inside that insisted she was being observed, a strong, almost visceral feeling that predatory eyes she couldn't see were watching her, sizing up the house.

She scanned the perimeter fencing and beyond, where the lamplight glowed dim, giving the surrounding grounds a gray, washed-out aura. The tall trees seemed to shift, leaves rustling in the slight breeze. And somewhere deep within the near darkness were those eyes, watching her.

You're just being paranoid. Stop it! Get over yourself!

She spied no one staring at her from the shadows, so she stepped back inside, locking the door behind her. She pressed against the steel, testing its strength.

In the kitchen she was able to slip a new liner into the trash can under the sink without turning on any lights. Then she started for the stairs, but she nearly bumped into the dog, who was standing at the front door.

"Come on," she whispered, but Shep didn't move, his head low, his hackles raised, a rumble of a growl in the back of his throat.

"What?" she whispered, then looked through the sidelight. No one was on the porch. But as she gazed farther, across the street, through the gauzy light from the lamppost, she noticed a dark figure standing just outside the weak pool of illumination.

Man or woman?

Friend or foe?

Innocent or evil?

Of course she couldn't tell.

But her heart stopped for a second and her fingers touched the lock on the door, making certain it was bolted.

Again Shep growled, brown fur at his nape standing on end.

The shadowy being stepped out of the light and disappeared.

There one second, gone the next.

She swallowed against a suddenly dry throat.

It's nothing! Nothing. This is the city. There are homeless and night owls and night-shift workers whose hours are turned around and—

The dog remained at the door, nose to the panels, black lips curling slightly. A warning that something—no, some*one*—was out there.

And, she decided, it wasn't someone good.

Heart knocking, she squinted as a car slowly passed, headlights glowing in the dark, flooding the road for a second as it passed. Then the street was empty. If not for the dog's tense body and growl, she would have thought whoever was out there had left. They were safe here, the three of them in the locked house with the dog. And then, Neal had a gun, secured in a safe in his den, never needed, never used. She took in a deep breath, calming herself, then touched the dog's head.

"Come on," she said softly. "Let's go." She snapped her fingers, and finally, Shep turned his attention to her and followed her as she quietly stole upstairs.

On the second floor Brooke checked on Marilee, silently opening her door to see that her daughter was burrowed under the covers, dark hair and one arm visible against the sheets.

Safe.

Good.

She didn't object when the dog stole inside and hopped onto the bed, curling at the foot before looking up at Brooke expectantly. "Okay," she whispered, "but just this once." She shut the door.

Back in her bedroom, she slipped noiselessly between the sheets, careful not to wake Neal.

As her head found the pillow, she closed her eyes, intent on forcing sleep.

A few minutes ticked by and she heard a creak in the old timbers of the house. No big deal. It happened all the time. Nothing was wrong. A hundred-year-old house still settles, aging joists sometimes squeaking or groaning.

You're letting your imagination run wild.

So someone was in the park in the early morning hours, so what?

It just so happens the park is directly across the street. Big effin' deal.

Get over yourself.

She quieted her mind.

Consciously relaxed her tense muscles.

Started to drift off . . .

Footsteps!

As if someone were running!

Down the stairs!

But no one was up.

Instantly alert, she rose on an elbow, her ears straining.

"You shouldn't do that," her husband admonished her.

She nearly jumped out of her skin.

What was he talking about? Then it hit her. He *knew*? *About Gideon?*

She didn't respond. Maybe Neal was just talking in his sleep, or—

"It's not good for you."

"What?" she asked, hardly daring to breathe, lying down again. No one was on the stairs. She had imagined the noise as she started to fall asleep.

"Smoking." His voice was stern. "You know how I feel about it, and all the health risks it brings with it."

Oh crap! He smelled it on her. She hadn't taken the time to wash her face and hands, or to use any breath mints, as she always did when she snuck a cigarette. But it was so long since she'd actually smoked, she'd forgotten. "Don't worry about it."

"But I do, Brooke," he said quietly.

She wondered if he was talking about more than her sneaking a cigarette. "You don't have to—"

"I always worry about you."

"Neal, what're you talking about?" she asked, deciding now, in the middle of the damned night, was when they were going to actually have it out. She braced herself for the midnight accusations. He'd only moved back into the house in the last few weeks and she was just getting used to him being around again.

Hence the imminent need to break up with Gideon.

She leaned closer to her husband. "Neal? What—?"

But he was already drifting off, his breathing becoming steady. In the faint light she saw that his eyes were closed. The conversation was over and that was a good thing, right? No confession necessary.

Soon he was snoring again and she was wound tight as the spring on a stopwatch. She got up and washed her hands and face, brushed her teeth and even flossed, all in the dark. Her features were ghostly in the bathroom mirror, pale, taut skin, accentuated by the dim glow of a single night-light. She splashed more water onto her face and was on her way back to bed when she passed by the bedroom window overlooking the backyard and the view of Seattle's lights and the dark waters of Elliott Bay beyond. Somewhere out there, presumably sleeping in the berth of his sailboat, was Gideon.

Once he'd been the spark in her life.

The hidden joy.

The little secret she'd kept hidden.

A fantasy that had become oh so real.

A dream.

And now he was a nightmare.

She leaned her head against the panes and glanced down at the yard to see him standing there, face turned up, right in the middle of the garden.

She almost cried out but bit back the scream, and as a cloud passed by the moon, allowing its luminance to play over the landscape, she realized it wasn't Gideon in the middle of her yard but the fountain, now broken and dry, standing in its usual spot.

He wasn't in the yard.

He never was.

"Come to bed," Neal said groggily, awake again. "I'm sorry I yelled at you."

"You didn't yell and what's going on? I thought you were asleep."

"In and out. Dozing." He patted the mattress softly. "Come on, Brooke."

Once again she slid between the bedsheets, the duvet thick and cozy over her, Neal's arm sliding familiarly around her waist.

This should be enough, she told herself. *This man, our house, the daughter we share; it should be enough.*

But was anything, ever?

And at that moment, not far away, she heard the sound of a motorcycle's engine fire.

Her insides congealed.

She heard the bike's engine whine and catch as the rider sped through the city, engine whining, then catching to rev again as the rider put the motorcycle through its gears.

Brooke's fingers twisted in the pillowcase.

He'd been there.

She knew it.

Gideon had been outside the house. Watching. Waiting.

And maybe he'd been inside, she thought wildly. Hadn't she heard footsteps?

The doors were locked, though. She'd double-checked. Did he have a key, or had he been trapped inside . . . watching her from inside the house rather than through the windows? Walking one step behind her as . . .

Oh God . . . but . . . no, the dog would have sensed him.

The back of her throat went dry as sand.

Why would he risk coming here?

For you, Brooke.

He wants you.

It's not that he loves you.

Don't kid yourself. You know better. He won't let you go. Not ever.

He wants to own you.

"Never," she whispered, and Neal stirred beside her.

She held her tongue then and stared at the window.

She couldn't let him destroy her life.

Somehow, some way, she had to get rid of him.

It was as simple as that.

CHAPTER 10

Sea-Tac was teeming as usual, the airport parking area filled with vehicles, cars weaving between taxis, buses, and hotel vans, all clogging the roadway.

Leah's flight, delayed by two hours, had finally landed.

She had texted Brooke that she was heading to the spot where they'd agreed to meet, in a parking garage where Brooke had squeezed her Explorer into a tight spot marked "Compacts Only."

Ten minutes later Brooke spied her sister. In a pink sundress, pulling a roller bag behind her, holding on to a floppy-brimmed hat with the other, Leah looked around, lost.

Brooke honked, then climbed from behind the wheel to wave and catch her sister's attention.

Leah started in her direction, stopped suddenly, and waited impatiently for a minivan to drive past before hurrying along the aisle between the parked cars.

"Good God, I forgot how cold it is up here," she said before releasing the suitcase handle so she could offer Brooke a huge, unexpected hug. "Brrr. I don't know how you stand it."

Brooke flinched a little as Leah inadvertently squeezed her hard enough to remind her of the bruise healing on one shoulder.

"Ooh, sorry." Leah stepped back and appraised her sister, her large eyes focusing on Brooke's scraped chin. "You look like hell."

"I missed you too."

"I mean . . . I forgot you took a header and—" Her gaze swept over the front end of Brooke's Explorer. She ran a finger along a huge dent. "Ouch."

"Yeah, 'ouch.' Let's go." She put Leah's bag onto the back seat.

"Wait!" Leah leaned in through the open back door, unzipped the bag, and found a sweater and a pair of casual shoes. Quickly, she took off her heels, closed the door, then climbed into the passenger seat, where she slipped her feet into her Skechers. "Sorry," she said. As Brooke climbed in behind the wheel, Leah wriggled into the oversize cardigan before snapping her seat belt over her slim torso. "It's freezing."

"It's sixty."

"Like I said, freezing."

"Didn't you live in Chicago?" Brooke started the SUV.

"Once upon a time, yeah. Eons ago. With Ryan." Leah glanced out the window as if she'd rather not talk about the time when she was married to her first husband, Ryan Connolly, whom she usually referred to as Ryan the Rat. "It's a dry cold there, you know."

"What? In Chicago? No. Cold is cold. And it really freezes there. I've seen pictures of ice on Lake Michigan." Eyes on the backup camera, Brooke reversed the Explorer out of the tight parking space. "You're just used to Arizona."

"I guess." Leah changed the subject. "All this"—she made a circular motion with her hand to take in Brooke and all of her injuries—"happened when you—what? Tripped?"

"Right."

Leah gave Brooke an exaggerated once-over as the sound of a revving motorcycle engine echoed through the structure. "You should be more careful."

"Ya don't say," Brooke said dryly.

"Seriously."

"I'm working on it." Brooke wound her way down the spiral ramp, other vehicles sliding behind her, the sound of the motorcycle still audible. For a second she thought about Gideon and his Harley, then tried to shove the idea out of her head. There were hundreds—no, make that thousands—of motorcycles in the area. And he hadn't bothered her in the few days since the fight. She was letting her own paranoia get the better of her.

"That was kind of a freak accident, right? You tripping like that. I mean, you've been running for years and never—"

"What?" Brooke's thoughts had taken her out of the conversation.

"Oh, when I fell down? I just lost my concentration." Brooke didn't want to talk about it, to keep lying, to think about the physical altercation with Gideon. "It wasn't a big deal."

Again, the wide-eyed and skeptical appraisal from the passenger seat. "If you say so."

"I do." Brooke's fingers tightened over the steering wheel. Leah had only been in the car a few minutes and already she was getting under Brooke's skin. Unfortunately, this had always been the case. As their mother had said when they were still in elementary school, "I swear, you two are like oil and water, or dogs and cats, or oil on dogs and water on cats! I don't understand why you girls just can't get along. You're sisters, for God's sake."

"You mean like you and Aunt Janey get along?" Brooke had reminded her.

"That's different. Jane and I are ten years apart, almost different generations. And different interests. You two, on the other hand, should be close. Not quite a year separates you."

Which, in Brooke's opinion, had only made it worse.

Brooke's jaw slid to the side as she remembered their mother turning from the front seat of their grandmother's old Chevy Impala, where the odor of once-smoked cigarettes lingered in the interior despite the fact that the windows were cracked slightly.

Nana was driving, a bit of a woman whose eyes, like Brooke's, were "as green as the Irish sea," according to their now-dead grandpa. Nana was clinging to what seemed an oversize steering wheel in her small hands, the rosary wound over the rearview mirror dangling and swaying, casting prisms of tiny lights onto the ceiling.

They were heading to the cabin on Piper Island. The road hugged the shoreline, the sound of the sea filtered into the car. From the passenger side Mom looked from one of her daughters to the other, searching for the culprit who had started the squabble that had been escalating ever since the Chevy had bounced off the ferry and onto solid ground. Brooke sat behind Nana in the wide back seat, Leah behind their mother. Though each girl was on her "side," the middle area between them was dubbed "no-man's-land," or more precisely, "no-sister's-land," was always the sought-after prize, one sister inching her fingers across the worn vinyl to touch or pinch the other.

Of course the response was a squeal of protest or a "She's hurting me!" cry, which was just what had happened as the sedan bounced over a pothole.

Carole Fletcher was at the end of her rope. "Stop it!" she'd ordered through clenched teeth, her narrowed gaze moving from one daughter to the other as Nana navigated the dusty, gravel road. "I mean it! Just . . . for once . . . stop fighting! Is that so impossible?" Her eyes, a golden shade that could darken with rage, pinned them to the backs of their seats.

Brooke thought the idea of getting along with Leah *was* impossible on that warm summer day. She'd looked past Carole to the windshield, where bugs had splattered and died quick and messy deaths.

But she and Leah held their tongues. They behaved until the end, when Nana drove into the tiny, shingled garage that tilted on its ancient foundation. For a final attack, Leah's fingers slowly dared to creep across no-sister's-land. Leah's index finger rubbed on the crack in the hot vinyl between them and inched even closer. It was all Brooke could do not to slap it away. Instead, she'd innocently curved her fingers so that the middle one was prominent, poking upright from her otherwise curved digits as she pretended to stare out the side window at the seagulls wheeling overhead.

Her quiet gesture didn't go unnoticed. From the corner of her eye Brooke caught her mother casting a glance at the gesture and frowning. Carole opened her mouth as if to chastise her oldest, then snapped it closed and fished in her purse for her cigarette bag. Meanwhile, stupid, pretty Leah remained unaware that her older sister had quietly but definitely flipped her off.

So that day Brooke was satisfied that she'd won.

Just as she had a few years later . . . but she didn't want to think about that now as she drove steadily north on the expressway and caught a rare glimpse of Mount Rainier rising in the east, the late October sunlight piercing the clouds to glisten against the mountain's snowy crest. As Leah started fiddling with the radio, checking different preset stations sputtering songs, ads, and news, Brooke thought she heard the whine of a motorcycle.

But wasn't that her new paranoia? How many times had it happened since her horrendous fight with Gideon? *Let it go*, she silently berated herself.

Still, she glanced in the rearview but saw only the grill of a pickup far too close—no, wait! Behind the truck, nosing as if to pass, the single headlight of a bike?

No way!

She was jumping at shadows.

Stop imagining things!

But the muscles in the back of her neck tensed.

Music with a sharp beat came through the speakers. "Geez, what is this? Rap?" Leah asked, pulling a face. "Really?"

"Marilee."

"Oh. Right." Little lines appeared between Leah's eyebrows. "Not my thing."

"Not mine either."

Leah kept switching channels while the traffic knotted and slowed as vehicles juggled to switch lanes. She went blithely on. " I'm kind of into country now." Short bursts of music spurted through the Explorer's speakers in rapid succession. "Sean got me hooked—oh shit, what's that!"

"What's wha—?" The sound of a motorcycle's engine roared from behind.

Brooke's gaze turned to the mirror again just in time to see a huge Harley cut from a lane on the left behind her, inching between her and the pickup. The truck braked just in time and the motorcycle accelerated, flashing past Brooke's Explorer on the right, unaware that a sedan had moved into the lane and swerved back just in time to avoid a collision.

"Jesus! What an idiot!" Leah cried.

Brooke's heart was in her throat.

Her foot on the brake.

She caught a glimpse of the reckless driver's helmet—matte black with a teal stripe.

Gideon.

He'd followed her?

Knew she would be at the airport?

Sweat broke out along the back of her neck. How had he known?

Her mind raced wildly. Was he at the park the other night? Had he overheard her conversation? But how? And what about the fact that he'd entered her house, that she'd actually heard footsteps? That he'd stolen her lingerie?

Then another sickening thought: *Her SUV. He must've put a tracker on it.*

Her blood turned to ice and she actually swerved a bit.

"Hey!" Leah shouted as she righted the SUV, keeping it in her lane. "What the hell's wrong with you?"

"Nothing," she muttered as he swung directly in front of her.

She hit the brakes. Her gaze immediately went to the rearview mirror, where she saw the truck behind her fishtail slightly.

"Jesus!" Leah yelled, now looking at the motorcycle less than a hundred feet in front of them. "What kind of an ass is that jerkwad?"

"I don't know," Brooke lied, letting up on the brakes.

Gideon, hunched over the handlebars, flew into the passing lane, roaring between cars crazily, weaving in and out, causing brake lights to flash and horns to honk.

"He's crazy!" Leah cried. "He's going to cause an accident! Someone should turn him in!"

"Maybe someone will," Brooke said, her heart racing as the motorcycle cut through traffic ahead of them.

"I didn't get his plate number, otherwise I would!" Leah vowed, then leaned dramatically back against the seat, her fingers splayed over her chest. "I hope to hell he gets a ticket. Would serve him right."

"Me too," Brooke agreed, trying to still her galloping heart. Her fingers still clutched the wheel in a death grip. What a stupid, reckless move! And Gideon knew what he was doing all right. She was sure of it. He'd probably figured Brooke was more nervous than usual when she was driving, the aftereffects from the accident with Gustafson.

"Pricks like that shouldn't be allowed to drive!"

"Amen." They were easing their way through the city, skyscrapers knifing upward between the freeway and Elliott Bay, huge ferries churning in the Sound.

"I need a drink after that. A double. And you? Geez, you've already had one accident this week! You don't need another."

"Right."

"And I'm kidding about the drink." Leah craned her neck to see the motorcycle disappearing through the crush of vehicles, then settled back into the seat.

As the crisis passed, Brooke became aware of the forgotten radio, which was now tuned to an eighties station, Bon Jovi's music wafting through the speakers.

"Holy shit, that was too close for comfort." Leah's phone chirped and she dug into a small clutch bag before sighing. "I was hoping it was Sean," she admitted sadly before clicking on, holding the cell to her ear, and pasting a smile on her face. "Hey, Dani, what's happening? . . . Oh right. If you could water the plants I would, like, owe you forever . . . uh-huh. Seattle, with my sister and her family . . . yeah, I know. No, he couldn't come. Work, you know . . ." She glanced at Brooke, who was negotiating her way to the off-ramp on the south end of Lake Union and still trying to figure out how Gideon had known she was at the airport.

No way it could be a coincidence; she just couldn't believe it.

By the time Leah disconnected, Brooke was turning onto the street where she lived. "Everything okay?" she asked.

Her sister sighed and looked up at the sky through the windshield. "Not really."

Uh-oh. Brooke braced herself. With Leah there was always drama. Hadn't she told herself that Leah didn't just show up because she missed Brooke? Wasn't there always an issue? "What's going on?"

Leah blinked rapidly. "It's Sean," she admitted, and Brooke's heart sank.

"What about him?"

"He wants a divorce."

Brooke turned into their drive. "Oh, Leah, why?"

Her chin trembled and her voice, quiet and higher than usual, cracked. "He says he doesn't love me anymore. In fact he says that he never really did." At that she broke down into sobs.

"Oh Leah, I'm sorry." Brooke pressed a button and the garage door started to roll upward.

Sniffing loudly, Leah said, "You're so lucky, Brooke. So damned lucky. You have Neal and Marilee and I . . . I have nothing."

"That's not true," Brooke said but trod lightly.

"It is!" Leah cried.

Brooke cut the engine, slipped out of her seat belt, and tried her best to hug her sister. Theirs might be a tense relationship, but she hated to see Leah hurting. Again. But it was too late. Now, as the garage door rolled down, Leah gave up all pretense of being in control and was openly sobbing, her face pink, tears running down her cheeks.

"Come on," Brooke said. "Let's go inside."

"I can't. Not like this."

"Sure you can. We're family." Feeling a stab of guilt for her negative thoughts about her sister, Brooke reached across Leah's lap and opened the glove compartment, where she found a small pack of tissues. "Pull yourself together. Okay?" She handed the package to her sister. "Everything's not as bad as it seems."

"Isn't it?" Leah plucked a tissue from the pack and dabbed at her eyes.

"Come on. Let's go inside and you can . . . have a glass of water or a soda or tea. Maybe that drink you mentioned earlier."

"I don't want anything." Leah blew her nose and didn't move. The garage door light went out and the only illumination seeping into the garage came through a tiny window grimy with dirt and cobwebs.

"What am I gonna do?" Leah said as more tears filled her eyes.

"You're going to figure it out. We'll go in the house. No one's home and you can go upstairs to the extra bedroom—the one next to Marilee's."

"I remember."

"Good."

Leah slumped in the seat as if she suddenly couldn't move. Now that she'd confessed her real reason for flying to Seattle, she was too weary to get out of the SUV.

Brooke was having none of it. She couldn't be late picking up Marilee again. She wouldn't. As far as she knew—and she'd asked friends and kept up with the school and neighborhood platforms on Facebook—Allison Carelli was still missing. Everyone was on edge.

So she couldn't deal with Leah's histrionics. She grabbed her sister's shoulders, her fingers digging into the soft cotton of Leah's cardigan. "Come on now. Pull yourself together." Dear God, how many times had she said those very words to her?

"I–I can't."

"You can and you will." Brooke was nose-to-nose with her sister.

"But—"

"You have before!"

Leah gasped, obviously stung, but they'd been through this time and time again. Brooke knew what she needed to do. Leah could use a shoulder to cry on, sure, but she also needed someone to toughen her up. To slap her back to reality. Brooke said, "I'll bring up your bag and get you settled, then I have to run and pick up Marilee from school and grab something from the deli. As I said, Neal's still at work, so you'll have the house to yourself for about an hour. Maybe a little longer."

"No, I just can't—"

"Sure you can," Brooke said, cutting off whatever wimpy excuse her sister could conjure. "Let's go." Reaching across Leah's lap again, she opened the passenger door and the interior light blinked on.

"You don't have to be so mean," her sister said, but she unhooked her seat belt.

"I'm not being mean," Brooke countered, "just reasonable." She wanted to explain that she too was dealing with stress, but now was not the time. "Come on, move it."

"Geez . . ." Leah said and, under her breath, she might have murmured "bitch" as she got out of the SUV.

Brooke didn't care. Right now she had bigger fish to fry, as Nana used to say, larger problems than Leah's forever revolving door of husbands. Muscles aching a bit from her struggle with Gideon, Brooke set her jaw and dragged the roller bag up the stairs, a step ahead of her sister.

In the kitchen Leah glanced out the back windows to the view. "I've always loved this place, you know." As she dashed the remainder of tears from her eyes, she looked around the cluster of rooms on the first floor: the kitchen, the dining area and living room, and the alcove to the side yard. Then she wandered to Neal's office, tucked in the lowest floor of the turret, and peeked inside before returning to the kitchen. She seemed more composed and asked, "Do you know how lucky you are?"

"Yeah. Yeah, I do." *And now more than ever*.

"This house—"

"I know. I love it too." And she did. So why had she risked it all—her marriage and her home, even her child's affection—for what? A summer fling with a man she barely knew, a sexy bad boy who touched a forbidden place in her heart? God, she'd been stupid.

Leah sighed, her gaze meeting Brooke's, and beneath the hint of a smile was there just a bit of something darker than sadness? Envy? Jealousy? "Really, really lucky." Then she made her way to the staircase by the front door.

Feeling slightly chastised, Brooke ignored the pain in her ankle and followed Leah into the guest room, where she deposited the roller bag at the foot of the old double bed she'd inherited from their mother.

"Make yourself at home," Brooke said, and again she saw that shadow of a darker emotion cross her sister's blue eyes.

"I will," Leah promised. "Neal's at work?"

Brooke was walking into the hallway but stopped short. Neal was always a difficult topic with her sister. "Yeah. He's usually home around six."

"Oh. Okay." The innocence in Leah's words belied what Brooke believed was something deeper, something a little less pure, but maybe it was her own guilt pricking at her conscience. Whatever the reason, she wasn't going to worry about it now. She was going to pick up her daughter from school and be on time for once, come hell or high water.

And then she was going to find out how Gideon Ross seemed to know her every move.

CHAPTER 11

Brooke arrived just as the final bell rang and students began streaming out of Allsworth High School. Cars started, kids laughed and pushed, some in tight clusters, others alone, striding away from the grounds. Cheerleaders in uniforms hurried out in a cluster, matching ponytails swinging behind them, and football players in letterman's jackets were also visible in a crowd of kids in hoodies, jeans, and backpacks.

Despite the fact that it was a brilliant October afternoon on a Friday with a home football game later in the evening, there was tension beneath the exuberant shouts and laughter of dispersing teens.

Students were being watched.

More teachers and aides were posted outside on the campus grounds. A police car idled across the street and there were more cars in the pickup lane than usual as anxious parents came for their kids rather than letting them walk or bike home. Despite the air of Americana and excitement for the weekend, almost everyone was on edge.

Because of the missing girls.

Brooke's cell phone rang and she jumped, checked the number, and froze because the digits meant nothing to her. Nor were they attached to any name in her contact list.

Gideon, she thought, remembering the mad driver on the motorcycle.

He had a new number.

Her insides twisted, yet she hit the Answer button, ready to tell him to go straight to hell. "Hello?" she said, her eyes still scanning the crowd of students milling between the school and the line of vehicles.

"Brooke?" a woman's voice inquired. Was it familiar? Maybe slightly?

"Yes."

"Oh good. I'd lost your number, but I got this one from Andrea . . . Andrea Davis; you know, Zuri's mom."

"I know her. And you are?"

"Oh, silly me. You don't recognize my voice. Of course you don't. It's been a few years. It's just that I'm so on edge," the woman said nervously as Brooke's heart rate returned to normal. "It's Joanna Nelson. Kinsey's mother."

"Oh, right. Hi, Joanna," Brooke said, leaning back against the seat as she recalled the tall, thin woman with short brown hair, oversize glasses, and a penchant for nervously picking at her collar or watch or whatever. Marilee and Kinsey were in a few classes together in middle school and Joanna was a PTA president or something. More personally involved than Brooke.

"I just wondered if Marilee said anything to you about what happened. I mean about Allison. Kinsey is freaked out and so am I. They were great friends in sixth grade. And Elyse; I can't imagine what she's going through. She and Tony—that's her ex, you know—have buried the hatchet, at least for now, until they find Allison . . . I mean if . . . I mean *when* they do. When they do. They will. They will find her. They have to. The police are on it and there are search parties being amassed and dogs and . . . they'll find her," Joanna rambled on, obviously trying to convince herself.

"Yes, I hope so," Brooke said, watching kids hurrying into waiting cars and buses, searching for Marilee.

"We all do. Of course. But Kinsey refused to go to school today and I don't blame her. She says everything's 'too weird,' and she seems to be coming down with a cold, so I let her stay home, but I haven't heard a word. So I'm calling around, seeing if anyone's heard anything. Dear God, I hope they find her. I can't imagine . . ." Her voice finally trailed off.

"Neither can I and I don't know anything. I'm just picking up Marilee now."

"Oh! Right! Of course. What was I thinking?" she said breathlessly, then added, "If you learn anything, anything at all after you talk to Marilee or from someone else, will you call me?"

"Sure. At this number?"

"Yes! Please. Thanks. This is such a nightmare!" And then she disconnected, probably to call some other person associated with the school or Allison Carelli. Like Joanna, Brooke couldn't imagine the anxiety and pain Elyse and Tony were going through. The loss of a child—could anything be worse?

"No," she said aloud and again scanned the area around the school, this time with renewed anxiety. Where was her daughter?

At last she spotted Marilee and her latest best friend, Tamara Paszek, walking out a side door.

Tammi was a petite girl with curly brown hair and dark eyes accentuated with thick eyeliner and mascara.

"Thank God," she whispered.

Before the two girls reached the front of the building, they paused near a cluster of birch trees shivering in the wind. At the sound of a door banging shut, they turned in unison to look backward, toward the tennis courts. Within seconds a tall boy with curly black hair and even features loped up to them.

It was Nick Paszek, Tammi's brother, in a maroon hoodie and black pants, a backpack slung over one shoulder.

An easy smile showed off white teeth against his olive skin, where a beard shadow was visible. At over six feet tall, he seemed more man than adolescent. Without a second's hesitation, he grabbed Marilee by the shoulders, pulling her tight against him.

Inside her Explorer, Brooke froze, her gaze fastened to her daughter, who didn't resist and didn't seem surprised by his actions. As if it happened all the time. Not a big deal, Brooke told herself, but wondered what the two of them would do if alone, not in the middle of a flood of kids in the schoolyard in broad daylight.

Tammi was chatting away, then caught sight of another knot of girls and, waving, peeled away to join the cluster of friends, some of whom Brooke recognized but couldn't name. That left Nick and Marilee alone as the tide of students flowed into cars, vans, buses, and trucks, the vehicles driving off, the noise of chattering voices quieting so that Brooke heard the clank of the chain against the flagpole as Old Glory rippled in the wind.

Brooke was about to honk but bit her lip as Nick bent down and gathered Marilee even closer to kiss her. Marilee tipped up her head, and as their lips met, kissed him back passionately. Yellowed leaves from the aspen swirled and pirouetted around them.

Oh no!

For a second Brooke was stunned.

Really? What did you expect? She's not a little girl anymore. Dear God, she can wear your shoes. Do you remember what you were like at that age? All hormones and curiosity, excitement and urgency? Didn't you tell your mother not to make you choose between her and Keith Turnquist when you were just a year or so older than your daughter is now? And that was around the time of your mom's cancer diagnosis.

Thinking of her own high school years and of Keith, a lanky kid with sleepy eyes, a fast car and even faster hands, her stomach knotted.

That had turned out badly.

So badly.

But it could have been much worse.

Absently, she rubbed the scar on the side of her throat, a war wound compliments of Keith and his temper.

Theirs had been a short-lived, highly charged relationship.

She felt a wave of heat climb up the back of her neck when she thought of the physical abuse and the resulting assault charges, and how lucky she'd been to get out of the relationship.

Passion was hard to rein in.

Didn't she know that?

In an instant she remembered a more distinct, recent scene, when she and Gideon were alone on the island, the wind swirling around them, the roar of the surf in their ears, the smell of the ocean salty and thick. They'd kissed on the beach and she'd felt the weight of his body as they tumbled into the sand in the dunes, so caught up in each other that they didn't know another couple was walking through the beach grass until a big, black, loppy-eared dog ran past.

She recoiled at the awkward memory, hitting the horn by accident.

Across the school lawn Nick broke off the embrace. He looked up and spied Brooke's car parked near the pickup lane. He said something and Marilee turned, her face red, her lips swollen, her eyes rounding. She said something more to Nick, then ran across the lawn toward Brooke's SUV. Flinging open the door, she said, "God, Mom, why did you do that?"

"Do what? You knew I was picking you up."

"You didn't need to honk. It's so . . . mortifying." Clicking on her seat belt, she slithered low into her seat.

"But making out in the schoolyard isn't?"

"Making out? We weren't—"

"Whatever you call it these days," she said.

Marilee buried herself in her phone and started texting like crazy.

"I'm serious, Marilee."

No response.

Brooke maneuvered the SUV around an idling minivan where three girls were climbing inside, then pulled off the school property. Calming a little, she realized she'd handled the situation all wrong. She shouldn't have come unglued, shouldn't have challenged her daughter at that moment. It would have been much better, much more sane to start an open-ended conversation about dating, about boys, and about sex, no matter how much she wanted to throttle Nick. Of course they'd had the basic biological discussion a few years back when Marilee had started to develop, and then again a year and a half ago when she'd started having periods, but this . . . this was different.

"Hey," she said. "I'm sorry." She kept her eyes on the road as she drove through the tree-lined streets, passing familiar landmarks and the back side of the park.

No response. Still more furious texting.

"I–I was surprised, that's all. I didn't mean to overreact."

Nothing.

"Marilee, this is new territory for me too," she admitted, stopping at the red light before turning the corner.

"Territory for *you*? Seriously? This is *my* life! Not yours." Her eyes flashed in anger, then she turned back to her phone.

Brooke turned onto their street, where their retired neighbor, Artemis Galanis, cigar clamped between his teeth, was raking leaves. Overhead a squirrel scolded loudly and raced along the branches of the maple tree.

"Maybe we should talk about this," Brooke suggested.

"About what? Nick?" Marilee said, then, under her breath, "Jesus."

"What did you say?"

"Geez," Marilee said more loudly. "You treat me like I'm a baby."

"I don't."

"Okay, then like I'm ten!"

Did she? Nah. But maybe she was being a little tougher than usual, frightened by everything that was going on. "You know Dad and I— well, all the parents—we're all on edge because of Allison Carelli." Brooke gave a quick wave to Artemis, then pulled into the driveway.

Marilee let out a puff of disgusted air. "Other parents still let their kids go in cars!"

"Other parents aren't Dad and me and that argument won't wash. I tried it too back in the day and Grandma didn't buy it either."

"Great," Marilee muttered, throwing her mother a look that could cut through steel.

Brooke stood her ground. "So, for tonight. You meet Nick at the dance. We'll pick you up. Then, later, we can have another conversation and maybe—"

"Oh yeah right!" Marilee was still seething. Still embarrassed. Still playing the victim. Brooke tried to compose her thoughts as she pulled into the garage, to keep calm. But as soon as she shifted the SUV into Park, Marilee was out the door. Without a word she raced up the steps.

"Your aunt is here!" Brooke called after her just as the door at the top of the stairs slammed shut.

"Fabulous," she said sarcastically, and Brooke felt a headache coming on. "Just effing fabulous."

This bratty behavior had to stop.

When Brooke made it into the house Marilee was nowhere to be seen, but Shep greeted her with his usual enthusiasm, cutting circles in the nook, toenails clicking frantically as she stepped into the kitchen. "I love you too," she told the dog and stroked his head. His dark eyes held hers and his tongue lolled to one side.

Leah, now composed, had changed into a thick gray sweater and navy leggings. She was seated at the table, her iPad open in front of her. Her hair was pulled away from her face by a navy band and her makeup had been restored.

"Hey," Brooke said, pulling up a chair. "How're ya doin'?"

"Better." Leah glanced up, taking her eyes off the screen for a second. "But what's with Mari? She barely said hi to me."

"It's a long story and she's mad at me, not you. Or maybe she's mad at the world."

"Why?"

"Basically, I called her out for kissing a boy in the front of the school."

"Oh. Wow. Like that's nothing you would've done?" She was typing, painted nails clicking, her gaze once again on whatever she was composing.

"At fourteen? No way."

Leah sent her a knowing look over the screen.

"You want a glass of wine?"

"Nah. Gave it up."

"You . . . don't drink?"

"No. Not much. I know I suggested one earlier, but that was just a joke. Maybe a bad one." Leah managed a thin smile. "Alcohol didn't help when Sean and I fought. So I cut back."

"You won't fight. Sean's not here," Brooke pointed out and found a bottle of red in the wine refrigerator Neal had installed just last year.

"But you are."

"Ooh. Ouch." Brooke scrounged in the drawer, found a corkscrew, and opened the bottle. "Someone's claws are out."

Leah sighed. "Yeah, you're right. Sorry." She put down her iPad as Shep settled into his dog bed near the window.

"Me too. I've been tense lately." Brooke let the wine breathe while she checked on the lasagna thawing on the kitchen counter. It was still cold, frozen in places, but it would work for dinner.

"You're tense?"

"Mm. A lot going on."

"The job hunt?"

That, fortunately, was the least of Brooke's worries, but she told her sister about the missing girls and her struggles with Marilee as she poured a glass of wine and sipped it while putting together a salad of spinach, red onions, and tomatoes.

Leah sighed, watching Brooke with an envious eye. "You've still got Neal and Marilee will come around. And hopefully they can find the girls. Maybe they just ran away. Doesn't that happen all the time? You know how emotional teenage girls are."

"I hope you're right and they come back."

Standing, Leah stretched her neck, then eyed the wine bottle. "Okay. I changed my mind. I'll join you."

"Good. You know what they say? That it's never good to drink alone."

"That had to be made up by an extrovert," Leah said as Brooke poured another glass, then handed it to her. "But maybe you should chill a little."

She took a swallow from her own glass and eyed her sister. "What does that mean?"

"Don't be so hard on Marilee." Leah clicked the rim of her glass to Brooke's. "She's just a kid trying to figure it all out, where she fits in in the world. You know, like you did once." She took a sip. "It's not easy being a kid these days."

"And it's easy being an adult?"

"Well, no. Of course not," Leah admitted. "Point taken."

"So, what happened with Sean?" Brooke asked, suddenly feeling a thread of connection to her sister.

"Oh God." Rolling her eyes to the ceiling, Leah sighed and shook her head, as if replaying an argument in her mind. "It's complicated."

"Is it?" To relieve some pressure in her ankle, Brooke leaned a hip against the counter while Leah returned to her chair, scooting it so she could look outside to the backyard and the view beyond.

"Maybe not so much," Leah confided and took a long swallow from her glass. "Out of the blue last week it all came to a head. Well, maybe not completely out of the blue. We'd been fighting for weeks. Over money."

Brooke remembered Sean's love affair with gambling.

"And then there was my insecurities—you know I have them— and I also want kids and he doesn't. His new job is a lot of pressure and, well, we fought about everything, I guess . . ." Her voice trailed off. Absently, she twirled the stem of her glass between her fingers, then cleared her throat. "Anyway, we got into it again. I found out he hadn't been paying the property taxes on the house, and worse than that, he didn't pay the IRS." She frowned, her eyebrows pinching as she glanced at her sister and confided, "They didn't like that much."

"No, they don't."

"I didn't know it, of course, I'd signed a return that he was supposed to file, but . . ." she shrugged, ". . . I guess I suspected. It's not like this was the first time. And he'd invested in some company on the advice of his 'friend.'" She made half-hearted air quotes. "Sean handles all the finances, but I'm not an idiot, I saw the past-due notices so, as I said, we got into it and he stormed out and I did some digging. Guess what?" She looked up at Brooke, tears forming in her big eyes. "He has a girlfriend." She sniffed. "A friend of mine—at least I thought she was a friend—and they've had this affair going on right under my nose for about six or eight months as near as I can tell." Her face collapsed in on itself and she let out a sob.

Guilt, hot and razor-sharp, cut through Brooke. She swallowed hard. "Oh Leah, I—I don't know what to say, except that I'm so, so sorry, but it sounds like you're better off without him."

"The worst of it was that he never loved me," she squeaked out, her voice an octave higher than usual as she reached under the nearby cupboard to the paper towel holder. Sniffing, she ripped off a towel and swiped at her nose.

Automatically, Brooke said, "No, no, no. That's not true."

"No? How would you know?" she demanded. "There's just something about me that men find attractive and then . . . and then don't." She was blinking, her face red. "This isn't the first time, Brooke. You more than most people should be aware of that, but I'm sick and tired of it!"

So there it was. The same old, awful point.

Leah took in a deep, shuddering breath. "My money's gone," she finally admitted.

"No." Brooke didn't want to believe it, but hadn't she suspected as much? Hadn't she expected some sort of dramatic revelation? Some reason her sister had insisted on visiting now? "You still have assets," Brooke ventured.

"Uh-uh. That's what I'm trying to tell you."

"But—"

"Everything I inherited from Nana?" Leah cut in, anticipating the argument. She looked at her sister and snapped her fingers. "Gone."

Brooke couldn't believe it. Didn't want to. She and Leah had each inherited a good sum from their grandmother. "But—but I thought you invested it."

"As I said, Sean took over. Handled *everything*." She looked away, embarrassed. Her neck and cheeks had flushed a darker hue. "Yeah, yeah, I know I was . . . stupid, but I loved him. I trusted him and . . ." Fresh tears rolled down her face.

Brooke was stunned. She'd seen Leah through a lot of tough times and some financial struggles. She and Neal had helped Leah out in the past, but over the years, no matter how bad things had gotten, Leah had assured her that her inheritance was safe, tucked away in some kind of government-insured bonds that couldn't be cashed in without big penalties, so she'd never touch them.

Leah angled her face upward while she played with the stem of her glass, twirling it between her fingers. "So now he wants a divorce and I don't even know if I can afford one." Her jaw hardened. "You know what they say about luck, that if I didn't have bad luck, I wouldn't have any." Her lips pursed, and Brooke felt the unspoken blame. Because nothing had changed with Leah over the years. She believed all of her problems, all of the sadness in her life and the bad choices she had made, were Brooke's fault.

And maybe Leah was right.

At that moment they heard the garage door roll upward.

Shep scrambled to his feet and his toenails clicked frantically as he raced to the top of the stairs to wait and whine for Neal.

Leah, calmer now, turned accusing eyes at her sister. "Guess who's home?" she said, as if she knew all of Brooke's secrets. "Daddy dearest." Her expression remained neutral as Neal's footsteps could be heard on the steps. "Tell me, sister," she asked softly, "is he still the love of your life?"

CHAPTER 12

With Shep at his heels, Neal appeared and took in the emotional tableau, then held up one hand. "I, uh, I didn't mean to interrupt."

"You aren't," Leah said. "We were just talking about you."

His jaw slid to one side and his eyes found Brooke's. "Nothing good, I guess."

"Oh, so you did eavesdrop." With a cool look, Leah scooted her chair back and retreated up the stairs.

"Ooh." He sucked in his breath. "What was that all about?"

"She and Sean are breaking up." Brooke poured him a glass of wine and topped off her own glass. "And it's bad. He took all of her money." She handed the glass to him. "Same old, same old. He's got a girlfriend." At the mention of Sean's infidelity her stomach churned.

"All her money?"

"And they owe the IRS, for starters."

Before Neal could take a sip Brooke clicked the rim of her glass to his. "To old grievances, may they never be resolved."

His eyebrows quirked upward.

"She'll never forgive me, you know," Brooke said.

"Honey—"

"Don't try to placate me. It's the truth. She's never gotten over it."

"Well, she blames me too."

"I know, but I'm her sister, the one who should have been taking care of her, and instead I stole her boyfriend."

"I was a part of that. And I wasn't really—"

"Oh, I remember, but she thinks I seduced you, got pregnant, and forced you to marry me."

"I wanted to marry you," he reminded her.

"And Leah will never forget it, or forgive me. Every time she has a breakup with a boyfriend or a fiancé or a damned husband, she blames me." Brooke took a big gulp of her wine. She didn't want to think about that time in her life, when she, the older sister, thought she'd intervene between Leah and a man too old for her. Leah had been a young, giddy seventeen-year-old and Neal twenty-six, just finishing law school.

No way should they have been together and Brooke had stormed over to his apartment to tell him to back off. She'd felt responsible as their mother had passed and their father, a man she barely remembered, was in the wind if even alive. Nana, who was their legal guardian until Brooke turned eighteen, was dealing with her own health issues.

Brooke had just come off her volatile relationship with Keith and the horrid assault, the brutal fight that had turned physical to the point of the police being called to intervene and charges leveled.

She had only to touch the spot on her neck where he'd wounded her to remember it.

The night that changed the course of their lives forever Brooke was supercharged when she learned about her sister being involved with a much older guy. And as her younger sister's protector now that both of their parents were out of the picture, she'd decided to take Neal Harmon on herself.

She remembered marching through the vestibule of his apartment building, past a couple of sickly looking potted plants and a row of mailboxes to the staircase. Gathering her courage, she mounted the steps to Neal's third-floor apartment and banged on his door.

Puffed up with self-righteousness and indignation, she'd been completely taken aback when he'd answered wearing scruffy jeans, a day's growth of beard, and a T-shirt that had seen better days. His black hair was in disarray and some U2 song from the eighties was playing in the background. The door was open wide and she quickly peered inside his studio apartment, a mess by Nana's standards and piled high with textbooks, old records, CDs, magazines, and news-papers.

He had the audacity to seem confused. "Can I help you?"

"I'm Brooke. Leah's sister. Leah Fletcher."

Then the light dawned. "Oh right." Brooke had never met Neal, but she'd caught glimpses of him as he'd dropped her sister off at night. He glanced over her shoulder as if he expected Leah to be lurking in the hallway. "Is she okay?" Concern wrinkled his brow and Brooke noticed how his too-long hair fell over his forehead.

"You tell me."

"What happened?" More concern.

"She's fallen in love with you, that's what happened."

"What?" He shook his head. "No." He backed up a step, held up a hand, and an are-you-crazy expression took over his features.

"No? Do you know that she's seventeen?"

"Yes."

"Well, of course you do. You made sure she was legal."

"What? Jesus, what're you talking about?"

"My sister!" she said. "You're too old for her! You need to back off!" she said, her voice raising.

A small dog started yapping behind the door of the apartment across the hall.

"Hey, shh," he said, patting the air around him to quiet her as the door to the neighboring apartment flew open and a woman of around sixty in a bathrobe and fuzzy slippers appeared. There were traces of a quickly rinsed facial scrub or mask on her face. Tucked under one arm was a little brown Chihuahua, big eyes bulging, black lips pulled back in a nasty snarl.

"What the devil is going on here?" she demanded.

"Nothing, Mrs. Quinlan," Neal said with a disarming smile. "It's all good."

She eyed him suspiciously, then swiped at a bit of green mask at her hairline. "Is that right?" she asked Brooke, beady eyes focusing on her as the little dog went off, barking and kicking, trying to escape Mrs. Quinlan's death grip. "Shh, shh, Punky," she said to the writhing beast in her arms.

"This is the sister of one of my students," Neal said quickly.

Brooke repeated, "Students?"

"Hmph! People coming and going all times of the night. *Girls* showing up in the hallway. I don't know what kind of a scam you're running over there, but I've talked to the manager about it and it wouldn't surprise me if you, Neal Harmon, were out on your ear by the end of the month."

Neal bristled but remained calm. "Do what you have to, but there are tenant rights, Mrs. Quinlan."

"I know and I have them!"

"Do you?" He eyed the dog. "Do you know about the pet restrictions? I'm pretty sure there's a no-dog policy. It prohibits dogs that intimidate other tenants and piss on the potted palms."

"You're an upstart, that's what you are. An overeducated, smart-alecky upstart and God, He takes care of the likes of you."

"Give Him my cell number the next time you talk to Him!"

"Well, I never!" Mrs. Quinlan gasped.

Neal replied, "Probably not. I believe it. That's your problem."

"My problem is you!" With that she stepped back and slammed the door. Several locks and dead bolts clicked loudly into place. A second later the little dog put up a loud fuss, growling and barking and scratching madly at the door.

"Wow," Brooke said. "Is she always like that?" She hooked her thumb at the apartment door.

"Nope. You caught her on a good day. Come on in," Neal said, stepping out of the way. "Don't mind the clutter."

Brooke was still stunned by the exchange, but she stepped inside and he closed the door behind her. "Have a seat." He motioned to a lumpy, green couch that he swept free of magazines. He snapped off a portable CD player and, as Bono's voice faded, swung one of his mismatched kitchen chairs from his desk, the only piece of furniture in the place that didn't look like it had come from a secondhand store at best and a dumpster at worst.

"So, you're here because of Leah," he reminded her. "What's the problem?"

"I didn't know you were her tutor."

"Mm. What else would I be?"

"She thinks you're her boyfriend."

"That is definitely not the case." He leaned back in his chair. Looked off through a window. "Wow. This is going to be awkward." There was just a hint of recognition that he might have sensed Leah's feelings, might have even encouraged them. Or maybe he was just used to younger girls falling in love with him. He shoved the hair from his eyes. "Well, I guess I'll have to set her straight, won't I?"

"Definitely."

That night was the first time she met Neal Harmon. From the start she'd recognized what her sister found so attractive about the older man, who had a sharp sense of humor and a deep-seated ambition. She'd learned about the scholarships, the loans, and the savings he'd put into his schooling, how he planned to become a lawyer to help others.

After that first angry, self-righteous meeting she made the pretense of seeing him as a tutor to raise her own grades, but they'd both known it was a ruse. She'd sailed through high school while her sister had struggled. When she finally admitted the truth to Neal, that she'd made up the excuse of needing help with her studies, he wasn't surprised. His smile told her that he'd seen right through her scheme.

He'd kissed her then. First a soft, questioning brush of his lips over hers. When she hadn't pulled away, had pressed her lips to his, he'd kissed her again. Hard. She'd felt a warmth inside, a melting that she'd never experienced before, and she hadn't backed away but kissed him back. Fervently. The warmth deep inside of her pulsing with each probe of his tongue. The fact that if Leah ever found out she'd be pissed and hurt had made it all the more seductive. The secret betrayal made it thrilling. For once, with that little edge of danger, Brooke savored the flirting, the kissing, the touching, the edge of danger that she and Neal might be exposed, that she was stepping over a dangerous, erotic line.

Forbidden fruit.

In the months that followed heated passion had turned to something deeper. She spent more time alone with Neal, and when he'd taken her to bed in a room lit by the weird, undulating light from a retro lava lamp, she'd lost her heart as well as her virginity to him. It didn't matter that he smoked weed, or that he had a pistol in a bedside table that his grandfather had bequeathed to him, or, the worst part, that he was Leah's fantasy boyfriend. Leah had still seen Neal as a tutor and still thought she was in love with him, though Neal swore he wasn't leading her on.

Brooke had never really been sure about that part. And she'd had a few trepidations due to her previous relationship and how it had crumbled emotionally as well as physically. But Neal was a pathway far from Keith and the horror of their last fight. So painful. So physical. Nearly deadly.

What she did know was that she and Neal had fallen in love and hidden their feelings from Leah, who only discovered the truth when Brooke ended up pregnant and was forced to confess.

"Are you kidding me?" Leah had raged, tears building in her eyes as she sat on the edge of her bed in her pink, spangled room.

"It's true," Brooke answered from the doorway.

"No! I don't believe you!" The devastation was written all over her face.

"It's true." Brooke met her sister's injured glare. "I—I'm sorry."

"Sorry?" Leah had sputtered. "And you're going to have a baby? Oh God." Tears ran down her cheeks. She glared at her sister with accusing, hate-filled eyes. "You're going to have a *baby*?" she repeated, then spat out, "Are you even sure it's his?"

"I'm sure." Brooke tried to sit next to Leah on the handstitched quilt that Nana had made, but her sister bolted from the bed, then turned sharply on her heel.

"You've been lying to me? Cheating behind my back! How could you? Huh, Brooke, how could you do this to me?" Leah broke into racking sobs, tears running down her cheeks.

Brooke had felt more than a twinge of guilt. "I said I'm sorry and I meant it," she repeated, the walls of Leah's small bedroom seeming to move closer. "It . . . it just happened."

"What? No! Uh-uh, Brooke. Don't give me that! It did *not* 'just happen'!" Leah insisted, mascara drizzling from her eyes. "That's the lamest excuse I've ever heard, the one every damned cheater in the world uses."

"No, I swear, I didn't mean to—"

"Of course you did, Brooke. You *meant* to. Neal *meant* to. Zippers don't just slide down by themselves!" She blinked hard and threw herself at Brooke, grabbing her around the neck. "You know what you are? You're a sick, pathetic bitch who has always been jealous of me. I'm prettier. Friendlier. More fun! Boys like me more. Teachers like me better and you can't stand it!"

"I really didn't—"

"Shut up! Just shut the—just shut up!" In a rage, she slapped her sister. Full force, across the face.

Brooke saw red, her mercurial temper spiking. And she remembered Keith Turnquist, and how she'd ended up with the scar on her neck, just to the back of her ear.

Her fists balled up and Leah sneered. "Go ahead, Brooke. Try it! I'll call the police and then what? Another report where you're involved. It won't look good, will it? What would Neal say then?" She paused for a second, then added, "I hate you!" Angrily, she yanked her pink roller bag from the closet, the one that matched Brooke's, the last gift they'd each received the Christmas before their mother died.

Stunned, Brooke stood by wanting to hit her, holding her sore jaw, needing to ask her forgiveness.

As if possessed by a demon, Leah began frantically ripping clothes out of her small dresser, throwing bras, socks and underwear, jeans and sweaters into the bag before storming to her closet and stripping the hangers bare.

"What're you doing?"

"What does it look like?"

"You're leaving?"

"See," Leah taunted, "you *are* the smart one."

Brooke grabbed her sister's arm as Leah tossed a pair of hiking boots and then sandals into the bag. She forced down her temper and said through gritted teeth, "Stop this!"

"No." Leah yanked her arm away, her eyes daring her older sister to hit her.

"You can't go anywhere," Brooke said. This had gone too far. Even for Leah.

"Why not? What're you going to do to stop me? Call the cops? I don't think so." She shook her head. "Or maybe you can call your boyfriend who knocked you up?" She paused for a second, then said, "Nope. You wouldn't. Too dangerous!" Then her face twisted in revulsion. "You disgust me!" She opened a drawer and pulled out a small zippered case of makeup which she stuffed into the bag. Then angrily crammed a plastic pouch holding some of her jewelry inside.

"You're not eighteen."

"Who cares?"

"I do."

"Oh right!" She narrowed her eyes as she forced down the top and struggled to close the zipper. "You care?" Leah made a disbelieving sound in the back of her throat.

Brooke reached out again and Leah spun quickly, slapping her hard across the face once more.

Brooke recoiled.

"Don't touch me!" Leah warned. "You hear me? Don't you ever fucking touch me again!"

Reacting, Brooke grabbed her once more. Hard. Her grip punishing.

Leah whirled around, and this time she spat. With vehemence. The spittle, warm and dripping, hit Brooke between her eyes and dripped down her nose as Leah jerked away again.

"You little—"

With that Leah was gone, the pink roller bag bouncing down the stairs before she marched into the kitchen, dragging the bag behind her, its wheels gliding noisily over the worn linoleum.

Hand pressed to her smarting cheek, Brooke was left standing in the middle of Leah's room with its blush-colored walls and posters of teen heartthrobs, a white bunny and a tattered teddy bear on her messy bed. Hot tears of frustration rolled to her chin.

She wanted to kill her sister.

Angrily swiping her face with her sleeve, she caught up with Leah downstairs in the pantry, where she was emptying out the ancient Maxwell House Coffee tin that Nana used to stash cash for emergencies.

"Don't!" Brooke commanded.

Leah ignored her. She stuffed a wad of bills into the pocket of her jacket and cast her sister another hateful glance before yanking on the roller bag's handle and disappearing out the back door.

It was all Brooke could do not to fly after her. And she might have, if not for the twinge in her abdomen, the reminder that there was new life growing inside her.

Brooke stepped onto the porch, where flies were buzzing against the screens and a wasp was busily working on a nest in the corner of the roof. Leah was already crossing the cracked sidewalk leading to an alley and out the gate.

As if the world weren't spinning off its axis, Nana's shaggy black cat was sunning himself on the broken concrete near the old tetherball pole. No ball was attached to the rusting chain, which rattled a bit in a small puff of wind.

Brooke squinted and shaded her eyes, staring down the open alleyway, where trash cans and old bikes were scattered.

Leah had disappeared.

She won't get far, she told herself.

But she'd been wrong. So wrong.

Leah had found a way to take a bus and hitchhike to Northern California. There she'd found solace with their grandmother's sister, a cold woman who had never forgiven Brooke for her part in what Leah insisted to this day was the turning point in her life.

Brooke assumed some of the fault, but Leah's problems were far more deep-rooted than the loss of a would-be boyfriend to her older sister. Far more.

At least, that's what she'd told herself so she could sleep at night.

It hadn't always worked.

So now Leah was back.

Taking up space in Brooke's house.

Again.

Just as she did every time her heart was broken.

Which, in Brooke's sister's case, was far too often.

CHAPTER 13

"Is Leah going to be okay?" Neal asked.

"You're asking me?" Brooke shook her head. "Is she ever?"

Frowning, Neal set his laptop on the table and left his jacket over the back of a chair. He glanced to the stairs, then turned back to Brooke and snapped his fingers, as if struck by a sudden thought. "Oh. A couple of things. Gustafson's lawyer called today. He's definitely talking about a lawsuit and damages above and beyond repairing the Porsche."

"Such as?"

"Whiplash, pain and suffering, you know, the usual suspects. He says you're a distracted driver." Neal brandished his hand in the air as if it was of no consequence. "The insurance companies will battle it out."

"Great," she said sarcastically. "You said 'a couple' of things. What's the other?"

"The adjuster is coming by today." He checked his watch. "In fact, he should be here any minute."

"What? Adjuster?"

"The insurance adjuster. To look at the car. See what the damage is."

"But—" No. This couldn't be happening! She hadn't searched for the tracking device yet. If Gideon had left a bug on her car and the adjuster found it, how would she explain it to Neal? Worse yet, her burner phone—the one she'd used to call Gideon—was in the car, tucked into its hiding spot. What if it was discovered when the adjuster was looking through the SUV? Oh. God. "Maybe it's not a good time," she said, motioning lamely toward the stairs. "With Leah upset and—"

"I'll check on her. Oh—he's here now." Neal was heading out of the room. "I'll meet you in the garage once I see that Leah's okay."

She doubted Neal could do anything to calm Leah down, but then again, maybe she was wrong. Leah always seemed to be looking for a man's opinion or approval. Brooke figured it was because of the lack of men in their lives growing up. Leah was always searching for a father figure because theirs had bailed early, leaving before Leah was five. Neither remembered the tall, blond man who had sired them. He'd flown to Spain, and the last Brooke had heard he was traveling with a woman half his age. That was years ago, when she'd tracked him down to tell him his ex-wife and the mother of his children had died.

Of course at the time she hadn't known he'd been married and divorced several times. When he'd asked, "Which wife?" and "Which children?" Brooke had cut the connection without answering.

Their mother had always said, "Fletch was born with a wandering spirit." As if that absolved him.

Nana had thought differently and sputtered, "Wandering spirit my ass! The man's a narcissistic son of a bitch who can't keep his pecker under control!"

Brooke figured Douglas Fletcher was somewhere between the two women's concepts of her absent father.

The doorbell rang. Shep started barking wildly and raced to the front door.

"Oh great," she said under her breath. There was nothing to do now but accept it and play dumb if the adjuster found the tracking device. Maybe there was no way to trace it. Did they come with serial numbers? Would Neal want to know why someone was following her? What would she say?

The person on the porch turned out to be a woman. In slacks, a sweater, and showing identification identifying her as Blair Johnson, claims adjuster for the insurance company, she smiled, white teeth showing against her dark skin. A satchel was slung over her shoulder, a clipboard in her hand, and she asked to see the SUV. Dreading what was about to happen, Brooke escorted the adjuster through the house to the garage, Shep eagerly leading the way as she flipped on the harsh fluorescent lights, illuminating the wide space where their two vehicles were parked.

Warily, Brooke answered a few of the adjuster's questions about the accident, though Ms. Johnson had a copy of the accident report on the clipboard where she made notes, then took pictures of the Explorer's dented bumper and crumpled hood.

"But it still drives?" Blair asked, her dark eyes sharp behind slim glasses.

"Yes. It pulls a little to the left, but I can drive it."

"And what about your injuries?" she asked, staring pointedly at the cut on Brooke's chin. "I saw you limp a little going down the stairs. You were hurt?"

"Not from the accident, no. I fell while running," she said. The lie, now repeated often enough to seem like the truth, flowed easily over her lips. "It's not been a great week."

"I guess."

Brooke heard Neal on the stairs. As he reached the floor of the garage, he was already grinning. "I told my wife that the next time she rear-ends a car she should pick out a 1986 Dodge or a rattletrap of a Chevy rather than a Porsche." His grin widened at his own joke. "Neal Harmon," he said, extending his hand.

Blair cast him a patient, I've-heard-it-all-before smile as she clasped her fingers around his and introduced herself. Then, all business, she continued surveying the vehicle, opening doors, taking notes of the interior as well as the damage to the exterior while Brooke began to sweat. The burner phone was right there, beneath the cup holder. All Blair Johnson had to do was lift up the false bottom.

Neal whispered to her, "Leah's going to be fine."

Brooke doubted her sister would ever be "fine," but she couldn't worry about it now, not with the adjuster scouring her vehicle.

Blair Johnson closed the driver's door without incident and Brooke let out her breath only to worry again as the adjuster got down on her hands and knees to peer at the undercarriage.

Brooke could barely breathe and hardly noticed as Neal opened the side door to let Shep into the yard. She watched the flashlight's beam move steadily under the SUV. Maybe she was wrong, maybe Gideon hadn't—

"Hey, what's this?" Blair asked, her voice muffled.

Oh. God.

"What's what?" Neal asked.

"Don't know," came the reply, a question in Blair's voice. It looks like—" There was the scrape of metal on metal. "Oh." She straightened up and held out a small black device.

Brooke thought she might be sick.

"Oh that." Neal gave a nervous little laugh. "I forgot all about that."

What?

The tiny black box had a short antenna attached to it.

"It's a tracker," Blair said, her voice clipped, all friendliness having evaporated from her face.

Oh God. Brooke steadied herself against the fender of her vehicle.

"Yeah, I know." Neal was nodding as Blair's gaze swept from husband to wife.

"Did *you* know?" the adjuster asked Brooke.

Of course not. Why would I track myself? Why would my husband? What the hell was Neal doing?

Her insides were shredding at the thought of what her husband had discovered with his secretive little bug, but she managed a bland expression and shook her head. "No. Had no idea."

Shep, picking up on the tension in the tight space, began to whine.

Brooke caught her husband's eye. Did she see just the hint of guilt in his gaze? Something darker? "Why would you be tracking me?" All too vividly she remembered the places she'd driven and how many times she'd lied about where she really was.

Neal knew!

And he hadn't said a damned word.

What in God's name was going on?

"No—no, not really." Neal held up his hands, as if embarrassed. "Geez, I forgot I even had it."

"You *forgot?*" Brooke said, disbelieving. Then again, why would Neal be keeping tabs on her unless he suspected she was lying about her whereabouts?

"Yeah, I mean . . ." Neal sighed, his shoulders slumping. "A client sells them and gave me one for free, said he'd hook it up for me. It's some kind of GPS deal, one of the first of his prototypes. At the time, when he was in the office setting up a new company, he asked everyone to give it a whirl and I told him I'd try it."

"What client?" Brooke demanded. This was too far-fetched.

"Bill Clayton. He inherited his dad's tech company a few years back and wanted to expand, get into surveillance."

"So you put a bug on my car and didn't bother to tell me?"

"No!" He shook his head. "I was driving the Explorer at the time," he said. "It was before I got the Range Rover."

"Well, you all," Blair said, waving a hand in the air between them, her eyebrows raised high over the frames of her glasses. "You figure it out. I think I've got everything I need." She zipped the small device into her satchel.

Brooke's palms were beginning to sweat again, just thinking about what information the device could reveal; no doubt it had GPS tracking abilities and probably a memory chip or something.

"You don't need the tracker," Brooke said to the adjuster, trying not to panic.

"I think it might help. If there's any data on this little bug, it could give us information about the accident. It's actually lucky I found it."

No, no, no! "But you have all the information. From the witnesses and the police report." This was a disaster!

Blair smiled. Without an ounce of warmth. "Think of it as evidence, then."

That thought struck Brooke numb.

Blair went on, "When it comes time to access responsibility and what happened just before and during the accident, you know, such as the speed at which you were traveling, from which direction? Who knows?" She shrugged. "It just might corroborate witness testimony if it comes to that and we land in front of a judge, which I hope we don't."

Brooke tried to tamp down her panic. "The accident wasn't that big of a deal."

"Well, we'll see. It might be that Mr. Gustafson will claim all kinds of physical and mental issues as a result of the accident, which he insists is your fault. It could come to big money." Blair offered a cold smile as she patted the side of her satchel. "We might need all the ammunition we can get, so the data on it could come in handy."

Brooke's heart sank. "But that will have personal information on it. You know, where I go with my kid, doctors' appointments, tutors and the like!" Frantic, she looked at Neal for backup.

"I'm only interested in the day of the accident," Blair assured her. "Once this is all settled, unless the police require it, you can have it back."

"The police? Why would they want it?" Oh Jesus.

"I don't think they will." Blair was now looking hard at her as if she were becoming suspicious, and Brooke felt strangled, all her fears knotting in her throat.

"Hey, don't worry," Neal said, though he too seemed serious, maybe a little concerned, the small tic near his eye appearing as it sometimes did when he was nervous.

Brooke's stomach was in knots. Everything was about to fall apart! She would have to confess, tell him the truth, which he might already know.

Neal said, "Maybe it'll help our case." He gave Brooke's shoulder a squeeze, a little harder than normal, just bordering on painful, then said to Blair, "I'll walk you out."

"No need. I'll find my way." She eased past him, then went to the top of the stairs, where she slapped the button that opened the garage door. As the tight space filled with the fresh air of the coming night, she hurried outside, her boots clicking a sharp tattoo on the driveway.

"I can't believe this!" Brooke walked from the side of the garage to the staircase, then stopped and faced her husband. "Why didn't you tell me?"

"Like I said, I didn't think of it." He shrugged, as if it were no big deal.

Should she be relieved? If, as he said, he hadn't been tracking her—and that was a pretty big if—he didn't know about her whereabouts, didn't know she had been lying to him. But, on the other hand, if he was covering up, there was something deeper going on here. And it didn't explain how Gideon had known where she was.

"I just don't understand."

Neal was walking toward the staircase as Shep reappeared and followed. "I've already explained it. It happened when I was still driving the Explorer. You remember. You had the PT Cruiser, right?"

That much was true.

"Anyway, so Bill comes up with the thing, and I thought—well, this is a little nuts, I guess, but I thought it might come in handy because our plan was that the Explorer is going to be the car Marilee drives someday, right?"

"Like in two years—four years from when you got the Rover?" she asked, closing the door to the yard and locking it.

"And that's why I forgot about it."

Shep had climbed the steps ahead of Neal and was scratching at the door to the house.

"Don't let him do that!" Brooke called up to him.

Neal was already saying, "Hey, stop that!" as he let the dog inside and Brooke, worried that the insurance company might come for the car or reassess the damage, took the time to swipe her burner phone from beneath the cup holder and shove it quickly into her purse, still sitting where she'd left it on the passenger seat. She swiped up the bag and cursed herself for not getting rid of the phone earlier.

Hidden burner phones and tracking devices.

What had their marriage come to?

She climbed the steps, hit the garage door button. As the big door rolled noisily down, she caught up with Neal in the laundry room and decided she couldn't hide her phone in its little niche. Not right now.

"How's the ankle?" he asked.

"Better, I think."

"You're still limping."

"Stairs—not exactly my friends these days," she said, then asked the question that had been nagging at her. "So, you never looked at the tracker?" She just couldn't quite buy that he'd installed the device, left it connected beneath the car, then ignored it.

"Nah. Couldn't figure it out. It was before every person on the planet had an iPhone with a billion apps. You had to hook up the camera, or feed, or whatever you call it through Bill's company— Clayton Electronics—and I never bothered."

He seemed sincere, but still, she doubted him. "And his company keeps a log of where the device has been?"

"Maybe. Probably. Or maybe it's within the device itself. I don't know. Why? Do you have something to hide?"

"Oh really, Neal?" she said, though her nerves tightened and her throat suddenly turned to sand. Somewhere, either in Clayton's company's electronic records or the damned tracking device, was a record of everywhere she'd been since she started driving the car. Or that information could have been wirelessly connected to Neal's computer. "Look, if you don't trust me—"

"For the love of God, Brooke, I'm kidding." He was walking into the kitchen. "Really, it was a joke!"

"Not funny."

"That's where you're wrong." His arm slid around her shoulders and he kissed her on the cheek as they reached the hallway. "And you know, come to think of it, you might ask him about a job. They're always looking for good salespeople."

"Not exactly my area of expertise."

"You sold software and you're a quick study. Really, you should look into it," he said, and she figured his enthusiasm was to change the subject. "Didn't someone say you could sell anything?"

"That was you," she said, remembering, but she still wasn't convinced and it must've shown on her face because she was still wondering about the bug in her car.

Neal said, "Come on, honey, lighten up."

Oh sure.

She told herself to take his advice.

She told herself to trust him.

If only I could, she thought.

If only she could.

CHAPTER 14

Upstairs, Brooke saw Leah seated at the table, a glass of wine resting near her phone. As she heard Brooke and Neal approach, Leah looked up, and she seemed more composed than she was earlier.

Good.

"Don't suppose you've got a cigarette?" she asked.

"Don't smoke," Brooke said, and when Leah's eyes narrowed she added, "I quit. Remember? When I was pregnant with Marilee. Never took it up again."

"Right." Leah leaned back in her chair and her eyes thinned in disbelief. "You don't smoke like I don't drink." She held up her refreshed glass and took a sip. "How about you?" she asked Neal. "Got any ciggies?"

"Me? Nah." He held up his hands. "Not for years. I'm clean. No more vices."

Leah clucked her tongue. "Look at the two of you, just paragons of effin' virtue."

"Give me a break," Brooke said under her breath.

Neal, sizing up the situation and Leah's mood, was already peeling off, backing out of the room, "I've got a little catch-up work to take care of, so I'll be in the office. But dinner? Your night."

"I know. I've got it covered." She noticed the questions in his eyes. "I pulled the lasagna out of the freezer earlier." She pointed to the foil-topped casserole dish on the counter next to the toaster oven. "I'll put it in soon. It should be done in about an hour, maybe an hour and fifteen. That gives Marilee time to get ready for the dance."

"So she's going?" Neal asked.

"Of course she is."

"With Nick?"

"No—well, not technically. We discussed this already. He's going to meet her there."

"And she agreed?"

"We came to an understanding." She turned on the oven to pre-heat.

"Okay. Good." He went to the refrigerator and pulled out a beer. "I'll be in the den." With a flick of his wrist he twisted off the cap and, to Brooke's utter annoyance, sent it sailing across the room.

"Really?"

"Old habits die hard."

"You're not in college anymore," she reminded him but managed a smile.

"Right." He picked up the cap from the floor and put it in the garbage under the sink before heading to his office located in the turret near the front door.

Leah watched him leave with the dog at his feet. "You two seem to be getting along," she observed.

"Why wouldn't we?" Brooke said, refusing to think about Gideon and her infidelity or Neal's . . . though his had been different.

"Didn't he move out a while back?"

So she did know. Of course. It wasn't a secret that they'd sepa-rated, and Marilee and Leah communicated.

"We've had our ups and downs. Currently up," she lied as the alert for the temperature gauge dinged. She slipped the lasagna in-side the oven and set the timer. Her ankle was starting to ache a lit-tle, so she sat down across from her sister.

"Take a look at this." Leah twirled her phone on the table so that Brooke could view the open social media app.

"What's this?" Brooke asked.

"Not what, but who." Leah cocked her head. "This is Isabelle Van Dyke's page, and if you scroll through her photographs and look closely, you'll see a familiar face."

"Don't tell me," Brooke said, already guessing the obvious answer. "Sean."

"Bingo! Give the little lady a prize." Leah blinked against another spate of tears, but none fell. "If I go back on this page, I can figure out about when he entered the picture, so to speak, and on his page too. So it's pretty easy to tell about when they became 'friends.'"

Brooke hated herself for asking but did anyway. "How does he know her?"

"He used to work with her, I do know that, but"—she turned the phone around again and scrolled through the online info—"Izzy— that's what she goes by," Leah explained, pulling a face. "She left the company about the time he got the axe. He said he quit, but I heard from one of his coworkers that he was fired, and then within a month of the time she started at a new company, he began investing in it."

Brooke thought of her own savings, which she'd placed in the start-up where she'd worked, how it was kind of a show of faith, how she'd believed in the business, and how it had cost her.

"So you think this . . . Isabelle, she got him to invest?"

"Pretty damned sure." Leah took a swallow of wine. "The timing is right," she said. "About the same time he showed up on her page he became less interested in me. In sex, I mean. And he's always been horny. Or was." She took another long swallow and drained her glass. She shoved her hair away from her face in frustration. "What is it with me and men?" she asked not just Brooke but herself and the universe as a whole.

"Don't go there," Brooke advised.

Leah scooted her chair back and found the wine bottle on the counter, then held it up. "Join me?" she asked, looking in Brooke's direction.

"No, I don't think so."

"Fine." Leah poured again, filling her glass to the rim. "More for me." She held her glass aloft for a second, some red wine sloshing over the rim. "Cheers," she said, taking a sip. "Fuck men."

"Right."

A cell phone jangled.

"Is that yours?" Leah asked, holding up hers. "Not mine."

"I'll see." Brooke's stomach clenched. Not a ring but a buzz. Not her cell phone but the burner.

Oh. Damn.

She reached into her purse and ended the call. She reminded herself to put it on silent and hide it in a small recess in the cupboard over the washing machine.

Leah glanced up at her. "Who was that?"

"Don't know. Probably a telemarketer," she said just as the timer went off and she turned her attention to the oven, where she rotated the baking dish, the scents of garlic and tomatoes wafting to her as the heat of the oven warmed her skin. "I'd say another fifteen or twenty minutes," she said, though Leah hadn't asked.

"That skank!" she cried. "Oh my God! Look what she just posted!" She set down her glass so hard that the stem cracked, the glass broke, and wine sloshed all over the table as well as over her phone. "No! No!"

Neal rushed back into the room.

Marilee too hurried down the stairs, Shep bounding behind her.

"My phone! Damn it, my phone!" Leah had picked up her cell and was wiping it with her fingers.

Brooke tore off two paper towels and, avoiding the jagged pieces of shattered glass, started blotting up the wine that was running over the tabletop and dripping to the floor.

"What happened?" Marilee asked, eyeing the broken glass and her mother busily mopping up.

"Nothing. An accident," Brooke replied.

Leah shrugged. "Just your lush of an aunt spilling her drink and ruining her phone. Just like she's ruining the rest of her life."

"Stop it!" Brooke said, sending Leah a hard look. As she did, a sharp pain shot through her palm. "Damn." A shard of glass had pierced her skin. "Holy—"

"Are you okay?" Neal asked.

Sucking in her breath through her teeth, Brooke plucked the wicked piece of glass from her hand. "Son of a bitch," she hissed as she quickly stepped to the sink. Blood trailed after her, but she turned on the tap and ran water over the wound. "It's fine," she lied, ignoring the pain starting to throb. "Not deep."

"Oh Brooke. I'm sorry." Leah seemed ready to cry again as she continued to dab at her cell with the towel.

"Put the phone in rice," Marilee said and walked to the pantry, returning with a canister of white rice. "It's supposed to draw out the liquid."

"Is it that bad? Let me see." Neal took the cell from Leah's hand.

As Brooke found a Band-Aid and tore open the little packet, the dog began licking up a few missed drops on the floor.

"Ugh! Someone get Shep out of here!" Brooke ordered and then did it herself after slapping on the Band-Aid. "There could be glass on the floor! Come on, boy!" She grabbed the retriever by his collar and pulled him into the hallway. "Stay!" she commanded, pointing a finger at the dog. "You, stay!"

"I think it's okay," Neal was saying as she stepped back into the kitchen. He touched the screen on Leah's phone and was nodding as he handed it back to her. "Here—try it again."

"Thank you." Leah was already typing and swiping.

Marilee glanced at her mother. "You okay?"

"I think I'll live," she said, needing a moment to pull herself together.

"You sure?" Neal asked.

"Yeah. I'm fine."

Neal didn't seem convinced, but he didn't press the issue and eyed the floor and tabletop, turning on the flashlight of his phone, trying to catch the glimmer of any tiny bits of glass still remaining.

Leah was still testing her phone.

"All clear," Neal declared.

"Mom, you're still bleeding." Marilee was staring at Brooke's hand. Sure enough, blood was soaking through the small Band-Aid. Marilee, to her credit, even found a damp towel and swiped the tabletop again.

"You should put some Neosporin on that," Neal said, motioning to Brooke's injured hand.

"Okay. Keep an eye on the lasagna, will you? It's got a few more minutes. And there's bread to heat and . . . a salad in a bag in the fridge."

"Got it!" Marilee said.

"Smells great." Neal gave her a wink as she snagged her purse from the counter, and she wondered how she'd ever not trusted him, ever thought they'd fallen out of love.

In the bathroom, she cleaned the cut on her hand and heard the conversation drifting up the stairwell. Muted voices, punctuated with laughter, her family. She applied the antibiotic gel to her cut, placed a large bandage on the wound and then, while everyone was downstairs, pulled the burner phone from her bag.

A voicemail.

Closing the bathroom door and locking it, she kept the volume on low and played the message. A raspy, whispered voice warned, "He's not who you think he is." Then the message ended.

Her heart stilled.

She licked suddenly dry lips.

Of course the number came up as unknown, and when she tried to call it no one answered. It cut off before the second ring. Who was calling her? Who knew? She felt cold inside and again heard a burst of laughter from the kitchen below.

She'd told no one of course, but Gideon could have told any number of people. He was reckless. Hadn't that been obvious just today as he, on his motorcycle, tried to cut her off in traffic? Showing up on her doorstep as a pizza deliveryman, for God's sake?

Unfortunately, his wild streak, his devil-may-care attitude, had been a big part of her attraction to him. The fact that she hadn't really tried to find out more about him, hadn't seriously researched him on the Internet, or had him scoped out by someone she trusted—

Like whom?

Who would you have trusted to look into a near stranger with whom you'd started an affair?

Face it, Brooke, you didn't really want to know him, wanted to keep the mystery going. You intentionally turned a blind eye.

You're an idiot.

God, she regretted every moment with him.

But you loved it at the time, didn't you? You wanted to step on the wild side and you dared to risk everything you loved for the thrill of the exhilaration, to feel young and wanted and alive once more!

Again, you're a fool.

The phone buzzed in her hand.

Gideon's number. Not a call but a text.

She froze, eyes wide as she read, **Liar! I thought you and Neal never made love. That the marriage was over. Isn't that what you said? And yet there you were, fucking the hell out of him.**

She stared at the message in disbelief.

Gideon knew that she and Neal had made love . . . no, wait, not just knew but had seen them?

She read the damning words: **and yet there you were, fucking the hell out of him.**

As if he'd been *watching, or in the room with them.*

Her stomach somersaulted.

No way.

That was impossible.

Or was it?

Fear oozed through her blood.

Hadn't the shades been open?

Hadn't she thought she'd seen someone in the backyard?

Hadn't she heard the roar of a motorcycle?

"Stop it!" she said aloud, jarring herself. He couldn't have seen them. Not from any position in the yard two stories down. No way. He was only guessing and she was letting her paranoia get the better of her.

Calm down.

He's out of your life.

Just because he buzzed you and Leah on the freeway doesn't mean he's stalking you. And you expected to hear from him after your showdown the other day. You knew he wouldn't just leave you alone. So this is how he's reacting.

Pull yourself together!

The uneasiness persisted, but she punched it down. Recriminations at this point were useless. She couldn't change the past, only the future. She turned off the phone, stuffed it into a pocket in her purse, and reminded herself to get rid of it. Splashing water on her face, she tried to cool off.

As she dried her cheeks with a hand towel, she heard the buzz of the timer for the casserole. Snagging her purse, she walked into the bedroom.

On the way out, her eye caught the glitter of something on her dresser. *What?* Something out of place. She stopped short. A small, bloodred stone winked from beneath the lamp. Her breath caught as she spied the bracelet Gideon had given her, the one she'd admired, with Marilee's birthstone and the engraved charm.

But she'd left it in the birdhouse.

Never brought it in.

Her mind spun.

Who had found it?

She snatched up the gold links and held them tight in her hand, then spun, searching the room as if she could find the perpetrator. Her heart was hammering, her breath trapped in her lungs.

Someone who knew about the bracelet, someone who had discovered it had been in her house and planted it where she would find it.

Once more she wondered if Gideon had been in her house, her home?

But he didn't have a key.

Or did he?

She'd heard footsteps, hadn't she?

Her underwear had gone missing.

Her heart was racing, her pulse thundering. Could he have somehow lifted her keys and made a copy when she hadn't been aware of it? But when? Frantically, she dug into her purse, found her set of keys, and identified the one to her house. She told herself she was grasping at straws.

Or was she?

He knew that she usually came in through the garage, with its automatic opener. Her key could have been off the ring for days, or weeks, and she wouldn't have noticed.

She started to hyperventilate, thinking how her life was destroyed, how he'd invaded every part of it. Nothing was sacred! No, no—

Get a grip!

Don't freak out.

You can't lose it!

Leah and Marilee are downstairs, and Neal . . .

Neal!

She froze.

Hadn't he been the one who sent her up here looking for Neosporin? Could her husband have found out the truth and decided to tease her, to gaslight her by leaving the bracelet on the bureau?

Neal was upstairs earlier.

Or what about Marilee? She was alone on this upper floor. Brooke had assumed her daughter was spending time in her own room, but maybe she'd found the bracelet earlier, even days ago, and sneaked into the room.

No, no. That was crazy. Marilee wouldn't even be paying attention.

Her mind went to her sister. Leah was alone in the kitchen when the adjuster was with Neal and Brooke. And she was upstairs. Could Leah have gone onto the deck and somehow found the bracelet? If so, why wouldn't she have mentioned it? Would she know the significance of this one piece of jewelry?

No.

None of Brooke's thoughts made any sense. So how had this happened? Her mind raced. Who had planted the bracelet on the dresser? As if to answer her question, she was sure she heard the sound of a motorcycle's engine revving in the distance. Then, when she listened more intently, she was certain she was mistaken.

Gideon hadn't been here.

Couldn't have sneaked into the house.

Right?

Frantically, she let her gaze scour the room as she turned in a slow, wide circle. He could have climbed in! Slipped inside and climbed up the back stairs? The ones they never used? Or scaled the exterior somehow; the drainpipe maybe? Hadn't she seen him scurry up the mast of his sailboat, perching high above her and looking down, laughing at her for her obvious concern. "Don't worry," he'd yelled, the sharp, salty breeze whipping his windbreaker and tossing his hair over his eyes. "I do it all the time."

Her stomach dropped.

The skin on the back of her arms pimpled.

All of a sudden she was back to her original fear: He'd been here. In this room.

Watching as she and Neal—

"Hey! Dinner's on!" Neal's voice boomed up the stairs.

She nearly screamed.

Hastily, she stuffed the bracelet into her pocket, nearly ripping off her recently applied Band-Aid.

She would throw it away, she decided, smoothing the bandage against the flat of her hand. The next time she ran, once her ankle was strong enough, she'd drop the phone and this damned bracelet into a public wastebasket, or heave it into the bay, or . . . somehow disentangle herself from the damning thing with its glittering stones and emotional ties to Gideon Ross.

At that moment the phone buzzed again, and her stomach twisted as another text from Gideon appeared on the small screen. She read the words and felt a chill as cold as winter seep through her bones:

Call me

"No way," she whispered.

And then the rest of the text appeared.

Or else.

CHAPTER 15

Brooke's heart leaped to her throat.
She stared at the damning message.

Call me or else.

"Or else what?" she whispered and was about to text the question but held off.

Don't engage.

That's what he wants.

He's trying to provoke you into dealing with him.

Ignoring him is the best defense.

Quaking inside, she replaced the phone in her purse and let out a slow, steady breath. She would not let him terrorize her.

Heading downstairs, she swore that Gideon would not ruin her life. She couldn't, *wouldn't* let him.

The scent of warm bread mixed with the tang of tomato sauce.

Dinner was already on the table, Leah sipping wine, Neal wearing an apron and slicing the lasagna, Marilee putting out the salad before slipping into her chair. Her bad attitude seemed at bay, though she was "too nervous" to eat and only managed a few bites before she flew back up the stairs to get ready for the dance.

Her sour mood returned once she found out that both her parents were dropping her off at the dance. Half a block before they arrived at the school, she insisted to be let out of Neal's Range Rover.

"This is sooo lame," Marilee complained from the back seat as Neal pulled to the side of the road.

"I think you'll survive," Neal said, shoving his SUV into Park in a spot not far from the school's gym, where exterior lights shone garishly, reflecting in the fog that moved slowly across the cracked asphalt and through the parked cars and teenagers milling around the open gym doors. Brooke caught sight of Nick Paszek hanging out with a couple of other boys in the drop-off area.

Before Neal or Brooke could say, "Have fun" or "Be careful" or "Text us when the dance is over," Marilee was out of the SUV and hurrying up a path to the doors.

"She definitely needs an attitude adjustment," Neal observed.

"You're on for that. I've tried and failed."

Nick, seeing Marilee, grinned widely and broke away from his group.

"That's Nick?" Neal was sizing up the six-foot-two-inch boy with the mop of black hair.

"Yeah." Brooke was nodding. "That's Nick all right."

"He's a . . . "

"Man?" Brooke supplied. "See why I'm worried?"

"Uh-huh."

But to Nick's credit, the boy caught sight of the Range Rover, lifted a hand in greeting, and smiled at Marilee's parents before she cast a look their way, said something, then took his hand and pulled him past a security guard who checked their ID before they disappeared into the gym.

Neal's brow was furrowed. "Maybe he's not such a bad guy. You know the family, right? They're okay?"

"I know Tammi, Nick's sister, and his mother, Renata. Not so much the dad." She lifted a shoulder. "I know Renata is involved in the school and goes to St. Andrew's, I think. As for Bruno?" She shrugged. "I've met him a couple of times and he seemed okay. But who knows what they're really like?"

"Who knows anything about anyone?" he said as Brooke noticed the news van parked near the student lot, harsh lights cutting through the night, a reporter in a red blazer and a microphone talking into the eye of a shoulder cam held by a thin man in a puffy coat and a knit cap. Beside them was the sign for the school:

ALLSWORTH HIGH SCHOOL
HOME OF THE FIGHTING ORCAS

"There's a grim reminder." Neal nodded toward a police cruiser, lights dark, parked at the far side of the lot near the empty tennis courts.

"I know." Brooke's anxiety ramped up again. "I just hope they find her, that Allison comes back soon."

"You and the rest of Seattle." He cast another look at the gym. The band was tuning up, the thrum of bass vibrating through the night. Flashes of strobe lights were visible through the open doors. The security guard was still checking each student's ID. "I guess we can go now."

Neal cranked on the wheel, making a quick U-turn, then drove away from the school. His expression was darker, more thoughtful than it had been on the way over, his features illuminated by the headlamps of passing cars, only to shadow until the next vehicle appeared and washed the interior of the Range Rover in the short-lived glow.

She thought about the tracking device found on the undercarriage of her car, of the fight with Leah *and* the spilled wine, of the bracelet feeling like a ton of bricks in her pocket, and of the warning that had been whispered from the anonymous caller.

He's not who you think he is.

She'd assumed the warning was about Gideon, but with a prick of dread piercing her brain, she wondered if the caller had been talking about Neal.

"I need to talk to you." Leah was waiting in the living room, a book on the couch beside her.

Brooke paused. She'd hoped to sneak the bracelet into a hiding spot until she could get rid of it, but she'd have to wait. Neal had already gone into his office shutting the door behind him, so now it was just she and her sister.

"Okay, about what?" she asked, taking a seat on a side chair.

Leah sighed. "What do you think?" She bit her lip nervously.

Brooke waited for Leah to finally cop to the real reason she'd flown to Seattle, because she didn't believe for a second that it was only about emotional support. It never was. It was about guilt. It was about payback. And it was definitely about money.

"I need a loan."

Boom. And there it was.

"Not much. Probably fifteen thousand?"

"Wow. Fifteen *thousand*?" Was she kidding? She'd never "loaned" her sister anywhere near that kind of money.

"Look, look," she said tentatively, then rushed on, "I know I haven't paid you back the last five, but I will. Seriously. I just have to get on my feet, and I've got a line on a job—substitute teaching again. It might lead to a full-time position if I get my certificate renewed and I've already applied."

Brooke had heard this before. "You think fifteen grand isn't much?"

"Well, for me? Yes. But you?" She motioned one hand to include everything in the house. "Look, I hate to do it, but I have to. Sean's gone through everything we had and then some. I need to pay for a lawyer and put up first and last month's rent."

"Sean is staying in the house?" she asked, astounded. "But it's yours; you paid for it with part of the money you got from Nana . . ." Her voice trailed off as she saw the pain in her sister's expression. ". . . or not."

Leah closed her eyes, battling tears. "I 'loaned' the money to Sean. We're leasing the house. The whole lease-to-buy thing didn't happen."

So it was worse than Brooke had suspected. "I don't have fifteen thousand," she said, thinking of her own bad investment choices.

"Neal?"

"Maybe, but probably less."

"Ten grand?"

"Money's tight, but you can ask him."

"No." Leah shook her head violently as she got to her feet and walked to the window at the front of the house. "You ask him for me. Please." Leah rubbed her arms as if a sudden chill had swept through her. "It's just so awkward." Leah didn't say it, but the silent reminder of *you owe me* hung in the air between them. Brooke didn't respond and Leah added, "Please, Brookie. You and Neal, you two are my last hope."

Brooke closed her eyes for a second. This was a mistake and she knew it, but she remembered her mother in those last days, thin on the bedsheets, her eyes sunken, squinting against the sunlight streaming through the windows of the hospital room. "You two girls, you take care of each other," she'd said, not asking, not beseeching but stating a fact as she'd grabbed each daughter's wrist in her bony fingers, her grip surprisingly strong. "Promise me."

And they had.

Now, Leah was staring at her with wide, worried eyes. Brooke couldn't stand it. "Okay," she finally agreed, "but this is the last time."

"Yeah, yeah, of course." Leah was nodding her head enthusiastically, blond curls bobbing around her face. She held up both palms as if in surrender. "Do this and I will never, ever ask again. Never. I swear."

"I'm going to hold you to it."

"I just—I just need to get through this divorce and then I'm done with men. I'm never going to get married again."

Brooke tossed her a give-me-a-break glance.

"Yeah, yeah, okay. I *know* I've said it before, but this time I mean it. I mean like *really*! And this time I'll sign a note for the loan for sure, make it official, and start paying you back as soon as I find a place and get that job."

"And you're staying in Phoenix?"

"For now. The area. Maybe Scottsdale, I don't really know. Like I said, I can work for the school district, so I'm gonna be there until the school year's over next June. By then I'll know what I'm going to do, if I'm going to stay or if I move again." She made a thoughtful face, her neatly arched eyebrows pulling together. "I just don't know yet. It depends on where I can get a permanent position."

In the past, whenever a relationship ended Leah had moved. She'd been in Chicago, San Diego, and Atlanta, as well as some obscure town in Oklahoma, before she'd landed the last time in Arizona.

"So you've filed for divorce?" Brooke asked.

"Not yet. Because I need the money."

"And he's agreed?"

Leah rolled her eyes. "We haven't actually discussed it. I can't afford a lawyer, but he'll agree to anything. He's already practically moved in with that bitch. And she's got a kid, did I mention that? A two-year-old." She blinked. "I can't believe it. Sean told me he never wanted kids. Never. Now he's going to be with her? Marry her?"

"You think?"

Leah's chin trembled slightly. "Oh, I know. We have a mutual friend who keeps me informed." She cleared her throat. "They're talking of having a baby together, a 'little brother or sister' for the one she's got!"

"Then you're right. The best thing you can do is get through this divorce as quickly as possible. Of course we'll help you."

Leah blinked back tears and crossed the room to hug her sister. "I knew I could count on you," she whispered, her voice cracking.

"I still have to talk to Neal."

"Yeah, yeah. I get it." She released Brooke. "I was just so worried about talking to you that I sat here kind of freaking out. I tried to read, but I couldn't concentrate, and then I just stared out the window, waiting for you, you know." She dashed her tears away. "It didn't help that the guy was back."

"What guy?"

"Some guy was across the street. Some weirdo. He stared at the house, you know, like he could see inside or something."

Brooke froze. "A guy?"

"No, no, I don't know. Maybe a man, but possibly a woman. It's probably nothing, somebody waiting for somebody."

Brooke walked to the window and stared out. A car drove by, its headlights glowing in the mist, but no one appeared to be loitering at the park or anywhere along the street.

"When was this?"

Leah shrugged. "Hmm. About fifteen minutes ago, I think. Yeah . . . the last time I saw him was right before I heard the garage door go down, when you and Neal came up the stairs, into the kitchen."

"So where was he exactly?" Brooke was still scanning the street and trying not to let her imagination run away with her. But she couldn't dismiss the unsettling thought that Gideon had been outside, as well as inside her house. She felt invaded, sick at the thought. "Over there?" She pointed to the park entrance.

"By the park entrance." Leah joined Brooke at the window, their pale reflections side by side, like ghosts wavering in the old glass. But the area outside the walls of the park was empty, no one standing near the gate, no one standing beneath the lamppost. She only saw a solitary man in a jacket and a driver's cap come out of the park. He was walking his dachshund and paused at the corner while the dog sniffed the stop sign. As he crossed the street, Brooke told herself it was nothing.

Losing interest in any activity, Leah picked up her book. "You'll talk to Neal?"

"Yes. Absolutely tonight."

"Good. Because I need to get back, much as I love it here. Things to do, you know. Not fun things, but"—she shrugged as she started for the stairs—"it has to be done. Again."

Leah headed to her room just as Brooke heard the faintest sound of a vibration coming from the kitchen. She turned to the nook where she'd dropped her purse on a chair.

The burner phone.

Crap!

Rather than take a chance on someone coming up and surprising her, she hurried down the steps to the garage, where she removed the phone from its zippered pocket. There, on the bottom step in the darkness, she read the message glowing in the dark:

I hope pretty little Marilee is enjoying the dance.

CHAPTER 16

A cold snake slithered down Brooke's spine as she read the message.

Gideon knew! Goddamn it, he knew about Marilee! Where she was.

Her heart kicked into overdrive as she raced up the stairs and into the house.

He wouldn't hurt her! He wouldn't dare!

But she'd seen the fury in his eyes, caught the bit of malice when she'd struggled with him.

How far would I go? he'd queried, as if it were a hypothetical question, one never to be tested. *I would do anything,* he'd said. *Anything.*

Her blood turned to ice.

"We have to go. Now!" Brooke was frantic as she pushed open the door to the den. "We have to pick up Marilee! Now!" Her stomach was in knots, her worst fears crystalizing.

Neal, seated at the desk, hastily closed his laptop. "What? Why?" He was on his feet in an instant. "Did something happen?" His expression said it all: He was suddenly panicked as he reached for his jacket, which was slung over the back of his chair. "Oh God." He glanced at the television mounted on the book case to the side of his desk, where a picture of Allison Carelli appeared, the number of a tip line beneath her smiling visage.

"I don't know," she said.

"What?" He was forcing an arm down the sleeve of his jacket.

"I mean I haven't heard of anything new. It's—it's just a feeling I have."

"A feeling?" He glared at her. "Did Marilee call? Text?"

"No."

"What?"

"It's just a feeling I've got that something is wrong." Even to her own ears, her reasoning sounded ridiculous, but she couldn't tamp down the panic that was bursting through her. Gideon knew. Somehow he knew about Marilee being at the dance. Her heart was pounding, dread riding on the back of the swelling alarm.

Neal was thoroughly confused. "Because she's there with Nick?"

"Because of everything!" she nearly yelled, motioning toward the television and the room in general.

"Hey, shh," he said. "It's okay."

"It's not okay, Neal. It's *not* okay."

"So you want to go to the school, force your way into the dance, and pull Marilee out of there?"

"Yes!"

"Brooke, that's crazy."

"Fine." She wasn't going to be dissuaded. She backed toward the door. "If you won't come with me, I'll go alone." She was racing for the garage when he caught her elbow and spun her back to face him.

"Listen to yourself."

"No, you listen to me!" She yanked her arm away. "I told you, I have this feeling that our daughter is in danger and I'm going to go get her."

"Just wait." He found his cell phone lying on his desk and scooped it up. "I'll text her."

"And you think she'll answer? She's with Nick, for God's sake! She won't answer a text from her father! She won't even have her phone on her."

"You don't know that. She always has her phone, lives with it. And she'll answer this text. Guaranteed." He was already typing.

"Oh sure."

"I'm going to tell her that her crazy mother is going to come flying into the dance and rip her out of there if she doesn't respond."

"What?"

He was still typing.

"No, Neal, don't!"

"Too late." He suddenly looked up at her. "I don't know what's going on with you, but you're acting like a damned lunatic. I thought we talked this all out in the car after we dropped her off. Has something changed?" he demanded, and for a second, when he looked into her eyes, she thought he knew more than he was admitting.

"I'm just worried."

"And it's over the top." He frowned and eyed his watch. "The dance is over at eleven. We'll go—together—at ten forty, so we're there in plenty of time, and we'll wait for her. Just as we planned." His phone dinged and he glanced at it.

"Marilee says she's fine." He rotated the cell so that she could read the screen, and she saw his text, just asking if she was okay—no reference to Brooke—and then Marilee's response: **I'm fine. Don't worry!** The text was accompanied by a cat emoji with hearts for eyes, Marilee's favorite. He slipped the phone into his pocket. "Satisfied?"

"No." But how could she explain her apparent hysteria? "I would just feel better if we went to the school now and saw that she was inside."

"Where do you think she is?"

"She could be anywhere. Just because she responded doesn't mean she's at the dance, just that she's close enough to a cell tower to get a signal."

"She's with Nick," he said again.

"And that's supposed to make me feel better?"

"Yes! She's not alone. He's a good kid, you said so yourself."

"Then suit yourself. I'm going now."

"Oh, for the love of—!" He shook his head and his expression turned to stone. "Fine. I'll come, even though the damned dance won't be over for an hour! Swear to God, Brooke, I don't understand what's gotten into you lately. Sometimes you're completely irrational."

She was already heading for the garage. "I guess, then, this is one of those times."

She drove. Fast. Like the madwoman she was.

With Neal hanging on for dear life.

Gideon's text was a threat. *Oh Jesus, if he hurt her daughter . . .*

Brooke's teeth clamped together. She thought about Allison. About Penelope. She didn't think Gideon was involved with their disappearance, but what did she really know about him?

Nothing.

She punched the gas through an amber light turning red, then screeched around a corner.

"Watch it!" Neal yelled. "What the hell is wrong with you?"

"It's just a feeling I have."

"You're acting like a crazy woman."

They made it to the school in record time. Her SUV bounced into the parking lot near the gymnasium.

"This is nuts," Neal said as Brooke slammed her Explorer into Park, threw open her door, and was out of the car in an instant. "Brooke! Wait! This is nuts! For the love of—"

She heard him cut the engine.

Let him think what he wanted. As she sprinted across the parking lot, she didn't care that her husband thought she was going out of her mind. She didn't care that her ankle was throbbing. She didn't care that she looked like she'd gone stark raving mad.

Not when her daughter's safety was at stake.

The security guard who had been posted at the gym door was nowhere to be seen. Good. But in his stead was a chaperone, a middle-aged, thickset woman with short hair and a fussy attitude, someone Brooke didn't recognize. The woman looked up from her phone as Brooke ran up. "Hi," she said. "Can I help you?"

Brooke barely broke stride. "I'm looking for my daughter."

"Oh. No problem. Who is she?"

Brooke sped past her and into the gym.

"Wait! You there, wait! I need to see some ID. We've had some trouble here at the school. Hey! Hey!" she screamed, her voice barely audible over heavy bass and wailing guitars.

Frantic, her eyes scanning the crowd in the dark gym, Brooke pushed her way through couples on the dance floor and singles or knots of kids crowding around the perimeter. "Marilee!" she cried.

"Hey!" one deep voice yelled.

Another muttered, "What the fuck?"

She ignored them, her eyes scouring the ever-moving crowd as she searched for her daughter or anyone she recognized. "Marilee!" she yelled, spinning wildly, the faces beginning to blur, the scents of sweat, perfume, and a hint of smoke mingling.

Where was she? Where? She started to panic but fought the urge to freak out.

Somewhere, over the din, she recognized her husband's voice. "Excuse me! Sorry—excuse me! Brooke! Stop!"

She didn't. Nor did she see Marilee as she moved through the throng. But they were here. Surely. They had to be. And Nick was a couple of inches over six feet, so he should stick out in the crowd. But nowhere did she spy the tall kid with the mop of dark hair.

Heart hammering, she spied Zuri Davis, Andrea's daughter, standing with a group of friends near one corner.

Brooke beelined to her daughter's friend. "Zuri," she said in a panic.

"Wha—oh." The girl's dark eyes rounded. "Mrs. Harmon?" The other kids, two girls and three boys, stopped their conversation. In fact, Brooke was vaguely aware of the music stopping and voices yelling behind her.

"Someone call security!" a woman—the chaperone—demanded, parting her way through the teenagers while kids backed away.

Brooke ignored her and caught Zuri by the arm. "Have you seen Marilee?"

Zuri's brown eyes widened. "Uh. Yeah. Earlier."

"Where is she? Is she still here?" Brooke released her grip, tried to gather her ever-fraying wits.

"I don't know." Zuri stared at Brooke as if she were an escapee from a mental hospital. She rubbed her arm and glowered. "I haven't seen her for a while."

"You!" The woman chaperone was still blocked by several couples, but she yelled loudly. "You stop right there!"

Brooke ignored her. "What about Nick?" she asked her daughter's friend. "Is she with Nick Paszek?"

Nodding, Zuri backed up a step. "The last I saw."

"And they didn't leave?"

"I don't know," Zuri said. But one of the boys with her, the short kid with an acne problem, glanced to an exit near the restrooms, double doors that opened to an inner courtyard.

Brooke didn't miss a beat.

She headed in the direction of the doorway. The door was propped open to let in a little air. No chaperone was posted nearby.

"Brooke!" Neal was closer now, but she kept plowing through the throng until she reached the door and shot through to a darkened courtyard. There, on a bench, huddled under a sapling devoid of leaves, was a couple, faces pressed together, bodies tight.

She recognized her daughter instantly. "Marilee!" she said, and the couple jumped away from each other as if electrocuted. "What the hell is going on here?"

From the corner of her eye, she caught a glimpse of two other couples who were startled by her voice.

"Mom!" Marilee turned wide, mortified eyes on her mother. "What the fu—what are you doing here?"

"Oh, um, hi, Mrs. Harmon." Nick shot to his feet and blinked wildly, as if he wanted to be anywhere but in this secluded courtyard.

"The better question is what're you doing out here?" Brooke replied.

Marilee's initial shock and dismay turned to anger. "Oh God, Dad too?" She got to her feet and stared past her mother as Neal caught up. "I can't believe this!" She looked as if she hoped to disappear, to just vanish into thin air.

Too bad.

To his credit, Nick said, "Uh, maybe we should go back inside." The other couples were slinking to the gym door.

"Let's go!" Brooke said to her daughter.

"What? No!" Marilee was having none of it. She sidled even closer to Nick.

"Right now!" Brooke wasn't backing down, though her heart was slowing and a sense of relief that she'd found her daughter alive and unharmed was coming over her. Thank God!

"Are you crazy?" Marilee asked, then, "Dad?"

"It's okay, honey," Neal said.

But Marilee was shaking her head violently. "It's definitely not okay! What're you two doing here?"

"Your mom had a feeling something was wrong."

"A feeling?" their daughter repeated. "Crap, Mom, really?"

It was more than a feeling, but what could she say? And then she spied a security guard approaching from the far entrance and her throat clamped shut. She recognized his frame, the way he walked in a straight line toward them.

Gideon.

No. Oh no!

"Oh, sh—oot," Nick said, spying the uniformed man quickly approaching.

"Mom!" Marilee's voice was a plea.

"Go back into the dance," Neal instructed. "I'll deal with this."

"This," of course, meant Brooke and whatever hassle the guard would give them.

Nick, his face ashen, was already heading for the double doors, Marilee scurrying after him.

Gideon, dressed in a full uniform, reached the bench.

Stricken, Brooke glared at him while Marilee cowered behind Nick.

"Is there a problem?" Gideon asked in a voice lower than usual. His face was shaded by a cap, his beard darker than usual, glasses with colored lenses covering his eyes. His clothing bore official-looking patches, and on his belt was a walkie-talkie and a holstered weapon.

"No problem," she said through gritted teeth, though panic pounded through her. What the hell was he doing here? How could he be so bold? So menacing?

"You're sure?" he asked, his voice authoritative.

"Nothing we can't manage," Neal assured him. "We were just checking on our daughter."

Gideon turned his gaze to Brooke. "And is she all right?" He nodded toward Marilee, still hiding behind Nick.

"Yes." Brooke's jaw hardened. "She's fine."

"No issue?"

"None," Neal assured him.

"You've got everything handled?" Gideon was still staring at Brooke.

"Absolutely." She stared right back, almost daring him to expose the truth. Trembling inside, fury melding with fear, she managed to keep her voice even. "We don't need any help dealing with our daughter." Brooke took a step closer to Neal and entwined her fingers in his.

"We've got this," Neal assured him.

"If you say so." Gideon finally broke her gaze to look toward the gym. The outraged chaperone, security guard in tow, was bustling through the door. "Well, you all keep tabs on your daughter. These days you can't be too careful." With that, he turned on his heel and headed for the outer gate.

"There she is!" the chaperone announced, wiggling an imperious, plump finger in Brooke's direction.

The same security guard Brooke had seen at the entrance when they'd dropped off Marilee was now with the chaperone. He didn't pause, just walked up to the group. "Is there any trouble?"

"No. We're just checking on our daughter," Neal explained. "We already explained it to the other guard." He motioned toward the far exit.

"What other guard?" The guard glowered toward the gate, now hanging open, Gideon nowhere in sight.

"The guy who was just here."

"I thought I was the only guard. I guess the service sent somebody else." He rubbed the back of his neck and scowled, then glanced at Neal and Brooke as if they were lying. "Look, we just don't want any trouble here."

"And we don't mean to cause any," Neal said, his fingers tightening over Brooke's, silently telling her not to make any more of a scene. "We're leaving now. We had a scare a little earlier and were worried about our daughter. I tried to reach her on her cell and couldn't. With all that's going on right now, with the Carelli girl still missing, we got worried and my wife, here, overreacted." He gave the guard an engaging, I'm-sure-you-understand smile meant for husbands of unpredictable wives.

As if! Brooke tried to yank her hand from his, but his grip tightened to the point of pain as he went on, "She's our only child, and when she didn't respond, we came down here, couldn't see her, and well . . . we're really sorry."

The guard glanced at the chaperone, but much of her bravado had deflated after hearing Neal's explanation.

Scowling, the guard said, "Maybe it would be best if you all went out this side gate; it's unlocked because of the fire code, you know. You can wait for your daughter outside in the parking lot. The dance will be over in about half an hour or so."

"We will," Neal agreed and pulled Brooke toward the exit where only minutes before Gideon had slipped out. As the guard ushered them past the smug chaperone to the gate and held it open for them, he said, "I understand about worrying about your kid. Got three daughters of my own."

"Thanks." Neal sketched out a wave with his free hand but didn't release Brooke for a second.

Once the gate clanged shut behind them, Brooke jerked her hand from Neal's punishing grip. "That was unnecessary!"

"No, that—what you did—was uncalled for. Jesus, Brooke, you didn't have to go charging in there like a raging lunatic!" They reached her dented Explorer and Neal opened the side door, motioning her into the passenger seat.

"This is my car."

"And you nearly killed me on the way over here! I'm driving home."

She slid into the passenger seat. "You're being an ass."

"Am I?" He slammed the door shut and rounded the car to take his position behind the steering wheel. "Well, at least I didn't act like a fucking psycho! You bullied your way into that gym like you were storming the damned Bastille."

She didn't respond. Just fumed.

And tried like hell to keep her real fears at bay.

Gideon.

Here.

At the school.

Pretending to be a security guard.

Knowing about Marilee.

Dear Lord, what a mess. She stared out the window past the leaf-less branches of the nearby trees to the sky above, where flimsy clouds wafted over a crescent moon.

But her thoughts were on Gideon and the lengths to which he would go to terrorize her.

She knew now he would never leave her alone.

And now he was involving her daughter.

She dug deep, found some resolve. Somehow, some way, she had to get rid of him.

Forever.

As that thought crossed her mind, she heard the whine of a motorcycle. Never had the sound been more ominous.

CHAPTER 17

"You absolutely mortified our daughter," Neal said after several minutes of icy silence. His fingers drummed angrily on the Explorer's steering wheel as they waited for the dance to be over. "I'd be surprised if she ever forgives you." Sending her a suspicious glance, he added, "And all because you had a 'feeling'?" Disbelief and anger colored his words. "There had to be something more for you to come that unglued!"

What could she say? "I was just worried."

"Beyond worried!" he threw back at her. "Everyone who has a kid in this school is worried, but did you see anyone else bullying their way inside and racing through the gym with their hair on fire? No! Just you, Brooke. Just you!" He pounded the steering wheel with a fist. "What the hell is going on with you?"

"Nothing."

"Bullshit! You've been acting like a crazy person for weeks!" He let out a long breath. "Or maybe even months."

She didn't respond.

"I feel like I don't even know you anymore," he admitted and watched the headlights of a pickup as the truck bounced into the lot.

"Maybe you never did," she said.

Other cars began to appear, creating a line of idling vehicles as it neared time for the dance to be over.

"Jesus, how did this happen?" he asked, but it was a rhetorical question that didn't require an answer. So Brooke remained silent, her eyes trained on the gym doors, her thoughts returning to the beginning with Neal. Maybe it was true what they say, that if you cheat with someone, you can never trust that person. Ever. Once a cheater, always a cheater. In their case the old saying cut both ways. But until Jennifer Adkins came along, neither Neal nor Brooke had crossed that invisible line of adultery in their marriage.

Well, as least as far as she knew.

She could only speak for herself.

There were times in the past when she'd suspected Neal was involved with someone else, though she'd never had concrete proof. In any case, though her suspicions had lingered nothing had ever come of it.

As for her?

She'd never looked at another man.

Until she found out about Jennifer Adkins.

And then all bets were off.

Brooke had heard rumors, a whisper at the company picnic when she'd first met the tall brunette with a retro shag haircut, her bangs fringing her huge brown eyes. She'd seemed shy and sultry, but Brooke had noticed how she'd lit up around Neal. While sitting at a picnic table drinking iced tea, Brooke had witnessed how he'd gone out of his way to be friendly to the newest member of the staff.

Then again, during the Christmas party at one of the partner's homes on Lake Union. When Brooke had finally extricated herself from a knot of wives whose conversation had turned to some charity art function, she couldn't find her husband. After a short search she'd discovered him alone with Jennifer on the deck facing the lake, smiling and laughing, standing a little too close, she thought. When the brunette caught sight of Brooke approaching, she'd taken a step back, her smile fading for a second before it widened again as she said, "Hi," before making an excuse about refilling her wineglass.

"What's the deal with her?" Brooke had asked.

"What?"

"Well, you're out here and it's what? Forty degrees?"

"Oh. She wanted to see where Troy Brent lives and you can see his home from here." He pointed across the lake. "It's the house all lit up, triple boathouse—there, to the left of those huge trees. See it? With the huge star on the roof?" He leaned close to her, adjusting her shoulders so she was facing the lake. "Jenny is working with Troy.

Well, not directly with him, but on his account." Troy Brent was one of the firm's biggest clients. Neal wrapped one arm around her and extended his arm, pointing to the largest house on the other side of the lake, but Brooke spun away.

"I know where the Brent complex is," she said. "You've shown it to me before."

"Oh, right."

Her eyes narrowed. "What's going on, Neal?" she asked.

He had the audacity to look innocent. "What do you mean?"

"You know exactly what I mean, with the newbie. Jennifer."

"Nothing." He actually smiled. "Don't tell me you're jealous?"

"Don't flatter yourself," she said. "And don't patronize me. I'm not an idiot," she'd said, then stormed into the house, plucked a drink from a waiter's tray, and tossed back the wine. A moment later she spied Jennifer giving her the side-eye from a spot near the grand piano, where a pianist was taking requests and currently playing "Hallelujah."

Brooke left her empty glass on an ornate table, then walked to the front closet, found her coat, and didn't wait for Neal, who caught up with her in the circular drive. "What do you think you're doing?" he asked, obviously upset.

"What does it look like? I'm leaving."

"But you can't. Not yet."

"Watch me!"

She reached into her purse for her key ring, then swore under her breath as she remembered she didn't have a key to his damned Range Rover.

"Brooke," he said more softly, and she let out her breath to watch it fog in the cold night air. "Come back in. I've got clients here. It's important."

She didn't want to but told herself that somehow she would get through the night. "Another hour."

"Yes. Sure. That'll do."

The rest of the night he remained by her side. Though she was wound tight, forcing a smile, sipping champagne, half listening to conversation. She heard as if from a great distance the piano renditions of "White Christmas" and "Jingle Bell Rock." She was aware of Jennifer Adkins's every move as she worked the room. Jennifer talked easily to the senior partners, engaged their wives, smiled, and fit in easily.

It was Brooke who felt like an outsider.

Still, she might have relaxed a little, but she noticed that whatever room she and Neal entered, Jennifer soon followed. Casually. At a distance.

A coincidence?

Brooke didn't believe that.

The hour went by excruciatingly slowly. As people laughed and glasses clinked and some, lubricated by liquor, sang the lyrics of the Christmas carols being played, Brooke counted the seconds.

Neal was at ease, and when she pointed out it was time to leave, he held up a hand until he'd finished his conversation with a junior partner and finally said his goodbyes.

Jennifer watched them go and—God, did she blow a kiss at Neal as she waved goodbye? Surely not. Brooke must've imagined it, but in the car on the way home, she barely spoke a word to Neal and then, two months later, she saw the text message and realized her husband had been unfaithful.

Tonight? At Harvey's? Can you get away?

Her stomach had dropped and she'd followed Neal to the bar seven blocks away from their house. After parking around the corner and crossing the street to the small tavern, she peered through the window. Quickly scanning the large room, she saw the two of them huddled in a booth near the back. They were close together, Neal's arm over Jennifer's shoulders. She leaned into him and tilted up her head for a kiss that he delivered so tenderly Brooke felt her heart crack. She backed up, stomach churning, and ran into a parking meter.

No! Her mind had screamed. *No, no, no!*

She'd suspected of course. All those late nights when he was "at work." But to be confronted with the bald truth was jarring. The door to the establishment opened, and for a split second she thought about striding inside and confronting her husband and the shrew who was with him, but as the door swung closed behind two men in similar Seahawks jackets and caps, she changed her mind.

What was the old saying? Something about revenge being best when served cold?

Well, she was hot at the moment. White hot with a fury only tempered by a sudden, icy onslaught of fear. What if Neal left her? What if he was emotionally entwined with this woman? What if the affair—if indeed their relationship had become sexual—was more than physical? What if, God forbid, her marriage, which had seemed to be foundering recently, was over? What about Marilee? Young, impressionable, on the brink of womanhood? Oh. No.

Brooke's stomach twisted as she stumbled backward, lurching onto the street, and slipping into a puddle. A passing car honked, nearly hitting her. It splashed up a sheet of icy water, drenching her clothes.

She didn't care and stared dully as the car flew down the street, taillights winking bright red. Tears blurring her vision, pain cutting to her soul, she stumbled back to her own vehicle, unlocked it, and before slipping into the interior, threw up on the asphalt.

"Shit." She fell back onto the seat and tried to pull herself together.

So Neal lied about work and met a woman at a bar.

So she saw him kissing that woman.

That didn't necessarily mean her life as she knew it was over. It just meant her husband was on the cusp of cheating on her—well, maybe beyond the cusp. But it wasn't the end of the world. Lots of marriages survived setbacks, including infidelity.

Big deal.

She turned on the ignition but let the car, lights on, idle as she pounded her head against the steering wheel. How had this happened? What had *she* done wrong? Had she been so disinterested in Neal that he'd felt compelled to—

No, no, no!

This is not your fault!

Brooke Fletcher Harmon, do not take the blame for Neal's weakness.

And don't accept the role of victim.

You're strong.

You can handle this.

Haven't you always done what you were called upon to do?

When Mama was sick and dying? Didn't you handle it, accept it, tamp down your own fear and heartache for the sake of Nana and Leah?

Yes, her grandmother eventually took control, but in those first few weeks of her daughter's diagnosis, even Brooke's gritty little grandmother had stumbled when faced with the loss of her child. As ever, Mary O'Hara had turned to God for answers and advice. She had stumbled, her grief and despair nearly swallowing her. Until the old priest came to the house a week after the funeral, when Mary, Brooke, and Leah had watched the coffin be lowered into a neat pit cut into the manicured lawn of the cemetery. They had all tossed white roses onto the casket, and Nana was like a zombie, only aware enough to whisper prayers.

She hadn't functioned, accepting visitors with casseroles and cakes as if in a fog, while Brooke kept track of who had come to offer condolences and meals. It was only after the old priest had visited and comforted her, somehow reaching the woman shrouded in grief, that Nana had returned to them.

Yes, Nana's emotional breakdown was short-lived, but in those few weeks, Brooke, as a teenager, had held the little family together.

As she stared through the windshield to the city street, it began to rain again, at first only a few drizzling drops, then faster and faster. Silently, she told herself that she could handle Neal's attraction to another woman. She'd find a way. No matter what it took.

She had to.

For her own sanity.

And for her daughter's well-being.

Marilee deserved better.

And so did she.

Washing out her mouth with a half-empty, watered-down Diet Coke in the cup holder, she spat on the street. Then, with renewed determination, she started the SUV, pulled onto the street, and pushed down any remaining shreds of self-pity. No way would she let some upstart young attorney ruin her life.

Even if she was beautiful and had her sights set on Neal.

No damned way.

CHAPTER 18

Now, as she watched teenagers climb into cars, Brooke realized her response to Neal's involvement with Jennifer Adkins had been way out of line. Not that she shouldn't have felt such a deep betrayal, but when she'd met Gideon, she'd felt somewhat justified in becoming entangled with another man.

How stupid.

Look what had happened.

Her gaze followed a group of kids climbing into an old Cadillac, a boy who looked too young to drive getting behind the wheel and peeling out of the lot. Farther up the street, she caught a glimpse of Austin Keller behind the wheel of his pickup, and when he saw his daughter approach he climbed out, no longer tall and lanky as he had been in high school but a little more muscular, his hair still a coffee brown and his beard shadow covering his jaw. At the sight of his daughter, Chloe, he waved his hand, and the girl with the straight red hair nearly sprinted across the lawn to him. They fist bumped and laughed, a widowed man and his seemingly well-adjusted kid. As if he'd sensed Brooke watching him, he'd turned and smiled, then given a wave as he climbed into his truck.

"There she is," Neal said and slid open the driver's side window to wave at Marilee.

She spotted her father, then looked back to the doorway where Nick held up a hand. Marilee smiled faintly, then turned and half ran to the SUV, where she quickly opened the back door and ducked inside.

"How was the dance?" Neal asked, and Brooke cringed. What a stupid question.

"How do you think it was? Don't you know?" Marilee charged. "You ruined it!"

"We didn't ruin anything," Brooke said.

"Oh yeah right! Are you crazy, Mom?" And then, without waiting for an answer, she said to Neal, "Can you just drive?" and slithered down in the back seat, as if to make herself invisible.

"Marilee," Brooke said. "I'm sorry. Your father's right, I did over-react a little bit, but—"

"A little bit? Jesus, Mom, you were a fu—a lunatic!"

"Hey! Language!" Neal barked as he pulled out of the lot.

"But the whole dance stopped. Everyone saw you!" She was starting to cry, tears sliding down her cheeks. "I can never go to school again!"

"Sure you can," Neal said. "By Monday no one will even remember."

"You really believe that?" Marilee was sobbing now.

Neal's face had hardened. Of course he didn't believe his platitude. None of them did. For a while no one spoke, the sound of the tires on the pavement the only sound as Marilee tried to stifle her sobs. Brooke's heart was breaking.

"You're right," Brooke finally admitted as they turned into their neighborhood. "I'm sorry. I was *waaay* out of line. I got spooked. Because of Allison Carelli and"—she glanced at Neal to catch his re-action—"and I thought I saw someone watching the house lately."

"What?" Neal said. "Who?"

"That's it, I don't know."

"Someone was watching the house?" Marilee said, sniffing loudly. "And so that makes it okay for you to go all psycho and ruin my life?"

"I'm not ruining—"

"You are!" she argued. "I was so embarrassed! And Nick. Why do you hate him?"

"I don't; we don't hate him," Brooke said.

Neal cut in. "Wait a sec. You said you think someone is watching the house?"

"I've seen someone, but I didn't think it was a big deal until—"

"When?" Neal demanded. "Where did you see him?"

"I'm not even sure it's a man, but it's a feeling I've had. And I've seen *someone* who seems to be lurking, and tonight Leah said she'd seen him—er, a figure—too. Near the park. By the gate."

"Across the street from the house?" Neal said. "There?" He pointed toward the hedgerow growing next to the fence surrounding the park.

"Yes."

Marilee said, "So you and Aunt Leah see someone on the street and that makes you think I'm not at the dance?" She let out a disgusted breath. "Like that makes any sense!"

Neal turned into the driveway. "It freaked your mom out because of the missing girls."

"You thought, what? That someone had kidnapped me or murdered me? Jesus, are you serious?" She was gobsmacked. "Mom, really, this is *sooo* over the top!"

Neal said, "We tried to text and call you, but you didn't respond."

"I did!" she argued, and Brooke remembered the text with the cat emoji and how she hadn't believed her daughter was really at the school.

"Well, later. We tried again."

"But I wasn't missing. I was at the dance!"

"Or," Brooke said as Neal hit the garage door opener and the door started to rise, "more precisely, you weren't at the dance but in the courtyard, making out with Nick."

"Ooh. Gross! You keep saying I'm making out," Marilee accused, unbuckling her seat belt.

"Because you were!" Brooke said as Neal drove into the garage and cut the engine. "And that only leads to trouble."

"You should know!" Marilee flung open the door and sprang from the car.

"Wow," Neal said, closing the garage door remotely.

Brooke couldn't argue. "I guess I had that coming." She and Neal had never hidden the fact that she was pregnant when they got married. Until now, it hadn't been an issue.

"She's right, you know," Neal said as she heard the engine tick as it cooled. "You were acting as if you'd lost your mind."

"If you say so," she said, more harshly than she'd anticipated. She didn't dare tell him the truth: that her lover—make that *ex*-lover— had been texting her, practically stalking her. The car's interior dimmed as she recalled how he'd had the nerve to confront her and Neal and Marilee. How he appeared as a fake security guard after posing as a pizza deliveryman. Gideon was definitely stalking her and ramping up his intimidation. Phone calls and texts were one thing. Pretending to be a deliveryman or a damned security guard and cutting her off in traffic was another thing altogether. And what about the bracelet? Somehow he'd found a way into her house.

How far would he go?

Hadn't he told her?

Her insides churned.

She had to find some way to stop him.

Before all of their lives were destroyed.

"Just try to keep a cool head," Neal advised.

"Okay. Great. Fabulous advice." She opened the passenger door and the interior light of the car switched on again. "From now on I'll try to get a firmer grip on my sanity." She was about to step out, but he grabbed her arm.

"You really saw someone outside the house?" His face was creased with concern.

"Yes." Irritated, she said, "Why would I lie about that?"

"You tell me."

She noticed the questions in his eyes. Ignored them. "If you don't believe me, ask Leah."

"I don't think that's necessary. I trust you."

Her heart wrenched, but she said, "Good. I hope so." Yanking her arm from his grip, she shot out of the car and up the stairs to find Shep wiggling and wagging his tail as he greeted her.

"Hey, I missed you too," she said.

Barking his exuberance, Shep greeted Neal too. While he walked through the kitchen, Shep dashed to the French doors in the kitchen. She got the hint and let him outside. Eagerly, the dog padded across the deck and down the steps to the backyard. "Good boy," she said as she heard the door to Neal's den click closed.

Good.

She was tired of fighting with him. Of lying to him. She stood at the French doors, watching the dog wander across the shadowy lawn and wondering just how she was going to get rid of Gideon.

There had to be a way to ensure she would never see him again.

Whatever it was, it would have to be final.

She would do it.

And she'd never look back.

The dog was taking his sweet time, so she left the French doors ajar for Shep, then made her way to the second floor. In the hallway she tapped lightly on Marilee's door.

No answer.

She rapped louder.

Still no response.

Opening the door, she poked her head inside. "I think we need to talk," but her daughter was at the desk, back toward Brooke and wearing earbuds. Marilee had her iPad on her lap, her computer monitor glowing on her desk, gaming controller and cell phone in the clutter of fingernail polish bottles and books and clothes.

"Marilee?" she said loudly and her daughter physically started.

Pivoting in her chair, she said, "Get out."

"What?"

"This is my room. *My* space. Get out!" Marilee's face was twisted in imperious disgust.

Brooke bristled. "This is my space too. I live here. I own the house."

"Daddy owns the house." She angled up her chin defiantly.

"Look, I was trying to say that I'm sorry I was a little over the top."

"A little?" She looked about to say something more disparaging but managed to hold her tongue.

"I'm trying to apologize."

"And I'm trying to accept it. But I can't. You know why? You seem intent on ruining my life! Do you know how embarrassing that was, or what it's going to be like for me at school on Monday?"

"You mentioned it, yeah."

Marilee ripped one of the Airpods from her ear and her face threatened to collapse in on itself, her chin trembling. "It's going to be horrible. Everyone will know what happened. Well, they already do. It's all over IG and TikTok and everywhere! But at school they'll be pointing and laughing and talking behind my back. And Nick . . ." Her voice drifted off on a sob. "Oh, just . . . just leave me alone."

"But—"

"Mom, *please*! Just go!"

"I'm trying to apologize."

"Are you?"

"You're not making it easy."

"Leave me alone!" She turned her back to Brooke again.

Knowing the fight would escalate if she stayed, Brooke finally did as she was bid and stepped into the hall. A split second before she pulled the door closed behind her, she thought she heard, "I hate you" whispered under Marilee's breath.

Her heart shuddered.

She'd blown it.

Pure and simple.

Everything she'd worked hard to create for decades was crumbling apart and it was all her fault.

Gideon had infiltrated her mind, her body, her soul, and now . . . now her family.

Before she could take a step across the hall, her cell phone buzzed in the back pocket of her jeans. She retrieved it and stared at the message on the screen:

Your daughter is as beautiful as you are.

Be careful.

It would be a shame if you were to lose her.

She couldn't breathe.

Gideon wasn't just threatening her; he was now threatening Marilee.

Oh no, you prick. Don't you . . . no, no, no! Her heart was thumping in her chest, fear running through her veins. He wouldn't dare. He wouldn't . . . for a second she thought of Allison Carelli . . . Oh Jesus, no! Gideon couldn't be involved in her disappearance. There was no way. But as she stared at the message, she wondered.

Should she go to the police?

She shuddered at the thought. She had her own memories of dealing with authorities, how things could be misconstrued, witnesses unreliable, charges brought . . . She couldn't go there. Not now.

But this was dire. Should she call in an anonymous tip?

Her mind was spinning with unthinkable, horrible scenarios. She leaned heavily against the deck's rail and tried to recall any evidence, any indication that Gideon could be involved.

She wanted to frantically type a text message, to warn him to back off, to leave her and her family alone. But she knew that he was baiting her, hoping to engage, and on her personal cell phone, the one Neal could access if he called the phone company.

Her stomach tightened and roiled and she felt the sudden burst of saliva bloom in her mouth. She was going to . . . oh hell! She raced to the bathroom off her bedroom and barely made it to the toilet before she heaved into the bowl. Everything she'd eaten that afternoon and evening came back up before she dry heaved twice.

Shaken, she flushed the toilet and sat on the cool tiles before finally realizing she wasn't going to hurl again. She stood on wobbly legs, turned on the tap, and leaned over the sink to take a drink, rinse her mouth out, and spit.

She caught her reflection in the mirror, pale and wan, hair a mess, and then her eyes rounded as she thought just briefly of feeling like this fifteen years earlier. When she'd been pregnant with Marilee. Her nausea hadn't been an early morning thing. There was no schedule. It had come day or night.

Gripping the counter, she told herself it couldn't be, then did a quick mental calculation. When was the last time she'd had a period? Her cycle had always been erratic, unlike so many of her friends. She pulled out her phone and confirmed the timing, her heart sinking.

Six weeks?

No, that couldn't be right. But she'd marked the date on her phone's calendar. She'd been late before. Often by a week, possibly ten days. Each time had proven to be a false alarm.

After giving birth to Marilee, she'd been prescribed the birth control pill to help straighten out her cycle, but on the medication she'd gained weight, suffered serious mood swings, and lost most of her interest in sex, even on a low dose. So she'd decided not to bother and accept that her body was different than most women's.

But now . . .

The cold reality was horrifying. She clutched the counter in a death grip, the sharp edges cutting into her palm. Her mind raced to the past several months and the times she'd been with Gideon in his bed, always careful, and yes, she and Neal had made love, but it had been very recent because they had been recently separated.

Her pulse pounded in her brain.

Sweat dappled her skin.

She couldn't be pregnant. She silently said as much to the woman in the reflection. No damned way. She was *not* carrying Gideon Ross's baby.

Bile rose in her throat again, but she swallowed it back and stared at the wan, frightened woman looking back at her with wide, horrified eyes.

CHAPTER 19

Rap. Rap. Rap.

"Brooke?" Leah's voice called from the hallway as she rapidly knocked on the bedroom door.

Brooke blinked.

Oh no. She'd forgotten about her sister.

How long had she been standing here, frozen in the bathroom, denying what was most possibly the truth? That she was pregnant? With Gideon's child. Her stomach churned as she attempted to collect herself. With a deep breath, she walked to the bedroom door and cracked it.

Leah was crying, dabbing at her eyes with a wadded tissue. "Is—is everything all right?" she asked. "I heard fighting and then someone getting sick and—" She let out a shuddering breath.

"That's not why you're crying." Brooke opened the door wide.

"No, of course not." She sniffed. "Sean texted me. He's been to an attorney and the divorce papers are coming through. He wants everything, Brooke: the house, the accounts, our time share, even my car."

"What? No. There must be laws in Arizona that split things evenly."

Her eyes slid away. Uh-oh. "What, Leah?"

"I, um, I may or may not have signed a prenup." She began blinking wildly and shredding the tissue.

"And—"

"It gives him everything."

"Including the money you inherited." Brooke's voice was a death knell.

"I was in love and, okay, stupid. I thought this one would really work out, but of course it didn't."

Brooke tried to concentrate, to let go of her own problems for a few minutes. "Let's not talk here," she said with a glance at Marilee's firmly closed bedroom door. "Downstairs." She ushered her sister into the living room. "I told you I would help."

"I know, and I appreciated it."

"Maybe you should talk to an attorney."

Leah was nodding. "I spoke with one in Phoenix, but he knows Sean and wouldn't touch it with a ten-foot pole. He said I should work things out with Sean. In his opinion that would be the least expensive, but there's no way that's going to happen." Her jaw tightened. "It's beyond that. I thought maybe Neal might help."

"Neal isn't a divorce attorney, and even if he were, he doesn't have a license in Arizona," she started to argue.

"But you know, he might know someone who knows someone, or at least he could give me some professional advice, like, off the record." She cleared her throat. "I just need to talk to someone."

And that someone would have to be a man, Brooke finally understood. That was the way it was with Leah, always seeking male companionship, male advice, male opinions. The sisters had grown up without a father figure in their lives and they'd taken different approaches. Brooke believed in womanpower and that a woman was equal if different from a man. Leah was always seeking male approval, searching for a daddy who didn't exist.

And right now they were both in trouble.

"Let's see what he has to say," she finally decided and tapped with one knuckle on Neal's closed office door.

"It's open."

She twisted on the knob and found him lying on the sofa near the window, his ankles propped on the arm, his iPad open. He straightened and shut the tablet as he saw the sisters crammed into the doorway. "What's going on?"

"Leah wants to talk to you."

"Okay," he said, "sure. What's up?"

"I need some advice," Leah said, walking awkwardly into the room.

To his credit, Neal didn't throw Brooke a beleaguered, oh-here-we-go-again look, even though this particular scenario had played out a couple of times before. "Have a seat," he said, motioning to the overstuffed chair. "What's up?"

Brooke took that as her cue to leave and shut the door behind her before heading into the kitchen. Her stomach was still on the queasy side and a headache was beginning to pound behind her eyes. She found a glass and filled it with water from the dispenser in the refrigerator, then took a long, cooling swallow before pressing the glass to her forehead. What was she going to do? As she set the glass on the counter, she saw the French doors hanging open and she paused.

Shep was curled in his bed near the table. She wondered how often she'd left the door ajar, allowing whoever to gain entrance. She wasn't the only one; they all—she and Neal and Marilee—left the doors open for the dog to come and go throughout the day. Though Neal usually made certain the entire house was buttoned up at night, a habit Brooke had relinquished to him once he'd moved back in.

All that being said, someone unwelcome had been inside.

Someone with evil intentions.

Someone named Gideon Ross.

Her stomach soured and threatened to convulse again, and she closed her eyes, counted to ten, then to twenty, then fifty before the feeling subsided.

Then she, rather than wait for her husband, turned the dead bolt to the French doors, her gaze scanning the empty deck as she did so. Afterward she confirmed that all the doors were locked, starting with the front door, then heading downstairs to the garage and laundry room. Near the washer and dryer she paused. Not only did the laundry room open to the side yard, it also was connected to the old staircase—the "fire escape"—though that door was never used. Locked tight. She double-checked, and sure enough when she tried the knob it held fast.

But the key to the lock was on a ring that hung inside the cupboard over the washer. She looked again. The ring was there, in its spot, partially hidden by a jug of bleach. She slipped the ring off its hook and fingered the individual keys. This ring was the spare set and not all the keys to the house were included. They'd had the original set since they purchased the house and some of the keys were orphans. They obviously went to locks they'd never found and were useless, but in the group she recognized the old-style skeleton key to the back staircase.

She hesitated just a moment before unlocking the door to the aging staircase and stepping inside the dark, closed area. The switch for the single light that hung over the landing worked, thank God, but the bulb was dim, the steps narrow, the thin rail wobbly against dingy, wood-paneled walls. Swiping at cobwebs, she wound her way to the first floor as dust filled her nostrils and she tried to avoid the planks that were visibly rotted. At the wide top step that led to the back of the pantry she tested the door.

Locked.

Good.

She heard the muffled sound of voices. Leah and Neal. She couldn't detect what they were saying; she could only make out a word here and there.

Heading upward, feeling a little claustrophobic, she heard the steps creak beneath her feet. Just as she'd heard the other night, her heart lurching at the thought.

At the landing on the second floor the stairs ended. She tried the door, but it didn't budge. Good. Located next to the linen closet in the upstairs hallway, it was locked tight.

Only one more space. With more than a little trepidation, she glanced upward to the rungs that disappeared into the ceiling and led to the cramped attic beyond—an area they never used.

In for a penny, in for a pound, she told herself. With her injured ankle protesting, she climbed up the ancient rungs, and as she ascended, sweating nervously, she told herself she wasn't being paranoid. After all, she had heard someone in the house. Could there be some kind of camera or microphone that Gideon had planted inside? Was he that obsessed? Or was she that paranoid?

Time to find out.

With an effort, she pushed the trapdoor up, its old hinges grating. Once it was open she eased herself upward into the musty, cold space. She located a light switch on a post near the entrance, but when she flipped it nothing happened, the old bulb burned out.

Great.

The space was dark as night, the ceiling low. As she felt around in the darkness, allowing as much weak light from the stairway below to enter the area, her eyes adjusted and she could barely make out the exposed joists with the ancient insulation packed between.

An uneven plank walkway had been set upon the cross beams to an area where the ceiling was the highest. There, the previous owner had nailed down a couple of pieces of plywood to create some rough flooring in the area.

The attic felt undisturbed.

She touched the nearest plank and discovered dust, cobwebs, and the desiccated remains of a dead insect. Nothing out of the ordinary. Nothing that appeared out of place.

And yet . . . she sensed someone had been in the house. Someone unwanted. Someone who had access and a key. As she shone the flashlight toward the rafters, she noticed some of the spiderwebbing seemed torn and was that a spot where the dust had cleared? An old mousetrap, scooted out of the way?

The skin on the back of her neck pimpled.

It had to be Gideon.

He knew too much.

Her heart pounded. Her thoughts swirled. Would he have really broken into her house? Spied on her?

Call me or else.

She swallowed hard.

Your daughter is as beautiful as you are.

Be careful.

It would be a shame if you were to lose her.

"No way," she whispered, a sense of terror gripping her. She fought it and tried to ignore the fact that the attic seemed suddenly cloying, as if the darkness were closing in on her.

The tense moment was broken by the sounds of life. She heard movement downstairs, people shuffling around, a toilet flushing, water running.

She didn't want to try to explain why she'd been on the back stairs, so she quickly climbed down the rungs, then paused at the landing of the bedroom floor, where she listened for a second. She didn't hear a thing. Letting out her breath slowly and being as quiet as possible, she made her way back down the stairs quietly and found Shep waiting for her in the laundry room. "Nothing," she said to the dog, as if he'd asked what she'd found. She quickly brushed the dust and cobwebs from her hair and clothes, replaced the keys, and took a deep breath.

Luckily, no one was in the kitchen.

She heard muffled voices coming from Neal's office, so she took a quick minute to step outside, across the deck.

Rain was starting to fall, the chill of deep autumn in the air as she stuffed the bracelet into the birdhouse to hide it. For now. Not that it was safe here, but for the moment she could think of nowhere else to stash it. She intended to get rid of it more permanently ASAP, but for now she didn't want to be caught with it in her pocket.

Back inside, she noted that Shep was sniffing for crumbs under the table and Neal was stepping out of his office, the lights already off. "Leah?" she asked.

"She went upstairs to her room, I think. She's leaving tomorrow."

"Tomorrow? But she just got here."

"I know." His smile was cold. Cynical. "I think she got what she came for."

"Your sage advice." She couldn't keep the sarcasm out of her voice.

"Yeah, that's it."

"And a check," she guessed.

He was nodding. "A significant check."

Brooke visibly cringed. "Ten thousand?"

"That would hardly get you into the door of a good divorce lawyer."

"So?"

"Twenty-five."

"What?" She sucked in her breath. "Twenty-five thousand dollars? Are you nuts? Where did you find that lying around?" she asked, trying and failing to keep her voice down. Her thoughts zeroed in on Marilee's college fund and her insides went cold.

"I can borrow. Against my retirement. I just have to pay it back soon."

"With what?"

He looked weary but managed a tight smile. "I'm working on a big case." When he saw her about to protest he held up a hand to stop the tirade he expected, "I know it's a lot of money. Don't worry about it. This is the last time."

"It had better be."

"I swear. And she signed a note."

Brooke leaned against the counter and slid him a disbelieving glance. "Another one?"

Sighing, he nodded. "Seems as if we're collecting them." He wrapped an arm around her. "It'll be all right. She'll divorce Sean and maybe be more careful before she walks down the aisle again."

As they mounted the stairs together, she threw him a glance. "People don't change, you know."

"She might, after this one."

"Wishful thinking."

"I talked to her."

"Oh good," Brooke said sarcastically. "And she actually listened? It sank in?"

"I think so."

"Wanna bet?"

He laughed and shook his head. "Don't think I can. I just loaned away my last dollar."

"Fool," she said, teasing, her lighthearted mood a mask as they entered the bedroom, and he snapped on the TV before kicking off his shoes and stretching out on the bed.

Brooke spent fifteen minutes in the bathroom, washing her face, brushing her teeth, and changing into a nightshirt. By the time she returned to the bedroom he was sleeping, softly snoring, his hair falling over his forehead, eyelashes visible on the blades of his cheeks.

She took the throw from the back of the chair near the dresser and tossed it over him. He didn't stir.

Quietly, she slid under the covers and snatched the television's remote from the bed near his hand. As she pointed the remote at the flat screen, intending to shut off the television, she froze and stared at the screen.

Neal had been watching the local news, which he'd recorded earlier, and Brooke recognized the people on the screen. Elyse and Tony Carelli were huddled together in front of the local police department. Tony's arm was around his ex-wife, and Josh McKrae, Elyse's son from her first marriage, stood a little behind to one side of his mother. Wearing a jacket with the Steadman Auto Parts logo emblazoned on it, Josh was tall and thin, the hint of beard shadow covering his jaw. He fidgeted, avoided looking at the camera, and appeared uncomfortable, as if he would rather be any other place on earth.

A detective from the police department stood front and center, fielding questions from several reporters while blond Elyse, in a long jacket and jeans, battled tears. Tony's stoic stare was betrayed by a wobbling, whisker-stubbled chin. He was a stocky man with a thick neck, and in his plaid jacket he appeared as destroyed as his gaunt ex-wife. The opposite of Jack Sprat and his wife of nursery rhyme fame, Brooke thought oddly as she sat on the foot of the bed and watched Elyse swiping at her eyes, her mascara running.

The questions came fast as a machine gun's spray.

"Are there any suspects?"

"None at this time."

"Does the police department have any idea what happened?"

"The investigation is continuing."

"What about leads?"

"We're following up on several. If anyone has any information, please call the department." She rattled off the number and reminded viewers that it was visible as a chyron running at the bottom of their screens.

"Is Allison Carelli's disappearance related to Penny Williams's?"

"The investigation in the Penelope Williams case is ongoing. So far we have not linked the two cases."

"But they're both teenage girls, both from Seattle. That can't be a coincidence."

The detective's gaze focused hard on the reporter who'd asked the question. "The department is looking into all possibilities. Again, if anyone has any information about Allison Carelli or Penelope Williams, please call the department at the number listed below. Thank you."

At that point the image on the screen switched to anchors who launched into a story about Halloween festivities planned in the area.

Numb, Brooke clicked off the TV, then lay on the bed, staring up at the ceiling, thinking of the missing girls, her daughter's animosity, and Gideon Ross, who seemed intent on ruining her life. For a second she thought about the tracker found attached to her car, then the knowledge that Gideon had been in her home, stealing some things and leaving others, letting her know that he'd invaded her space.

She remembered the warnings she'd received, hissed and harsh: *He's not who you think he is.*

Who sent them?

Who knew?

And then she touched her flat abdomen and considered the fact that new life might be growing inside her.

Gideon's baby.

She closed her eyes.

Dear God, she hoped not.

CHAPTER 20

Somewhere in the distance Brooke heard a baby crying.

She ran to it, through the darkness, propelled by fear for the child—an infant, it seemed. City streets streaked by and rain peppered the ground as she ran, splashing through puddles, the water icy and cold, her legs leaden.

Where?

Where was the sound coming from?

She saw something, deep in the shadows of the park.

Who would leave a helpless child in the—

Scrape!

She heard the sound of footsteps hurrying past.

Creak!

Her eyes flew open.

She was in bed, in the dark, the digital display of the clock announcing it was 1:57. The dream faded and her heartbeat slowed, but she knew something had awakened her, a noise that didn't fit into the house and broke into her dreamscape.

Hardly daring to breathe, she strained to listen. Above the beating of her own racing heart and the soft, steady breathing of Neal lying beside her, she heard the quiet hiss of air moving through the ducts as the furnace clicked on. Outside it was quiet, just the occasional sound of a passing car's engine.

Was it her imagination or did she hear footsteps? Soft and muted but moving quickly?

Noiselessly, she slid from beneath the covers, snagged her bathrobe from a hook on the bathroom door. Pushing her arms into sleeves, she slipped into the hallway. Nothing seemed out of place amid the darkness. But still . . .

Cinching the robe's tie around her waist, she crept along the darkened hallway and stopped at the top of the stairs, her eyes straining. Yet she didn't switch on a light, didn't want to warn whoever might be lurking.

Slowly, she descended.

The first floor was as still as the second. Had she heard a nocturnal bird or a bat on the rooftop? Or maybe just the wind causing a loose shingle to clatter?

Or had it been nothing?

Just the vestiges of her disturbing dream?

In the kitchen she looked outside, but the garden far below, dark with the night, appeared undisturbed. Quiet. Shep barely lifted his head as she passed by his bed near the table, the spot he'd claimed for the night. His eyes did blink open for a second, and he gave two soft thumps of his tail before tucking his nose into his body again.

You're losing it, that nagging voice in her head chided as she eased through the living room just as she'd left it earlier. *Go back to bed.*

She crossed the foyer, but on her way to the stairs she paused at the door of Neal's office, then noiselessly opened it and stepped inside.

This small room, with its couch, his desk in the curve of the turret, and a chair squeezed between the bookshelf-lined walls, was her husband's private sanctuary. It was an unwritten rule that no one was allowed in without him because of the sensitivity of the files of cases on which he was working. Most of his work was digital, though she knew he had more than a few manila files locked in the fireproof cabinet in the corner. The safe where he kept the family's personal documents along with the small caliber pistol Neal had brought with him into the marriage. The gun had been left to him by his grandfather.

Again, something that was uniquely his.

Though she was the co-owner of the house, she considered this room Neal's domain, and she always felt as if she were trespassing when she stepped inside without his knowledge. It didn't happen often, just for her to drop mail onto his desk or dust or vacuum occasionally. Even then she felt as if she were an intruder. She didn't bother snapping on any light; her eyes adjusted to the dim illumination that sifted through the window from the streetlight outside. An old clock sat on a shelf and rhythmically ticked off the seconds. She spied his laptop and had the urge to open it and peek inside.

He was always quick to close it whenever anyone walked into the room.

Had he been lying about receiving footage from the tracker in her car?

Was there any chance that she would find a secretive email from Jennifer Adkins or some other woman? Someone she didn't know about? She told herself she was being paranoid. Yes, she'd doubted Neal in the past, half believing that Neal had cheated on her once or twice before, but she'd found no solid proof. Once when Marilee was two or three and she confronted him about his long hours, he'd claimed he'd been distracted by work and was determined to prove himself to the senior partners.

Then came Jennifer Adkins.

Oh, as if you have any reason to snoop or cast the first stone?

Her relationship with Neal was tenuous, hanging by the proverbial thread. He had moved out for nearly three months after the Jennifer Adkins debacle and now they were trying to piece back together what they once had held so securely. Only she hadn't stopped seeing Gideon before Neal had returned.

Big mistake.

And now . . . she quickly stepped around the desk and flipped the laptop open. The screen jumped to life and she bit her lip. He hadn't shut it down. She pressed a button and saw a menu appear. The top file was marked *Leah*. She clicked on the folder and it opened to a digital note.

No surprise there.

Except for the amount.

Not for twenty-five thousand dollars, as he'd said earlier.

Fifty thousand dollars. She thought she had read the amount incorrectly, but she hadn't.

Stunned, she let out her breath slowly and sat down in his desk chair.

Why would Neal lie?

Why would Leah?

What the hell was going on here?

She scrolled through the info in the file and found other "loans" that she hadn't known about. One for ten thousand dollars eleven years earlier, then another ten grand four years ago, and then five thousand just three months earlier this year. During their separation.

Brooke had known nothing about the loans—not these.

Leah had frequently borrowed a little money from her here and there over the years, never more than a few hundred bucks at a time, all of which she'd always promised to pay back and never had, and finally there was the five grand once before, but this?

So why had Leah come to her for money when it seemed she had an unending source with Neal, all behind Brooke's back?

Don't jump to conclusions. There could be a justifiable reason for this.

But why so much this time?

What kind of hold did Leah have over Neal? Was she blackmailing him? Or just preying on his guilt for dumping her years before? Why was Neal—a tough attorney who spent his days negotiating with litigants—such an easy mark for her? Why would he buckle, give her the money she asked for and not confide in Brooke, unless he had something to hide?

That part runs in the family.

"Oh shut up," she whispered just as she heard footsteps overhead.

Crap!

Someone was coming?

Neal?

She had to get out of here.

She was about to close the file when she caught sight of an addendum and hit the link that led to the legal description of property in Tillamook County, Oregon.

A lien on the cabin on Piper Island?

Nana's house?

From Leah to Neal?

What the hell?

Her mind spun. Why had Neal kept this a secret? Why would Leah give up her interest in the idyllic childhood spot where they'd vacationed? Why had neither of them confided in Brooke?

Brooke stared at the computer screen, dumbstruck.

More footsteps and a door opening.

She should get out now. How could she explain herself? But she couldn't tear her eyes away from the screen.

Why was he securing loans with equity in the beach house?

No wonder she had come to Neal.

No way would Brooke have made such a deal.

Their mother and Nana wanted them to have the property on the island together, and it was the one place where they had shared childhood memories. Where Brooke had learned to ride a bike and swim, where Leah had built sandcastles and chased seagulls.

The last, fleeting memories of their father were caught in the pine-paneled walls, exposed beams, and wide back porch overlooking the sea.

And Leah was ready to give it up.

Quietly, she closed the file but didn't get up, her eyes on the screen as she pushed off the memories of a childhood that was filled with innocence and promise.

She listened.

No more footsteps.

What else could she find in Neal's files?

Possibly information from the tracker on her car? She glanced up at the door, half open, feeling like a criminal, but she scrolled up and found a file marked *Clayton Electronics*. She opened the file, and there was information on the WCTracker Series 6.

She clicked on the file but was sent to a link that included the listing of a serial number that she thought probably matched the bug that had been placed in her car. The file had options, including one marked *History*. Probably a history of every damned place she'd been in her car for months.

Sweat collected between her shoulder blades and she heard muffled little yips coming from the kitchen: Shep having one of his doggy dreams.

She stared at the screen, her throat dry.

Neal knew.

He had to know.

Unless he'd never been to the site, never bothered to set up a password, never checked on the Explorer's whereabouts.

Yeah sure. What were the chances of that?

Slim and none and wishful thinking.

Maybe it was just time to come clean.

Her marriage would be over.

Marilee would have nothing to do with her.

Her life as she knew it would be destroyed and—

She stopped that runaway train of thought.

If he had been checking up on her, why had he never asked her about where she'd been? When her car was parked at the marina when she'd claimed to be at job interviews or running errands? Did he know? Did he not? Her stomach twisted. After several attempts to break into the log she gave up and was about to close down the computer to continue to check the house when she saw the file marked *JA*.

Jennifer Adkins.

Jesus.

She clicked on the file.

Sure enough, there were documents inside.

Biting her lip, her nerves strung so tight they ached, she opened the first.

A divorce decree.

For Jennifer and her husband, dated and signed three months earlier, during the time when Neal and she were separated.

She was about to open the next document when she heard the creak of a door opening and footsteps overhead again.

She froze for half a beat.

Then quickly closed the file.

The footsteps were heading for the stairs.

Damn!

She shut the computer and silently prayed that the screen was returning to its normal default.

A step groaned as someone headed downstairs.

Damn!

She slid back the desk chair, stepped to one side, and pushed it noiselessly into place.

"Brooke?" Neal called, and she slipped around the desk to the couch.

She could keep quiet and hope he went into the kitchen first. If so, she could move hurriedly from his office through the entryway to the living room.

"Honey?" he called at the base of the stairs. "Are you down here?"

Shep gave up a soft "Woof" from his spot in the kitchen.

"Hey, boy," Neal said as she heard him start for the back of the house. "Have you seen Mom?"

She didn't hesitate, just silently eased out of the room down the short hallway past the staircase and into the living area. As she reached the window, she said, "In here."

Neal appeared from the darkened dining area.

"What're you doing?"

"I heard something and came down to look around the house. Make sure I locked all the doors."

"What did you hear?" He was crossing the room, and even in the semidarkness she could see that his eyebrows were drawn together, his eyes dark.

"I don't know." She sounded breathless and cleared her throat. "That's what I was checking."

"Probably the dog," he said and placed an arm around her shoulders.

She thought of the sounds she'd heard. "Definitely not Shep."

He snapped on a light and she realized he was still dressed in the clothes he'd worn all day, the wrinkled shirt and pants, his beard shadow dark on his jaw, his hair askew. "Well, let's look around. Nothing in here."

"Don't make fun of me."

"I'm not." As he walked across the foyer to his office, his frown deepened into a scowl. "I know I closed this," he said, touching the door to his office. "I remember doing it." He walked inside, then came out quickly, pulling on the knob and testing it. His eyes found hers. "Did you go inside?"

"No! Well, yeah," she equivocated from the living room, her heart knocking. Dear God, was she really afraid of her own husband, of his reaction? Is that what they'd come to? "It was closed. I opened it, poked my head in to make sure no one was inside, then came in here."

She should tell him the truth. Ask him about the loans to Leah. The file marked *JA*.

Neal rubbed a weary hand over his face, scraping at his beard stubble. "If it makes you feel better, I'll test all the doors again." He started toward the kitchen, then held up a hand behind him, as if expecting her to call after him with more directions. "And the windows." He yawned. "I'll test them too." He walked in stocking feet to the staircase leading to the garage and laundry room.

"I'll take the upstairs, double-check the windows." She was up the steps in an instant, wondering if she was going crazy, afraid that her paranoia and guilt were distorting her reality. Slowly, she cracked the door to the guest room, where she found Leah curled in the fetal position in the bed. The old quilt Nana had pieced together half a century earlier partially covered her body. Her roller bag lay open near the small closet, clothes spilling out.

The next room she verified was Marilee's. Quietly, she pushed the door open, and in the half-light from the windows saw the bed, covers mussed, sheets falling to the floor, but empty and cold to the touch. "Mari?" she said softly, her eyes scanning the room where the computer screen was constantly changing with underwater scenes. "Marilee?"

Brooke's heart began to thud with a new, terrifying dread.

She snapped on the light and quickly turned around, certain she'd missed her daughter, but the room was empty.

Half running, she went into the hall and then the guest bath, littered with Marilee's toiletries, Leah's floral Dopp kit hanging from a hook on the back of the door. "Marilee!" she yelled louder as she threw back the shower curtain on the old claw-foot tub, the hangers scraping noisily over the rod.

Nothing.

Oh. God.

Two girls had gone missing. Both around Marilee's age. One just recently.

"Neal!" she yelled and ran into her own bedroom, hoping against hope that her daughter would be there.

She wasn't.

Nor was she in the bathroom.

"*Marilee!*" she screamed at the top of her lungs.

The only response was the sound of footsteps clamoring up the stairs and the dog barking. She ran into the hallway again as the door to Leah's room flew open.

Brooke's sister, bleary-eyed, fingers clutching her robe together, glared at her. "What in God's name is going on? It's the middle of the frickin' night!"

Neal rounded the corner at the top of the stairs, Shep on his heels.

"Marilee. I can't find her! She's not in her room!" Brooke said, panicked.

"What?" In three long strides Neal was at the open door to their daughter's bedroom, as if he could find her.

"She's not here!" Brooke cried.

Leah shook her head. "Maybe she's downstairs."

"Neal was just downstairs."

"Marilee!" Neal yelled, his voice booming through the house as he followed Brooke's earlier path inspecting the upstairs rooms, including the closets. Nothing. Next he made a thorough search of the main level as Brooke and Leah went into the kitchen.

Neal hurried down to the laundry room and then the garage. Brooke heard him calling for their daughter and the garage door roll up. She went onto the deck and yelled her daughter's name, then hurried inside, located her purse, pulled out her phone, and noticed it was about out of juice.

No text from Marilee.

Brooke dialed her daughter's number.

The call went straight to voicemail.

"Hey—you missed me. Leave me a message or text," in Marilee's voice.

"It's Mom. Call me!"

Then she texted a similar message:

Where are you? Call me ASAP!

"You think she snuck out?" Leah asked. "Or—?" Her face paled as she finally caught onto Brooke's fear.

"I don't know what she did!" Brooke snapped just as she heard

Neal coming up the stairs, taking them two at a time. She looked up expectantly as he rounded the corner, but he shook his head. "Nothing. Except that . . ." Worry cut deep grooves into his forehead.

"What?"

"The gate was open."

"The gate," she whispered.

"To the alley."

Her heart sank. Tears formed in her eyes.

"That doesn't mean anything," he reminded her. "I searched the backyard and there's nothing! Shep was with me. I think he would've run to her if she were out there. But I've texted her and called and left a message. She'll get back to me."

"I did too." She was shivering inside. "Maybe we should call her friends? Zuri or Tammi?"

He glanced at his watch. "It's three twenty in the morning. Let's give it a little time."

"We don't have any," she argued.

Neal nodded, his brows drawing together. "Maybe she's just out."

"With Nick," Leah said. "That's my bet."

Brooke was dying inside. "I hope you're right," she said, though she wouldn't have thought she'd ever hope that Marilee, in an act of rebellion, had left the house behind her parents' backs to be with a boy. "But we can't take a chance." She turned horrified eyes to Neal. "Not when Allison and Penny have gone missing."

"Don't even go there," he warned.

"Have you checked the fire escape?" she asked suddenly.

"The what?" Leah, the lapels of her robe still clamped in her fingers, looked confused. "Fire escape?"

"The back stairs." Neal was already heading to the door on the second floor.

Brooke hurried alongside him, stride for stride. "The door is locked."

"I've got a key." He fished in his pocket and extracted a jingling key ring.

"You have a key—to the—?"

"Of course I do. I have keys to all the locks here and at the office." He sorted through the keys, extracted one, and slipped it into the lock before pushing open the hallway door and stepping into the back staircase. A few seconds later a light snapped on, spilling a weak shaft of illumination into the hallway.

"All this time I thought that was a closet," Leah said, poking her head inside, then, "Ooh, ick. Spiders!" She swiped a hand in front of her face as if she'd stepped into a web.

"We don't use them."

"Maybe you don't use the back stairs"—Leah gestured toward the door yawning open—"but it looks like maybe he does. Why else keep a key on his ring?"

Brooke was wondering the same thing and as she did, all her worries congealed.

"The things you don't know about people," Leah observed.

"Amen," she whispered as Neal reappeared.

"Nothing," he said to Brooke's unspoken question, "but I think someone has been in there. The dust was disturbed. I saw footprints."

My *footprints*, Brooke thought.

"What are you talking about?" Leah demanded and he explained that they never used the back stairs because they were unsafe.

As he spoke, Brooke's legs gave out and tears began to drizzle down her face. Her girl was gone. Her baby. Fear curdled through her blood. *Don't do this*, she told herself. *Now is not the time to fall apart. You need to find her. You* have *to find her!* Blinking, she swiped her sleeve over her nose.

Neal crouched down beside her, his worried eyes holding hers, and as if he'd heard her thoughts, vowed, "We'll find her." He gathered Brooke into his arms. "We'll find her." His fingers tangled in her hair as he held her close.

She choked out a sob.

"Shh," he whispered.

She closed her eyes and got lost in his strength.

"Come on." He pulled her gently to her feet.

Brooke sensed Leah staring at the two of them huddled at the top of the stairs, their world crashing in around them.

Leah cleared her throat. "Look, I think she probably just snuck out with Nick," she said. "I know, I know with the other girls going missing that you're freaked. I am too, but really, she was here. In her room. She's probably with Nick."

"Let's hope," Neal said.

Leah went on, "I know you're out of your heads panicked, but I really think you should wait until morning to make those calls. If she hasn't shown up by five or six, snuck back in, start calling around. If you wake up her friends, big deal. This is serious."

Brooke barely heard her. Buried in Neal's arms, her face crushed to his wrinkled shirt, she told herself that everything would be all right.

That Marilee would be found.

That Gideon would go away.

And that she wasn't pregnant.

But she couldn't convince herself.

CHAPTER 21

"Oh, Brooke, no, I'm sorry," Andrea was saying on the other end of the connection, her voice clogged with emotion. "I'm sure she'll be all right."

That was a lie and they both knew it. Andrea wasn't an idiot, and with Allison Carelli missing, the situation looked bleak. "Look, I asked Zuri if she had any idea where Marilee could be and she told me she doesn't have a clue. But I'll keep pushing her, keep seeing if any of their friends know anything."

"Thanks." Heartsick, Brooke slouched onto the kitchen table while Leah fussed with the coffee, muttering under her breath as she waited for the pot to brew.

Neal was gone, off in his Range Rover, searching for their child. He had scoured the park across the street and was now calling the local hospitals and police department while driving around to the places that were Marilee's favorite haunts.

As if she would go to any of them.

Brooke was left calling Marilee's friends. She'd started with Andrea, Zuri's mother, without any luck. Now she called the Paszek residence, or at least she hoped it was. The number she had was old, from a list of volunteers at the elementary school that she'd kept on her phone. Meanwhile Leah, finally satisfied with the coffee, poured a cup and set it on the table in front of Brooke.

"Thanks," Brooke said automatically, but her stomach curdled just looking at it.

A groggy female voice answered the phone after four rings. "Yeah, who is this?"

"Brooke. Brooke Harmon. Your son met my daughter at the dance last night."

"Oh yeah. Marilyn."

"Marilee."

"Right. Right. Sorry. Friend of Tammi's, I know. I guess I'm still half asleep. Holy God, what time is it? Six a.m.? On a Saturday?" Irritation had crawled into the muddled voice. "I need coffee. Strong coffee. Vats of it."

"I know, I know it's early, but listen, Renata, the thing is, Marilee didn't come home last night," Brooke said as Leah poured cream and sugar into a second cup of coffee and stirred, obviously listening. "I mean she came home, but now she's gone."

"What?" the woman said.

"Could you please just talk to Nick—ask him if he knows where she is?"

"Nick? Why would he know anything about it?" Renata asked, suspicion seeping into her words. Brooke heard the sound of a lighter clicking, then a deep inhalation as Renata lit a cigarette.

"Just ask him about it. Please. They—Marilee and Nick—met at the dance. She didn't leave the dance with him, we picked her up, but I thought he might have some idea what happened." Brooke tried to keep the panic out of her voice as she explained about not finding Marilee in her bed in the early morning hours. "She and I had a fight, a mother-daughter thing, you know?"

"I do know. Tammi? My daughter? You've met her, right? Then I don't need to tell you. That girl can give me fits!"

"Yes, so, Neal and I, we're calling all her friends. My husband has checked with the hospitals and—"

"Holy shit! Are you saying she's missing—like Alli Carelli? Oh my fu—oh my God!" Renata was finally getting it. "Wait a sec. Just a sec. I—I'll go see. Nick's still asleep."

Brooke heard footsteps and a door opening, then, though muffled, as if the phone was being held to her chest, Renata's sharp voice, which had elevated an octave, "Nick! Nick! Jesus Christ, for the love of—And what're you doing here—Holy Mother of God. Nick! Get out of bed and you—your mother is worried sick about you!"

"Mom! Get out!" a deep male voice yelled. "What the hell are you doing?"

"Saving your ass, that's what I'm doing. Holy crap, Nick!"

Renata Paszek was back on the line, her voice clear if a bit unsteady. "She's here. With Nick. Jesus, Mary, and Joseph! She's here!"

"Thank God," Brooke whispered, her knees buckling as she imagined her little girl sleeping in the boy's bed. . . . At least she was alive. And safe. And hadn't disappeared. "We'll be over to pick her up right away. Thank you."

She disconnected. "She was with that boyfriend, Nick, right?" Leah asked, taking a long swallow of coffee. "What did I tell you?"

"Fine, fine, you were right." Brooke was already on her feet, picking up her purse and searching for her keys.

"You're driving her away."

"What?" Brooke asked, barely hearing her sister.

"All your rules, and your distractions—like not picking her up from school on time, when you don't even have a job?"

"I'm looking. And—"

"Distracted! If you ask me, you're driving her right into that Nick kid's arms."

"No one did ask and you don't know what you're talking about."

"Don't I?" She glared at Brooke. "I remember being young. Being in love. Thinking that the boy who paid attention to me was the 'one,' my Prince Charming. And then, of course, I found out differently," she added bitterly. Her jaw was set and there were deep-seated recriminations in her eyes.

Brooke grabbed her jacket from the back of a chair and ignored Leah's unspoken accusations. Right now she didn't have time for any of her sister's histrionics. She headed down to the garage.

Shep, on alert with all the activity, tried to follow her. "Not this time, buddy." She left him in the laundry room, then made her way down the final half-flight to her Explorer.

The damaged SUV that had been fitted with a tracking device, she reminded herself as she climbed behind the wheel. She opened the garage door, backed out, and tore out of the driveway. On the way to the Paszeks' home, she called Neal, who answered on the second ring.

"Tell me you found her," he said desperately.

"I did." Heart hammering, she maneuvered through the still-dark city streets and gave him an update as she slowed for a light that shimmered blood-red on the wet pavement. A truck pulled up behind her, headlights glowing as the Explorer idled and she waited for a pack of early morning joggers to run through the crosswalk, barely noticing them as she was ranting to Neal. ". . . in his bedroom and his bed, from the sounds of it. My God, she's only fourteen and . . . and . . ."

"And it could be statutory rape."

"Don't even say it!" she cried as a car horn behind her blasted and she finally noticed the light had changed. She hit the gas and thought she heard the sound of a motorcycle.

"I'm on my way!" Neal said.

"No, no . . . just meet me back at the house. I'll bring her there."

"I want to talk to that horny son of a bitch!"

"I know, me too, but maybe we should let his folks handle him for the time being. We can talk to them or him later. Let's just get her home safe!"

He argued with her and she understood it. She wanted to throttle Nick Paszek too. He was older, should know better, but Marilee wasn't a complete innocent. They'd had "the talk." Make that many talks. And two other sets of parents weren't as lucky as they were this morning. The Carellis and the Williamses would be jumping for joy just to have their daughters back regardless of where they'd been. "Look, Neal," she said, trying to calm him down, calm them both down. "Just meet us at home, okay? Then, once you've talked to Marilee, if you still feel compelled to confront Nick? Have at it."

Was that the sound of a motorbike's engine? Or was she just stressed and imagining it?

"Fine," Neal said, disconnecting, and she could tell he wasn't fine. Not at all. Well, neither was she. "'Fine'" would be a long time coming.

She turned off the main street and the truck behind her went straight. Only then did she notice the headlight glowing behind her, a single lamp bearing down on her.

A motorcycle!

Her heart dropped.

Gideon!

"No," she whispered, her heart nearly stopping until she realized it was an older car with a single headlamp because the other had died.

Thank God.

The last thing she needed this morning was to deal with Gideon. *Just concentrate on Marilee. That's all that matters.*

She had to get control of her runaway emotions, pull herself together, and deal with her daughter.

Grinding her teeth and telling herself over and over that she could handle this, she took in several deep breaths and forced her hands to relax on the steering wheel. She couldn't handle this. But she had to.

At the Paszeks' house, she pulled into the leaf-strewn drive of the split-entry home. A porch light was glowing in the still dark morning. The second Brooke made her way to the brick steps, the front door opened, and Renata, Nick's mother, stepped outside, a glowing half-smoked cigarette in one hand. Disheveled, her dark hair mussed, she was wearing a once-aqua-colored bathrobe that had paled with time. "Come in," she said with a final puff before poking the remainder of her cigarette into the soil of a potted, untrimmed boxwood and motioning Brooke inside. No reason for introductions; they knew each other, if only as acquaintances, mothers of girls who ran in the same circle. "They're in the family room," she said "and Nick's in trouble. Big trouble."

She guided Brooke down the half flight to the basement, where she found Marilee seated on the opposite end of a worn leather couch from Nick.

Nick's father was leaning against the bar at the far end of the long room. Scowling and unshaven, he nodded at Brooke. "Bruno," he said by way of introduction. "We've met?"

"A time or two." Brooke nodded, her focus on her daughter.

Marilee, wearing a sweatshirt with the hood pulled up over her hair, looked upward and at least had the grace to seem embarrassed. Nick too glanced at Brooke, then looked quickly away.

"What's going on?" Brooke asked.

Silence.

To her daughter she said, "You snuck out and . . . came here?"

When Marilee didn't respond, Renata said, "We had no idea. I mean, we didn't hear Nick go out again after the dance, and we didn't hear them come in."

Marilee looked up. "Can we just go now?" Before Brooke could answer, she shot to her feet and was out of the room and up the stairs.

"I guess we're out of here," Brooke said. "I'm sorry for all of this mess."

Renata was nodding, reaching into the deep pocket of her robe and coming up with a crumpled pack of cigarettes. "Me too. Nick here is grounded."

Nick's head jerked up. "That's not fair."

"For life," Renata added, shaking out a cigarette. "Longer, if I can arrange it with God."

"Oh Mom!"

"Apologize to Mrs. Harmon."

"For what?"

"Sneaking her daughter out of the house. For God's sake, she's only fifteen!"

"Fourteen," he corrected.

Renata's face fell. "Fourteen? A frickin' baby? Well, that's worse! Jesus H. Christ, Nicholas, what in heaven's name were you thinking?"

"He wasn't," Bruno said. "At least not with his head."

Nick sputtered. "Oh Dad, gross!"

"Yeah, maybe." Bruno hitched his thumb toward the stairs. "Let's go to your room right now. We'll go over the facts of life and the facts of the law again."

"Fuck, Dad, we didn't do anything!" Nick growled and ran stiff fingers through his dark curls. "Why don't you believe me?"

"Because I was nineteen once and I remember."

Brooke said, "Look, I'm sorry for all of this, all of the trouble. I'm going to have a talk with Marilee too."

"Teenagers," Renata muttered under her breath, as if that single word said it all. Then she added a world-weary, "Whaddaya gonna do?" and lit up.

Brooke let herself out and found Marilee slumped in the Explorer, already strapped in, her arms crossed belligerently over her chest. As Brooke slid inside, Marilee said, "We didn't do anything, okay? I know what you're thinking, but we were just together. That's all."

"In bed."

"With our clothes on. It's not like we were—you know!"

"Having sex?"

Marilee had the decency to look aghast. "It's not like that!"`

It's always like that, Brooke thought but held her tongue. She cast her a glance as she started the car and tried a gentler approach. "Marilee—"

"Don't, Mom! Just don't!" Marilee turned to face her, and in the darkness the girl's skin was white as death. "I don't need a lecture. I know you're 'disappointed' and all that, and that you're going to ground me or whatever, but *nothing* happened."

Brooke's jaw slid to the side. She wanted to believe her daughter but couldn't.

She started the Explorer and backed onto the street. Traffic was picking up, the sky turning to a deep gray, the mist having turned to rain, the silence in the car thick and deafening.

Marilee turned on the radio.

Brooke switched it off.

"Maybe we should talk before we get home and have to deal with your dad." She switched on the wipers, but they didn't move. *Damn*. She tried again. Nothing. Just the click of the switch.

"He knows about this?" Marilee was doodling in the condensation on the passenger window.

"Of course he does."

"Ugh."

"You thought he wouldn't know?" She tried the wipers again; the windshield was difficult to see through. Once more they failed.

"I hoped he was asleep." She was doodling on the fogged passenger window, writing Nick's name with a finger.

"Marilee, what were you thinking?" Brooke demanded.

"That I love him!"

"For the love of God! You're fourteen!"

"You keep saying!" She drew a heart around Nick's name.

Sooo frustrating!

"Look, this is serious. I was worried sick. So was your dad!"

She was squinting, trying the damned wipers and cursing under her breath as the rain distorted everything in her path. Obviously the wipers had been damaged in the stupid accident she'd had days earlier. They were barely working.

"What do you mean?" Marilee grumbled.

"I mean, what were you thinking when you were sneaking out behind our backs and meeting Nick?"

"You wouldn't let me see him."

"Wrong! I wouldn't let you *drive* with him."

"You treat me like a baby."

"And so you act like one. Your father and I were worried sick." Futilely, she worked the switch, but once more the stupid wipers hardly moved. They couldn't keep up with the rain. Still, she tried to drive, splitting her concentration between the road ahead and the conversation.

"I don't want to talk about it," Marilee said.

"We're talking now." Brooke was beyond irritated with her daughter's petulance and demands. "We were scared to death. We didn't know what had happened to you. There are girls missing, you know! Girls from your school."

"I know, Mom, but I'm not!" Marilee said angrily.

Brooke was trying to keep her tone even but was failing. "With Penelope and Allison missing—"

Marilee gave a little snort.

What?

"Don't you care?" Brooke almost screamed. "No one knows what happened to two of your classmates and you're not concerned?" She was almost screaming now.

"God, Mom . . ." Marilee rolled her big eyes.

Brooke wanted to strangle her.

Marilee looked away quickly and added a shaky arrow to the heart she'd drawn in the condensation.

And then Brooke felt the hairs on the back of her neck lift. There was something going on here. Something Marilee wasn't telling her. "You know where they are?" she asked, dumbstruck.

"No . . ."

But it wasn't sincere.

"Marilee, if you know anything, and I mean *any*thing about where Penelope or Allison are, you have to tell me."

"I don't."

"You don't know?"

"I don't have to tell you," she said petulantly, her eyes sparking in defiance.

"That does it!" Brooke yanked on the wheel, pulled over to the curb, and put the car into Park. "What the hell do you know?" She faced her daughter, who was shriveling against the door.

"I'm not sure—"

"And we're not moving until you tell me what it is." She cut the engine. Then she laid a hand on her daughter's shoulder. Marilee shrank from her touch. "I mean it," Brooke said, trying to keep her tone even. "Tell me everything you know about Allison right now or, I promise you, I'll make sure you never see Nick again."

Marilee gasped and reached for the handle of the door, but Brooke anticipated the move and hit the automatic door lock. "Tell me!"

"I can't."

"You damned well can and you will!" For the love of God, what did her daughter know? What kind of secret was she keeping?

Marilee burst into sobs. "I hate you!"

Brooke let the painful barb slide.

"You're awful!"

She waited, the engine ticking. "I'm serious."

Marilee cast her a look of pure loathing, tears and mascara running down her cheeks. She sniffed loudly, then wiped her nose with her hand. Brooke didn't move, just stared at her daughter as the rain pounded on the hood and roof and the beams of her headlights caught the slanting drops. "I can stay here forever. In fact," Brooke said, "I'll call your dad and he can bring me coffee—"

"No!" Marilee screamed as Brooke fished in her purse for a pack of tissues and handed the entire package to her daughter.

"Then talk."

"Okay," Marilee finally said angrily. She plucked out a Kleenex, dabbed at her eyes, and blew her nose. "Alli's okay."

"Where is she?"

Silence.

"Marilee, where is she?" Brooke demanded. "And how do you know?"

Her daughter looked up at the ceiling of the car. "She's hiding," she whispered, sniffing and fighting back more tears. "Somewhere. Swore us all to secrecy, okay? I don't know where, so don't ask me. But her father . . ." She sniffed again. "He was trying to get custody, and her mom was saying all sorts of things about him. Lies. That he like . . . touched her or whatever, and it's not true, but she didn't know what to do and so she's hiding."

"Where?"

"I—I don't know."

"Where?" she said again.

"I said I don't know! She's—she's with a cousin, I think." Some of the fire had left her and her shoulders slumped, as if she were totally defeated.

"And Penelope?"

"Don't know. No one does." She slid her mother a glance. She looked frail and scared and oh so young. "It's the truth. No one that I know has any idea."

"Okay. I'm calling Elyse. Right now. She'll want to talk to you." As a bicycle whizzed by, she found Elyse Carelli's number and punched it in. The phone was answered after one ring.

"Hello?" Elyse answered breathlessly.

"Hey, Elyse, this is Brooke Harmon, Marilee's mother," Brooke said, her gaze pinned on her daughter. "Marilee thinks she may know where Allison is."

CHAPTER 22

Brooke heard a gasp on the other end of the wireless call. "What? Marilee *knows*? Oh my God, I can't believe it!" Elyse Carelli's voice cracked. "For the love of God, where is she?"

Glancing at her daughter, who seemed to want to melt into the floorboards, Brooke said, "Allison may be with a cousin."

"What? A cousin? No way? Like Diane?" Elyse's voice faded, as if she'd turned away from the phone. "Tony!" she yelled. "Tony! Get the hell in here! Marilee Harmon says Allison is with Diane."

"What?" a male voice said faintly. Then, more clearly, "Diane? Are you shittin' me? We talked to her! That little liar—"

"No!" Marilee cut in, shaking her head violently as she heard the conversation. "It's . . . it's . . . a guy cousin, I think. And that's . . . that's all I know."

"Did you hear that?" Brooke asked. "Marilee said she thinks it's a male cousin."

"Yeah, but she doesn't have any boy cousins. All girls . . ." Elyse muttered, her voice drifting off. "Oh fuck, is she talking about Robert?" she said on a gasp. "Holy shit! Tony! We need to check with Robert ASAP—no, better yet, go there! You drive over there. Just show the fuck up! That little son of a—oooh!"

Marilee slunk down further in her seat.

"And Allison. Why would she do this to us?" Elyse's voice was clogged, as if she were fighting sobs. "Why would she put us through this? I thought . . . I mean I was almost sure that she was . . . that I would never see her again!"

"Tell them everything you know," Brooke instructed her daughter as she put the phone on speaker.

Haltingly, shooting daggers at her mother with her eyes, Marilee repeated what she'd told Brooke a few minutes earlier amid gasps and expletives from the other side of the connection. She heard Tony say, "I'm going over there right now!" just before a door slammed, while Elyse started crying in earnest.

By the time the call was over, Marilee, pale as death, cowered against the window, where her heart drawing was disappearing. "Can we just go now?"

"I guess." Brooke put the car into gear and pulled away from the curb.

"And I can still see Nick?"

"I can't believe your priorities! Allison has been missing for what? How many days?"

"I don't know."

"And you—"

"But—" Marilee's big eyes were round, pleading.

"Once we straighten a few other things out, we'll talk about you seeing Nick."

"You promised," Marilee charged.

"I haven't forgotten. Now, who else knows about this—about Allison?" she asked, still squinting; the rain wasn't letting up and the windshield was immediately awash again.

"Just me and a couple of other friends. Zuri and Katie Chen."

"And Nick?" Brooke prodded, seeing her daughter in a new light. Gone was the innocent girl and in her place was a scheming, sullen teenager.

How many other things had Marilee lied about? She prayed there was nothing as monumental or catastrophic as this.

When they reached the house Brooke noted that every light shone from the windows, the porch lamp illuminating the arch of the porch, where one of the rocking chairs was moving slowly back and forth, though no one was sitting on it.

Was it swaying because someone had just been rocking?

Was there something on the cushion? A red splotch against the yellow twill? Brooke squinted.

"Weird," Marilee said, noticing the chair as well.

"Maybe your dad was on the porch waiting for us." Brooke turned into the drive.

"And then he saw your car and went inside?" Marilee looked directly at her for the first time since getting into the Explorer. "I don't think so."

Neither did Brooke.

"Like I said, 'weird.'" Marilee glanced back to the front of the vehicle. "Oh shit!" she yelled. "Mom! Watch out!"

"What!" Brooke stood on the brakes.

The SUV skidded on the wet pavement.

From the corner of her eye Brooke caught sight of a shadow darting past.

The Explorer jolted to a stop, headlights glowing in the downpour.

Through the watery glass she saw something indistinct—someone? A dark figure?—scurrying around the corner of the garage.

"What the hell was that?" she whispered, her heart clamoring, her pulse jumping as she pounded on the button to open the garage door.

"I don't know." Marilee's voice was weak, her eyes round.

Loudly, the garage door clambered up, the light switching on, illuminating the surrounding area.

No one was visible in the apron of light.

"You saw that, right?" Brooke asked.

"I saw something. Or someone."

Pulse pounding, Brooke drove the Ford into its bay. "Go into the house," she ordered, then switched off the engine and was out of the SUV in an instant. "Close the garage door. Lock it!"

Running, she rounded the corner to the backyard and to the short fence where she'd seen whatever it was disappear. The gate was ajar and she slipped through, squinting against the rain as she scanned the uneven yard, the grass in tufts, the old broken fountain. But no movement. No dark figure scuttling near the fence line or around the corner of the house.

Something rustled in the shrubs near the deck and she whirled to face the noise, only to spy a shaggy raccoon squeezing beneath the fence.

Above, on the deck, the French doors flew open. "Mom!" Marilee ran across the deck, her footsteps overhead quick and light. She leaned over the rail. "Is Shep with you?"

Brooke held up a hand to shield her eyes from the rain. "What? Shep? No!" She was shaking her head, feeling cold drops on her cheeks as she squinted upward.

"He's not in the house."

"No. He's not in the yard," she said nervously. "Look again. He probably got locked in a closet or something."

"Wouldn't he bark?"

Yes. "I don't know."

But a new fear was growing within Brooke.

"I'm telling you, he's not here!" Marilee's voice was high and pan-icked.

"He's got to be!"

This couldn't be happening; she couldn't lose her kid and her dog in one night!

Leah appeared on the deck next to Marilee. She held a jacket over her head and looked frantic. "I swear, Shep was here earlier. I saw him, but now we can't find him."

"No one let him out?" Why? Why was the dog missing? Brooke scanned the yard again. Dawn was breaking, the cloud-covered sky offering some pale illumination, rain pouring and running noisily down the gutters. "You're sure?"

"Yes!" Marilee yelled, obviously near tears again.

"Okay, okay! Let's not panic," she said, though she already felt her pulse quickening. "I'll check out here."

She saw Leah try to urge Marilee inside, but the girl remained at the rail, her head swiveling slowly as her eyes searched the sodden shrubbery and lawn.

"Shep!" Marilee yelled. "Shep. Come!"

Brooke too walked the perimeter and called for the dog. Using the flashlight app on her phone, she scoured the dripping rhodo-dendrons and hydrangeas, then searched through a hedgerow of arborvitae and a small pile of forgotten pots near the corner of the house. "Shep!"

But no wet, bedraggled dog lumbered out from a hiding spot. As she traveled along the fence line, rain running down her neck, her shoes sinking into the bark dust, mud, and weeds, she saw no sign of him.

The gate to the alley where they kept their garbage cans was un-latched and hanging open.

Why?

They never unlocked it.

This was wrong. "Shep!" she yelled as she stepped into the alley, her voice ringing down the empty lane. "Damn it." Then, more loudly, "Shep! Come, boy!"

A startled, bedraggled cat leaped from a trash bin to run along the fence before climbing into the overhanging branches of the neigh-bor's lilac tree.

But there was no sign of their shaggy retriever.

First the kid went missing.

Now the dog.

Could the morning get any worse?

The answer was yes.

Because she saw him then.

Through the pouring rain.

Standing at the end of the alley.

Dressed in black leathers.

His motorcycle parked near a neighbor's garage.

Gideon stared at her for a long moment, then climbed onto his bike and with one searing look over his shoulder, kick-started the en-gine.

With a roar, he tore out.

"You bastard! You sick, sick son of a bitch!" She kicked at a rock in the driveway and sent it reeling into the hedge. Her hands clenched into fists and if she saw him now, she swore, she'd kill him. Why, for the love of God, was he tormenting her and terrorizing her family?

Thoughts of how he'd targeted, stalked, and taunted her spun through her mind, memories rotating sharply, cutting into her brain.

He'd been at the school posing as a security guard.

He'd been in her house riffling through her drawers, leaving the bracelet, stealing her underwear.

He knew the name of Marilee's boyfriend.

That she would be at the dance.

That *Brooke* would be at the dance.

In fact, he knew more about her and the family than she'd ever divulged.

How?

Not by a tracking device on her car. Neal had claimed that awful little bug as his own and she'd seen the information about it on his computer. So how had Gideon known where she was? How did he know what was going on in the family?

And where the hell was Shep?

Angrily, she left the gate open on the off chance that the dog returned on his own, then crossed the yard, swept the rain from her face, and mounted the steps to the deck. Pausing at the birdhouse, she decided to destroy the remainder of her cigarettes—no smoking now that she was pregnant. She reached inside and crushed the pack out of frustration and then remembered the bracelet.

She'd left it in here earlier, but now, as her fingers explored the inside of the little house, she touched something else: not metal and stones but something wet and soft and squishy and—

She pulled out her hand as if she'd been burned.

Her fingertips were red.

Blood!

What?

Looking into the birdhouse, she saw the dead rat, its nasty little teeth visible and tinged red beneath scraggly whiskers, its eyes dull, its fur matted, its long, naked tail curved to fit into the recess.

"Oh." She recoiled.

Bit back a scream.

"Oh . . . oh . . . no." She backed up, sick to her stomach, horror curdling her insides. Bile climbed up her throat and it was all she could do not to retch.

"You fucking bastard," she said, her skin crawling, her stomach convulsing as she clung to the deck rail and stared in horror at her bloodstained fingers. *No, no no!* What kind of a sicko would kill a rat and leave its carcass where she was certain to find it? She thought of her dog and closed her eyes at the thought of what Gideon might do to the retriever.

Don't even go there!

Even he wouldn't hurt the goofy, loving dog.

But the image of the dead rat with its slimy, wet fur superimposed itself over her mental picture of Shep.

It was all she could do not to scream.

CHAPTER 23

"I don't know how it happened," Leah was saying as Brooke, shaken to her core, walked into the kitchen from the garage stairs. Pulling herself together after the shock of finding the dead rat, she'd hurried down the deck staircase, quickly crossed the yard, and entered through the garage so she could wash the blood from her fingers in the laundry room basin. She'd dried her hands and counted to ten, then twenty, then fifty.

She was calmer now. Determined. But Leah was still upset and dabbing at her eyes with a napkin at the table.

Neal was at the coffee maker, measuring grounds for a fresh pot. "He'll come home," he said but shot Brooke a worried glance.

"I left the back gate open, if he does."

Neal said, "I thought I saw you on the deck."

"Yes—yes, I was," she said, "but I got my hands dirty and went back through the laundry room to clean up."

Neal eyed her speculatively, but before he could ask anything else, Leah said, "What about the blood?"

She knew?

"The blood?" Brooke repeated.

"Yeah." Leah swung her gaze from Brooke to Neal, who was adding water to the reservoir of the coffee maker. "You saw it, right?"

"What're you talking about?" Neal asked.

"There's blood smeared all over one of the pillows on the front porch. Marilee told me about it. She said you," Leah glanced at Brooke, "saw it when you drove in, so I checked." Leah shuddered visibly, then pressed her lips together. "I pray to God it's not Shep's."

"Why would it be his?" Neal asked, but there was trepidation in his voice.

But Brooke knew it belonged to the rat.

She remembered now seeing a smear of red on the yellow cushion as she turned into the drive.

Brooke headed for the front door and porch, where she saw the yellow cushions on the rockers, one smeared red, the stain looking like blood—rat's blood—but she couldn't let on about the dead rodent. Not yet.

Leah followed Brooke to the front porch and stood in the doorway.

"Am I cursed or what?" Brooke said, then bit her tongue. Her dog was missing, yes, but her daughter was safe, even if Marilee was in big, big trouble.

"Why in God's name would there be blood here?" Leah paced along the front porch. "Maybe Shep got out, stepped on something—glass or whatever—and came up to the porch and . . ."

"And then ran off?" Brooke asked.

"I guess." Leah looked across the street to the park and Brooke followed her gaze. A jogger in sweats raced by before disappearing through the open gate. A squirrel scampered out of his path and scurried up the bole of a fir tree. A few vehicles passed, and she heard the sound of a leaf blower from the house next door. It was Mr. Galanis, who wouldn't give up his Saturday morning routine of cleaning his driveway and smoking a cigar even if the leaves were sodden from the previous night's storm. She smelled the acrid smoke that seemed at odds with the clear air, fresh after the rain, then caught a glimpse of a police car rolling slowly through the intersection.

A typical Saturday morning for most Seattleites.

But not for Brooke, nor anyone else who lived here.

Not here.

Brooke picked up the smeared pillow and carried it inside, where she sniffed it and eyed the stain more closely.

"You think it's Shep's?" Leah asked, a tremor in her voice.

Neal shook his head. "Dunno."

"No—it can't be," Brooke insisted. "I saw a raccoon in the backyard. Maybe some creature was hurt and bled on the rocker."

Neal shook his head. "There weren't any tracks. No blood across the porch, I looked." He frowned, rubbing the back of his neck thoughtfully. "It's been a weird, weird morning."

"Amen. I'm just going to get rid of this." Before anyone could object, Brooke carried the pillow to the trash bin outside and dumped it. Her skin crawled when she considered the rat's blood, but she forced herself to remain calm. She would take care of the rat's bloody carcass the same way once she was alone. But for now she didn't want to explain about finding it, why she was even reaching into the birdhouse in the first place, or what it could mean.

Because she knew what had happened and who was behind it.

When she got back to the kitchen and had again washed her hands, she heard the coffeepot sputtering and hissing. Steam was rising from its vents, the smell of roasted beans permeating the air. Any other morning the warm scent would have made her smile. But not today.

"I just don't get how blood ended up on that pillow," Neal said, his eyebrows pulling together.

Brooke said, "We may never know."

"Well, we will the next time."

"Ugh," Leah said. "You think there will be a repeat?"

"Dunno. But I'm going to get a security camera. Make that two," Neal said, finding three cups and placing them on the counter. "From Bill Clayton—remember, he's the guy who makes all the security devices?" He poured coffee into the first cup.

"Yeah, I remember. The tracker on the Explorer."

"Right. If I had taken his advice and gotten the entire security package for the house, we would have videos of the porch and the yard. We'd probably know what happened to Shep," he said as he placed a mug on the table for Leah. "And we would have seen Marilee sneak out with Nick, so we wouldn't have been so panicked."

"Speak for yourself," Brooke said. "Yeah, maybe we'd know more about what happened to Shep. Maybe. But I would have been worried seeing Nick and Marilee together."

"But at least we would have known who she was with and not that she was kidnapped by some pervert or worse."

Brooke had to agree. "Good point." But had there been a camera, Gideon would have appeared on the screen, and there would have been all kinds of questions. Questions she didn't want to answer.

When Neal offered her a cup of coffee, she shook her head and held up a hand. "I'm good." The last thing she needed was more caffeine pouring through her already jangling bloodstream. "I think we need to talk to our daughter."

"Didn't you do that on the car ride home?"

"I tried." When she caught him looking at her over the rim of his cup she added, "It was pretty tense. She didn't exactly appreciate my advice. Nothing penetrated." And then she told him about Marilee knowing where Allison Carelli had been for the better part of a week, and her conversation with Allison's parents.

"Other kids knew this?" Neal asked, stunned.

"I guess."

"I'd better have a chat with Marilee," he said, taking a long swallow, then setting the coffee aside. "God, I hate these talks."

"But you're so good at them," she said, and he shot her a look to tell her he knew she was giving him the business before heading up the stairs.

"At least she's safe," Leah said as she stirred cream and sugar into her cup.

"Yeah, I know." For that Brooke was grateful, but Marilee was still very much a worry. It seemed that day by day, the fragile relationship Brooke had with her daughter was unraveling faster and faster.

"You should count yourself lucky."

"I do," she said, even though she had a mountain of worries and was heartsick that Shep was missing.

Yes, thankfully—oh yes, thankfully—Marilee was home and safe, but there were other issues, big ones.

"Remember what I'm going through, Brooke," Leah said, turning the conversation back to herself, as always. "Look where I am. A cheating husband who's leaving me for a slut, no home, no money, no kids . . . nothing! I would kill to have what you do." She frowned a little, looking pitiful.

Brooke could stand it no longer. "I heard Neal gave you the loan."

Leah stiffened.

"Quite a lot, in fact."

Leah's gaze darted away, a trace of shame showing before defiance resurfaced. "Neal understands what I'm going through."

"Again, that's a helluva lot of money."

Leah's lips pursed. "I wouldn't have asked for it if I didn't need it."

"You've asked before. And received."

Her sister stiffened, suddenly uncomfortable.

"What is it, Leah? Why do you keep running to Neal?"

"Whoa," Leah said, finding her tongue. "You said yourself to ask him, so I did." ·

"For more than you asked from me."

"Yeah." She lifted a shoulder as if to say, *so what? Big deal*. "Yeah, I did. And he gave it to me." She lifted her cup to her lips and stared over the rim. "So sue me."

"*Loaned* it to you."

"Yeah, yeah, that's what I meant." She took a long sip, and Brooke walked to the French doors to stare out at the deck and the yard beyond. Morning had broken, the rain abating, the clouds still threatening, but she could see the entire enclosure.

No Shep.

And somehow Gideon was involved.

She heard an almost inaudible buzzing as she walked into the kitchen.

Leah, standing near the open door to the stairs, said, "What's that?"

Oh. Crap. She always did have good hearing, had, even as a kid, been listening in everywhere, a regular little snoop.

"My phone," Brooke said, realizing Leah didn't know she had two phones or would recognize the subtle difference in the sound of the vibrations between the different cells. But Brooke did instantly. And this time it was her burner phone that was buzzing.

"Probably one of the moms I phoned earlier. I'd better make some calls or at least some texts and explain that Marilee is okay."

"Oh. Sure. But . . . can you still take me to the airport? My flight's at eight tonight. I should get there, what—before seven, maybe six forty-five."

"Yeah, of course." Brooke's mind was already racing ahead. Taking Leah to the airport would be a good excuse to finally have it out with Gideon. She would have time alone. Time away.

Leah's phone rang and she walked to the table and picked it up. Her face twisted. "It's Sean."

"Don't answer it," Brooke advised.

Leah hesitated.

"You're divorcing him, right? That's why Neal loaned—we loaned you the money."

"Yes, yes, I know, but I still want to hear what he has to say."

"I wouldn't," Brooke said, just as Leah said a crisp, "Hi," into her phone.

Glancing up at Brooke and obviously not liking her older sister's expression, Leah cradled the phone to her ear and took her cup with her as she walked to the French doors, stepped onto the deck, and shut the doors firmly behind her. Brooke watched as she leaned over the rail, right next to the birdhouse. All she would have to do was open the lid and she'd see the rat.

If so, Brooke would play dumb.

Let Leah scream and go into hysterics and have Neal wonder how in the world the bloodied rodent had ended up there.

But Leah wasn't interested in anything other than the phone call. It was obvious as she held the phone close, nodding and whispering. In that instant Brooke realized that Leah would give her husband another chance, that all Sean had to say was that he wanted to make things work and Leah would be into him all over again. She thought of the money Neal had loaned her sister—a small fortune—and if Sean the gambler found out, why wouldn't he play on Leah's already ragged emotions?

She made one step toward the deck to warn Leah but stopped.

Who are you to give advice? It's not like your life isn't crumbling around you. Forget Leah, the money, and her marriage. Concentrate on your own problems. It's not like you don't have enough worries of your own.

First and foremost she needed to find Shep. That was her top priority now that Marilee was safely home.

Secondly, she had to buy a pregnancy test and take it. She had to know if she was pregnant or it was a false alarm.

Finally, she had to figure out how Gideon knew her every move and was one step ahead of her.

She believed with all her soul that he was involved in Shep's disappearance.

She was certain he was at the end of the alley, loitering beyond the open gate.

And he left the dead rat, not just to freak her out but to let her know just how dangerous he could be. She didn't doubt it for a second. She'd seen the darkness in his gaze, the cruel glint. If she were to square off with him, she suspected she would need a weapon.

Neal had one. A gun that was locked away. A pistol that Brooke hated even being in the house.

Until now.

Out on the back deck, Leah stood leaning over the railing and appeared to be looking out at the lights of the city winking in the distance, but Brooke suspected Leah's vision was turned inward; she was deep in conversation with Sean, oblivious to the world.

As for the rest of the family, they were upstairs. She heard muffled voices coming from Marilee's room, so while everyone else was busy, she quietly eased her way into Neal's office again and closed the door, hearing a soft click. Moving noiselessly, she slipped around her husband's desk and knelt in front of the safe.

With an ear tuned to the sound of voices and an occasional creak of the ceiling, indicating someone was walking on the floor overhead, she tried to open the safe. Her fingers were trembling so badly, she overshot as she spun the dial and had to reset it twice.

Sweat collected on her forehead and fingers.

Come on, come on!

She tried more carefully again, and she heard the door to the deck open just as the tumblers fell into place.

Crap! Leah!

The door shut.

Brooke's heart was pounding so loudly she could barely hear Leah's footsteps in the kitchen.

"Hey!" Leah called, her voice coming closer. "Where is everybody?"

Hastily, Brooke tried the handle on the safe.

It didn't budge.

Damn!

Neal must've double-locked it with the key. She rocked back on her heels. Yes, they always kept the safe locked of course. But she couldn't remember when it had been double-locked. Not for years. And she didn't even know where the key was. She glanced rapidly around the room, trying to guess where it was hidden. What had

Neal said just the other day when she'd asked about the keys to the unused staircase and he'd withdrawn a ring from his pocket?

"I have keys to all the locks here and at the office."

So the key was with Neal.

Shit!

"Brooke?" Leah called again.

Frantically, Brooke tugged on the handle just in case she'd been mistaken.

Nothing.

She heard Leah in the living room, closer now.

No time.

Swiftly, she rounded the desk, slipped out of the room, and pushed open the powder room door. She flushed the toilet and noisily turned on the taps, water rushing into the sink.

Calm down. Just calm the hell down!

But her stomach had twisted into knots and her lungs were tight. She made noise, turning off the taps and yanking the towel from its metal ring, then glanced into the oval mirror mounted over the cabinet.

Dear God.

She blinked at her reflection.

She looked like death warmed over, as Nana used to say, as if she hadn't slept in days. Her hair was mussed, her eyes haunted, her skin pale. The cut on her chin was a thin reminder of her fight with Gideon, how physical it had gotten.

Pull yourself together!

Find the dog.

And find out if you're effing pregnant.

Stepping into the hallway, she nearly ran into her sister.

"There you are!" Leah said, little lines puckering her eyebrows together.

"Yeah, here I am." She was heading for the kitchen. "But I'm going out. We need a few things for breakfast—I guess we could call it brunch soon—and I want to search for Shep now that it's light."

"If you call this light," Leah said, looking through the windows to the gray day beyond.

"Says the woman from Arizona. I'll be back within an hour or so. Tell Neal I'll text all the people we called earlier about Marilee being missing. No doubt gossip is running like wildfire through the kids at school, freaking out their parents."

"Yep." Leah was nodding. "All over the Internet."

"You know this?" Brooke asked as they walked into the kitchen. She grabbed her purse. "How?"

"I told you, I'm friends with Marilee. She already posted and her friends commented, so I'm pretty sure everyone at her school—what's the name of it? Ainswell?"

"Allsworth."

"Oh, right. Right. I remember now."

"You remember?" Brooke was skeptical. "How?"

"From all the posts!" Leah said, rolling her eyes. "I just told you."

"I'm not into it."

"For the love of God, weren't you, like, in sales? Of a tech company or something? You should be all over it."

"LinkedIn."

"And that's it?"

"No—yes. Well, I mean LinkedIn was the biggie. I had a presence on other platforms—we were encouraged—but I'm not on the job any longer, so . . ." She shrugged. Why was she bothering to explain all this to Leah right now when she had so much to do and her life was falling apart?

"Well, you should get online more. You won't believe what you can find there." Her grin faded and she added bitterly, "Even your husband's girlfriend if you want, apparently."

"You're getting over him," Brooke reminded her sister as she found her keys. "Remember? You're divorcing the guy who robbed you of your inheritance and cheated on you. The one who is trying to kick you out of the house? That guy."

"I know, I know, but—"

"No 'buts,' Leah. It's over. You said so yourself. Don't let that con man sweet talk you. And don't," she pointed a finger at her sister, keys jangling on the ring as she did, "don't let him know you borrowed from us. Okay? If he thinks you've got a dime, he's gonna want it."

Leah sucked in her breath. "Ooh, harsh, Brookie."

"I'm just reminding you. I'll be back soon."

Leah's eyes darkened and her eyes narrowed. "You might want to check your messages. I heard your phone . . . well, someone's phone was buzzing," she said, seeing that Brooke's cell was poking out of the back pocket of her jeans.

The burner! She'd forgotten about it. Again.

"Yeah, it's going nuts," she said, holding up her iPhone, which she'd put on silent; the parent text chains about Allison Carelli's return had been on overload. But what about her burner phone? In all the mayhem she'd let it slip her mind. With all the chaos she'd been careless, leaving it in the niche in the laundry room. She closed the door at the top of the stairs and, on her way to the garage, retrieved it from its hiding spot behind the dusty containers of bleach and spray starch. Then she hurried down to the garage, her ankle twinging in protest.

Leah was right, Brooke realized as she slid behind the wheel and hazarded a look at the screen.

There were several messages, two from Gideon.

Call me.

As if.

Obviously he hadn't gotten the message.

And later, when she hadn't responded, in the hours before Shep went missing:

If I don't hear from you, you'll be sorry.

What? Seriously? An out-and-out threat?

And then Shep disappeared. And he'd left the dead rat in the birdhouse. Enraged, she fought the urge to phone him and call him out, tell him what a lowlife son of a bitch he was. But she didn't. Because that was exactly what he wanted: a reaction. He was taunting her, daring her to call him back, and it was all she could do not to take the bait.

The last message, sent from an anonymous number only minutes before, was much more disturbing:

He's not who you think he is.

She swallowed hard at that.

The anonymous caller was now texting.

She didn't have time for this, not for Gideon and his threats nor these dark, vague warnings from an unknown person.

A person who knew she had this phone number, this *private* number, but wanted anonymity.

A mixture of anger and fear swept through her blood, but she fought the anxiety and set her jaw. She'd figure out who was behind the eerie warning and when she did there would be hell to pay. Right now Brooke had to keep moving. Who knew when Gideon would strike again?

She didn't have the time or energy to deal with Leah's screwed-up marriage. Brooke had her own relationships to deal with, along with a shitload of other problems.

Disturbed, she hit the interior remote for the garage door opener and, as the door rolled up, texted Neal to let him know that she was running to the store for a few things and would be on the lookout for the dog.

As she pulled out of the garage, she thought of Leah's advice about social media and mentally kicked herself for not being able to use the different platforms to check on her daughter or search out more information on Gideon. After her initial fascination with him and a shallow Internet search, she'd told herself it didn't matter; it was a fling that would die a quick death and the less she knew about him the better.

But that had been a lie. The truth was she didn't want to know too much about him, didn't want to delve too deep in case she discovered something that would end the affair. Or something worse. Something she didn't want to know.

She'd been careless, reckless, and stupid.

Now she and her family were paying the price.

But at least Marilee was home and safe. Brooke took heart with that, even though recriminations followed her as she took off through the neighborhood, searching for Shep, looking down streets, in alleys and across yards as she drove to Northeast Seattle, far enough away from her neighborhood that she wouldn't chance running into anyone she knew. She located a strip mall she'd seen in passing and parked at an unfamiliar pharmacy. Once inside she bought a pregnancy test, then crossed the lot to a mom-and-pop grocery for milk, bagels, cream cheese, and eggs.

So far, so good.

Yet anxiety fired her blood.

Her next stop was for gas and then a coffee shop still far enough away from her house to guarantee it was unlikely she would run into friends or acquaintances.

After ordering a latte from a girl with tricolored hair and a nose ring she left her cup at a booth next to the bathroom and went inside. Hands shaking, she promptly took the pregnancy test and waited while she heard someone come and go in the next stall.

Please, no, she silently prayed, not even contemplating what a baby would mean. The irony of it didn't evade her. How long had she and Neal tried for a second child? Five years? Six? There were two miscarriages early in the pregnancies, one when Marilee was three and another a year later. Since then, nothing. Over the years it had become a nonissue. Brooke had thanked her lucky stars that she'd gotten pregnant young and become a mother and had never expected to have life growing within her again.

She heard the other woman wash her hands and tear off a couple of towels, just as two more women entered—friends, from the sound of it—chatting and laughing as if neither had a care in the world.

The door to her stall rattled. "Oops, sorry," a young voice said through the door, then to her friend, "That one's occupied."

Brooke closed her eyes. Ignored the continuing conversation about their toddlers and kids in elementary school, though she did hear the fear in their voices when they spoke of "that teenager who's missing."

"Probably a runaway," the voice in the stall said.

"Then what about the other one? From the same school. She's been gone over a year."

"If you ask me, she's dead," came the horrible conclusion from the woman flushing the toilet.

"Don't say that! She's just a kid."

"A kid who should've had parents paying attention."

They traded places, the stall door opening and closing.

"Those parents have to be devastated."

"Good. Then if they have any other kids, they'll be more careful."

"Not everyone can be a helicopter parent," said the woman now in the stall.

"These days everyone should be."

Brooke bit her tongue. Parents of toddlers and kids in primary grades had no idea what the challenges of trying to control, protect, and mete out independence to teenagers entailed. She hadn't. She'd been as cavalier as these women. And just last night she'd thought she'd lost her daughter.

The toilet flushed, the taps turned on, the electric hand dryer roared, and the women left, door clicking shut behind them. And Brooke waited, trying and failing to keep her thoughts from racing to their inevitable conclusions and the despair that came with them.

She knew there was a chance the baby, if there were one growing within her, was Neal's. A slim chance. She'd been careful with Gideon, as had he, though not always . . .

With Neal, the results of a positive test provided some promise. They could reconcile, make things work, deal with Marilee's horror of becoming a big sister at fifteen, find the joy and anticipation that comes with pregnancy.

With Gideon . . . oh Lord. She foresaw the end of her marriage, the loss of her daughter. And the child would forever hold her to a man she didn't love, didn't want, and couldn't trust. She knew nothing about him. Nothing. And she'd been an utter fool. She'd thrown away everything for a few hours in his bed.

She faced the threat of him grasping onto her forever. Threatening her. Terrorizing her.

It had to stop.

One way or another.

It *had* to stop.

She touched her flat abdomen.

A baby? With a man who seemed darker, eviler by every passing moment?

"No," she said aloud in the bathroom as she stared at the window of the tiny wand in her hand and noticed it was trembling. Her throat went dry and she felt her pulse ticking up with anxiety as, sure enough, the results became clearly visible: She was pregnant.

And there was little doubt the father was Gideon Ross.

CHAPTER 24

"Shep's still not back?" Brooke asked, dropping the sack of groceries on the kitchen counter. She'd known he was still missing of course. If the dog had returned, Neal or Marilee or Leah would've texted or called and the retriever would have bounded to greet her.

"No." Leah shook her head. She'd found her spot at the table once more, only now there was no dog curled in his bed nearby and she seemed perturbed, angry about something. But then, didn't that always happen?

Brooke couldn't worry about her sister, not when there were too many other things on her mind. On the way home she'd driven slowly, studying and searching side streets and parking lots, peering into carports and garages with open doors. She'd also called the local vets and animal hospitals when she hadn't been talking with her friends, assuring them all that her daughter was home and unharmed.

"Thank God she's safe!" Andrea had said when Brooke phoned earlier. "Zuri just told me that she was home. I guess she posted it on Insta or something."

"So the word is out."

"Yes. And Allison Carelli is home too. Finally. Again, it's all over the Internet, and I think the police are talking to her and her cousin, Robert Barrone. It's just crazy. Zuri finally fessed up that she had an inkling of what was going on and let me tell you, she is sooo grounded."

"I know. Neal and I have to talk seriously with Marilee. Again."

"I hear ya. I don't know what gets into these kids' heads," Andrea admitted. "And Allison? What was she thinking? Does she have any idea what kind of hell she put her parents through?"

"Maybe that was the whole idea," Brooke said.

"Dark, Brooke, but I hear ya. Who knows? Look, I've gotta run, but I hope you find your dog."

"Me too," Brooke said, her heart twisting as they ended the conversation. She suspected that Gideon had taken him or let him loose, and she was heartsick all over again. If anything happened to sweet, goofy Shep and Gideon was behind it? She'd kill him.

Really? You'd murder the father of your child?

For now she pushed that homicidal thought aside and took a deep breath. At the moment she needed to concentrate on her family. Maybe Leah was right. It was time for Brooke to become more media savvy. If she wanted to know what was going on in her daughter's life, she needed to scan the Internet and social media, dig a little deeper by checking on her friends and acquaintances, the places they met, where they went.

"What took you so long?" Leah eyed the single sack of groceries.

"I drove around looking for Shep and ran a couple of errands, including getting gas and coffee, you know," Brooke said, not admitting how long she'd been at the coffee shop with its free Wi-Fi connection, where she'd tried and failed to do a deeper search into Gideon Ross. Once again she'd failed. It was as if he were a ghost. A ghost with evil intent.

She forced her mind to the here and now. "You hungry?" she asked her sister.

"Not really." Leah held up her cup. "I've had this. It's enough for now."

"Okay. And Neal's gone?" She had noticed his car wasn't in its spot in the garage.

"Yeah. He just said he was going out."

"To . . . ?"

"What am I, his keeper?" Leah asked sarcastically, an edge to her voice. "Isn't that your job?"

Brooke looked up sharply. "Geez, no. And I just thought he might've said where he was going."

"He didn't tell me, okay?" she said, obviously in a bad mood. "He just said something about being back in the afternoon."

"Odd," Brooke said aloud as she slid the package of bagels into a cupboard. Then she remembered it was Saturday. Golf. She checked the time. "Maybe not so odd." Nothing came between her husband and his standing tee time, not even, apparently, a family crisis with their daughter or the dog. Nope. Not when his two handicap was at stake.

Leah's lips pinched a bit. "He said you'd know where he was."

"I do." She nodded. "I just didn't think that he'd go to the course today. Not with what's going on with Marilee and Shep missing. I mean, we were up all night worried sick about our daughter."

Leah let out a huff of disbelief. "Yeah, yeah, I get it. But you know that boys will be boys, especially when it comes to boys and their toys," she said before taking a sip from her cup.

Brooke slammed down a carton of milk. "I hate those old expressions! They're just antiquated excuses giving men a free pass. You know, to play or to get out of responsibilities or chores or even be sane. Whatever happened to women's lib?" Under her breath Brooke muttered, "'Boys will be boys.' Ugh!" She stuffed the carton of milk into the refrigerator.

"Tell me how you really feel!" Leah tossed back. "Why are you so touchy?"

"Why are you?"

Leah just glared at her. Sipped from her cup.

"Okay, okay, I'm on edge, okay. It was a long, hard night." *Harder than you know*, Brooke added silently. "And it's not just Neal, it's . . . everything."

Leah's voice softened. "I get it. We all feel it. It was a long night." Frowning, she glanced out the French doors. "Looks like it's gonna rain again. I think I'd better go for a walk now before the skies open up. Maybe I'll find Shep in the park."

"I hope so," Brooke said without much hope. "Neal tried last night. I'm sure he scoured the place."

"Yeah, I know, but dogs wander. And a lot can happen in eight hours."

Amen to that, Brooke thought hopefully as she emptied the grocery sack and folded it. "Has Marilee been down?"

Leah shook her head. "Still in her room as far as I know."

"Okay." Brooke stuffed the bag into a cupboard, then headed upstairs. Quietly, she poked her head into her daughter's bedroom. Breathing evenly, Marilee had burrowed herself under the covers as if she were blocking out the world.

Now wasn't the time to disturb her.

What was the old saying from one of the Roosevelts? *Speak softly and carry a big stick?* Something like that. So maybe in this case it was walk softly and let sleeping dogs lie, or some such amalgam of words of wisdom. In any case she closed the door.

Hearing the front door close, she made her way to the guest room and picked her way around Leah's scattered clothing to the window. Looking out, Brooke spied her sister wearing one of Brooke's jackets. With the hood up against the rain, Leah had crossed the street and was hurrying into the park.

Marilee was dead to the world for all intents and purposes, so Brooke was alone in the house.

She took advantage of it.

She didn't have much time because she wasn't certain how long Leah would be out. Marilee could sleep forever, and Neal wasn't going to return from the country club for hours, so Leah was the unknown. She could be gone for two hours or return in fifteen minutes.

Remembering how Gideon had made comments about her and Neal making love, she went to their bedroom. If, as she suspected, he'd somehow invaded her home either physically or electronically or both, she wanted to find out how he got in, what surveillance equipment he'd installed, and where.

As rain drizzled down the windows, she stood in the middle of the room and scoured the walls and ceiling for any hint of a tiny camera or microphone. Slowly, she rotated, surveying every inch in the plaster walls and dark window casings with her eyes. If there was a camera hidden, she'd certainly see a flaw, something disturbed in the room.

Nothing.

And time was ticking by. She wouldn't have the house to herself forever.

She looked under pictures and lamps and searched beneath the bed, where she came up empty. But there had to be something here.

Undeterred, she studied the closet doors and the line of sight when they hung open.

Again, she didn't find anything obvious, nothing seemingly out of place.

If the spying equipment was in this room, it was well hidden or, conversely, hidden in plain sight and she was missing it.

Where, where, where?

"Come on, Brooke," she said under her breath.

Her cell phone buzzed and she jumped. Leah's number appeared on the screen. "Hey," she answered, her eyes still scanning the room. "What's up?"

"I thought I'd walk over to that little restaurant for a deli sandwich. It's almost noon and my coffee's wearing off. Want anything? I could bring it back."

"Al's Bistro?" The little café was on the far side of the park.

"Yeah. That's the one."

"No . . . I'm okay," Brooke said, her stomach uneasy as she stepped back for a better view of the room.

And she saw it.

What appeared to be a small beetle or spider or some kind of insect at the baseboard near the foot of her bed.

Her insides froze.

"Suit yourself." She heard Leah's voice as if from a distance. "I'm going to window-shop, I think, and ask around about Shep."

"Good. Good. Yeah." Brooke was barely listening. "Let me know if you find him."

"Will do." Leah cut the connection and Brooke ran to the side of the bed to kneel down so quickly she felt a twinge of pain in her ankle, a sharp reminder of her fight with Gideon.

She leaned down, ignoring the dust bunnies, and fingered the spot in the baseboard. Definitely a small hole and coming from it, almost invisible to the eye, was a clear wire that ran between the baseboard and the carpet.

She felt a moment of triumph, quickly replaced by dread as she followed the wire along the floor to the doorframe, where it met the corner of the room. From there the wire disappeared into the wall.

On the other side was the unused staircase.

She practically flew down the stairs to the laundry room, where she pulled out the key ring and a flashlight, unlocked the door, and quietly started to climb. She switched on the dim overhead light, then clicked on the flashlight with its intense beam. Slowly, she ran the bright light around the edges of the staircase, across the low ceiling with its myriad of spiderwebs to the dusty steps, where dead bugs and traces of mice were visible. Shuddering inwardly, she moved up the stairs to the landing on the second floor.

Nothing had appeared on the lower steps, but as she shone the harsh light on the wall that backed the master bedroom, she saw it. A thin, nearly translucent wire was stretched across the top of the doorframe.

"Son of a bitch," she hissed, keeping her voice low; Marilee's room was just on the other side of the door and across the hall. She searched for a camera or listening device but found none. Could it be wireless? On battery? Still, it would have to be able to survey, to view, or to listen in.

The thought was nauseating.

She concentrated on the wire and noticed that it rounded a corner, then ran upward.

Leading to the attic.

Holy shit!

She'd known it, damn it, she'd known it!

Holding her flashlight in her teeth, she carefully climbed the unsteady rungs. All of her muscles were tense, her legs aching as she paused to open the trapdoor in the ceiling before poking her head into the empty space. Cool air, dust, and darkness greeted her.

She heard the sound of rain pinging against the roof and water running in the gutters.

Standing on one of the rungs, she swept the beam of the flashlight around the perimeter of the attic, where the roof joists met the crossbeams at the floor. Then she directed the light over the interior of the roof itself.

Nothing.

Wait . . .

Where would the camera be?

Over the bedroom?

Or . . . with a gut-wrenching realization, she understood that she might not be searching for only one camera and/or microphone. There could be more than one, perhaps dozens. "Oh, please," she whispered to herself. For a few disgusting seconds scenarios of her private life spun through her mind. Not only the intimate, private scenes, but just the normal, day-to-day conversations and interplay of the family; the private jokes, the recriminations, the playful banter, the silly talk to the dog . . . all so personal.

Then she considered something more disturbing. Darker. She remembered the comments about her daughter.

I hope pretty little Marilee is enjoying the dance.

And then:

Your daughter is as beautiful as you are.

Be careful.

It would be a shame if you were to lose her.

Could Gideon have been watching as she undressed or showered or listened in on private conversations about her hopes, her dreams—

Bile rose in her throat.

Oh. Dear. God.

Gideon?

Or someone else?

More than one sicko?

Her throat went dry at the thought.

Don't go there! Not now!

First things first, she told herself as she tamped down her fear and found the spot where the wire should have run through the attic floor. Carefully, her skin itchy where it rubbed up against the insulation, she dug, silently cursing herself for not wearing gloves. Nothing. She reached deeper, to the attic floor. The tips of her fingers scraped against plywood.

It had to be here!

It had to.

Craning her neck to see into the small hole she'd dug in the insulation between the joists, she searched the area. She shone the light into the hole.

Nothing.

But it had to be!

She twisted the flashlight a bit and the beam caught a glimmer of something: a taut strand strung below the plank that ran the length of the narrow wooden pathway through the attic. It led to the island of plywood in the center of the garret where old magazines, records, and discarded, long-forgotten boxes were piled.

Anticipation mixed with dread.

She hoisted herself up to a crouching position and started to inch forward.

As long as she walked on the planks or balanced on the floor joists, she would be okay. In between, should she trip, she would fall through the sheet rock of the ceiling below.

Not good, she told herself and focused the flashlight's beam on the wire. Its shimmering edge peeked over the joists. Whoever had strung it hadn't bothered to drill through the beams.

Bent down and teetering, telling herself she was a certified idiot, she made her way over the planks to the plywood platform where she tested the makeshift flooring with her weight, then lowered herself to a kneeling position.

She located the end of the wire. Sure enough, she found what she assumed was a dime-sized camera attached to it. The insulation had been cleared from a spot at the edge of the platform, and when she lifted the camera she discovered a small hole right above what she knew was the overhead light of her bedroom.

"Terrific." Despite being alone in the dark attic, she felt herself flush with a mixture of embarrassment and outrage. "Son of a—"

Oh shit!

She noticed that just on the other side of the camera the wire split in several directions. Slowly, painstakingly, she followed each thread, her blood pounding in her ears as she located a tiny camera mounted at the edge of the platform. When she lifted it she found it had been placed in the ceiling over Marilee's bed. Just as she'd speculated and dreaded.

"You bastard," she whispered. "You lowlife, fucking bastard." She tore the camera from its hiding spot, ripping the wires, hating the man who had done this and hating herself for allowing him to get close.

Rage pulsing, she crawled along the planks and discovered yet another tiny camera nestled in the insulation over the staircase. *You sick prick!* She tore it from its wires. Then she found another located over the guest room, again hidden in the overhead light fixture. Well, no more! She yanked that camera as well, then, gritting her teeth in frustration, ripped out all the effing spy equipment.

Were the cameras attached to a router, something that would forward images to a computer somewhere? Or were they somehow connected wirelessly to some unknown computer? If so, why were the wires here?

Who cared?

It didn't matter.

What did matter was the fact that Gideon had slipped into the house and set up the whole nest of minuscule cameras.

Her blood pounded through her veins at the thought of him spying on her, watching her make love to Neal. Or gaping at Leah as she primped or slept? Worse yet, playing the voyeur and observing Marilee in various states of undress, staring at her young, supple body.

Oh. God.

Her stomach heaved and she fought the urge to vomit.

In her mind's eye she saw Gideon on his sailboat, alone, leaning back in a chair, sipping a beer and watching the images on his computer. Was he getting off on what he saw? Or becoming quietly furious?

Either way, you did this, Brooke. It's your fault.

She was ill at the thought of what she'd done to her family, how she'd let him into her life, how he'd taken her trust and abused it.

What kind of psycho was he?

She thought about going to the police. Immediately she discarded the idea, but her stomach churned when she realized he'd overheard their private conversations, their whispered secrets. He'd even watched as she'd found the bracelet, and when she'd sneaked into Neal's office. He'd probably watched her freak out when she'd found the dead rat and had smirked in satisfaction at her panic about losing the dog.

Sick, sick, sick!

Her stomach churned.

She considered confessing to Neal, but again thought better of it.

She couldn't tell Leah or any of her friends, and especially not Marilee.

No, she had to solve this problem. Alone.

And she would.

Her teeth ground together and rage burned through her blood as she ripped out the wires, hearing the pop, pop, pop of staples being splintered from wood.

No way could she let him get away with this!

A dozen quick ideas of dealing with him swirled through her mind, all of them murderous. She would stop him if it was the last thing she ever did. How in the world had she ever gotten involved with him? When she thought of their stolen hours together, their private trysts, the way she'd abandoned herself to him, she wanted to scream.

And then there was the baby.

What a mess!

After stuffing the damning cameras into her pockets, she eased her way back along the plank to the ladder to the trapdoor. She had just started down the rungs of the ladder to the attic when she heard the sound of the front door opening and Leah's voice.

"Brooke! Brooke!" she yelled, and Brooke slid down the ladder and sped down the staircase as quietly as she could.

"Brooke!"

Shit.

In the laundry room she closed the door and shoved the key into her pocket with all the small spy equipment.

"Brooke!" Leah was walking fast, her footsteps reverberating through the house.

What now?

Frantically, Brooke brushed the cobwebs from her hair as she hastened up the half flight to the kitchen.

"What?" she asked, rounding the corner from the kitchen to the foyer.

Leah was in the hallway, her hair wet from the rain, her eyes shining.

Next to her, bedraggled and muddy, Shep shook himself before galloping up to Brooke.

"Oh my God," Brooke cried, falling to her knees. Her heart cracked as she petted the wet dog, who eagerly washed her face. "I missed you too," she said, her throat thick, tears burning her eyes. "Marilee!" she yelled. "Marilee!" Then, still petting the dog, she looked up at her sister. "Where did you find him?"

"In the park. On my way back from the deli."

"Really?"

"Yeah. I might've missed him, but some guy yelled at me and asked if I was looking for a dog."

Brooke's insides congealed. "What guy?"

"I didn't get his name. He was far away, straddling a motorcycle at the curb. I guess he heard me calling for Shep, you know. I yelled back that I was searching for Shep and he said he saw one and pointed in the direction of the gazebo. And there he was, his leash caught in one of the benches, which was weird because I'd been by there not five minutes before."

"And you didn't get the guy's name? Or see who he was? Get the license plate of the motorcycle?"

"Are you kidding? It was raining like hell, my damned hood fell off, and I wouldn't have recognized him anyway. He was wearing a helmet and before I could say anything, even thank him, he took off."

"Don't you think that's weird?"

"Or lucky!" Leah said. "Who cares who he is? The important thing is that Shep's back."

"Right, of course," Brooke said, but her emotions were roiling and she did care; she cared a lot. Straightening the wet dog still dancing at her feet, she yelled up the staircase to her daughter, "Marilee! Come down here."

She heard a thump and then slow footsteps.

A few seconds later her daughter, disheveled and squinting, a blanket wrapped around her, glowered down the stairs. "What?" she demanded crossly before her gaze landed on the dog. "Shep! Oh! Oh!" She dropped the blanket and as she ran down the stairs, Shep bolted up, dripping water and mud. The two met at the center of the staircase. Marilee, almost bowled over, knelt down and embraced the wriggling mass of dirty fur.

"Shep, Shep," she said, burrowing her face into his neck as he whined and wiggled in excitement.

Tears streamed down Marilee's face and Brooke's heart melted.

No matter how angry, worried, and downright scared she'd been the night before, she felt nothing but joy and relief seeing her daughter and her dog together.

"Thank you," she said to Leah.

"Don't thank me, I just happened to be in the right place at the right time. Thank the guy who found him."

"If only I could."

"What? I thought you found him," Marilee said to her aunt.

"I did, but I had help." Leah brought Marilee up to speed as she peeled off Brooke's jacket and hung it in the closet. "As I told your mother," she said, shutting the closet door, "the important thing is that Shep is back and unhurt. So I guess it doesn't matter."

But she was wrong, Brooke thought.

It mattered.

It mattered a lot.

And it had to end.

Now.

"Hey, what's this?" Marilee asked as she fumbled with Shep's collar. The dog yipped as she yanked something free.

Brooke asked, "What?"

"Some kind of necklace—no, a bracelet, I think." Marilee unwound the gold links and red stones and held it up to a nearby lamp, where it winked bloodred, the tiny sailboat charm catching the light.

"What the devil?" Leah said as Brooke felt every muscle in her body go rigid. "Is this some kind of a joke?" She glanced up at her sister. "Do you think it belongs to the guy who found Shep? Or . . . or someone else?"

"I have no idea," Brooke lied, her stomach grinding. "I guess we have to keep it until he comes back to claim it."

"How can he do that?" Leah asked while Marilee studied the bracelet. "I didn't even give him my name, much less this address."

Oh, he knows.

"Maybe it has an inscription," her daughter said, hopping to her feet. "I'll check."

Oh no!

"Look," Marilee said, glancing up at her mother. "On the sailboat. A date, I think."

"Let me see." Leah took the bit of jewelry from her niece's hand to study the charm. "You're right. Just this past spring. It must be important."

Brooke swallowed hard and wanted to argue about the bracelet and the importance of the engraving, but she held her tongue.

"Should we take it to the police?" Marilee asked.

"I don't think so." Brooke shook her head and tried to keep her voice even. "It doesn't look valuable."

"Not to you, maybe. But to someone—I mean, with the date on it." Marilee was fingering the bauble. Then she grinned suddenly, "I know! I'll post it online. See if anyone recognizes it," she said. She turned to Shep. "Come on, boy! You can be in the picture too! After a bath!"

No! Don't give him the satisfaction!

"Do you think that will work?" Leah asked as they heard the creak of old pipes and the rush of water as Marilee turned on the spigots in the hall bath. "Putting it online?"

"Probably not," Brooke said, filled with dread at the thought. If Marilee put the picture out on the Internet and Gideon saw it—was even looking for it—he would be back. And satisfied. Smug in the fact that he'd toyed with her, made her uncomfortable, his presence noted to the family, the threat of exposure all the closer.

And there was no telling what he would do to up his game.

She had to find some way to stop him.

Forever.

CHAPTER 25

She needed a gun.

If not Neal's, another one.

Which she didn't have.

But to intimidate Gideon, which she fully intended, she'd need a weapon. A serious weapon. One that didn't require her to be close to him. Yep, Brooke thought, she needed a gun, and even though the thought was foreign to her, that never in her wildest dreams had she thought she would want to be near a firearm, she had to get her hands on a gun.

Neal's little Beretta would do.

If she could get it.

The problem was that she needed the key to the safe to get Neal's pistol and she didn't want to explain to him why she wanted it. So, despite the urge to confront Gideon right this very minute, she had to force herself to be patient, to bide her time, and to come up with a plan.

As luck would have it, Neal came home from his weekly golf game earlier than expected. "Rained out. Had to stop at the turn," he explained as he stepped through the door and was met with a yipping, excited Shep. "Hey, who's this?" He crouched to pet the dog. "Who's a good boy, huh? Who's a good boy?"

Shep whined and excited and was rewarded with major scratches and pets.

Looking up from the excited dog, Neal asked, "How did this happen? How did you find him?"

"Leah ran into a guy who had him," Brooke said, trying to keep the acrimony out of her voice. "In the park."

"Really?" Frowning, Neal glanced to the windows looking out on the street and the wooded park beyond.

As if she'd been listening at her bedroom door, Leah ran downstairs.

"You want to tell him what happened?" Brooke guessed, and Leah did. Eagerly. Detail by minute detail. When Marilee joined them she added in the part about the bracelet wound through Shep's collar, even showing it to her father, including the charm with the sailing ship and engraving.

He eyed the date. "Beginning of summer. June."

"Right." Her throat went dry.

"I've already posted pictures of the bracelet on the Internet," Marilee said as she snagged a box of Oreos from the cupboard. "Social media—hoping someone will come forward and claim it. Then maybe we'll figure out who the guy is so, you know, we can, like, reward him or something."

"Good idea," Neal said.

After taking several cookies from the package, Marilee whistled to the dog and headed back up the stairs.

Neal watched her leave. When she was out of earshot he asked, "How's it going?"

"Between Marilee and me?" Brooke asked and, at his nod, said, "Better. Though I think being up all night is taking its toll. On all of us. But Marilee's perked up since Shep came home, and at least she's talking to me again."

"That's good." He took a swallow. "Did you talk about last night?"

"No." Brooke shook her head. "For now—this afternoon—I'm letting it pass. I thought I'd give it some time. Ferment, you know. Let us all think about it. But we do have to emphasize that what she did was wrong. And I'm not just talking about sneaking out with Nick, but the whole Allison Carelli thing." She sighed. "I don't know how she could keep it from us, from the Carellis."

"She's not the only one. Several kids knew."

"Yeah, but she's *our* daughter."

He nodded, raking his hand through his hair. "Teenagers. Sometimes you don't know what they're thinking."

"Peer pressure," Leah chimed in.

Neal said, "But we have to talk to her tomorrow. Before school on Monday. I take it there's no word on the other girl?"

"Penny Williams?" Brooke felt that same old worry she always did when the girl's name was mentioned. It had been so long since any-one had seen her, hope was fading that she was alive or would turn up again. "No," she said. "I've been on a text thread with some of the moms from school. There's lots of speculation, but it seems to me that the two incidents are totally unrelated."

"God, I wish she could be found."

"Me too."

He blew out a long breath of air. "It's exhausting."

"And really scary. I know." She leaned a shoulder against the re-frigerator. "I'm tired too. Don't want to fight with Marilee. I mean, I will. Just not right now."

He frowned, as if mentally wrestling with something, but finally nodded as he walked to the refrigerator. "Yeah. Sure. We should give Marilee a little space to think things over."

"I'm trying. But she's still in trouble and knows it. Big trouble."

He found a bottle of Coors in the fridge. "So, am I supposed to be-lieve you're learning patience in your old age?"

"Old age?" She made a sound of disgust, and as he flipped the top of the beer bottle across the counter and it bounced against the cof-feepot, she sent him a knowing look. "And then there are those of us who are immature beyond their years."

Neal actually laughed aloud, some of the tension finally breaking. "You're right!" He wrapped one arm around Brooke's waist and swung her around the room while still holding on to the bottle of Coors with the other.

"Stop!" she protested but actually giggled as he set her on the floor again. How long had it been since they had been this comfort-able with each other, had teased each other playfully?

He took a long swallow from his beer, gave her a wink, then gave her a quick pat on the rump before he announced that he was going to "hit the showers."

Only then did Brooke see Leah in the archway to the living room. She'd obviously watched the entire exchange. All joy in her face had drained.

"What?" Brooke asked.

"I wish I had that," her sister whispered as she gazed to the staircase where Neal had disappeared.

"Had what?" Brooke asked.

"Oh, you know. I didn't mean . . . not Neal, but . . . I was thinking aloud that I wish I had that—what you and Neal have—with Sean," she corrected, obviously flustered and stumbling. Her cheeks turned pink.

"But it's over with Sean. Right?"

"Yes, yes. Right. Uh, look," she swept a glance at her watch, "I'd better get back to packing up." And with that she too went upstairs, though Brooke couldn't imagine how much packing she would need to do after being here so short a time.

It didn't matter. Brooke had a small window in which to do what she had to. So she went up the stairs into the master bedroom, and when she heard Neal turn on the shower she found his damp clothes in a pile on the chair in the bedroom, riffled through his pockets and, praying she had time, extracted his keys. In a flash she was downstairs, in the den, sorting through the keys until she came up with the smaller key for the safe. Her heart was pounding, her nerves strung tight as she listened to the sound of water running. Her fingers fumbled with the combination and muffed it, spinning past the final number.

Biting her lip, one ear cocked to the noises outside the door of the den, she gave it another try, heard the tumblers fall into place, inserted the key, twisted, and opened the safe.

The Beretta was inside.

A small pocket pistol.

Perfect.

She picked it up, snagged two clips next to it, and closed the safe just as she heard the water stop running overhead.

Damn.

She had to work fast.

Barely breathing, she closed the safe and stuffed the keys and ammo into her pocket. Pistol in hand, she slipped out of the room, across the hall, and down the stairs to the garage, where she stashed the weapon and clips under the passenger seat of her Explorer.

Stealthily, she mounted the stairs, swept through the laundry, and up the final half flight to the main level.

Leah was in the kitchen at the sink. Uncapping a bottle of Tylenol, she started when Brooke appeared and dropped the bottle, nearly knocking over a glass of water. "Jesus, you scared me." Scraping up the pills that had escaped, she eyed her up and down. "What're you doing?"

"Just getting something from the car."

"What?" Leah asked, tossing back a pill and chasing it down with a big gulp.

Brooke realized her hands were empty. "I mean, I thought I left my phone in the car, but I didn't."

"Oh." Leah took another swallow of water and tossed the rest into the sink.

"Headache?"

"Yeah." Leah nodded. "Trying to get rid of it. I get these some-times. Probably tension. You know, I'm going to have to deal with Sean. Or his lawyer. And . . . well, whatever."

"And it's been kind of a wild twenty-four hours."

"Kind of?" Leah shook her head. "I couldn't live this way. Much as I envy you, as I said . . . but . . . Brooke, this"—she stretched her arms to include all of the house—"this is pure chaos!"

You don't know the half of it.

"Usually not so much." But she recalled that Leah had lied to her about the money she'd borrowed, and that Neal had equivocated as well. With everything else going on, Brooke had put it out of her thoughts. But there it was again. Front and center.

Her sister was definitely part of the chaos, much as she dispar-aged it.

"I'd go out of my mind," Leah said.

"Sometimes I think I am."

"Well, I don't blame you." She glanced at the clock and said with more than a hint of sarcasm, "I really hate to leave when we're having all this fun, but I'd better go up and finish packing." She paused. "You're still up for driving me to the airport?"

"Of course." Brooke planned to use the time to not only ask Leah about her deal with Neal but also to confront Gideon once she'd dropped her sister off at the airport. After all, there was no time like the present.

She was done with him.

Done with his calls.

Done with his motorcycle roaring past.

Done with his charades of cop and pizza deliveryman.

Done with his damned bracelet.

Done with his spying and threats.

Done with his dead rat left to intimidate and terrorize her.

This time, no matter what else happened, she'd make sure he got the message.

Neal's gun would see to it.

CHAPTER 26

Two hours later Brooke was behind the wheel of her Explorer, navigating the clog of traffic near the airport, her sister in the seat next to her. Night had fallen and the storm was in full force, rain coming down so hard that the wipers could barely keep the windshield clear, cars, buses, and trucks jockeying for position, the red glare of taillights stretching in an undulating line ahead of them. Fortunately, her headlights still worked.

While Brooke tried to maneuver the Explorer through the lanes, she told herself not to think about the gun and ammo tucked under the seat, nor the spy equipment and bracelet stuffed into the pockets of her jacket. She was tense, thinking ahead, calculating how much time she would have after dropping Leah off, then driving to the marina and confronting Gideon.

How would he react?

And how far would she go?

She intended to scare the liver out of him, to turn the tables on him, but what if, God forbid, it didn't work? White-knuckled over the steering wheel, she forced a calm she didn't feel. Leah and her bad mood weren't helping. She'd been spoiling for a fight ever since seeing Neal and Brooke getting along, teasing each other, assuming they were in love and their problems were only a recalcitrant teenage daughter and a dog that had wandered off.

If she only knew.

Leah kept drumming her fingers against the armrest, then checking her watch pointedly, then futzing with the radio.

"I knew we should have left earlier," Leah complained for the third time since they left the house. She'd been snappy and tense, nervous about the flight and about her upcoming battle with Sean.

Which was nothing compared to what Brooke was dealing with.

For the dozenth time Leah switched radio channels, stopping at a song by U2.

Good.

Mouthing the words Bono was singing, Leah checked her phone as if hoping to get a text that her flight to Phoenix was delayed. It wasn't. "Didn't I say so? Didn't I tell you I always have anxiety about missing my flight—that we should have left half an hour earlier?" she spat out, highly agitated and not bothering to mask it.

Brooke had seen her this way before, recognized the signs, told herself to tread carefully despite the fact that her own nerves were frayed to the breaking point. "You've got lots of time. Over an hour." Brooke flipped on her blinker and aimed the crumpled nose of her Explorer toward the off-ramp, but the driver who she'd hoped would let her in ignored her signals and stared straight ahead, inching his Dodge van forward. "Come on," she said.

As the van moved past, she eyed the driver of an older Volkswagen, a woman with puffy gray hair and a tiny dog lounging on her shoulder. The woman eased off the gas and Brooke waved as she wedged into the tight spot and exited the freeway. "See," she said to her sister, "you're going to make it."

"Next time we leave earlier!" Leah huffed and Brooke tried to tamp down her irritation. "Didn't I say so?" Leah flipped down the visor and peered into the passenger mirror, its tiny light illuminating her face. "If you'd listened to me. I said I would take an Uber, but oh no . . ."

Brooke braked as the traffic slowed to a crawl, taillights glowing in an unending stream.

"Now what?" Leah said on a disgusted sigh. She snapped the visor up again and glared out the windshield. "I don't know why I let you bully me around."

"Bully you?" Brooke repeated.

"You know you do. You always have!" She was steaming, still itching for a fight.

"Bully?"

"You know what I mean. You've always been bossy, telling everyone what to do. Get everyone to take the blame for you."

"What?" Where was this going? Why was it coming out now?

"Just ask Keith Turnquist," Leah said with a knowing smirk.

"Keith?" Brooke said. "What does he have to do with any of this?"

"I know what happened that night, Brooke. So does everyone else. He saved your ass."

"He nearly raped me," she replied.

Leah shot her an oh-really glance and Brooke turned her attention to the brake lights burning ahead.

"You assaulted him," Leah said. "I heard Mom and Nana. The only reason you weren't charged was because you were underage."

"That's not the way it was."

Leah snorted her disbelief, and for a few seconds Brooke remembered that night. The party. The crowd . . .

She and Keith had been drinking and arguing. They'd been at a teen party outside the city in a house in the woods, somebody's relatives' house who were away for the weekend. They were drinking and high when Keith talked her into stepping into a bedroom with him. She'd known it was a mistake the minute he'd opened the door, where two twin beds were positioned on either side of a window. In one a couple was already naked and going at it, moaning and so out of it they didn't know anyone had entered or just didn't care.

But Brooke wanted nothing to do with sharing the space and making out on some little girl's bed with unicorn sheets and pink-striped wallpaper. She spied a Barbie Dreamhouse tucked into one corner, tiny dresses hanging in the closet. As Keith used his body to block the door and walk her backward toward the vacant bed, she tripped over some toy, a sharp plastic dinosaur.

"You need to take me home," she insisted.

"Come on, Brooke," Keith said, pulling up her blouse and pushing her onto the rumpled unicorn sheets. Some little girl slept here.

"No." She wasn't about to give her virginity to him on a twin bed where some unknown child slept. Even half drunk she knew better than that, and she really didn't like the idea of the other couple, naked and groaning on the matching bed.

"It'll be good," Keith promised and was working at his fly, lowering the zipper.

"No, not here." She pushed hard, throwing him off her and stumbling out into the living room, filled with smoke and loud music and people she didn't know. Keith followed after her.

"What's wrong with you?" he demanded.

"I want to go home." And she was out the door, determined to walk the three miles if he didn't take her.

"Brooke!" he yelled through the hot summer night. "Goddamn it, Brooke. Well, fuck!" and he was jogging closer to her. "Okay, I'll take you home."

But she didn't believe him. Freaked out, she took off, running across the side yard, past the parked cars and into the surrounding woods. Moonlight pierced the leafy canopy, but she was drunk and scared and he was thundering behind her, catching up.

She didn't see the exposed root and stumbled. His hand caught her shoulder, twisting her back, but she went down, landing hard, a sharp rock piercing her neck.

Pain screamed through her shoulder.

And there he was, leaning over her, just like he had in the bedroom. "Get away from me!" she screamed.

But he kept coming, on his knees, touching her. "It's going to be all right," he said, a dark shape. Oh God, was he unzipping his fly again? She didn't wait to find out.

She felt the rock beneath her hand. Sharp on one side, wickedly sharp on the other. Her fingers curled around it, and as he got closer she swung, smashing the sharp edge into his face.

He howled.

Blood spurted, warm and raining.

She struck again.

Bam!

Bone crunched.

Again.

"You fucking bitch," he screamed, rolling away from her. "You goddamned, fucking—" And then there were voices and lights and the world spun as she passed out. Only later did she hear that she'd broken his nose and cracked the orbital socket around one eye. He'd nearly lost his vision, which she'd thought was tit for tat because she'd nearly lost her virginity.

Except the police hadn't seen it that way, nor had his parents and their lawyer. She'd been accused of assault, but she was underage, the records sealed, but everyone knew. And Keith, in the end, convinced his parents to let it go.

"You could have gone to JD," Leah said, switching the radio to a country station. "That really would have screwed up your life, wouldn't it? To spend time in juvie? Don't think you would've married Neal then. Just think where we would all be if you'd served your time?"

"I don't know why you're bringing this up now." Brooke never wanted to think about that time in her life.

"Because you always think you can twist things around to the way you want, pretend life is different than it is and boss people around just to get your way."

"What does that have to do with—?"

"I'm just saying you can't tell me what to do. No more."

"You're being irrational." Brooke turned her attention to the upcoming exit. "Is this really because we didn't leave when you thought we should?" Of course not. It was years of resentment piling up and finally erupting.

Leah checked her phone again. "I'm just letting you know that I'm not putting up with your BS anymore."

"Like you ever do."

Leah pronounced, "Next time I'm not letting you tell me what to do!"

"Next time?" Brooke repeated, her own irritation growing.

"If there is one. I don't think I'll be back!"

"Wow." Brooke snapped off the radio. "So, let's talk about the next time you come to visit."

Leah snorted, as if there was no chance she would be returning. She flipped down the visor with the mirror *again* and touched her finger at a smudge of lipstick at the corner of her mouth. "What about it?"

"Maybe it won't be for money." There, it was out.

"What?" Eyebrows knit in frustration, she was still rubbing at a bit of lipstick.

"I know Neal loaned you fifty thousand dollars. And that was just now. Before that, there was more."

"A little," she admitted with a lift of a shoulder as she pushed up the visor.

"A little? Are you kidding?"

Leah let out a breath. "It doesn't matter. It's secured."

"I know. By some sort of lien on the cabin. *Our* cabin. Yours and mine. The one we inherited."

"And your point is?"

"You lied. You both lied. You said you needed fifteen."

Leah threw up her hands. "Okay, so you caught me. Big deal. I could use the money. More than you."

"I'm not sure about that. Marilee's going to college in a few years." She eased onto the approach to the airport.

"And I'm dead broke, okay? But you don't care!"

"Of course I care."

Leah scoffed, "What's it to you anyway? The loan's secured. You never want to sell the damned cabin, so I figure it's a win-win! You end up with 'our' cabin and I get a little cash."

"A little? Leah, I don't see—"

"Of course you don't!" Leah cut in. "You never do! You never see anything from anyone else's point of view!"

"Wait a second. What are you doing? Why is this all coming out now?"

"Because I saw with my own eyes how fucked up you've made everything with Neal, and with Marilee, and with me. So, okay, I'm finally doing what my therapist said and telling you how I feel."

"Now?" Brooke said, disbelieving, as traffic started moving again as the terminal loomed ahead at last, the tower lights visible in the rain.

"Why not? The truth is, Brooke, you just take what you want and don't care what happens to anyone else!"

"That's not true!"

"Of course it is!" Leah charged angrily, her emotional floodgates, shut too long, suddenly overflowing. "It always has been!"

"I'm trying to drive, damn it!" Brooke said. "I can't do this right now!"

"You started it," she pouted. "Bringing up the money."

"You started it by coming up here just to get money! I don't know what the hell you have over Neal, but he sure seems like your personal ATM."

"Oh Jesus. Is that what you think?" Leah let out a breath of disgust and yanked her purse from the floor to her lap. "That's sick, Brooke."

"That's what it looks like!" Brooke tried to maneuver to the curb while arguing with her sister. A convertible, vying for the same space, honked loudly. "Shit!" she yelled, yanking on the wheel. "Prick!"

The sleek car squeezed ahead of her with inches to spare. The driver, a woman in her twenties, shot a finger into the air.

"Idiot," Brooke muttered.

Leah didn't notice. She was too hot. "You just don't know how to count your blessings. You have a good man in Neal. A damned good man!"

"I know that." She eased toward a space at the curb.

"And yet you don't appreciate him."

"What? Of course I do."

Leah let out a breath of disgusted air. "I don't know why you don't divorce him and get it over with!"

"What're you talking about?" Brooke hit the brakes and the Explorer jerked to a stop. "Seriously, do we need to do this now?"

Leah was undeterred. "I've seen what's going on!" She opened the passenger door, and the noise of the airport under the portico—echoing voices, running engines, horns, tires humming on pavement—seeped inside the vehicle. "I know what you're up to, Brooke." She stormed to the back door and flung it open. "And, by the way, Neal does too!" She jerked her bag from the back seat.

"What?" Jesus God, did Neal know about Gideon? Did Leah?

"So you're not getting away with anything."

"I don't know what you mean."

"Sure you do." Leah glared at her for a minute, her eyes a dangerous shade of blue. "You know, Brooke, things would've been different, a lot different, if I married Neal."

"What!" Brooke said, stung to her core. "You're still upset about that? Oh my freaking God, Leah! It's been years."

"And three marriages for me. How many do you think it would've been if I'd had the chance to marry the man I loved all those years ago?"

"You were too young—"

"But I knew what I wanted! Too bad for me! It's the story of our childhood. If I wanted something, you took it!"

"This is crazy!"

A horn behind her blared.

"I have to go," Brooke said.

Leah wasn't finished and her eyes snapped fire. "Take my advice, Brooke. If you're so damned miserable in your marriage, just get it over with and get out."

"You're being irrational."

"Am I? I don't think so." All the repressed anger of fifteen years burst to the surface.

"And don't worry about having to put up with me again. From now on I won't bother you."

"Don't say—"

"I'm serious, Brooke. I'm done with you!"

"Even if you need money again?" Brooke threw back at her.

Leah gasped.

The guy behind her laid on the horn again.

"Wow," Leah said. "Harsh. But I should have known. You know what, Brooke, you're a heartless bitch!" She was nodding, agreeing with herself, as if she were alone under the canopy crawling with vehicles and travelers. "You always have been. Always will be. I'm over this. So don't worry about it because I'm not your problem. Not anymore. And you should be happy because I promise you, you'll never have to deal with me again. In fact, you'll never see me again!" She slammed the door.

Brooke pounded the steering wheel. Damn it all! Why now? Why? And what the hell did she know? What did Neal know? The two of them had lied to her about the loan. Had they discussed Brooke's affair? Neal's fascination with another woman?

Tears of frustration burned in her eyes as she watched her sister head into the terminal. Did she believe she'd never see Leah again? No. But still, it was hard to accept that they couldn't just move forward, have a normal relationship, whatever that meant.

Brooke put her SUV into gear and caught one last look at her sister.

Dragging her roller bag, Leah strode away, pushing her way through the crowd and never once looking back.

Don't worry about ever having to put up with me again.

How many times had Leah threatened to stay completely out of Brooke's life over the years? Every time the anger had simmered for months, sometimes years, but this time . . . Did she mean it?

I'm done with you!

You'll never see me again!

Brooke watched Leah disappear into the throng as she swept through the glass doors. What the hell had set her off? Why did she have to bring it all up here? Now?

Pull it together, she told herself, viciously cranking the wheel as the attendant stepped back, whistle in mouth, making rolling gestures to the traffic in general. Brooke forced the Explorer into the thick traffic and threaded her way away from Sea-Tac.

She told herself she didn't care what Leah threatened. It wasn't the first time and she doubted it would be the last.

Trying to convince herself that she was better off without her needy, drama queen sister, she blinked back tears and ignored the scar over her heart that Leah always seemed to rip open.

She'll be back, she told herself as she switched lanes and headed north. *Like a bad penny*, Nana used to say. Brooke told herself she had to forget about Leah at least for the moment, let her younger sister have her self-serving proclamation of independence.

Right now Brooke needed to focus on Gideon and finding a way to get rid of him.

Forever.

She had a gun.

If only she had the guts.

"One way to find out," she said to the empty car as she drove through the South End of Seattle, the wipers slapping the rain from the windshield, headlights bright on the shimmering pavement.

At the first stoplight, her stomach in knots, her muscles tense, she reached under the seat, found the pistol, and slipped it into her jacket pocket. She followed with the clips, listening to the wind howl over the rapid beating of her heart.

"God help me," she whispered, the interior of the Explorer turning an eerie red from the stoplight.

You can still change your mind. Just go home to your family and cozy home on the hill overlooking the city. Give this up.

But then she'd never be free.

She swallowed back her fears.

The light turned green.

She hit the gas.

CHAPTER 27

You can do this, she told herself as she sped north, the city of Seattle towering on the hillside, skyscrapers knifing upward lighting the dark night. She couldn't put up with his intimidation a second longer. She couldn't spend the rest of her life jumping whenever the phone rang, or a motorcycle raced by, or her damned doorbell chimed. She couldn't continue with her family at risk.

You can do this. You can do this. She glanced in the rearview mirror and saw the determination and fear in her eyes. *You have to*.

"Give me strength," she whispered when the marina came into view, vessels shifting on the dark, ever-moving water, the rain sheeting down the windshield. The single, tall security lamp cast a bluish glow over the scattered vehicles and uneven pavement, rain swirling in its weak illumination.

Brooke threw herself out of the car and into a wall of cold rain. She ignored it. Propelled by determination and fury, she strode along the dock.

The *Medusa*, moored as it always was between other craft, rocked in the pitching water. A few vessels showed tiny spots of illumination visible through their portholes.

Gideon's boat was dark.

Fine.

If he wasn't here, she'd wait.

Before she walked up the gangway she turned and squinted into the rain, just to make sure. And yes, his motorcycle was parked in its usual spot, chrome handlebars and exhaust pipe glinting in the poor light.

Good.

She felt the hard weight of the gun in her pocket and, in the other, the lighter, malleable package.

It was time to turn the tables.

She stepped onto the decking, the rain pouring down, sliding down her jacket. The icy wind snatched her hood.

"Gideon!" she yelled, shielding her eyes against the rain.

The boat creaked as it moved with the tide rolling into the sound.

"Gideon!"

No response.

Damn it!

When he didn't answer Brooke slid her burner phone from the back pocket of her jeans and texted:

I'm here.

On your boat.

We need to talk.

Face-to-face.

That should do it.

Throw his own demands back at him.

Water dripped on the screen, but it remained dark.

The seconds ticked by.

Come on, damn you, answer!

Minutes passed.

No response.

She blinked against the rain.

Checked her watch.

Obviously he wasn't going to answer and she couldn't stand out here all night, bracing herself against the storm.

But his bike is here.

He must be somewhere.

Fine.

She eased around the deck, shouting his name, peering into the dark, shivering from the cold.

Where are you?

The surrounding boats undulated with the ripple of the water. Tall masts, spindly and skeletonlike, knifed upward to the roiling sky.

But all aboard the *Medusa* was quiet.

Circumnavigating the wet deck, she stepped carefully, bracing herself in case he was hiding, involved in a sick game, ready to pounce from some hiding place. Carefully, shoulders soaked, she made a full rotation.

Nothing.

Just the wind battering the boats, rain pattering the deck.

Was he in the dark cabin?

Asleep at this early hour?

Or lying in wait? The hairs on the back of her neck prickled upward, her pulse jumped, but she clamped down on her rising sense of panic. She hadn't come all this way for nothing. Now that her nerve was up she wanted to end it.

Setting her jaw, she started for the stairs to the dark cabin below.

One step.

The boat rocked.

Two.

She heard the mournful cry of some seabird and her skin crawled as she made her way lower, out of the wind and rain. With one hand in her pocket around the butt of the gun, she eased into the pitch-black cabin.

Her cell phone buzzed and she jumped.

Yanking it from her pocket, she saw Marilee's number:

Where are you?

Time was passing.

No time to respond. She hit the flashlight app, illuminating the small room with the weird gray light. She rotated slowly, running the beam over the familiar built-in couch, the galley. The boat creaking and rocking slightly, she tried to orient herself, her gaze piercing the nooks and crannies where he could be.

"Gideon," she called, her voice a whisper, every muscle in her body tense. "Gideon? Are you here?"

She waited.

Nothing.

She eased into the berth, shining her light, expecting him to lunge out of the darkness because that seemed to be the new kind of game he liked to play, to terrorize her.

"Gideon!" She yelled his name and saw a flash of light.

A small beam.

Pointed directly at her.

A dark figure barely silhouetted behind it.

Gasping, she ducked down, her heart in her throat. Nerves jangled, she cut the light on her phone. Fumbled in her coat pocket for the gun. Grabbed the pistol. Yanked it out.

Finger on the trigger, she aimed. Into darkness. The light disappeared. The flash no longer there.

Desperately, she twisted, looking into all the dark crevices, her gaze scraping every shadowy corner.

No sight of him.

No sound either.

No sign of the intruder.

Not the intruder; you're *the intruder! You never should have come here!*

Shit, shit, shit!

She'd seen a spark, like the flash from a gun's muzzle.

Why was there no blast? No sharp report or bullet whizzing past her head?

She trained the pistol toward the spot where she'd seen the figure.

Only then did she realize she'd caught sight of her own image, her own shadowy form holding not a gun but a phone, its flashlight app catching in the porthole and reflecting on the glass.

For the love of God, Brooke, you're jumping at shadows! Get an effin' grip! You're acting as if Gideon's out to do you physical harm when all he's done is threaten you psychologically. Yeah, he's been brutal with his mental torture, and there was that one fight that got physical, but remember, you *came here.* You *boarded his boat.* You *brought a gun. Did it ever cross your mind that maybe you're playing right into his hands?*

Still crouching, her nerves stretched tight as bowstrings, she rocked back on her heels and took several deep breaths. Her heart was pounding a desperate tattoo. Nervous sweat collected on her back.

She was freaking herself out. She'd been keyed up already and then the fight with Leah had hyped her up. But here, cowering on his sailboat in the middle of a storm, expecting him to leap out and what—slash her throat?—was crazy.

Pull yourself together.

And get the hell out. Coming here was a mistake.

She made her way up the stairs and to the deck, where the storm had abated, the wind dying, the rain a steady drizzle. What had she been thinking coming here—and bringing a gun? He was making her act like a lunatic, driving her crazy. She had to get a grip and just forget him, or if he kept ramping up the harassment, go to the police. Face the consequences.

Like a sane person.

She pocketed the stupid pistol, and her hand brushed against the surprise she'd brought Gideon, the dead rat she'd put in a Ziploc bag next to the bracelet, both of which she intended to—*Thud!*

He landed right in front of her.

Gasping, feet sliding on the wet deck, she scrambled backward as she stared at him, dressed in black—pants, jacket, gloves—still in a crouch, as if ready to spring.

"What the hell—?" She glanced upward and realized he'd been on the mast, hidden in the dark, and had probably been watching her the whole time.

He *was* a psycho.

"What're you doing here?" he demanded. His hair was plastered to his head, his skin shiny with rain.

Well, now she was in it. Time for the truth. "I came here to end it with you."

Even in the darkness she saw him cock a skeptical eyebrow.

"Really?" he mocked. "By coming to my home?"

"It was a mistake." She started for the gangway, but he blocked her path.

"Was it?"

"Yes. For God's sake, Gideon, it's over and you won't accept it. I found your damned cameras and the rat and the bracelet. For the love of God, I know you've been in my house, stalking me, okay?" she said, and rather than be intimidated she took a step toward him. "I'm tired of you playing your sick little games, all right? It's over. No more fake delivery guys and security guards, no more stealing my dog, no more leaving things in my house where you want me to find them!" She was angry, her pulse jumping.

"You love it."

"I hate it! And that's why I came here. To tell you to leave me and my family the hell alone. Texts and phone messages don't work," she said. "So I thought I'd do it face-to-face. Isn't that how you wanted it?"

"What I want," he said distinctly, "is you."

"Fuck that. What *I* want is for you to leave me alone."

"Liar," he accused, coming closer. Too close.

"It's over."

"It will never be over. You know that."

"Of course it will. Right here. Right now!"

"No," he countered. "One way or another, you and I, Brooke, we will be together. Forever. I will never let you go. Never."

"You're nuts!"

He actually smiled then, that crooked smile that once had seemed full of sexual promise and now was only evil. "You came here because you want me." Another step. "You're enjoying this."

"Bullshit!" She retrieved the bracelet and held it over the rail. "Don't you ever come near me or my family, even my damned dog, again!" She let the bobble dangle for a second before releasing it into the water. "No more!" She reached into her pocket and took out the nest of tiny cameras, some with wires still attached. "No more spying! No more fake pizza drivers and security guards." She shot her arm over the rail and dropped the spy equipment into the water. "Got it? And for God's sake, no more damned dead rats!" She reached into her pocket and withdrew the Ziploc bag. Inside the plastic was the lifeless rodent, tail wrapped around its curled body. "No more anything!" She dropped the rat in its plastic shroud over the side of the boat.

A gust of wind snatched at her hood, pulling it off. "I won't be terrorized by you, Gideon," she warned him and swept her burner cell from her pocket. "We. Are. Done." Her eyes scorched him in her fury. "You got it?" She warned, "If you don't, if you make one more call, step onto my porch, contact me in any way, I'm going to the police."

He actually laughed. "Don't think so." He'd moved closer now and she reached into her pocket one final time, her finger surrounding the butt of Neal's gun.

"And why not?" she asked, taking the bait.

He seemed smug. "Because, Brooke, I have evidence."

"Evidence?" What the hell was he talking about?

"That you've been stalking me."

"That *I've* been stalking *you*? No way. No one would believe that. Not after what you've done."

"What proof do you have?" he asked, and she glanced overboard where the rat, the cameras, and the bracelet were now presumably at the bottom of the bay.

When she didn't answer he said, "Yeah, too bad, eh?" and followed her gaze to the water.

Her heart turned to stone. She thought of Marilee in the shower, or her underwear, or naked in her room. Or of her and Neal making love. "You bastard."

His eyes sparked as he stepped closer. "Oh, more than what you're thinking," and the smugness of his expression was a warning.

"You don't know what I'm thinking."

"Don't I?" He was close now. "You're a fake, Brooke! You and your precious little postcard-perfect family," he mocked. "The perfect husband who never strayed; the teenager who's kept up her grades and athletics and never dabbled in alcohol, pot, and boys. The loving wife who's never so much as looked at another man, much less warmed his bed and begged for him to fuck her?"

She slapped him. Hard. The smack against his wet skin resounded in her ears.

"That's right, Brooke. Attack. Hit and kick and bite. Like before. You're such a hot little bitch." She reached back again, but he caught her wrist in his gloved hand and drew her close. "That's your problem, isn't it?" he said, almost in a snarl. "Good thing I've got pictures of our last fight. Of your attack. How you coldcocked me and drew blood."

"What?"

"Not only did I catch it all on camera, but I've got a witness. My neighbor on the next boat." He hitched his chin to the little sailboat where she'd seen the balding man with the pail of fish.

"No one would believe you!" she spat and tried to pull her hand from his.

His fingers were a manacle. Kept her bound.

"And just now, while you were snooping around the cabin of my boat, prowling around and trespassing. And with a weapon? A gun?" He made little tsking noises and she wilted inside. "I've got pictures

of that too. A video. Amazing what technology can do these days."
He yanked her even closer. "So don't be so sure of yourself. The police aren't going to buy it."

How diabolical was he? How depraved?

"I don't think you'd want to risk going to jail. What would Neal
think? Does he know? And what about pretty little Marilee? How
would she feel if her mother were behind bars? A second offense."

"What?" she whispered.

"Old records could come to light."

"I don't know what you're talking about," she lied, but fear grew
within. As little as she knew about him, he seemed privy to everything about her. She glanced to the docks, hoping to see someone,
anyone, out, but the vessels moored to their berths were, for the
most part, dark. No one had ventured out in the storm.

"You haven't talked to Keith Turnquist lately?"

No! Oh no! Immediately, he had her full attention again. He didn't
have to say anymore. She was shaking her head in disbelief. "That's
old history and sealed and—"

"And the truth, Brooke." To prove his point, he pulled her so close
his breath was warm against her face. Startled, she felt his hand on
her waist. What?

His free hand snaked into her pocket.

She tried to tear herself away.

Too late!

He came up with the gun.

"You should know better than to play with firearms."

He held the Beretta—*Neal's* Beretta—to her chest. Would he really
shoot her? Risk wounding himself? Dear Jesus, she had no idea.

"As long as there's a breath of life in my body, I will never let you
go," he vowed.

"Please, Gideon, if you ever loved me, please, just let me and my
family be."

"Love?" he repeated and his eyes, dark with obsession, bored into
hers. "Is that what you think this is?"

No, she knew better now! This *was* obsession. Power. Love had
nothing to do with it.

She had to get away.

Now!

She had to get off this boat and—

She threw herself backward, her feet slipping on the deck. Still he held on. They slammed against the wet rail, pain jarring through her body. "Help!" she yelled, no longer worried about the consequences as they banged into the rail again. He was crazy. Maybe willing to kill them both. "Help!"

"Shut up!" he yelled, his face twisted in rage. His visage demonic in the light from the security lamp. Still unsteady, he hauled back with the gun, intent on striking her. "Shut the fuck—"

She kicked. Hard. Connected with his shin. He yowled. Pain ricocheted up her leg. She tried again and he moved quickly, too quickly.

"If I can't have you," he growled, his face a mask of determination, "no one can!"

She didn't think, just threw herself backward.

Over the rail.

He didn't let go.

Struggling, they splashed into the frigid water of the bay.

As they hit the water, his grip loosened.

Desperately, she kicked. Away. Hard. Fast. Deeper into the cold, cold depths, twisting and flailing.

But he was right there. She saw his menacing form, silhouetted by the thin light of the security lamp. She started to swim away and then she caught a glimpse of it.

Falling between them.

The gun!

Sinking fast.

Bubbles swirled around them, but she saw the dark glint and swam for it. Closer to him. Deeper.

Where, where, where was it?

Still sinking.

Frantic, she propelled herself downward.

Touched the barrel as it sank.

Felt the swirl of water nearby.

Gideon!

He was so close.

Again, she dove deep, her lungs beginning to burn. She saw the Beretta as it reached the bottom. Made a swing for it. Juggled it as it slipped through her fingers. She pirouetted through a cascade of bubbles. Where was it? Where?

From the corner of her eye she saw Gideon reach for her.

Diving closer.

She kicked back, felt his hand graze her shoulder.

Find it! Find the damned gun!

She saw a glint in the surrounding detritus.

Shot forward, lungs on fire.

Come on!

Gideon clamped a hand on her arm.

She grasped frantically for the weapon with her free hand, scraping the muck.

The gun rotated, spiraled upward with a plume of silt.

She grabbed for it, fingers scraping metal, just as a strong hand grasped hers, grappling for the weapon. Bubbles released as her lungs began to scream for air, but she wouldn't let go, wouldn't let him win.

They struggled, the water churning around them, legs striking legs as they swirled together in this macabre water dance, the Beretta clasped between them.

Heart pumping, lungs ready to explode, she felt his fingers peeling hers away from the gun.

God, no!

She kicked as hard as she could and felt something rend within her, a tearing, as she held tight to the Beretta, her index finger slipping through the trigger guard.

His finger tightened over hers as they fought.

The gun fired.

Her body jerked.

The gun sank.

Gideon lost his grip.

His fingers fell away.

His face turned ashen, a ghastly mask.

Drifting backward, he stared at her, his eyes round and disbelieving.

Blood clouded the water between them.

Brooke didn't wait.

Through the pain and horror, she kicked like hell, shooting upward, her lungs about to burst.

Swim!

Kick!

Get the hell out of here!

She focused on the security lamp, an orb growing brighter as she swam upward.

She broke the surface.

Gulped air frantically.

Gasping, choking, searching the black water.

Where was he? Where?

She spun, searching the darkness. Expecting to see him rise to the surface near her and drag her down.

Don't wait. Just get the hell out of here! Now!

Still dragging in precious air, she began to swim to the shore, toward the boat ramp near the parking lot. As she dragged herself onto the sloped asphalt of the ramp, she took one last look back to the black, undulating water.

No sign of another person in the depths.

She closed her eyes, felt tears mingle with the rain running down her face, then pushed herself to her feet.

She didn't know if he was dead or alive.

Either way she prayed she would never see him again.

Never.

PART TWO

CHAPTER 28

Piper Island, Oregon
Now

Walking into Nana's cabin on Piper Island was like stepping back in time. The stone fireplace, pine-paneled walls, and wood floors were battered but familiar, the scent of lemon from its recent cleaning detectable. The cabin was on the eastern shore of the island, facing the bay and the fishing village of Marwood on the shoreline of the mainland. Piper Island and the mainland were connected only by a ferry that shuttled vehicles across the narrowest stretch of water. On the other side of the island the Pacific Ocean stretched to the horizon, but here the view was of the forests climbing up steep hills beyond the small town.

Neal pocketed his keys as he followed Brooke inside. "Look at this place. It hasn't changed since when? Maybe, if I'm guessing, the seventies. A long time before I was in the picture," he said as he set down his roller bag and duffel in the entry hall near the base of the stairs. "Or earlier than the seventies." She, too, eyed the cast-off furniture that they'd added to Nana's worn leather over the years.

"I can't remember the last time I was here," he said.

Brooke could.

It had been the summer before last, sunlight had bounced off the waves, the air had been fresh and exhilarating, the sand warm against her bare feet, the cabin—this cottage—warm and inviting.

Now, outside, the sky was gray and threatening, the rumble of the sea audible, the wind gusting cold, promising snow.

Neal whistled to Shep and the dog streaked inside to explore.

"We came four years ago," she reminded him. "Summer. Marilee had to give up that gymnastics camp to come."

"Oh, right." Neal nodded and walked into the short hallway to fiddle with the thermostat. "Too long."

With a rumble, the old furnace engaged.

While Neal unpacked the car, she put things away. "What time is Marilee getting in?" he asked, setting one of the two coolers they'd brought from Seattle on the counter that separated the kitchen from the living area.

They'd been over this before, but Neal had been distracted lately, a new, "big" case that required him to work late nights and some weekends. "Later," she reminded him. Marilee, now a student at St. Bernadette's, a private school in San Diego, was flying into Portland and had assured her parents that she had a ride to the island.

"We could've picked her up at the airport."

"I know. Or she could have flown to Seattle and come down here with us, except you had us leave before the crack of dawn."

"We beat the traffic, didn't we?" he asked. "And made the first ferry."

She couldn't argue. They'd left at four a.m., pushed the speed limit in their Honda CR-V, the replacement for the Explorer, which hadn't been totaled but never drove quite the same after the accident with Gustafson. The insurance company had handled the claims and, fortunately, Brooke had never heard from him again.

Now, it was still morning and Neal was grousing about their daughter living apart from them, a source of their continued discontent.

"Flying up here on her own was the way Marilee wanted it," Brooke reminded him. "Her choice."

"I know, but I don't like it."

"Me neither."

"Maybe sending her away was a mistake," Neal grumbled.

"We did not send her away. Moving out was Marilee's choice."

"And she's too damned young to make those choices."

Amen, Brooke thought, *but here we are*.

Neal headed back to the car for another load.

Allowing Marilee to go to school in Southern California had been a tough decision, one she'd begged for.

After the whole Nick Paszek debacle, Marilee's pregnancy scare, and grades that had tumbled, their daughter had gotten into vaping, alcohol, and marijuana. Marilee had declared she wanted to move out. Of course she wanted to live with Nick. Even though she was fifteen.

"That's ridiculous!" Neal had told their girl, Brooke standing at his side.

Nick's parents too were horrified and both families had ended up blaming the other. "She's going to get pregnant for real," Brooke had told her husband.

"Jesus. She's just a kid."

"I know, but she thinks she's in love." They shared a glance, each remembering their own circumstances.

"You were older," Neal said to the nonverbal argument.

"So were you."

"Then what do you want to do?" Neal had said, and for the first time in their marriage he seemed to be at a loss, unable to plot a course of action.

"Boarding school." Her answer was automatic. One she'd heard about growing up. "St. Bernadette's. It's far. Outskirts of San Diego. Where my grandmother went."

"I don't know," he'd said, but Marilee had overheard the conversation from the stairs and burst into tears. Only after Nick had broken up with her the next week had she agreed. In fact, she was eager, then, to leave Allsworth High School, Seattle, and her parents. She had embraced the idea of moving as far away as possible. Southern California had seemed ideal.

At least that was what Marilee had claimed.

In reality, things hadn't gone that smoothly.

But after the first two weeks of tears during FaceTime, Marilee seemed to be thriving. In their phone and video calls Marilee had evolved from angry defiance to sad-eyed loneliness, then, more recently, newfound confidence. She'd made friends, loved the weather, and complained about the teachers but had regained her interest in school.

She had opted not to come home for Thanksgiving but had reluctantly acquiesced for Christmas break. Neal was the one to suggest they spend the vacation here on the island, and the idea was that the cabin was a neutral zone, where they'd all gotten along, and not the war zone that their Seattle home had become.

And it was two hundred miles away from Nick.

Which was a good thing, at least in Brooke's opinion. Nick had graduated, moved out of his parents' home, and now shared an apartment with two roommates. Still, Brooke knew how easily old sparks could rekindle.

Brooke carried Shep's bag with his leash and dog food into the laundry alcove, a small space that doubled as a kennel and sometimes office when Neal opened his laptop on the counter and dragged in a chair from the dining room.

"I don't suppose there's any way we can talk her into moving back home," Neal said, continuing the conversation.

"We tried. Remember? And that kind of defeats the purpose."

"I know. But she's only got a couple of years of high school left. The only time she has to live with us as a kid. For us to be a family."

"You can bring it up again," Brooke said, fighting her own urge to bring her daughter home. She too missed Marilee terribly and felt the years of her girlhood slipping by rapidly. "But I don't think it's gonna fly."

"So, what about you? Can you try to talk to her?"

As if she never had. She replied, "I'll follow your lead this time. You know I'm not crazy about the whole boarding school thing, but we agreed to give it a try for a year. It's only been a couple of months."

"Feels like a lot longer," he said and she nodded.

Their home in Seattle, the house she'd loved forever, had become quiet, almost tomblike without their daughter's chatter and whirl of activity. Marilee's empty room, with its neatly made bed, organized bookshelves, clean desk, and dark computer, was a place where Brooke had shed more than a few tears. Alone. Burying her face into the stuffed bunny that had once been Marilee's favorite.

Because they had empty nested early, if hopefully just temporarily, Brooke had thrown herself into her new job, another sales position. After a few months of looking, she had taken Neal's advice and landed an outside sales position with Clayton Electronics, where she'd had to learn the ins and outs of security equipment, including parts and installation. She couldn't help but find it ironic that she was selling the very security equipment that had been attached to her Ford Explorer. In fact she had her smallest sample case tucked into the compartment under the passenger seat of her Honda.

The new job helped keep her busy, but it didn't fill the emptiness that plagued her.

Brooke tried to remind herself that wasn't so, that Marilee was alive and well in San Diego, that they were lucky, unlike Penelope Williams's parents who, to this day, had no idea what had happened to their daughter. Runaway? Kidnap victim? Who knew. The case had gone ice cold.

Brooke reminded herself that she and Neal were fortunate.

So maybe it was best if they all met here.

Despite the fact that this cabin had its own worrisome ghosts—Nana and Mama, even her father. And of course, Gideon.

As Neal carried the bags upstairs, Shep whined at the back door off the living room. He shot across the porch and through the tall grass of the backyard to startle a couple of crows that had been perched on the rocks of the firepit. They flew into the surrounding trees, cawing their displeasure.

The dog nosed around the woodshed before trotting back inside. "Remember this place?" Shep too had been here when she and Gideon had visited.

Gideon.

The last time she'd seen him was that horrid night at the marina, when they both had nearly drowned. She'd dragged herself up the boat ramp, then run to her car. Shaken, shivering, still psyched out, she'd made it to her Explorer and told herself it didn't matter if he lived or died.

Call 9-1-1!

You have to call 9-1-1!

Fingers trembling, teeth chattering, she'd fumbled for her phone, still in her jeans' pocket, and started to make the call, but of course it was waterlogged. Wouldn't turn on. Crap, crap, crap! She decided to run to the nearest boat where lights were glowing behind closed curtains. She'd let the chips fall where they may.

Then his head popped out of the water.

She gasped, dropped her phone, and watched horror-struck. In the security lamp's glow, he swam to a ladder and pulled himself up the rungs to the dock.

She started the engine.

He turned, focused on her, and seemingly dazed or wounded or both, lumbered along the dock toward the parking lot.

"No!"

She tromped on the accelerator. The Explorer lurched forward in a spray of gravel and water. She drove crazily, shaking and fighting tears. She had to go to the police. She had to confess to Neal. She had to admit everything to Marilee. To everyone.

She found herself sobbing as she reached her health club.

Pull yourself together!

She swiped at her eyes.

She forced her jaw to keep from chattering.

She told herself to be mentally tough.

And then she noticed the blood.

Her blood.

Smeared on the driver's seat.

But she wasn't wounded. No bullet had struck her.

She remembered the rending, not just of her body but of her soul.

The baby.

Shivering, Brooke threw on her coat and made her way into the locker room of the club, signing in as usual, ignoring the concerned look of the girl of about eighteen who watched her from behind the desk.

Then she half ran to the showers, where she peeled off her wet clothes. As she stripped off her water-soaked jeans, she located the source of the blood, a thick red river running down her legs.

She stifled tears in the shower, the noise of the spray muffling her sobs, the hot water needle-sharp against her skin and steam rising around her in a cloud. Deep inside she felt a loss and an unexpected despair. Fighting the heartache, she'd closed her eyes, reminding herself that this was for the best. With a steely resolve, she rinsed off the seawater, lathered off the blood, and washed Gideon Ross from her life forever.

Driving home later, she'd been surprised at the pang of bereavement she experienced for a baby who'd barely been conceived. How many years had she wanted another child? But not this way. Still, there was some sorrow—even grief—for the baby that never was. She carried the thought of that loss with her in the next few days, when she drove past the marina and noticed that the *Medusa* was no longer moored in her berth. She called the marina and was told that the owner of the sailboat had left in the middle of the night, the woman on the other end of the connection irritated because there was money owed.

But when she inquired if there was a forwarding address for Gideon Ross, the woman seemed confused for a second, asking, "Who?" Then, before Brooke could explain further, the woman had clammed up, muttering something about privacy before disconnecting.

Brooke had double-checked with the local hospitals, asking if he'd been admitted for care. The answer had always been the same: *We have no patient registered under the name of Gideon Ross.*

Hadn't he been wounded?

Surely all that blood in the water hadn't been from her miscarriage . . .

But he hadn't been admitted to a hospital, nor had there been any mention of Gideon Ross or some unidentified man in the newspapers.

And so she'd let it go.

Told herself that he'd somehow survived to sail out of Elliott Bay and her life.

"Brooke?" Neal's voice broke into her thoughts. "A little help?" He had dropped the second cooler onto the counter and was staring at her.

"Oh, right."

"You looked a million miles away."

"I was just thinking about Nana and Mom," she said, which wasn't a total lie. "How we used to come here at Christmas." She began unloading the coolers.

"With Leah," he reminded her.

"Right. With Leah." She ignored the concern in his eyes. That she and her sister were still estranged wasn't a surprise.

"Maybe you should do something about that."

"Maybe I will."

"It's Christmas," he reminded her.

"In a few days." She opened the refrigerator and began filling it. "So what are you saying, that I should call her? Because it's Christmas?"

"Wouldn't hurt."

"I've tried, remember?"

"What's the old saying, 'If at first you don't succeed, try, try again'?"

"Spare me the antiquated pat phrases," she said sarcastically as she slid a carton of eggs onto a shelf in the fridge. Then she paused to meet his gaze. "You're really pushing this."

He was handing her a quart of milk. "'Tis the season, but it's up to you."

"Then I'll handle it my way." She was more than a little irritated but didn't want to fight. "I'll finish here," she said, motioning to the kitchen, "then I think I'll take Shep to the beach so we can stretch our legs." She glanced out the window to the gray day. "Before the storm."

"It's cold."

"I know." She sent him a reproachful look. "I can handle it."

"Right." He nodded and headed for the front door. "I'll finish unloading the car."

She unpacked the rest of the groceries and went to the alcove off the kitchen that they'd dedicated as Shep's when he was just a puppy. A leash hung on the inside of the door and toys and blankets were stuffed into a basket on a shelf. She located his water dish and filled it, leaving it in its usual spot on the floor near the stacked washer and dryer.

"No?" she asked when he ignored the chance to drink. "Suit yourself." She slipped on running shoes and a windbreaker, then scraped her hair back into a loose ponytail. "Let's go." Together, they took off through the back door, jogging across the clearing and cutting through the woods along a trail that ran from the east side of the island, where the cabin was located, to the western shore.

A tinge of exhilaration flowed through her as she circumvented the wet branches of fir trees and the rocks and roots buckling the path. Within minutes the trees gave way to the dunes, where beach grass shivered in the wind. From the sandy crest she viewed the ocean, vast and wide, gray as the sky, white caps roiling as huge waves pounded the shore.

She'd forgotten how much she loved it here: the salt air, the wild sea, and the dull roar. All so exhilarating. She'd missed it. More than she'd imagined.

"Come on," she said to the dog, and together they raced to the shoreline and took off to the south. Shep shot ahead of her, streaking near the water's edge as she jogged behind him.

How many times had she run on this beach, playing tag with the waves, chasing her sister and splashing in the icy water, dodging the icy waves as Nana and Mama had followed after? Even her father, his khakis pushed up to his knees, was here a few times, but of course, she thought, kicking at a bit of crab shell that had washed onto the shore, Douglas Fletcher's last visit to this sandy stretch of beach was a lifetime ago.

This had been her summer home, a place of solace, and she decided it was time she'd returned, forgot about her few hours with Gideon here and reclaimed her connection to Piper Island. Neal had pressed her to make the trip.

She'd been reluctant to return. Hadn't wanted to face the memories that lingered. She'd tried to talk Neal out of the trip, but he'd been adamant, surprising her.

"Come on," Neal had insisted as they'd watched rain drizzle down the window of their home just last week. "We haven't been there in years and it will be good for us to reconnect with Marilee."

She hadn't put up too much of an argument even though she'd had more than her share of trepidations. There were just too many memories here, good and bad, too many ghosts from the past. And yet she was opposed to selling the cabin on the island that Nana and her mother had loved.

That *she* had once loved.

"It'll be fun. An adventure." He'd slung his arm around her shoulders and squeezed. "God knows we need one." Then he'd gotten serious. "It'll be good, Brooke."

She hadn't been convinced. "I have a bad feeling about this," she'd admitted as they'd left Seattle in what seemed the middle of the night. The entire trip down in the predawn hours, she'd been anxious, no doubt because the last time she was here it was with Gideon. She'd thought his ghost would haunt the place, but she'd been wrong. She had a connection here to this island, and it wasn't one that could be destroyed by one fanciful trip with a man she hoped to forget.

As she ran, ever faster, her blood pumping, she told herself it was time to cleanse.

Time to wash away the past and her nightmares of Gideon.

Time to look to the future for their small family to heal. She and Neal still weren't as in love as they once were, but at least Jennifer Adkins was in the past. Brooke had found out that she had left the firm and moved to Boise. If she and Neal had been intimate, it appeared to be over.

Just as Brooke's relationship with Gideon Ross was in the past.

Maybe the closeness, that unity Brooke had once felt with Neal, would never return. And maybe that was okay. They each had stepped over the vows of marriage, so it was likely those bonds would never be as strong as they once were.

She caught up with Shep at a tangled mass of seaweed and eased her speed. "Let's head back," she said and whistled to the dog before turning and heading north, the muscles of her legs beginning to protest. She glanced up at the few houses that faced the ocean, rarely occupied except in summer. And she thought she spied the trail up the dunes that led to "the cave," as she and Leah had dubbed it. It wasn't a real cave, just a ravine splitting the dunes where Scotch broom had grown into a canopy, leaving a space beneath where they could play—when they got along.

Shep followed her at a trot, then took off like a shot to startle a flock of shorebirds that scattered as he bounded to the water's edge.

Halfway back to the path leading to the cabin, she slowed to a walk.

A lonely gull was skimming the waves, crying plaintively over the thunder of the surf, and Shep had discovered a wet stick, black and sodden, which he carried in his mouth.

"Kinda gross," she told him over the crash of the waves. The sky was darkening with the promised storm. There had even been talk of snow, a rarity on the coast, especially at Christmas.

She felt the first icy drops of rain just as Shep, stick in mouth, came loping back.

"Let's go," she said, flipping up her hood and jogging across the wet sand to the path.

Shep ran ahead. By the time she came upon the cabin he had dropped his prize on the back porch, where he shook the rain from his coat and scratched at the door. "Hold on. You're a mess." But so was she.

The rain was turning to snow now, still gurgling in the gutters and soaking the ground, but the temperature was dropping fast.

She stepped inside, the cabin seeming still. She grabbed an old towel from a hook in the laundry room, then dried Shep's wet fur. "There ya go," she said as she straightened and threw the wet towel in the old laundry basket sitting on the dryer. "Neal?" she called and kicked off her sodden, sandy sneakers, leaving them near the back door. No answer. As she hung up her windbreaker, she noted that his parka wasn't on a hook. A glance outside the dining room window revealed that their SUV wasn't in the drive.

Odd.

He hadn't said anything about going out and where would he go?

She found her phone and texted him:

I'm back. Where are you?

When he didn't answer immediately Brooke said to the dog, "Just you and me, eh?"

As if in answer, a gust of wind rattled against the old windows.

The cabin felt suddenly empty and cold.

"Come on, I've got something for you," she told the dog and he followed her into the laundry room again. She rummaged in a cupboard and found a dog toy she'd spotted earlier, a once-orange crab, one eye missing, a claw hanging oddly because she'd sewn it back into place. "You used to love this—" she started; then her voice faded, eyes rounded.

"Oh Jesus!" She jumped back, dropping the toy and staring at it in disbelief.

Brooke's world shifted.

Her knees threatened to give out.

Wrapped tightly around the once-severed claw was the bracelet, red stones winking, tiny sailboat charm visible.

"No," she whispered, denial raging through her brain. "No, no, no!"

He couldn't have! He wouldn't have! But how . . . ?

Shep picked up on her distress and whimpered.

"Get a grip," she said aloud. "Get a damned grip!"

Heart thudding, she reached down and picked up the bracelet. Unwound it from the stuffed toy. She had no doubt who'd placed it here as she studied the little sailboat with the engraved date of her first meeting with Gideon.

Not the same piece of jewelry, she thought; it was too pristine, too shiny to have been somehow scavenged from the murky waters of Elliott Bay. But this bracelet was an exact replica, probably bought at the same shop at Pike Place Market in Seattle and engraved with the date by the same hands.

Her knees threatened to buckle.

Gideon had been *here*.

Inside this cabin.

Standing in the very spot where she stood now.

And he'd left her a little gift, a reminder.

His words during their desperate fight that last night came back to her, echoing through her mind:

One way or another, you and I, Brooke, we will be together. Forever. I will never let you go.

Never.

CHAPTER 29

"You sick fuck," she whispered to the empty cabin. With quivering fingers, she picked up the bit of jewelry with its tarnished sailboat and damning date.

When had he been here?

Months ago?

Yesterday?

She felt her heartbeat kick a little faster.

How long had he stayed?

Had he stayed here? Slept in their bed?

Don't do this, Brooke. Don't let your imagination run wild. He probably dove for it that very same night, sailed south, and left it here months, possibly a year ago. Maybe by now he wouldn't even remember doing it. If it was the original.

She snorted out loud.

Didn't believe her own rationale for a second.

Turning slowly, she looked around the kitchen, then stepped into the living room. She eyed every inch of the living room, with its built-in bookcases and battered, hand-me-down furniture. She imagined him walking through here, an apparition she'd never wanted to envision.

He'd known how to get inside of course. Because she'd shown him. On the weekend they'd come down here, she, still giddily in love or lust or whatever, had retrieved the hidden key from the spot where it always hung behind a crossbeam in the woodshed.

He'd seen her play with Shep, feed him, and stash his toys in the cupboard.

And all the while he'd taken note.

To use the information to haunt and terrorize her.

As she passed through the dining area, she imagined him possibly putting on his wet suit and diving down to retrieve the bracelet where she'd tossed it into the frigid waters of the marina. That was how laser-focused he was. But when he couldn't find it? He'd just had another made.

Who would do that?

Who would go that far?

Who would then come down here and break into the cabin and stash the bracelet here, where it might not be found for years, if ever?

A man obsessed.

She shivered, cold from the inside out.

That was just plain crazy.

What if she hadn't been the one to find the bracelet? What if Neal or Marilee had discovered it? They would have recognized it in a heartbeat, remembered finding it on Shep's collar the day he'd disappeared for a while.

And yet Gideon had left it for her, a brutal reminder.

She found herself still clutching the bracelet so tightly the beads left impressions in her palm.

She had to get rid of it.

She heard the front door open and quickly slipped into the kitchen and laundry room.

"Brooke?" Neal called.

"In here," she yelled back.

Quickly, she shoved the bracelet along with the stuffed toy back into the cabinet. She would get rid of the bit of jewelry permanently, throw it into the sea or bury it deep in the sand on the beach when she had the chance. Forcing a smile, she stepped into the kitchen while Shep bounded across the dining area and wiggled wildly.

"You're doing laundry?" he asked, scratching the dog's ears before walking into the kitchen and dropping a small bag on the counter.

"Checking to see that we had detergent," she lied, then gestured to her wet, sandy running pants. "We're about out."

"Damn." He snapped his fingers. "I was just at the store, almost home when I got your text."

"You went to the store?"

"Yeah, while you were out with Shep the lights flickered a couple of times. I checked the flashlights, all dead. So I ran to the store to get some batteries. While I was there I picked up a quart of eggnog, because it's the holidays and all. Didn't think about laundry soap. Sorry. The trip took longer than I thought because I left my wallet there, so I had to turn around to go back to retrieve it. I thought I'd be home before you, but . . . guess not."

"Doesn't matter, but . . . eggnog, really?" she asked, surprised. She'd never known him to pick up anything that wasn't on a list. At least not recently.

"Yeah," he was saying. "I saw it in the dairy case and thought, why the hell not?" He grinned, and in a flash she remembered other holidays, usually parties where they would sip eggnog laced with rum or brandy and topped with a dash of cinnamon.

"Why the hell not," she repeated, puzzled. "Okay, sure. But later, okay? I need to shower and unpack and settle in."

"Take your time." He was peeling off his jacket. "I'll see if there are any Christmas decorations around."

"Should be—somewhere," she said, curious about his enthusiasm, his newfound Christmas spirit. It was odd, but better than workaholic Neal who was worried about his growing business, or disappearing Neal who spent endless hours at the golf course. "I'll be down soon."

It was a lie.

She was still freaked out at finding the bracelet.

The words that she'd tried so hard to forget, returned:

One way or another, you and I, Brooke, we will be together. Forever. I will never let you go.

Never.

She didn't bother unpacking.

After stripping off her wet clothes she gave herself a quick sponge bath while trying to convince herself that Gideon hadn't been here recently. Certainly the bracelet had been left months ago, and by now he'd long forgotten about her. In the past year he'd had to have found some other woman to obsess over.

She scraped her hair away from her face, snapping it back in a ponytail, and didn't bother with makeup. Rather than unpack, she found a pair of yoga pants and a sweater in her suitcase, threw them on, then flipped on her laptop. Wi-Fi on the island was iffy at best, and with the storm the connection kept failing. The wind howled outside, and as she took a look outside, she noted that the rain had given way to a steady snowfall. Still, she had to find out if Gideon had resurfaced somewhere. "Come on, come on," she muttered, biting her lip as she searched the Internet.

She scoured websites for any information she could find on Gideon Ross and sailboats named the *Medusa*. She searched local Oregon newspaper websites, along with those in Seattle. In the back of her mind she knew she was grasping at straws. She would find little information on the man she knew as Gideon Ross, but she couldn't help herself. She had to try. She had to do *something*.

Then there was the simple fact that his name, common enough to be confused with so many others, could be an alias. That could account for a lot of things, questions that had no answers. Maybe he'd been seen at a hospital the night of their near-death struggle under a different name. Hadn't the woman at the marina been confused and stopped talking when she'd mentioned Gideon Ross? What if—no, she'd seen his driver's license. She was letting her wild imagination get the better of her and that was what he'd hoped to do by leaving the bracelet: to remind her. To never let her forget. To mess with her mind.

Don't let him!

In those weeks that she'd been seeing him, she hadn't cared about his past and had thought any mystery surrounding him was all the more intriguing.

"Idiot," she muttered under her breath.

After their last brutal struggle, she'd hoped she'd never hear from him again.

No such luck.

Now she prayed that this reminder was the last.

And now she knew for certain that he hadn't died that night. Even though she'd seen him haul himself out of the water, she'd wondered if he'd survived his wounds or bled out later. There had been so much blood.

Her only confirmation that he'd survived had been the fact that he'd sailed out of Seattle. She also hadn't trusted the woman she'd talked to at the marina. She was too anxious to get off the phone. Brooke had double- and triple-checked that Gideon hadn't returned. She'd driven by the marina several times and taken note that the *Medusa* had not returned to her berth, or any other one that Brooke had noticed. Also, she hadn't found any death notices, no hospitalizations she'd unearthed, no police reports posted. She'd checked for what seemed weeks on end and finally accepted that he'd left, that he was out of her life.

Until now.

A chill ran down her spine just knowing he'd been here, had walked down these hallways. Possibly he'd been in this bedroom. On her bed. Fantasizing and—

"Stop it!" she growled under her breath. Gideon loved mind games and she was letting him get to her, falling right into his trap.

The lights flickered and she glanced around the pine walls nervously.

Great.

The last thing they needed was to lose power. The last!

Checking her watch, she realized that nearly two hours had passed. She closed down her laptop, preserving its battery life.

The house was quiet aside from the storm outside and the quiet hum of the old furnace. She didn't hear Neal downstairs.

Weird. She'd heard signs of life earlier, the creak of his footsteps on the stairs, his off-key whistling, and Shep's claws on the old hardwood.

But as she opened the bedroom door, she sensed she was alone.

"Neal?" she said, the scent of coffee reaching her as she padded barefoot downstairs. She reached the archway to the living room and stopped short. "What the hell?"

While she'd been upstairs Neal had put up some Christmas lights around the window, strung another set over the Christmas tree, such as it was, a little artificial pine that made Charlie Brown's look like it belonged in Rockefeller Center. And he'd found the crèche. The Nativity scene with its miniature creatures sat on the mantel. Except something was wrong. Baby Jesus, who usually appeared on Christmas Eve, was already in his manger—a common mistake in Nana's opinion—but there was no Joseph. Mary was in the stable, shepherds and animals were all situated around them, the Magi farther away. Even the perennially broken angel was in her spot over the stable's roof.

The back door opened with a gust of cold air and Neal, wearing his parka and heavy work gloves, deposited a basket of firewood on the hearth. "Hey!" he said. "Thought you'd died up there." He hitched his chin toward the ceiling.

"What on earth are you doing?" She motioned to the decorations he'd arranged, all old, some cracked, all filled with memories. Dusty boxes lay open and she recognized a string of oversize bulbs and ancient glass decorations that Nana's mother had purchased long ago at a sale in a Woolworth's in a previous century. "I didn't even know we still had these."

"Rescued them from the attic."

"Really?"

"Um-hmm." He smiled, pleased with himself. "I figured we'll have a retro Christmas! Do you know there's an old portable stereo up there and some LPs from fifty-sixty years ago?"

"Probably longer," she said, remembering her grandmother with a mug of hot chocolate laced with peppermint schnapps in hand as she decorated the forlorn little tree while singing along with the recordings of "White Christmas," "Rockin' Around the Christmas Tree," and a host of other favorites.

Brooke recalled those Christmases past with Leah, Mom, Nana, and Nana's lazy cat, Tabitha. They'd spent many Christmas vacations on the island, weathering winter storms, dealing with power outages, and even cooking chili and cornbread in the massive fireplace once when they'd lost power. She'd been six or seven the last time she'd seen snow on the island, a rare occurrence.

As a child she'd been thrilled by the snow; she and Leah had built a snowman that listed far to one side. They'd created snow angels in the small open area off the deck. They'd been freezing cold, ice clumps hanging on their matching wool caps and gloves, which Nana had knitted for them.

Those thoughts touched a part of her that she'd pushed down deep, stirring happier memories of a childhood that had been partially tragic but also a little magical. As taciturn as Mom had been at home when they were in school, here on the island she'd let them run free. Brooke and Leah were allowed to explore the island with few restrictions and they'd felt a freedom and connection to the wildness of nature that few children, including Brooke's own daughter, had experienced.

And now?

What about this Christmas?

She was "celebrating," if that was the correct word with a husband who had become a stranger and a daughter who, at "almost sixteen" thought she was an adult.

"So where's Joseph?" she asked, touching the edge of the mantel where the ceramic characters were displayed. "We're missing a key player here."

Neal followed her gaze and lifted a shoulder. "I know. All of the other figurines were wrapped in plastic, but Joseph has left the building." He paused, then said, "Maybe he realized that his wife wasn't faithful and just took off."

Did his eyes darken just a tad? A silent accusation? Or just a bad joke?

She felt the muscles of her neck tense but managed a half smile. "That's sacrilegious."

"Since when do you care?" Again, he seemed more serious than the conversation warranted.

"I just think it's a little odd." Was there something more to his words or was she just overreacting because her nerves were frayed, her emotions strung out from finding the bracelet?

"Things sometimes get lost," he said as he dusted slivers of wood from his gloves.

Once more the underlying meaning. "We are talking about this, right?" she said, touching the mantel above which the crèche was displayed.

"What else?"

"I don't know, but it seems like you're saying something more here."

A beat.

"Something metaphorical," she clarified. If they were going to have this discussion, it may as well be now. Before Marilee arrived.

Another bit of hesitation. Then he shook his head. "No."

She folded her arms over her chest and stared at him. "This"—she motioned with one hand to include the entire house—"the decorating, the whole getting into the Christmas spirit, is so not you."

"Maybe that's part of the problem," he said.

"The problem?"

"*Our* problem."

"Oh. So now we *are* talking about something else?"

The intensity in his expression softened a bit. "Maybe we—both of us—have lost our ability to have a little fun."

That's what this is about?

"What do you mean?" she asked but remembered how the two of them had once enjoyed being together. Simple things were a part of their lives: playing cards or video games or drinking cheap wine and beer with old friends who seemed to have disappeared over the years.

Once all-encompassing and filled with expectation, the holiday "season" had slowly eroded to a company party, maybe an open house, and a small celebration with their tiny family on the big day. No midnight mass, no caroling, no eggnog drinks by the fire, no hiding presents or playing Santa Claus, no feeling of eager anticipation as the holidays approached.

He raised his eyebrows, daring her to argue, but she couldn't.

"Okay," she said, trying to get into the spirit and tamp down her anxiety about Gideon Ross. She was here, now, with Neal, waiting for Marilee, hoping to mend fences and strengthen their little family. She couldn't let anything get in the way. "Okay, I'm in! Retro Christmas it is."

"Good!" One side of Neal's mouth lifted. "Let's get started. I'll be right back." He picked up a second basket and headed for the door. She watched through the window as the dog followed him to the woodshed that angled off the porch.

Relax, she told herself. Everything was going to be fine. Despite finding the bracelet. If Neal was more into the holidays and the family thing this year, that was good, right? Odd, yes, but good. She poured herself a cup of coffee, considered adding a shot of booze if she could find one, and glanced at the woodshed through the windows. The shed's plank door was hanging open, the light inside on, but Neal wasn't visible near the stack of dry cordwood.

No big deal, except that Shep was standing at the edge of the porch, ears cocked, looking behind the door expectantly. His tail wagged slowly, brown fur ruffling with a gust of wind.

Again, not all that odd.

She took a sip, her gaze glued to the window.

Soon Neal hurried from around the door and stuffed something—his phone?—into his jacket pocket. He paused to slip on his gloves before stepping inside to take up the axe again.

So what? He took a call. But why hide behind the screen of the door?

He didn't hide, that's just where he was when the call came in. For the love of God, don't go all hypersuspicious.

Her cell phone buzzed and she swept it from her pocket.

Marilee's number and smiling face, a picture taken her freshman year at Allsworth High School, flashed onto the screen.

Brooke braced herself, expecting her daughter to try to bag out. No way. She wasn't going to let her daughter weasel out of coming to the island. They'd already had the discussion two days earlier when Marilee had called with different plans.

"It's just such a hassle getting to the island from here," she'd complained, "and Wes really wants me to go skiing at Mount Baldy." Wes Inskeep was Marilee's current boyfriend, a senior, and as far as Brooke knew they had only been dating for about six weeks.

"I thought you planned to go for a day after Christmas."

"Yeah, I know, but his parents were able to get the condo for the whole two weeks. You understand, don't you?" Marilee had wheedled. "It's our first Christmas as a couple."

Brooke had been bitterly disappointed, as had Neal. She hadn't said, *But you're only fifteen*, or *You don't know the family*. They'd already had that conversation. She and Neal hadn't budged. They'd insisted she come and spend the holidays with them as a family and grudgingly, over pained protests, Marilee had acquiesced, but now—

Brooke answered, "Hey, hi."

"Hi, Mom." Marilee sounded tense, no lift to her voice, and of course here the connection wasn't the best; the Wi-Fi signal on the island was always iffy and, with a storm brewing, it was even worse.

"What's up?"

"There's kind of a change of plan," Marilee said, a touch of rebellion in her voice.

Brooke didn't let the argument start. "You're coming," she said, forcing a smile into her voice. "Tonight. We discussed this."

"Of course I'm coming. Duh! I'm already in Portland. Just landed. What's wrong with you, Mom?"

"What, then?" Brooke asked as she heard the back door open. Shep galloped inside. Neal, carrying a basket of wood, followed.

"I've been talking to Aunt Leah."

Uh-oh. "O-kay."

"Yeah, well, you know we keep in contact."

Brooke did, though she wasn't privy to how close her sister and daughter were these days.

"Whatever's going on with you two, that's not on me. Right?" Marilee pointed out. "Whatever happened, I mean." Then more clearly, "Your fight with her."

"I know what you're talking about," Brooke said but tensed. Neal had dropped the basket onto the hearth and was obviously listening as he removed his gloves.

"I think it's stupid that you two don't talk," Marilee said.

Brooke didn't say anything. Couldn't argue the fact. Just set down her cup on the counter.

"Anyway, she called the other day, and I told her I was coming up to the island for Christmas, and she . . . Mom, she wants to come and spend the holidays with us."

CHAPTER 30

So there it was. Brooke hadn't talked to her sister in over a year, and the last words Leah had said to Brooke, "You'll never see me again," had rung true. So far. No phone calls. No email. No texts. Even the birthday card and last year's Christmas package had been returned, first by Leah herself, then by the post office, with a note that the mail couldn't be delivered as there was no forwarding address.

After a few tries Brooke had given up.

She'd known Leah was alive and presumably well, that she had some kind of long-distance relationship with Marilee, and she had never stepped between them. Brooke's erratic, love-hate relationship with Leah didn't include her daughter. And eventually, Brooke had thought, Leah would show up again, the old bad penny syndrome.

It seemed that time was now.

"Mom?" Marilee said, the sounds of the busy airport terminal audible in the background.

Brooke hadn't realized she'd been caught dumbstruck. "Oh, right. I guess so—"

Did the lights just flicker again?

"For crap's sake, Mom. She's your sister. You two need to work this out. And she said that last year you practically begged her to get together at Christmas."

That had been before she'd come to visit Seattle early to weasel money out of Neal. Brooke's suggestion was just to shine her sister on. Now she was using it as leverage with Marilee.

Marilee sighed audibly. "Do you know what I'd give for a sister or a brother?" she demanded. Brooke's fingers clenched over the phone. Her daughter had no idea how close she'd come to having a sibling, or a half sibling. If things had turned out differently, if she hadn't miscarried on the dock of the *Medusa*. Even now, she remembered the blood running down her legs in the shower at the gym.

"Christmas is in two days," she heard herself saying. "How would Leah even get here? Flights are booked and it would be nearly impossible—"

"That's on her," Marilee pointed out sensibly.

"I know, but—Leah should call me," Brooke said, watching as Neal closed the door and walked into the kitchen.

"Okay, right. That's the attitude, fight over who should call whom," Marilee was saying, unable to hide her disgust. "You know that sounds absolutely ridiculous? Like you're still in kindergarten? Phones work two ways, you know! And there's FaceTime and Zoom and oh, I give up. Geez, aren't you two, like, adults? Shouldn't you both just grow up? Do you even know that she finally divorced Sean or that she moved to San Francisco?"

"Of course I do, but—"

"Forget it! I've said what I had to. Look, I gotta go; I see my ride." And with that she disconnected.

Brooke clicked off, stunned by her daughter's attitude. Not yet sixteen and more adult than both Leah and her. At least on this issue. Marilee was right. After her first attempts to reach out to Leah, she'd barely kept up with her only sibling. The only real facts she knew about Leah were from bits and pieces she'd gleaned in conversations with her daughter.

"Marilee?" Neal surmised. "Don't tell me she's trying to weasel out of coming again."

"No. No." She shook her head. "She's already landed in Portland and should be here in a few hours. She was calling about Leah." There was a sudden flicker of some emotion in Neal's features— worry? Fear? Anxiety? It disappeared in a heartbeat as he pulled off his gloves and unzipped his jacket.

"What about her?" Kneeling at the fireplace, he stacked yellow, wadded newspaper, kindling, and a few large pieces of oak in the grate.

"She wants to come here. For Christmas."

He glanced over his shoulder. "Seriously? Like, in a couple of days?"

"I guess. I didn't know what to say." She filled him in on the sketchy details that Marilee had conveyed and added, "Marilee thinks I should call her."

"What do you think?"

There was the question. She took a sip of her tepid coffee and shrugged as he found a barbecue lighter on the mantel and tried to ignite the fire. The lighter just clicked, no spark visible.

"I don't know," she said, "but she's right. It's stupid that we don't even talk."

More clicking of the lighter and Neal gave up. "Don't suppose you still carry a lighter?" he asked.

"Not since I really quit smoking. But I think I saw matches in the junk drawer in the kitchen." She retrieved the old matchbook and handed it to Neal.

"Thanks." He struck a match and held it to the dry paper. Within seconds eager flames ate through the paper and reached the tinder-dry kindling.

"Oh shit." Neal reached into the firebox and opened the damper so that the smoke that was starting to seep into the living room was drawn up the chimney. "Damn. I always forget that," he said. "Now, what were you saying about Leah?"

"I don't have her number anymore." The last time she'd tried, on Leah's last birthday, the call didn't go through and she was informed by a robotic voice that there was "no new number."

"So you gave up?"

"Two-way street," she said, almost echoing her daughter's point.

He rocked back on his heels, the fire growing, flames licking upward and crackling. "Yeah, that argument doesn't hold a lot of water. Marilee obviously has no trouble keeping in touch. I'm sure she has Leah's phone number."

"I'm sure she does."

"Then?" he nudged.

What was that old saying about holding a grudge? Brooke mused. *That it's like poison? You drink it and hope it harms the other person?*

"I'm on it." Brooke texted her daughter, asking for Leah's number.

When she didn't get an immediate response she texted again, asking Marilee to pass the word to Leah that she was welcome.

Even if it was a bit of a lie.

"Done," she said, ignoring the uneasy feeling that had lingered ever since finding the bracelet. She spent the next few hours making certain the guest room was ready, that the sheets were clean, and the pillows plumped. Then she washed most of the dishes. Though she'd had the house cleaned by the local housekeeper before she and Neal arrived, Brooke didn't trust that all of the old cutlery, pots and pans, and dinnerware were dust- and/or spider-free.

More than that, she had to stay busy and keep her mind off the fact that at any second she could find some other reminder that Gideon had been in the cabin.

Eventually, Marilee texted both her parents to let them know that she'd been dropped off in Marwood on the other side of the bay and was boarding the ferry to the island.

"You're not coming with me?" Neal asked as he slid his arms into the sleeves of his parka and patted his jeans pockets to make certain he had his keys.

"No, you go. Have a few minutes alone with your daughter. I mean, how often does that happen?" Brooke said.

Neal's forehead wrinkled and the look he cast over his shoulder told her that he thought she was acting out of character.

She was.

But she had to.

She needed time alone.

"I thought you'd want to come," he said, stuffing a pair of gloves into his jacket pocket.

"I do, but I'll get everything ready," Brooke assured him. "Marilee will probably be starved. I'll get dinner together."

"Dinner can wait."

"It's already late," she argued. Why was he being so damned obstinate? She made waving gestures with her hand. "Just go! Go! She's already on the ferry."

"Okay." He gave her one more puzzled glance, then said to Shep, "Maybe you want to come along."

And then he was out the door, the retriever bounding ahead of him.

Brooke wasted no time.

She turned on the oven.

Then, the second she heard the engine of the Honda rev and tires crunch on the drive, she flew into the laundry room, retrieved the damned bracelet, and dashed outside. Using the flashlight app on her phone for illumination, she darted into the woods and along the path toward the sea. She didn't have time to get across the island and back again, so, for now, she raced to the bend in the path by the old stump. There, between the roots, she stuffed the horrid bit of jewelry in the same spot she'd hidden her diary as a child. Later, as a teen, she'd tucked in one of Nana's Mason jars for the cigarettes she'd swiped from her mother's pack, and the stash of weed she bought off the kid down the street, back in the days when she got high.

Now she pushed the sand off the rock that hid the hole, then jammed the bracelet into it, replaced the rock, and covered it with bits of leaves and small branches, before running back to the house, washing her hands, and trying to calm her jangled nerves.

The oven was hot and she slipped in a frozen potpie.

She tried to convince herself to calm down. With the bracelet out of the house, she could relax.

Or could she?

What if Gideon had left more little "surprises" for her?

What if she—or Neal—or even Marilee found something else he'd planted, some little reminder of the time they'd spent together?

Or Leah? What if her sister went nosing around?

She thought of the missing panties and bras she'd never found. Of the cameras and burner phone she'd chucked into the waters of the marina.

Or the gun.

Neal's pistol.

Her stomach turned to lead at the thought.

It had taken two weeks after she'd lost it in the dark water of Elliott Bay for Neal to ask about it. He'd been frantic, searching the house from top to bottom, accusing everyone. Brooke, Marilee, and Marilee's visiting friends had been scrutinized as potential thieves. Nick Paszek's name had come up more than once, to Marilee's horror.

When Brooke had suggested that maybe he'd moved it, he'd asked her if she were crazy, reminding her that the firearm was not only dangerous but an heirloom of sorts and he would not forget moving it. Panicked, he'd vowed he was going to report the loss to the police.

But if he'd notified anyone in law enforcement, she didn't know about it. No one from the department had phoned or stopped by and she'd let the subject drop.

He'd eventually quit mentioning it. End of story.

Yet she couldn't stop worrying as she opened one of the bags of salad she'd brought from Seattle.

What if Gideon had found the pistol? It probably had landed somewhere near the bracelet on the bottom of the bay. She'd always assumed the gun, along with the cameras, burner phone, and bracelet were lying at the bottom of Elliott Bay, or possibly drifting into the deeper waters of Puget Sound.

She'd never expected any of it to surface again, but she had learned not to underestimate Gideon. She flashed on the wet suit she'd seen hanging on a closet hook on his boat, the diving gear nearby.

"Shit." Her blood pressure was skyrocketing. *Don't go there*, she told herself.

Gideon had left one item to make a point, to remind her, to have the last word. Only one point. And he hadn't scraped the bracelet off the bottom of Elliott Bay, so the other items that had landed there were probably safe.

Probably.

She heard Shep barking and car doors closing as she tossed the salad, dumping the packet of dressing onto the greens.

Marilee breezed into the house. "Oh my God, it's cold here!" She shivered and raced to the fire to warm the backs of her legs.

"It's Christmas. Well, almost. It's supposed to be cold." Brooke couldn't help but grin at the sight of her daughter. She'd missed everything about her, including Marilee's sometimes caustic tongue and bad attitude.

"But not freezing!" Marilee protested. "And not *inside*. Dad says it's gonna snow." Marilee shot a worried look out the back window to the gray day beyond. "I didn't think it ever snowed here."

"Rarely but yeah. And wouldn't that be great? A white Christmas?"

"Ugh!" Marilee bit her lip. "I can't be trapped here. I told Wes I'd be back on the twenty-sixth."

"You just got here." Brooke walked into the living room and gave Marilee a hug while Shep was losing his mind, dancing and wiggling at her feet, crazy for her attention. "Don't worry about leaving yet."

"Says the woman who worries about everything." Then, to the dog, "Didn't I give you enough love in the car? Geez, Shep, chill!"

Brooke let out a short laugh and sniffed back emotional tears. "He's missed you." Then added, "I have too."

Brooke braced herself for a snarky reply, but Marilee's chin wobbled. "Me too," she said, and tears welled in her eyes.

At their feet Shep whined. "Yeah, and of course you too!" Marilee let go of her mother to sit on the hearth and rub the dog's shaggy coat. "Especially you!"

Brooke's heart melted. "You could come home, you know."

"Yeah," she said, still petting the dog. "I know, Mom. I've thought about it." She bit her lip. "I really wanted to when I first got there, was really homesick, you know? But I think . . . I think for now this is better." She wiped away her tears and smiled. "Maybe next year. But can we talk about it later? I just got done with finals and then had to get to the airport. I just want to crash."

"You're not hungry?"

"Got something at the airport."

"Did you get hold of Leah?"

Marilee nodded. "Yeah, she's coming. Didn't she text you?"

"No."

Marilee rolled her eyes. "Maybe it was supposed to be a surprise?" She thought for a second. "Yeah, maybe I wasn't supposed to say anything. Oops." She pulled a face, then shrugged. "My bad. Pretend you're surprised, okay? Like over the moon with shock."

"Will do."

Marilee headed upstairs to "her" room, the smallest bedroom of the three, little more than a nook built over the front porch, complete with a dormer and round window that faced the mainland. It was still furnished with the bunk beds that Brooke and Leah had shared growing up. Brooke had spent hours in the upper bunk or staring out the window or reading, while Leah, on the lower bed, had played with her Barbie dolls and plastic horses, caught in a world of her own.

And now Leah was coming back for Christmas, presumably to mend fences.

After over a year of ice-cold silence.

What could possibly go wrong?

CHAPTER 31

"Oh, wow. That's pathetic," Marilee said. She was eyeing the Christmas tree as Neal, on his knees, plugged in the lights. Only a few in the string actually winked on. "Can't we, like, have a real tree?" She looked from the little artificial pine to Brooke. "Like we did at home?" She gestured toward the fake tree with its sagging limbs. "I mean, look at it."

"It is sad," Brooke agreed and remembered the giant, festive firs they'd decorated in their home in Queen Anne. The tall trees had always been placed near the staircase so the highest branches could be reached from the upper landing and the star placed on the very top of the tree.

Marilee scoffed, "Mom, it's *beyond* sad. Way beyond."

"Okay, okay. I've heard enough about this from the both of you." Checking his watch, Neal said, "Maybe we can find a better one in a lot in Marwood. Maybe even at a discount, considering tomorrow's Christmas Eve. The next ferry leaves the island in twenty minutes. We can make it if we hurry!" He rolled to his feet and looked at his daughter. "You in?"

Marilee was still staring at the tired little tree. "Oh yeah, I'm in. I'm in big-time!"

Brooke held up one hand. "I've still got some chores here, you guys go."

"Really?" Neal said. "First you didn't want to come to the landing and now . . ."

"Come on, Dad!" Marilee was already stepping into her boots. "You said the ferry was gonna leave."

"Okay. Yeah. Let's go." But he sent one more I-don't-get-you look at Brooke.

He slid on his jacket again, Marilee her coat, and then they were off, dashing outside, where the ground was now covered with a thin layer of snow.

Brooke heard the CR-V's engine roar to life and checked the window, watching as Neal drove like a madman down the rutted drive, mud and water spraying from beneath the SUV's tires.

She checked her watch.

Neal and Marilee wouldn't be gone long—a twenty-minute ferry ride each way and an hour in town, a total of less than two hours—so she had to work fast.

This was her opportunity.

Enough time to search the house and make sure Gideon hadn't left her any more little surprises.

While Shep followed after her, she walked through the rooms on the first floor, her gaze scouring every inch of the cabin, every small crevice. She remembered those tiny cameras hidden throughout the house in Seattle, the little eyes that had silently watched and recorded her every move.

Could there be more here, sprinkled about the house, hidden in dark corners and tucked into unlikely niches?

She located a small flashlight in the kitchen junk drawer and jammed it into her pocket. In the upstairs hallway she drew down the ladder, then climbed into the attic.

"Déjà vu all over again," she told herself once she was in the cramped space and remembered her last foray into an attic, where she'd found all the spy equipment. Undeterred, she shone the tiny, bluish beam from the flashlight around the ancient joists and over the old, forgotten bins and crates. A few were broken, clothes and books and records from a previous era spilling out. Cobwebs glistened, and in one corner she discovered evidence of a rodent's nest, now abandoned. The layer of dust was disturbed of course; Neal had been rooting around up here, searching for the Christmas decorations. She spied candles and photographs, a broken desk chair and cracked ceramic lamps, pictures of relatives she couldn't remember and memorabilia from Nana's high school: diploma, cap and gown, and yearbook, all slowly disintegrating.

Her breath visible, Brooke riffled through the piles, scanned the floor and short walls, and studied the wide expanse where she had to crouch to inch forward. A small window was cut into the peak of the roofline and she checked, only to find it cracked, rain leaking inside, the wall beneath it soft where the water had penetrated and rotted the wood.

Worse yet, she discovered evidence of bat droppings along the wall and on the floor. "Great," she muttered as she searched an old file cabinet that held stacks of papers addressed to Mary Flannigan O'Hara. As if Nana would need the bank statements, letters, and reports any longer. Sooner rather than later she would have to clean this attic, as well as the basement.

Not today, she told herself. *Definitely not today*.

Something darted across her feet.

Brooke screamed. Dropped her flashlight. Scrabbled backward.

A mouse, disturbed and squeaking its surprise, scurried across the floor to duck into a knothole where the floorboards didn't quite meet.

"Crap!" Brooke's heart was beating wildly as she followed the little rodent with the beam from her small flashlight. She didn't see anything. Not even a pair of beady eyes reflecting in the harsh glow. Good. Nerves tight, she went back to work, crawling around the perimeter of the attic, searching for wires or cameras or microphones or transmitters or anything suspicious.

Nothing.

At least nothing that caught her eye in a first, quick appraisal.

Unless Neal already found the bugs when he was up here looking for the Christmas tree and lights.

Was that possible?

Would he?

"Don't even go there," she said, trying to tamp down her paranoia as time ticked by. Why would Gideon set up surveillance here, when he knew they rarely came to the island? It would have been a lot of work for very little if any reward.

She was jumping at shadows.

"Stop it!" she hissed so loudly that Shep, in the hallway below the open trapdoor, let out a worried "Woof."

"It's okay, boy," she called down to him, though of course it wasn't. It wasn't okay at all.

Yes, Gideon had been here. The bracelet was evidence enough of that. But most likely it was a one-time shot, a last-gasp effort to one-up her if and when she ever returned. She tried to force herself to relax.

It's over, she reminded herself as she gave another quick look at the belongings left and forgotten up here. She climbed down the ladder and pushed it back into the ceiling, the old springs groaning as the trapdoor snapped into place. She couldn't let Gideon's last desperate play get to her now. She refused to let his actions scrape her emotions raw. It was his final mind game and she wasn't going to play.

Still, she went outside, letting Shep explore the backyard while she hurried down the exterior stairwell to the basement, where a key was hidden in a rusting flowerpot. The door was heavy and swollen, but she shouldered it open and stepped into a space that was dank and musty. The light switch worked, though only one of two single bulbs gave off any illumination. She ran her flashlight's beam over shelves of gardening equipment, canning jars, old newspapers, and fishing gear. All the old possessions in the basement seemed as if they had been undisturbed for years. When she shone the light over the exposed beams of the ceiling and cracked cement of the walls, she didn't see anything out of the ordinary. Just a lot of junk that needed to be cleared out.

Satisfied that nothing was out of place, she locked the basement door behind her again.

She'd been on a fool's errand.

Finding the bracelet had unnerved her, made her a little crazy.

Brushing the cobwebs from her hair and clothes, she decided to shower before Neal and Marilee returned. Quickly, she stripped off her dusty sweater and smudged jeans, her sweat-soaked bra and panties. The old pipes groaned in protest as she stepped under the spray that was little more than a fine mist but at least washed the perspiration, grit, and fear from her body. *Pull it together*, she told herself and suddenly craved a cigarette, though she had completely given up the habit.

Ignoring her sudden need for a shot of nicotine, she lathered and shampooed, closing her eyes as she rinsed the suds from her body and hair. Her tense muscles finally relaxed and as she twisted off the taps, she let out a long breath, then reached for a towel.

Just as she spied a little dark spot above the showerhead. Barely visible from her height. It was nothing of course, she told herself as she toweled off, but she didn't remember seeing it in years past. *Don't go there*, she told herself firmly. *Do not!* But she couldn't help her heightened sense of worry. After slipping on a clean bra and panties, she found the old stool they'd used years before when Marilee needed a step up to use the sink or toilet. She positioned the stool inside the tub and stepped up, balancing herself against the shower curtain rail. Then she reached up and poked a finger in the hole. Was there a bit of glass there? The eye of a minuscule camera?

"No," she whispered, her skin prickling. Maybe it was an old wasp's nest or a hole made by some kind of burrowing insect or . . . She stepped off the stool suddenly, hurried back to her bedroom to retrieve the flashlight, and was back on the stool in an instant. Under the flashlight's beam there was a reflection, some minute lens, smaller than a pea. "Shit!" she said, her pulse jumping as she realized whoever had set the little camera in place could watch her naked and wet, as he could watch Neal or Marilee if they used this shower.

Gideon.

It had to be Gideon.

"You son of a—ooh!" So furious she nearly lost her balance and fell off the stool. She grabbed the hook where she'd hung her towel just as she heard the sound of an engine.

Neal and Marilee were returning.

And she couldn't tell them about the camera, wouldn't be able to explain it. Not that they would think she would have an explanation, but there would be questions—lots of questions—and possibly the police called in if Neal thought it necessary. No, no, no. Better they didn't know. At least not yet. But she couldn't leave it the way it was. Frantic, she found a bar of soap and shaved off bits of it with her fingernail. The shavings were soft and malleable and she pressed the opaque bits into the tiny cavity until the lens was completely covered.

A temporary solution, but it would have to do for now.

Shep gave off an excited bark just as she heard the front door open.

"Mom!" Marilee's voice carried up the stairs.

"In the bathroom," she yelled back. She quickly washed her hands, then pulled on a clean sweater and yoga pants.

"We got a tree!"

Was there a touch of excitement in Marilee's voice? Childlike merriment?

Brooke hoped so.

"Fabulous!" She forced a smile on her face and made her way downstairs to find her daughter grinning, finally caught up in the spirit of Christmas.

"A real one," Marilee said. "On sale!"

"Even better," Brooke said, though her insides were trembling and she couldn't forget that someone—Gideon, she believed—was spying on them.

Neal had already dragged the fir into the house and gone back outside. He now appeared with a dented Christmas tree stand and a rusted handsaw he'd found in the woodshed. "This close to the holiday the pickings were slim, but the salesman was thrilled for a sale. Let's see how this works." He sawed off a few of the lower branches and placed the little fir into the stand. Holding it in place, he said, "Tell me when it's straight."

Marilee giggled at how far the tree leaned to one side. "Uh—sorry—not yet, Dad." She gave him directions on adjusting the listing tree.

Fifteen minutes later Brooke had added water to the base of the tree stand and swept up the sawdust while Marilee had begun opening boxes of ornaments that seemed from the same era as the ones they'd found in the attic.

As Brooke eyed the glass balls and spherical shapes right out of the nineteen fifties or sixties, Neal said, "As I mentioned earlier 'retro.' Maybe even retro cool." He was adding wood to the fire, flames crackling.

"There wasn't anything more up-to-date?"

Neal shook his head. "Not unless you wanted Smurfs circa 1985 or trolls with matted hair."

Marilee was already stringing lights and decorating with a garland of fake popcorn and cranberries.

Nearly an hour later Neal surveyed their work from the kitchen. "Not exactly Currier and Ives."

"Currier and who?" Marilee asked.

"No one you'd know," he said.

"Didn't think so." Marilee stuffed the packaging in a front closet.

"It's better than what we had." He cast a glance at the smaller tree that Brooke had tucked into a corner near the dining table.

Brooke followed his gaze. "Mm. Just by a little." She held up her thumb and forefinger, almost touching to indicate a smidge. She was trying hard to find some exuberance, to forget about the ugly reminders of Gideon Ross, but she couldn't. Her skin crawled at the thought that he was out there watching.

"Brooke?"

She snapped back to the present and caught Neal's eye. "Did you say something?"

"Just asking about dinner."

"Oh. I thought we'd eat late, you know, a light dinner, because lunch wasn't that long ago." Truth be told, she hadn't even thought about their next meal.

"I'm not hungry," Marilee said, "but how about clam chowder tomorrow? For Christmas Eve?"

"Right." Another one of their yuletide traditions: Manhattan clam chowder and hot bread. The next day she and Neal would work together on a stuffed turkey with "all the fixins," as Nana had said their last Christmas here with her. Nana had been making a pumpkin pie, her Virginia Slim forgotten and burning in an ashtray on the counter. Her eyes had twinkled behind her glasses. "Who cares if it's all a Thanksgiving redux?" she'd asked while sliding a pecan pie into the oven. "We all love it! We'll have the best Christmas ever." They hadn't of course, not with Mama already having passed.

As for this year?

With Leah on her way?

Who could guess?

Without really thinking about it, Brooke crossed her fingers.

CHAPTER 32

The bakery smelled like heaven.

The aromas of fresh ground coffee, cinnamon, and baking bread melded together in the tiny shop, where booths lined the walls and a few tables were scattered in front of the glass case displaying pastries. A few other customers were seated with steaming cups and strewn newspapers or open laptops.

"I'd like a tall pumpkin spice latte," Brooke said to the barista. In pigtail buns, a nose ring, and a white apron emblazoned with *Gina's Bakery* in bright red embroidery, she asked, "For here?"

"No, no. To go. And a loaf of sourdough. No, wait, can you add half a dozen cinnamon rolls?"

"Sure," she said brightly. "You got it."

Brooke had been the first one up. She and Shep had left Neal and Marilee sleeping as they'd caught the first ferry into town for a few last-minute things. She'd already picked up fresh clams from the fish market located next to the bait store at the marina and then made her way past empty buildings, a few secondhand shops, a local realty company, and the two 1950s-era motels. There were other small businesses as well: a craft shop displaying quilts and macramé wall hangings and a pub, closed at this hour. Farther along, behind a sporting goods store, the white spire of the Catholic church downtown rose to the dark heavens.

Now, inside the bakery, she waited, looking past a man in a stocking cap to the paned window and the storm brewing outside. The sky was gray and dark, dawn offering little light, so that the Christmas decorations on the light poles—starfish and seahorses—were still glowing.

"Brooke?" she heard and turned around to find the owner herself, Gina Duquette, standing at the open window separating the counter from the kitchen area, where large wooden tables and two huge ovens were visible. "Brooke Fletcher?" the little woman asked. With her white hair pinned beneath a net and rimless glasses over wide blue eyes, she was eyeing Brooke.

"It's Harmon now," Brooke said.

"That's right, that's right!" Gina was nodding. "Of course. I knew that. Though I've never met your hubby."

"Seriously?" Brooke said.

"I'm sure I would remember. I never forget a face, you know. Names—well, I've never been good with them, but faces—that's different."

Brooke decided she was probably right. Most of their time here in Oregon was spent on the island and if she or Neal ever ran to town for supplies, they usually made the trip separately. "I'll introduce you," she promised.

"Good. So you're here for the holidays?"

"That's the plan."

"You picked a good time. We've already got snow falling and they're forecasting more on the way—a possible blizzard, if you can believe that! Anyway, we're having a white Christmas! Isn't it just wonderful?"

"Great," she agreed.

"I live on the island, you know, just down the street from your place. I have to boat over here myself because Zeke, he's the ferryman; you know, Zeke Owens? Well, he doesn't want to make a three a.m. run, you know. Baker's hours." She chuckled at her little joke. "I hate to see your house so empty. Your grandma wouldn't like it, you know. Good Lord, what's it been since you've been here?"

"A while," Brooke said evasively. "A couple of years or so."

The old lady was nodding. "Good thing your sister comes up to check on the place."

"What?" Brooke eyed the woman as the espresso machine hissed. "Leah?"

"Mm."

"I don't think so." She had to be mistaken.

Gina's silvering eyebrows pinched together. "I'm sure I saw her. With her husband. Yes." Scratching the side of her face thoughtfully, she nodded, as if agreeing with herself. "What was it? Now I remember. Just after Labor Day, I think; the tourist season was winding down. I remember because she bought the last of the peach tarts and another customer came in wanting some. Dorothy Latimer, and boy, was she mad that she'd missed out." She chuckled to herself. "I went to school with Dot. She's got a temper, that one does!"

The bell over the door tinkled as a couple in ski jackets, gloves, and wool caps entered.

"I don't think Leah's been here in years," Brooke clarified.

"No?" Gina worried her lip. "Hmm. I'm pretty sure I saw a car at the house in the drive, you know, and lights on inside, and them walking on the beach, but maybe I was mistaken and—" A timer buzzed behind her. "Well, whatever. Merry Christmas." She turned away. "Holy Toledo! Is anyone getting the cardamom rolls out of the oven?"

"Pumpkin latte?" The girl behind the counter offered Brooke a steaming paper cup and a crisp white sack filled with her order of baked goods before she turned her attention to the next customer, a lanky man wearing a hat with earflaps and a too-tight jacket.

Brooke thought Gina had gotten it wrong about Leah. And as far as she knew, Sean Moore was out of the picture and Leah hadn't married again. She'd barely had time. Then again, with her sister, anything was possible.

As for Labor Day, that was a whirlwind time. St. Bernadette's had barely started for the year and Brooke had been on the phone with her daughter and the school almost every day while still navigating her new job. Neal too had been super-busy, flying to the Bay Area because of a new case.

As for Leah, who knew?

Still lost in thought, Brooke drove to the ferry and wedged her car in the last slot behind a battered pickup with plastic taped over the back window. The first flakes of snow were beginning to fall. She watched them melt against her windshield while sipping her latte. The ride across the water was a little rough, the water in the bay choppy, and by the time they docked on the island she realized she'd forgotten to pick up a lighter and laundry detergent, so she took a chance that she could find both items at Piper's Landing, a small store located near the ferry slip.

The shop was small and compact, with wood floors that were from a previous century and two coolers that weren't much younger. The limited shelves were filled with convenience items, but she was lucky enough to locate a small box of laundry detergent and a pack of disposable lighters.

Brooke paid for the items at the register where Hank Thatcher, son of the original owners, was working the register while watching a small TV mounted above the cereal racks. Currently a game show from the seventies was airing. "Hey," she said as he handed her the purchases. "Thanks for returning Neal's wallet."

"What?" Near seventy, he was a tall, bearded man with an advancing waist and receding hairline. He favored flannel shirts, rubber boots, and jeans held up by suspenders. "Neal?" he said.

"Right. Neal. My husband."

"Oh right. He was in here yesterday." Hank nodded, as if remembering. "But I don't know anything about a wallet."

"He said he left it here but came back for it?"

"Huh." Hank wrapped a meaty hand behind the back of his neck and looked out the window in thought. "Nope. Didn't happen. I waited on him. I remember because he wanted cash back off his card and we don't do that here. Never have."

"Oh."

"I do remember he bought coffee and drank it while he was on the phone for a while. Outside. Pacing on the porch there." He nodded at the plate-glass window with its neon OPEN sign visible in reverse. "Then, when he got in his rig he talked for a while before he took off. I remember because he was still on the phone when he got out again and threw away his cup in the trash can by the door, there," Hank pointed to the tall trash bin nearby. "Then he took off."

"So how long was he out there on the phone?" she asked, trying to piece together what was happening, why Neal had lied.

"Geez, I dunno." Scratching at his chin, he narrowed his eyes. "Fifteen, maybe twenty minutes, I'd guess."

She remembered seeing Neal on his phone behind the open door of the woodshed. She hadn't thought too much about it and told herself not to worry about it now. He could talk to whomever he wanted to.

But why lie about it?

For a second she thought of Jennifer Adkins, and her stomach knotted painfully as she sprinted through the snow to her car. Had Neal taken up with her again?

Or was it something else?

Something completely innocent?

She fired the engine and caught a glimpse of her own eyes in the mirror, eyes dark with suspicion. Because of the simple little deception. Her first instinct was to drive home and call him out, to demand to know what was going on, but she told herself to wait, not make trouble.

Their little family seemed more solid than it had been in years.

She didn't want to ruin that, not with Marilee, not at Christmas.

With Leah coming to visit it would be tough enough.

She clicked on the wipers; the snow was falling steadily now, flakes collecting on the windshield.

The lies, she thought, *it always came down to the lies*.

Once home, Brooke found Marilee curled on the couch with a blanket, Shep at her side, a fire burning. Earbuds in place, blanket wrapped around her, Marilee was deep into her iPad, while coffee perked in the kitchen.

"Good morning," Brooke called and Shep lifted his head, stretched, and yawned, finally deigning to climb to his feet and follow Brooke into the kitchen. Marilee too finally glanced up and smiled.

"Morning."

"Hungry?"

But Marilee was already involved in her iPad again, and as Brooke set the groceries on the kitchen counter she spied Neal in his makeshift den, little more than a desk shoved under the single window in the laundry alcove.

"I'm going to run before the snow starts to pile up," she explained to her husband. "But I'll warm up some cinnamon rolls when I get back."

"Sure." He didn't bother looking away from his screen, so Brooke took advantage of her family being caught up in their electronic devices. She snapped on Shep's leash and took him on the same path as the day before, noting as she passed the stump where she'd buried the bracelet that it seemed undisturbed, snow beginning to cover the blackened wood and brambles.

On the beach she and Shep ran a short distance, then she circled back to the house and eyed the exterior of the upstairs bathroom bump out. Sure enough, there was a wire that ran up the side of the firebox and chimney, then tucked beneath the weathered shakes to the area where the shower was located. So far, it seemed, Gideon hadn't invested in wireless technology.

"You miserable son of a bitch," she muttered. "No more." She made her way back to the shed, located the old toolbox, rummaged through the interior, and finally located a rusted pair of wire cutters that she hoped would do the job. With only an old rhododendron as a screen she knelt down and cut the damned wire near the ground where it was buried. God knew where it led.

She didn't care. All she needed to do was dismantle the damned thing.

Mission accomplished.

Whistling to the dog, she grabbed two chunks of dry oak from the shed as her excuse just in case Neal or Marilee had been watching. Then she headed inside.

As it was, neither seemed to have even noticed she was gone.

Over the next few hours she had a light brunch of cinnamon rolls and fruit with her family, wrapped the few presents she'd brought from Seattle, laid them under the tree, and decided a bottle of wine would have to do for Leah. Though on her last visit her sister had claimed to be off wine, that had proved to be untrue, so the Merlot would have to do.

Once the presents were set she pretended to reorganize and clean the cupboards, all the while looking for any other spy equipment.

"Didn't the cleaning people do a good enough job?" Neal asked as he caught her ostensibly polishing the doorknobs and dusting the doorjambs and window casings as she searched.

"It's been years since this place has had a real top-to-bottom scrubbing," she explained. "Nana believed that cleanliness was next to godliness."

"Then she must've always been washing stuff," Neal observed because he understood how deeply religious the older woman had been. Even still, the cabin held more than its share of holy artifacts from the days when Mary Elizabeth Flannigan O'Hara had been the matriarch in charge. He hitched his chin toward the Celtic cross mounted over the archway near the front door.

"Amen," Brooke said and just kept working.

A few hours later she was satisfied that the house was swept of bugs or as clean as she could get it. She set out cheese, crackers, and cut vegetables with ranch dressing in lieu of lunch.

As promised Neal had set up the record player, and Marilee found a spot on the couch. Rather than view TikTok videos or text friends, she picked up her e-reader and settled in while Neal headed upstairs for a shower.

Just like old times, Brooke thought, pushing aside her anxiety for the moment. Humming to the likes of Nat King Cole, Bing Crosby, and Mariah Carey, Brooke started the soup stock of tomatoes, spices, and clam juice. Soon the scents of garlic and basil and tomatoes filled the room. As George Michael sang about "Last Christmas," she sliced clams and vegetables and tossed them into the simmering base. As she slid the sourdough round to reheat in the oven, she thought about her conversation with Gina Duquette at the bakery.

"Marilee," she called from the kitchen, then shouted a little more loudly until Shep gave off a bark and her daughter looked up from her e-reader.

"What?"

"You talked to Leah. Right?"

"You know that."

"Did she ever mention coming here?" she asked, the old timer clicking loudly as it wound down. "You know, in the past couple of months or so?"

From the corner of her eye she saw Neal coming down the stairs. "Something smells good." He headed to the kitchen.

"Hope so," she said.

To her surprise he stepped behind her and pulled her tight against him, then kissed the top of her head, something he rarely did.

Marilee winced. "Ugh! Stop."

"Okay." Neal took a step back but patted Brooke on the rump and winked at her.

"Oh, Dad, no! I don't need to see that!" Marilee said, pulling a face as she shook her head and turned to her mother, "You think Aunt Leah was here? Like on the island?"

"No, I doubt it, but . . . well, I'm just asking."

Did the arms around her waist tense?

"Dunno." Marilee shrugged. "She never said anything to me about it." She turned back to her electronic book. "You can ask her when she gets here. Isn't she supposed to be here, like, any minute?"

Brooke checked the old Kit-Cat Klock positioned over the archway to the dining area, its bulbous eyes and tail clicking in tandem. Her nerves tightened at the thought of Leah's arrival. It shouldn't be such a big deal, but considering the terms on which they'd last seen each other, Brooke couldn't bury the concern that the holidays wouldn't go as planned. Everything could even be ruined.

But that was stupid. She should have more faith. For her part she would try, really try to get along with Leah.

"Why do you think Leah was here?" Neal asked, plucking a slice of cheese from the cutting board and plopping it into his mouth.

"Just something Gina Duquette—you know her, the woman who owns the bakery in town? Something she said."

"The owner of the bakery?"

"You've met her, right?" Brooke clarified. "She lives about five doors down, here on the island."

He was shaking his head. "Never met her, not that I remember."

"But you've been to the bakery." He had to have in all the years they'd been together, all the times they'd come to the island.

He shrugged.

"Oh, well, it doesn't matter. It's just that she mentioned seeing a car here, and the cabin lit, and maybe Leah with her husband. Around Labor Day."

"Really?" he said, frowning. "I think she was already divorced by then."

Was that the tiniest of tics near his eye—the tell that he was nervous? But why? "Long divorced, as I understand it," Brooke said. But did she really know? She picked up the wooden spoon and stirred the chowder again. "Anyway, I don't think Gina's the most reliable source. She seemed a little confused."

"Maybe some car parked in the driveway and she just assumed it was Leah."

"Why Leah? Why not me?" she asked. "Here, taste this." She offered him the wooden spoon with some of the chowder.

"Who knows?" He blew across the spoon, then sipped. "Mm. Good."

"Doesn't need more salt?"

"Nope." But he seemed a bit distracted.

Before she could ask him what was on his mind, Brooke saw the wash of headlights flashing through the windows.

Shep let out a sharp bark and scrambled from his bed.

Brooke heard the crunch of tires on gravel.

"She's here!" Marilee yelled, hopping from the couch. Grinning widely, she raced barefoot to the door, Shep bounding beside her.

Brooke felt a pang of guilt for ever fighting with her sister, for letting her own personal issues with Leah become a barrier between them.

Well, no more. It was time to bury the hatchet and let bygones be bygones. They were family, after all. Quickly, she turned down the burner, letting the chowder simmer, then stepped into the living area just as the doorbell pealed through the house.

Marilee threw open the door.

Shep bounced in happy circles.

A blast of icy wind whooshed inside.

The fire glowed brighter as Leah stepped into the cabin. She was wrapped in a cream-colored coat, a red scarf draped around her neck, sleek gloves covering her fingers. Her blond hair gleamed, snowflakes melting in the gold strands. Her face was flushed and she was beaming. "Merry Christmas!" she cried, hugging Marilee as Brooke and Neal reached the entryway. "God, it's great to be here!" Leah was breathless, her cheeks rosy, her eyes sparkling. "I brought a special present with me!"

At that moment Brooke's heart sank.

She'd seen this glow around her sister before.

No doubt about it; Leah was in love.

Again.

Leah glanced over her shoulder and wiggled her fingers, indicating someone should step inside.

"What is it?" Neal asked.

Brooke bit back a gasp.

Big as life, wearing a leather jacket and jeans and sporting three-days' growth of beard that didn't hide his sardonic grin, Gideon Ross stepped inside.

CHAPTER 33

"This is Eli!" Leah announced breathlessly as she extracted herself from Marilee's embrace and wrapped her arms around the waist of the new man in her life. "Eli Stone." Then she glanced at the surprised group. "Marilee, my niece; I've told you about her." She waved a gloved hand at Marilee who stood, her smile fading, appearing as shocked as Brooke felt. "And Neal . . . my brother-in-law," Leah went on, obviously on cloud nine and beyond.

No! No! No!

Brooke stared at the man, shocked to her soul.

This man wasn't Eli Stone.

He was Gideon Ross. In the flesh.

Visibly taken aback, Neal managed to step forward to shake Eli's hand. "Neal Harmon. Glad to meet you," he said, though he didn't sound it. And he hesitated, as if remembering Eli's face but wasn't able to place it. Then he shook his confusion off, his face becoming welcoming again.

". . . and of course my sister, Brooke," Leah went on, and Eli leveled his gaze directly at Brooke.

Her breath caught in the back of her throat. She swallowed hard and felt the color drain from her face.

Leah went on, "I've told you all about her."

"Yeah." Eli nodded. "You have."

Dear God!

He took Brooke's hand in his icy fingers. "Glad we finally meet. Face-to-face."

She nearly gasped and caught the cruel glint in his eye. Her knees threatened to buckle, but she forced a fake smile and stared stiffly at him. He was a little different than she remembered and she told herself that she was imagining things, that because of discovering the bracelet and camera she'd been obsessing about Gideon and this man was not him. Couldn't be.

Yet the differences were subtle. Lighter hair grown out longer and showing just a few strands of silver. Brown eyes rather than gray. His nose not quite the same—broken maybe? And possibly about an inch taller? But that jaw, even masked by a scruffy, three days' of beard shadow, appeared nearly identical, as were the eyebrows and cheekbones and the off-center, easy grin . . . If Eli Stone wasn't Gideon Ross, he was his damned twin.

She swallowed hard, heard the timer ticking off the seconds of her life. "Let's just say I'm surprised to meet you," she forced out and her voice came as if from a distance. She felt woozy as she said, "Leah didn't mention bringing a guest." *Don't pass out! Don't!* The words rang through her mind while dozens of images, snapshots of the time she'd spent with him flashed in rapid-fire succession behind her eyes: Gideon at Pike's Place Market. Gideon in the coffee shop. Gideon at the helm of the *Medusa*. Running on the beach. Making love in the bed upstairs. In the very bed she was now sharing with Neal. And Gideon with Neal's gun, threatening her life, the last words he'd ever spoken echoing through her mind:

If I can't have you, no one can.

"Brooke?" Neal's voice, sounding far away, brought her back to the here and now. "Are you okay?"

"Fine," Brooke managed, though she was anything but fine as she stared at the man she'd once so foolishly trusted with her life.

And there it was, that glint in his eyes, a mischievous spark that she'd once found so intriguing and now made her blood run cold.

"My bad," Leah said, pulling her head into her shoulders like a little kid knowing she was cute. "Mea culpa. I didn't say anything because I wanted it to be a surprise."

"Beyond a surprise," Brooke managed, trying to tamp down her anxiety. Why would he come here? It had to be on purpose. What did Leah know? From the look of her, nothing. Was it possible? Could she be innocent in all this?

Eli said, "I've been looking forward to this." The voice—a little raspier, but . . . She realized he was still holding her hand. She yanked it away. Blinked back to reality. This couldn't be happening. It could not!

Recovering slightly, Neal finally pulled the door shut behind them. "Well, come on inside and settle in."

No! Oh, no, no, no! He couldn't be here! *No way! No how!*

"I—we have a big announcement," Leah said, taking Eli's hand in hers.

Brooke knew what was coming before Leah even said a word.

"Eli and I are getting married." She pulled off the gloves and held up her left hand, fingers splayed, a bright diamond winking on her ring finger. "He asked me just last week and I said 'yes'!" She squeezed Eli's hand and he bussed her cheek though, Brooke noted, before he closed his eyes during the quick kiss, he shot a glance directly at her, almost mocking her.

Oh, Jesus. Stunned, Brooke couldn't say a word.

"Wow." Neal took a step back. "That's fast."

"When you know, you just know!" Leah gushed and twined her fingers in Eli's. "Isn't that right?" she asked her fiancé, but he was already nodding, his eyes catching Brooke's.

"Yeah," he agreed. "When you find the one you should never let her go."

Leah nearly swooned against him. "I won't," she said.

"Me neither." And again he cut a quick glance at Brooke. "I'll never let go. Just like I promised."

Brooke visibly started.

"Well—then, I guess congratulations are in order." Though at first visibly taken aback, Neal was trying to pull himself together, while Marilee hadn't yet said a word. She appeared as shocked as anyone.

Neal said to Brooke, "I think we have a bottle of wine here, don't we?"

When she didn't respond he nudged her. "Brooke?"

"Yes." Dear God, what was she supposed to do? She couldn't have Gideon in the house and she couldn't allow him to marry Leah. No damned way. Her mind was racing, her heartbeat frantic.

"No worries. Of course we brought champagne to celebrate. And two of my best friends, Jim Beam and Jack Daniels just for good measure." Leah shrugged off her coat and hung it on one of the pegs in the front hall. "This place hasn't changed a bit. And oh! Look! You found Nana's little Christmas tree!" She hurried to the corner where Brooke had tucked the little fake pine. "I used to love playing with the ornaments. Remember? It was sad-looking then, but now—wow. Still, I *love* it. And—wait!" She made a big production of closing her eyes and sniffing the air. "You're making clam chowder? Manhattan, right?" Her eyes fluttered open. "Perfect." Her blue eyes twinkling, she linked arms with Eli. "And it's snowing outside. Gonna be a white Christmas. I take it as a good omen!"

"Really? An omen?" Brooke said, working hard to think clearly as she put the pieces together in her mind—finding the bracelet in the cupboard, discovering the camera's eye in the shower, hearing that Leah had been on the island within the last few months, and now this—Gideon Ross posing as another man.

What the hell was happening?

Dragging her gaze from Eli, she kept telling herself over and over again that he was *not* Gideon Ross; a dead ringer, yes, but *not* the man she'd left bleeding in Elliott Bay a little more than a year before.

"And another tree too!" Leah said as she stepped into the living room to survey all the decorations and the fir tree trimmed with old-fashioned ornaments. "I've got presents! And . . ." Again she grinned and hunched her shoulders like a mischievous little girl. "Another surprise."

Dread crawled up Brooke's spine as they all went into the living room. "I don't know if I can take another one."

Leah ignored her. "Come here, come here," she said to Eli, motioning him into a spot in front of the stone fireplace. The embers in the grate glowed red while flames licked the chunks of blackened oak. Linking her fingers with his again, she announced, "We're getting married here on the island."

"No," was Brooke's immediate response.

"What?" Neal didn't bother to mask his shock.

Marilee blinked and took a step backward. "Here?" she whispered. Her face had drained of all color. "You're getting married? Really? Now? Here?"

"On New Year's Eve." Leah hugged Eli fiercely.

"Wait—what?" Brooke said, aghast. "This New Year's?"

"Yes, yes! You heard me. We're getting married here, in this cabin. I've already spoken with the preacher in Marwood. And the florist. And a caterer—well, she's really just a woman who works at the restaurant—but it's going to be small, so it shouldn't be a problem! It'll just be us . . . Oh, Marilee, you'll still be here, right?"

"I—I—" Marilee was slowly shaking her head. Obviously dumbstruck, she said, "I was heading back. I have plans. With my boyfriend."

"Well, call him. Get him up here!" Leah said. "We can handle one more."

"I don't know. . . ." Marilee glanced at Brooke, as if she was looking for a lifeline.

Brooke didn't have one. "Wait a second. You can't be serious," she said, trying to keep the panic from her voice.

But she saw from the determined gleam in her sister's eye that Leah had made up her mind. Brooke stumbled on. "I mean, it's just that this is so sudden. I didn't even know you were dating."

"Neither did I," Neal said, as if Leah should have confided in him.

Marilee didn't say a word.

"Well." Leah's lips pulled into a tiny little smile, as if she'd been holding on to a little secret, a guilty little pleasure that she'd been savoring. "I admit, it's been pretty quick, really. I met Eli when I moved to San Francisco, just this past September, the twentieth to be exact, after I got the job at Central. That's the private school where I teach."

"So, how did you meet?" Neal asked.

"I swear it was kismet, or fate," Leah said, a little more seriously. "We literally ran into each other. Down on Fisherman's Wharf!" She cuddled closer to Eli. "Didn't we, babe?"

Marilee had dropped onto the couch and Shep found a tennis ball that had rolled under a side table and carried it across the room to drop it next to Eli.

Neal took in the dog's antics and didn't say anything, but Brooke knew what he was thinking—that Shep rarely initiated play with a newcomer.

"I don't think so, boy," Eli said and scratched the retriever behind the ears, just as Brooke had seen Gideon do in this very room.

Bile crawled up her throat.

Leah nudged Eli. "You remember how we met at the waterfront?"

"Of course." He wrapped his arms around his fiancée, so that he could stare over Leah's shoulder, his gaze finding Brooke's.

A chill slid down her spine.

This man was a poser.

A diabolical manipulator.

"We had coffee," Eli said.

Brooke's stomach dropped.

Leah agreed, nodding, and before he could go on, she added, "In that little shop on PIER 39! And we've been together ever since!" She wrapped her arms around Eli and hugged him close.

Oh. My. God.

"So you've known each other for what—a couple of months?" Neal asked, his gaze moving from Leah to Eli.

"Almost three!" Leah piped up, the diamond in her ring winking in the firelight. "And trust me, it was like something out of a fairy tale. Magic, you know. I turned and saw him and I knew, I just *knew*. It was almost as if we'd met before. A weird déjà vu. Like in another lifetime or something."

Not in another lifetime, but when a stranger on a motorcycle pointed her in the direction of a missing dog.

Leah giggled, twisting her face up to stare at Eli. "Isn't that right, babe?"

"A little different for me," Eli said, "but basically, yeah."

"It was love at first sight for me," Leah assured everyone. "Like I said, almost as if it were preordained. I mean, what were the chances that we would meet like that?"

"Exactly," Brooke said, trying to keep the disbelief from her voice, tamping down the fear in her heart. Eli Stone had to be Gideon Ross. He had to be. Not just his nearly identical twin. "A fairy-tale romance."

Leah looked up sharply, as if she'd caught the sarcasm in Brooke's words. "I know, I know, I've said it before," she admitted, little lines creasing her brow. "And let's be clear, Eli knows all about my previous marriages, but this time is different."

"Of course it is," Brooke said flatly. "And what about you, Eli? Been married before? Any kids? Or old girlfriends?"

Leah's mouth dropped open.

Neal shot Brooke a look that warned her to be careful and Shep settled in next to Marilee, who stroked him absently, her attention fixed on Leah and the new man in her life, her future husband.

Eli took the questions in stride. "No ex-wives," he said with the lift of one shoulder. "And no kids. At least none that I know of." His cocky smile hardened a bit, and Brooke remembered the miscarriage, the blood visible in the water near the marina where the *Medusa* was docked. "There are a few women in my past, of course," he admitted. "One in particular I always thought was the one who got away." Leah's smile faded for a second and she glanced sharply at him. "Then, though, I met Leah and everything changed." He gave her a squeeze and her smile returned, though it didn't seem to shine quite as brightly as it had earlier.

The ancient timer on the stove buzzed loudly and Brooke turned back to the kitchen, grateful for the distraction. Her head was pounding with a headache, her thoughts spinning, and it was all she could do not to panic.

This was all so wrong.

So very wrong.

"Look—the snow's really pilling up!" Leah pulled Eli to the window overlooking the backyard. "There must be two inches already!" Leah was as delighted as a kid who thought she would miss school for a snow day. "Look, babe!"

Eli did stare out the window but, Brooke noted, as he looked at the glass, she sensed he wasn't caught up in Leah's enthusiasm.

Nor was he surveying the snow.

Instead, his reflected gaze caught hers. Cold. Piercing. Ruthless.

It turned her blood to ice.

"Brooke?" Neal's voice brought her around. "The bread?"

"Oh! Crap! Right," she said automatically as she turned to the stove, opened the oven door, and fumbled with the hot loaf. She dropped it onto a cutting board, but her mind was reeling. She was not about to serve goddamned Gideon Ross Christmas Eve dinner and . . . and . . .

"The soup?" Neal said, looking at her strangely.

"Oh. Sorry, sorry," she said and saw that the chowder was at a roiling boil. She picked up the wooden spoon and dropped it into the pot, splashing hot broth onto her hand. "Ouch!"

"You okay?" Neal asked.

Brooke was already reaching into the freezer for the ice but found the old cubes frozen into a solid block. "Fine." A lie, but one she could live with as she found an ice pick in the old knife rack and chipped off some ice, jabbing at the block ferociously.

"Taking out your frustrations?" Leah said from the living room.

"Something like that," Brooke bit back and slid a knowing glance in Eli's direction.

Sensing the festive mood on the verge of being destroyed, Leah said, "As I said, we brought champagne! It's in the car—?" She motioned to Eli and in that cutesy voice she sometimes used when she was wheedling a favor, a high-pitched baby voice that Brooke detested, she said, "Maybe you can bring it in? With the luggage?"

"Sure." He winked at her and turned on his heel to walk outside.

Brooke held the ice to her fingers.

The minute the door closed behind him, Leah rushed into the kitchen. "Isn't he fabulous?" Then, finally understanding that Brooke was tending to the burn on her hand, said, "Are you okay?"

"Yeah, yeah, I'll be fine," Brooke snapped. "But tell me, what is all this about you getting married to this . . . this man you barely know!" Her hand smarting was making her more irritable than she was already feeling, feeding the panic she'd felt since the moment she saw Gideon posing as Eli. Now that he was out of the house Brooke saw no reason to dance around the subject.

"I know, I know, I know! It's fast."

"Speed-of-light fast!" Brooke countered as the ice melted, drizzling down her fingers to her palm.

"That's the way it happens sometimes!" Leah said as Brooke found a plastic bag and loaded chipped ice into it. "I can't believe how we met just when I'd sworn off men for good." She let out a sigh. "It's funny how life works, isn't it? How fate steps in and makes decisions for you?" She glanced up at the crucifix still mounted on the wall, a relic from the past, and crossed herself fervently. "Nana would've said it was God's work."

"You think God was involved?" Brooke asked skeptically as she replaced the melting chip with the plastic bag.

"Some greater force, yeah." Leah had that dreamy look in her eyes that Brooke found irritating. "This time, Brookie, it's different. With Eli. I mean it. He's definitely 'the one.'"

"What do you know about him?"

"Everything I need to." Some of her dreaminess evaporated. "Why?"

"Have you checked on him? Met his family? Any of his friends?" She tossed the nearly melted ice chip into the sink.

Leah didn't answer, but her blue eyes darkened.

"I knew it!" Brooke said. "You can't marry someone you don't even know!"

"We connected immediately and—"

"Do you even know if that's his real name?" Brooke said, feeling herself unravel. "I mean, really, what do you know about him?"

"Enough!" Leah said. "I know enough. And I know the way I feel when I'm with him. Happy. Special. Safe. Loved." Her voice was rising. "You could be happy for me, you know. Would it be that tough? Why do you always want to ruin my life?"

"No, no! This isn't about me ruining anything. This is about him." Brooke pointed to the door. "And you planning to marry a virtual stranger!"

Neal stepped between them. "I think what Brooke is trying to say is that this is all so sudden. So fast."

Leah angled her chin upward to glare at Neal. "Well, sometimes fast is better than slow! At least I know where I stand with Eli."

"Isn't that what you thought about Ryan and Harrison and Sean?" Brooke reminded her. "Dear God, you married them all. And you almost walked down the aisle with Robert Whatever-his-name-was!"

"You left one out!" Leah charged and stared straight at Neal.

"For God's sake, I'm just saying that you should slow down," Brooke said.

"Why?"

"To be sure."

"I *am* sure. That's what I'm telling you. And I came here to make up with you and to share my happiness and spend the holidays and have you witness my wedding and . . ." She started to choke up, tears filling her eyes.

"I can't stand this," Marilee said from the living room. "It's all . . .

it's all just crazy." Not looking back, she ran up the stairs, Shep following.

"Why can't you just be happy for me?" Leah demanded.

"I want you to be happy, but I just want you to think, Leah," Brooke said, grabbing her sister's upper arms. "And this time with your head instead of your heart."

"Think? Like you did, when you started fucking Neal behind my back, when you stole him away from me by getting pregnant?" she spat.

Brooke released her grip, pushing her sister away.

"Whoa, whoa, whoa," Neal interjected.

"Not true?" she threw back and Neal's jaw tightened as she stared at him.

A vessel pulsing by his eye, Neal said quietly, "Ancient history." But a fleeting shadow of guilt passed over him.

Leah finally broke the stare down. "I knew this was a mistake. Coming here. I told Eli we should just elope. Go to Vegas. But *he* wanted to come up here. Practically insisted on it. 'Let's start out strong,' he said. 'I really want to meet your sister and her family,' he said, and I thought he was right! Obviously I was mistaken!"

The front door opened, a gust of icy wind following Eli inside. With a bottle of champagne tucked under one arm and a duffel bag over his shoulder, he dragged a huge roller bag behind.

"This conversation is over," Leah muttered between clenched teeth, then pasted a smile on her face and spun to face him. "Let me help you!" she said, rushing to the front hall.

"Got it."

"Is there anything else?" Neal asked, making his way to the door.

"Are you kidding?" Eli paused at the bottom of the stairs, setting the champagne bottle on the console table next to an Immaculate Heart of Mary figurine. "Leah doesn't know what it means to pack light."

Leah snagged the bottle of champagne, carried it into the kitchen, and placed it in the refrigerator. "Let's open this later, after we settle in." Then, to her husband-to-be, "Come on upstairs!" Her mouth twisted into a naughty grin. "Let me show you to your—er, our room." She cast a questioning glance at Brooke. "And that's—?

"I set you up in Mom's old bedroom," Brooke replied dully. This couldn't be happening. The thought of Leah and Gideon/Eli sleeping together and making love in their mother's room made her stomach turn over.

But worse than that was the fear, the feeling that at any moment he could do something rash. Something dangerous.

How far would he go?

"Ah." Leah was nodding. "I figured." She took Eli's free hand and led him up the stairs. Neither one looked back.

CHAPTER 34

*D*on't freak out! Don't freak out! For God's sake do not freak out!

But Brooke felt her entire world imploding. Gideon was here? Posing as Eli Stone? Intending to marry Leah? After leaving the bracelet and putting up a spy camera?

She felt as if she might hyperventilate.

"I don't know about you," Neal said to Brooke, "but I could use a drink." He turned to the hutch by the dining room, where one lower cupboard had always been used as a liquor cabinet. Crouching and rooting around inside, he said, "Well, shit! All that's in here is peppermint schnapps. Oh no! Wait a second! What's this? Here we go!" He let out a long whistle as he stood to dust off a blue bottle. Eyebrows lifting, he said, "Bombay Sapphire! As you know, I make a mean martini." He eyed the bottle and muttered, "Let me see." Then searched again. "May the gods of booze be with us and . . . ah yes!" He pulled out another bottle and wiggled it. "Vermouth! Now we're in business." Grin stretching, he looked up at her, "Want one?"

She shouldn't. It would be far better to keep her wits about her, but she couldn't stand it and she needed something, *anything* to help her calm down and slow her heart rate. "Sure," she said, throwing caution to the wind. "And while you're at it, make it a double."

"Your wish is my command." Neal found a small pitcher, rinsed it out, and chipped ice from the frozen mass of cubes in the freezer with the ice pick while Brooke opened a fresh jar of olives. "Note to self," Neal said, "pick up more ice."

"Or make some. It's Christmas tomorrow, remember?"

"And this is Christmas Eve—oh, hell." He handed her a glass and they clinked rims. "Merry Christmas."

"You think?"

"We can try."

"Right." She touched the rim of her glass to his again but knew she was lying. She might fake it for the family, but the last thing this Christmas was going to be was merry. Inside her mind was screaming, her heart palpitating from the shock of seeing Gideon again, but she had to think, to figure out what to do, rationally. Calmly. Without freaking out.

Yeah right.

She took a swallow and felt the welcome warmth of the gin on her throat.

"What do you think about Eli—the new guy?" Neal asked, scowling into his drink.

I think he's a lying scumbag capable of God knows what! She remembered Gideon with the gun, how she'd felt he was going to kill her on the deck of his sailboat. But she couldn't mention any of that. Instead, she settled for, "Don't trust him."

"That makes two of us."

"Three if you count Marilee."

"Yeah, I know." Neal took a swallow of his martini. "She looked as if she'd seen a ghost when he walked in. Well, so did you."

I did! "It was a shock." She took another swallow and tried to gather her wits about her. Why would Gideon play this charade? Why change his name? Why try to infiltrate the family? Why go to such lengths of deception? Why go as far as marry Leah under an assumed identity? None of this made any sense.

"Yeah," Neal said and finished his drink in one long swallow. "I just don't get it. Leah never said anything."

"To you?" Brooke said. "You've been talking to her?"

"To Marilee." But the way he said it made her wonder. She remembered their fight when she'd confronted him about the loans to her sister, about the lien Leah had signed against this very cabin.

It had been less than a week after her final near-death blowup with Gideon. Brooke had been on pins and needles, half expecting Gideon to show up on her doorstep again. To find him lingering in the park, or see his number show up on her phone as he tried to text or call her.

There had been nothing.

Radio silence.

The same was true of Leah. Once she'd walked through the airport doors at Sea-Tac, she hadn't communicated with Brooke at all.

They'd gone about their lives.

As if none of the drama had happened.

Except that Neal had let it slip about the loan to Leah.

Brooke had stepped into his office and his laptop was open, Leah's name visible. Neal had snapped it closed.

Too late.

Brooke had seen the lien again. But now Neal knew it.

"Fifty thousand dollars?" she'd said.

For once, Neal didn't try to change or dodge the subject. It was almost as if he'd expected the confrontation.

"It's secured." He'd waved her into a side chair and she'd dropped into it.

Brooke couldn't believe that he'd gone behind her back. "It's Marilee's college fund."

"Not all of it. We'll be okay." But as he'd sat in his desk chair, he'd twiddled a pen between his fingers and the little tic at his temple, the telltale indication that he was nervous, became visible.

"Why, Neal?" she'd asked. "And why didn't you talk to me about it?"

"Because you and Leah were already at each other's throats and she told me that you were against it. In fact, she said you told her to talk to me."

"But it's so much money."

"And she lost everything she had," he said, rubbing the back of his neck, having the decency to at least look a little uncomfortable. "Everything," he repeated. "Including her inheritance."

"By letting her dumbass husband get his hands on it!"

"She has nothing, Brooke, and we have so much. God, could you have a heart? She's your sister!" And he'd seemed agitated then, the tic pulsing more visibly. She'd wanted to argue, to remind him that Leah was a victim of her own making. But Brooke had sins of her own. When she thought about what she'd been through, how she'd put her family as well as her own sanity at risk, she decided to drop it.

"Okay, fine," she'd finally said. "But in the future before we loan out a penny, we discuss it."

"Agreed." He was nodding, looking out the window. "If we have to, we can take a loan out on the cabin."

"What? No!" she'd argued. The cottage on Piper Island had been in the family for decades and all the while unmortgaged, owned free and clear. "Let's not get crazy. I'll have a new job soon and we'll figure it out."

"You should talk to Bill Clayton," Neal had said. "They're expanding, doing all things wirelessly, cutting-edge technology. You like that stuff. You and Marilee. I can call him."

"No. Don't. I'd rather do it myself," she said.

"Always."

That was true; she had a habit of trusting her judgment over others, creating her own path, and it had worked out for her—until Gideon.

So she'd called Bill Clayton, had been hired within a week, and she and Neal hadn't mentioned the money that Leah had owed them again. Marilee's boarding school was expensive, but they managed to get by, as they would when she went off to college.

"How about another?" Neal now was already pouring himself a second drink.

"I'm good." Brooke put her hand over the top of her glass. She couldn't take a chance on getting buzzy and losing control of her lips. She had too much to do.

No, now that the shock was wearing off, she had to be clever, to expose Eli as a fraud without exposing herself. Somehow she had to trip him up, to get rid of him, before Leah made the mistake of marrying him.

Somehow they got through dinner. As surreal as it was.

It had been touch and go, but Eli had convinced Leah to come downstairs and Brooke had managed to convince Marilee that she would try her best to get along with her sister, even though it was probably impossible, especially considering the circumstances and how freaked out Brooke was. But she pulled it together. "It's Christmas," she said, and Marilee had finally deigned to join the tense group seated around the old oak table.

Leah wanted to pout. Brooke recognized the signs. Her slightly protruding lower lip, the dark looks sent Brooke's way, and an overly dramatic slump of her shoulders. But Leah really couldn't give into her usual poor-me routine with Eli at her side. She had to portray herself as the ebullient bride-to-be, a tough act when she was also the preyed-upon victim.

If only she knew that in this case, tonight, her two roles had truly melded into one.

Marilee, though quieter than usual, held up her part of the conversation as they consumed spicy chowder, slices of hot bread, and a salad made with kale, pumpkin seeds, and dried cranberries, which Marilee steadfastly picked out and slid to the edge of her plate.

"So, Leah says coming up here to the island was your idea?" Brooke said to Eli.

He was seated across the round table, the small arrangement of pine cones, holly, and greens separating them. The drink had taken the edge off, and she could actually speak to him face-to-face. But damn, he looked like Gideon. He *was* Gideon. She just knew it! And it scared the hell out of her.

"Yeah, I thought it was a good idea."

How could she call him out? Expose him?

Brooke was still trying to slip him up, to make him admit that he was a fraud and, possibly, Leah was an innocent victim. A mark. She hated to give Leah the satisfaction of being used because of her history and her outright envy, if not jealousy, of her older sister. Still, would Leah try to ruin Brooke's life as she claimed her older sister had destroyed hers? Would she really be so brazen as to bring Gideon here to claim he was someone else, someone she intended to marry?

None of it made sense, but her wits weren't as sharp as usual. Neal's martini was strong: a double shot of gin with just a whisper of vermouth along with two olives. And she'd downed it quickly. Then there was the wine with dinner. She'd had a glass, maybe two, but definitely not three . . . or . . .

Leah filled in the blanks. "Eli found out that you and I weren't on the best of terms and he didn't like it." Seated next to him, she reached out and touched his hand.

"Didn't like it?" Brooke repeated.

"Uh-huh." Leah nodded, her eyebrows arched, almost daring Brooke to argue. "He knew we weren't speaking, and then when Marilee said she was coming up here for Christmas, he suggested we all get together. That we sisters should, you know, mend fences. How did you put it?" she said, glancing Eli's way, "embrace family?"

For the love of God. "Is that right?" Brooke said and caught a warning glare from Neal.

"It is," Leah insisted and stood. "It's what he does. He's kind of a counselor."

"A psychiatrist?" Neal asked.

Eli shook his head. "Not a doctor." Anticipating Neal's next question, he added, "Not a psychologist either. It's not really what I do."

"What then? What is it you *really* do?" Brooke asked, expecting him to squirm under the scrutiny.

He didn't. "I give free advice to my clients. I'm a personal trainer."

"What kind of advice? Like, do you solve marital problems?" she persisted. "Family issues?"

His lips pulled into a tight smile. "More like using common sense. Clients come to me and start talking, that's all." He sent a meaningful glance at Leah. "I'm *not* a trained counselor."

"He's a life coach," Leah said.

"Without a degree," Brooke pointed out, and while Leah seemed to fume, Eli—or whoever he was—let a slow smile crawl across his lips. He was amused by all the underlying tension.

"What exactly does a life coach do?" she asked, pushing it.

"Helps people!" Leah's eyes narrowed.

"So you didn't go to college or some special school to become a personal trainer? Don't you need to have some certification if you're planning to 'coach' people on how to live their lives?"

"He doesn't need a degree for that!" Leah was getting angry.

"Doesn't he?" Even though alcohol was loosening her tongue, Brooke figured he would need some formal training. "What about sailing?" she asked.

Did the muscles in his neck tighten a bit?

"A little."

Brooke asked, "Ever own a sailboat?"

"No." He shook his head, but a bit of a smile touched the corners of his lips.

"For Pete's sake, just stop," Leah said. She forced a cold grin, and if there ever was a look that could kill, Brooke would have been dead five minutes earlier. "Let's have some champagne," Leah forced out. "I think we need to celebrate!"

She scraped her chair back, found the bottle she'd put in the fridge, yanked it out, and hauled it back to the table. "You can do the honors," she said to Eli, then rummaged around in the hutch and came up with five champagne flutes, part of a set their mother had owned since her marriage, a gift from a close friend. "I know you're not legal," she said to Marilee as she quickly rinsed the stemmed glasses and returned to the table, "but we can fudge a little."

"Because it's not every day you decide to get married?" Brooke asked.

Leah took in a swift breath. *Wow*, she mouthed. *Low blow*.

Brooke was about to say something more, but Neal placed a hand on her thigh, his fingers tense. The tiny shake of his head was almost imperceptible. But she caught his message: This wasn't the time.

What he didn't understand was that there would never be a good time. Ever.

"Pooh, Brooke. Get over it. I already told you, Sean—er, Eli— knows everything about me. About my marriages."

"And you know everything about him?"

"I'm not going to let you ruin everything!" Leah insisted. "Eli— please. Let's do this thing!"

"I'm not trying to ruin anything," Brooke argued as Eli took the champagne bottle from Leah's quivering fingers. "I'm just asking."

"Sure," Leah said icily. Her jaw was set, her lips flat.

"Maybe Leah doesn't know everything about you," Eli said to Brooke.

"What?" Brooke couldn't believe his nerve.

"It happens. Siblings keep secrets from each other," Eli said and Leah, idiot that she was, actually seemed pleased, as if he'd come to her rescue.

Oh save me!

While Marilee looked as if she wanted to melt into the floorboards and disappear and Neal sat tense as a bowstring, Eli tore away the foil, twisted the wire holding the cork in place, then quickly worked the cork from the bottle. The champagne erupted with a loud pop that sounded like a gunshot.

For a second Brooke was thrown back in time, remembering the gun going off in that cold, dark water. The explosion. The blood. His ghostly face as he drifted away. He was injured that day. He had to have been. There was just too much blood for it to have all been from the miscarriage . . . and yet she'd seen him pull himself from the water. She remembered punching the gas, freaking out, driving away while her insides cramped.

She swallowed hard and felt her own face drain of color. Blinking, she found Eli staring at her as he poured the glasses.

She'd expected to hear from him.

Or the police.

Or someone.

For weeks, if anyone came to the door she'd freeze inside, certain to see him on her doorstep, or a cop on the porch with dozens of questions.

Instead, there had been silence.

Blessed but cold silence.

He didn't show up at her door, or at the school, or in her vehicle, waiting for her.

He didn't call or text.

No email.

And all those raspy warnings from an anonymous caller had stopped.

The silence had been deafening, and, in the first few weeks, put her on edge. She'd barely eaten, jumped whenever the phone or doorbell rang. Not even the sight of the empty berth, the knowledge that he'd sailed off, could ease her mind.

Eventually, her fears had faded.

But she'd never forgotten his vow: *I will never let you go. Never.* And now he had caught up with her when she'd least expected it.

"Brooke?" Neal brought her back to the present and she saw that Eli was trying to hand her a glass of champagne.

"Oh. Sorry. Daydreaming, I guess."

Leah gave a disgusted little snort as Brooke accepted the flute from Eli's outstretched hand.

"To us!" Leah said, holding up her glass before taking a sip.

Brooke couldn't add so much as, "May you have years of happiness together." Nor could she force out, "Welcome to the family, Eli." Because she just didn't feel it. And it would be a lie. She knew he was an imposter. He was playing some mind-bending, macabre game.

Neal managed a weak, "Hear, hear," while Marilee, her glass lifted limply in a toast, looked as if she would rather be anywhere else on the planet.

"To family," said Eli. "May we always be together." He looked at his bride, then his gaze skated around the table, lingering, she thought, a beat too long on Brooke. Or was it her own anxiety, her painful memory? Or maybe the alcohol she'd already drunk settling into her bloodstream?

"'Til death do us part," Leah whispered and Brooke almost choked on her champagne.

Hell no!

"Awkward," Marilee whispered under her breath before sipping and setting down her glass.

The whole scene made Brooke's blood run cold, but she managed to get through the rest of the meal despite the fact that her insides were churning. She even choked down one of the hand-decorated petits fours that Leah had brought from "the most darling little bakery" she'd discovered in San Francisco.

"Absolutely charming—oh, Marilee, you would *love* it. It's not far from the Presidio. You'll *have* to come up and visit. We'll show you all around."

Over my dead body! No way in hell was Marilee going to visit them. Again Brooke caught the glimmer of dark amusement in Eli's eyes.

This was all too much.

The whole scenario seemed so staged.

Leah was trying too hard and Eli—what was up with him? He looked like Gideon and kind of sounded like Gideon. Whenever she caught him watching her, she had the same feeling she'd experienced when Gideon stared at her a little too long.

"I've been to San Francisco," Marilee said.

"Well, come again. There's just so much to do, to see, to explore. Bring . . . uh, that new boyfriend of yours. What's his name?"

"Wes."

"Yes, bring Wes!" she said enthusiastically and polished off her champagne. "We'll make it a party!"

Never, Brooke thought.

Marilee looked wan. "Sure," she said weakly. "Can I be excused?" Before anyone could answer she scooted her chair back and shot up the stairs.

Leah watched her go. "Is she okay?" she asked.

"I don't know," Brooke said. "I'll check."

Neal put down his napkin. "Maybe I should—"

"I've got this." Brooke was already pushing away from the table and hurrying up the stairs.

Marilee was already in her room, flopped on the bottom bunk and texting on her phone. "You okay?" Brooke asked.

"As if!" Marilee let out a short huff. "Are you?"

Brooke lifted a shoulder. "Maybe."

"Liar." Her phone pinged and she glanced at a text. Her fingers flew over the tiny keyboard. "I'm fine," she said in a flat tone and finally looked up. "I don't like that guy," she admitted.

"Eli."

Her jaw slid to the side. "Yeah. Eli." But there was something in her tone that caught Brooke's attention.

"Do you know anything about him?"

"What? No. Why would I?" Marilee said a little defensively as another text chimed. "Just a feeling. I don't know." She was typing again. "And let's face it, Aunt Leah doesn't have the greatest taste in men."

"I won't argue there."

"It all seemed so fake. I just had to get away. You know, be alone." Marilee's attention was dragged to the phone again and Brooke took the hint and let her be, closing the door softly behind her.

She heard the sound of voices downstairs, of dishes being collected, a flurry of activity. She glanced at the door to the guest room. Ajar. Beckoning. Her chance to find out more.

But she had to work fast. Who knew how long anyone would stay on the lower level?

Noiselessly, she entered the guest room. Inside she looked for Eli's wallet—not visible on the dresser or nightstands, but his duffel was open beneath the window and she quickly went to it and riffled through its contents. Her heart was thudding as she strained to listen.

Hurry, hurry, hurry! Was that a footstep on the stairs?

Oh crap!

Another thought went through her mind. What if whoever had put the camera in the shower had placed another one somewhere in this room and if that person were Gideon/Eli?

Well, tough.

Too late now.

This was her chance.

She might not get another.

Sorting swiftly through the duffel, she discovered nothing but jeans, socks, boxers, and shirts. Was that faded T-shirt familiar? Were the battered jeans the same ones Gideon had worn? She couldn't remember, had no idea, and was about to give it up when she saw that the duffel, faded green, had a patch of darker canvas where something that had been sewn on was now obviously missing. An ID patch? For another man? Had she seen this duffel in the cabin of the *Medusa?* A corner visible in one of the small cabinets where the door had been ajar? She wasn't sure. She felt along the sides and on the bottom and . . . what? Something hard. In a nearly invisible zippered pocket.

Throat dry, listening for any sound from the hallway, she reached into the zippered area, a false bottom, and found a sheathed hunting knife. She extracted the knife and felt further. Nothing.

Why would he bring the weapon and somehow smuggle it here?

She could think of no good reason.

Again she thought she heard a footstep, so she eased away from the bag.

"Brooke?" Neal was calling to her and he was close.

Damn!

How could she explain herself?

And then she saw it. Eli's wallet, on the floor as if it had been knocked from the nightstand. But she didn't have time to go through it. Without thinking, she swept the worn leather wallet from the corner of the rug and hid it, and the knife, under the hem of her sweater. Each was too bulky to slip into her pockets and would show a bulge she couldn't explain.

A door opened in the hallway. "Hey," Neal said and she nearly jumped out of her skin.

She sneaked across the room.

"Have you seen your mom?" Neal asked.

Heart in her throat, sweat beginning to collect on her palms, Brooke cracked the door noiselessly. She peered through the opening and saw her husband leaning into Marilee's room.

"Yeah," Marilee answered, "she was just here."

"Must be in our room."

Pulse thundering in her ears, she watched through the slimmest of cracks as Neal crossed the hall.

The second he was inside the room and calling her name, she stepped into the corridor, slipped the door shut, and then said, "In here," as she slid the sheathed knife behind her back, under the waistband of her jeans. Moving stealthily, she kept the wallet pressed against her body.

A second later Neal was back in the hall. "What're you doing?"

"What does it look like?" She hitched her chin toward the bathroom.

"I know, but . . . why not use ours?" He cast a glance toward their room, with its small, attached bath.

"Dunno. Is it a problem?"

"Well, no. 'Course not." He shrugged, the expression on his face letting her know he considered it odd.

The wallet slid downward.

She clamped it tighter to her side just as Leah climbed up the stairs.

"Oh," she said, spying Neal and Brooke huddled together. "What's this? You two having a little tête-à-tête?"

Keeping her arm pressed against her side, hoping to secure the slick leather wallet, Brooke said, "Just checking to make sure there was soap and hand towels out in the bathroom. I—uh, forgot ear-lier."

Leah, more than a little tipsy, seemed to buy it.

"Where's Eli?" Brooke asked.

"He went for a walk." Rolling her eyes, she mimed puffing a ciga-rette. "Needed some fresh air, you know. As if I don't know he's go-ing out there to smoke." She sighed. "I guess he's not perfect."

Not by a long shot, Brooke thought, the wallet wedged tight against her, the knife at least unmoving.

"He's taking Shep with him," Leah announced as she stepped into the bathroom.

"What?" Brooke was thrown back to the panic of the night Shep went missing and a "stranger" brought him back to Leah in the park. The wallet slid, pushing past the sweater's hem.

"He loves that dog," Leah said with a disbelieving expression. "How weird is that?"

Not so.

"I guess we'll have to get a puppy." Leah pulled the door shut be-hind her.

Still pressing the wallet tight against her, Brooke was already head-ing for the stairs.

Just as she reached the top step she heard the click of the French doors opening to the back porch. Damn it all! She nearly tripped as she raced to the first floor and grabbed her jacket from a hook near the front door on the fly. Then, looking around to make certain no one was nearby or watching, she jammed Eli's sliding wallet into one of the pockets, the knife in the other.

At the back door she hurried outside but saw no one. "Shep!" she called and heard a soft woof at the side of the house. She sped around the corner and found Eli, leash in hand, with the dog. "Hey! Wait!"

He stopped, turned to face her, and in the light cast from the snow, he looked exactly like Gideon.

"What do you think you're doing?" she demanded, darkness sur-rounding them, only the reflection from the light in the windows on the snow giving any illumination.

"Just needed a break, I guess."

"With my dog?"

"He wanted to come."

"Like before?"

"What're you talking about?"

"I know who you are."

His eyes were shaded, his entire face in shadow, but she swore his jaw tightened. "Good."

"Not Eli Stone." Her pulse was pounding in her brain.

"No?" He didn't sound surprised.

"Give it up, Gideon. What the hell are you doing with my sister? Why are you here?"

"Gideon?"

"For the love of God!"

"Again, what are you talking about?" His voice was harsh. Offended. And in the darkness she couldn't be sure.

"I know you're posing as Eli Stone."

There were a few minutes when he didn't answer, when the wind rushed through the surrounding trees, when, farther away, the surf was a dull, ever-present roar. "Why would I 'pose,' as you put it, as someone I'm not?" he asked. "Are you out of your mind?" He stared at her as if he really did think she was crazy.

And then she stopped.

What if, after all, she was wrong?

What if this man was a doppelgänger of the man with whom she'd been involved? What if he were someone who was almost identical to Gideon? There were those people in the world, but the odds of Leah being involved with a Gideon look-alike were astronomical. Impossible. No, she wasn't wrong.

"Why?" he repeated.

"To get back at . . ."

"At? Who?" He let out a low whistle. "Oh, at you." Shaking his head, he reached into his pocket and pulled out a pack of cigarettes. He lit one as if he'd had the habit for decades. "That's pretty self-centered, don't you think? Leah warned me about that."

"I know who you really are."

"No. You don't know a thing about me. Obviously." He offered the pack to her. "Want one?"

"No, I don't . . ." Of course she saw that the brand was Marlboro Lights, the brand she'd smoked once after making love to Gideon. He'd never even taken a drag. "Get that out of here," he'd said. "There's a reason my dad used to call them coffin nails." And she'd never smoked around him again.

But now . . .

Eli drew hard on his cigarette, the tip glowing red in the night, noticed her staring. "Leah hates these things," he said. "I said I'd give 'em up once we're married." He leaned against the post supporting the porch. The voice—too low for Gideon. From the cigarettes?

Nah. If he were Gideon—and he was—it was too soon to have developed a smoker's voice. He was just disguising it.

"Look. I don't know how, but for some reason we got off on the wrong foot." Another long drag, then he threw the rest of the cigarette onto the lawn, where it fizzled and died in the snow. "Maybe we should start over."

And the way he said those words caused her heart to freeze.

"Start over?" she repeated, slipping her hand into her jacket pocket, feeling the security of the knife—his knife. Just in case. "I don't think we can."

His smile was disarming. "It's never too late."

He took a step toward her.

Her breath caught and the look he sent her—so intense, so dangerous—made her heart nearly stop.

The door opened with a loud creak.

Leah stepped onto the porch. "There you are!" she said before spying Brooke. "What—what's going on here?" She wrapped her arms around her body and shivered dramatically. "God, it's cold."

"Just getting to know your fiancé," Brooke said quickly.

Eli said evenly, "She's confused me with someone else."

CHAPTER 35

"Who?" Leah asked. "Who did Brooke confuse you with?" She shot Brooke a suspicious glare, then said, "And for the love of God, come inside. It's freezing out here." She shivered and held the door open.

Well, the cat was out of the bag now. "Eli is a dead ringer for a guy I used to know when I was selling hospital software," Brooke said, quickly coming up with a partial lie as she walked into the house. "His name was Gideon Ross."

"I get that a lot," Eli said as Shep streaked inside and he closed the door behind them. "People thinking I'm someone else."

"Really?" Leah shook her head. "Well, you must have gotten it wrong," she said to Brooke. "Hard, I know, to think that you made a mistake, but there you go." Then she turned to Eli. "Besides, I think you're pretty unique-looking." She winked. "And, of course, rakishly handsome."

"Of course," he replied, grinning at her but sliding a glance Brooke's way.

Not wanting to be witness to the sickening display, she walked into the kitchen, where she found a towel and started wiping down the counter just for something to do. Thankfully, Marilee was still upstairs.

She started to take off her jacket, then hesitated, considering the contents in her pockets. She considered hiding the knife and wallet in her bedroom and started for the stairs. As she did, she saw Leah kiss Eli lightly on the cheek, then wrinkle her nose. "You promised you would quit."

"After we're married," he reminded her.

"I'm going to hold you to it." Her eyes were sparkling again as she linked her fingers through his and pulled Eli into the living room, where her gaze landed on the stereo. Apparently, she hadn't noticed it before, probably because she was so wrapped up in her fiancé. "Oh my God, are these Nana's old records?" she asked, picking up the sleeves for the LPs and shuffling through them.

"Of course." Brooke shrugged out of her jacket and, with the intent of taking it upstairs at the first chance, kept an eye on Eli.

"I remember her playing these over and over. Do you?" she asked Brooke. She was already setting up the stereo, adjusting the speakers, and slipping an LP onto the turntable. A few seconds later Elvis's voice filled the room as he crooned "Blue Christmas." "Oh man," she whispered, stepping away from the stereo. "Mom used to play this right after Dad left." She seemed wistful. "It always made her so sad."

Neal stepped out of his office area and said, "Maybe we should listen to something a little more uplifting."

"Yeah," Brooke agreed. The last thing she needed was for any of them to get maudlin.

But Leah refilled her champagne flute with the end of the bottle she found on a side table, then began dancing slowly in front of the fire. "Nana used to get so mad at her."

"True." Brooke didn't want to think about it. She wanted to stop the record from spinning and sending out its sad notes, but because of Leah, she tamped down the urge and went back to polish the kitchen counter until it gleamed. She preferred not to think about their mother's grief when Douglas Fletcher decided he was a free spirit who couldn't be caged, that he no longer needed or wanted to be tied down by a wife and two daughters.

Thankfully, the song ended, but all of a sudden Leah was at the turntable again, lifting the needle intending to replay the song.

"Don't," Brooke said. "This is a celebration, right? No need to think about unhappy times."

"But I *love* this song! It was Mom's favorite!" And Elvis's voice began singing again. She began to sway. "That's your problem, Brooke," she said. "You never want to face the pain in your life so you never get over it."

"So now *you're* a psychologist."

"I've had a lot of counseling," she admitted.

"From a trainer?"

"And certified psychologists!"

"Because of all your divorces?" Brooke said and wanted to call back the words when she noticed Leah flinch.

Then her sister rounded on her. "Sure I got help dealing with my anger and despair when I went through the breakup of my marriages, all of them. But every time I went to a counselor it came out that most of my 'problems' "—she used air quotes with her fingers— "were mainly because of you, Brooke. My feelings of inadequacy and my need for love stemmed from our toxic relationship and what you did to me."

"Because of me?" Brooke shook her head so hard her ponytail loosened. "Save me! That's BS and you know it. I didn't put a gun to your head and force you to marry any of those losers!"

Leah sucked a breath through her teeth. She looked like she'd been slapped. "You started it all!" she accused, venom lacing her words. "With Neal."

"Oh whoa. For the love of—" Neal said, coming out of the laundry area, as he stopped short. "Don't," he warned.

"Why not?" she countered, her eyes narrowing on him. "Don't tell me you still feel guilty."

"Leah," he warned.

Brooke caught Eli silently watching the display, his eyes taking in the whole scenario.

Leah was on a roll. "He does, you know," she said to Brooke. "And if you ask me, I think he's never really gotten over me." Her chin was angled defiantly. "Right?" she threw out at her brother-in-law. "Come on, Neal. Admit it."

Neal frowned. "I think you've had a little too much to drink."

"Sure. Blame it on the alcohol. Or me. Or even Marilee, because you knocked up Brooke when you were still seeing me, but why the hell aren't you man enough to admit the truth?" she accused before knocking back the remains of her drink and attempting to set the flute on the mantel. The slim glass teetered. Leah made a grab for it, but it toppled and smashed on the rough stones of the hearth.

"Oh no! Mom's champagne flute!" She glared at Brooke, tears sprouting. "Look what you made me do!"

"Me?" Brooke rounded the peninsula, and while Elvis kept singing about loneliness at Christmas, she used a towel to pick up the shards and dab at the bits of spilled champagne. "I didn't make you do anything."

"Of course you did! You're the reason my life is the way it is! You always try to ruin everything!"

"What?" Brooke was immediately incensed. "Don't blame me!"

Leah threw an angry look at the kitchen, where Neal, standing on the other side of the peninsula, was watching the ugly drama unfold. Then she snarled at Brooke, "You started it all!" Her voice was low, almost menacing, barely audible over the stereo, but Brooke heard it loud and clear. "I shouldn't have listened to Eli! I should never have come back here!"

"Maybe you shouldn't have!" Brooke said. And before Elvis could sing another note she stalked to the record player and clicked it off, the needle skipping over the old grooves with an earsplitting shriek.

"You're horrible!" Leah said and left the room, stomping quickly up the stairs and down the short hallway. A second later a door slammed so hard it shook the entire house.

"And Merry Christmas to you too!" Brooke flung the towel and broken glass into the kitchen sink as Eli took off after his fiancée, his boots ringing on the stairs.

"Christ, Brooke," Neal said. "Can't you ever give Leah a break?"

"Yes. Yes, I can. When she gives me one! What kind of stunt is she pulling, huh? Springing a surprise fiancé on us whom she intends to marry right here, on our vacation. A guy we've never heard of, let alone met! Who does that?" she demanded.

"Maybe someone who wants to be a part of the family again."

Stunned, she stared at him, this man she'd married years before and sometimes didn't think she knew. "Why do you always do that?" she demanded, thinking of the way Leah had goaded him. "Why do you feel some inner need to defend her?"

"Maybe because she needs a champion."

"She's got Gid—Eli! He can be her champion!"

"What's going on?" Marilee called from the top of the stairs before quick, light steps could be heard and she and Shep came into the living room, where Brooke was still picking up pieces of glass. "Wait, don't tell me!" She held up a hand for dramatic effect. "Mom and Aunt Leah are fighting. Again."

"That's about it," Neal said. "Look, I'm out of it." He held up his hands and walked backward toward his makeshift office. "This is between your mother and her sister." Then he closed the heavy pocket door to the laundry room, a door rarely used.

"As if you aren't in the middle of it," Brooke yelled, and Marilee sent Brooke an I-can't-stand-this look.

"Figure it out," Marilee said, her chin jutted out angrily. "And both of you—you and Leah—grow the fuck up! Thank God I didn't invite Wes into this shitstorm!"

"Wow!" Brooke was stunned at Marilee's language. "Don't you ever talk to me like that again!" Brooke warned, but Marilee was out of the room and up the stairs, Shep at her heels.

"Great. Just . . . great." A headache beginning to throb behind her eyes, Brooke leaned against the kitchen counter and took deep breaths. First two. Then five. Then ten. Until she felt her blood pressure returning to normal and some of her mercurial anger subside. She was still pissed beyond pissed at her sister, still didn't trust Eli Stone, and was furious with her daughter, but she tried to rein in all her fury.

It was Christmas.

They were a family.

And Leah, whether Brooke liked it or not, was marrying Eli Stone. Whoever the hell he was.

The headache fueled by the aftereffects of the alcohol, arguments, and head-splitting memories was really taking hold. She found some Tylenol in the kitchen cupboard near the sink and uncapped the bottle just as she heard a door close upstairs and then heavy steps as Eli returned.

Perfect, she thought, shaking out two capsules and swallowing them dry. For the first time they were relatively alone. Dangerous as that may be, there was a chance she could get some answers, or that he might slip up and reveal himself.

"Where is everyone?" he asked, glancing around.

"They all retreated to their corners. Leah's upstairs, right?"

He gave a short nod. "And pissed."

"She and I got into it," she explained. "Too much alcohol. Too little good judgment. And then there's the problem of the mystery fiancé."

"No mystery," he insisted, but beyond his innocence she saw something darker—or was she imagining it all?

"I just want you to know that I don't believe a word you say. Why aren't you with your family? It's Christmas."

"Don't have one."

"Convenient."

He winced. "That's harsh."

"Okay. Maybe." Was he playing her? Of course. "So why don't you have one?"

"Car accident. Long time ago."

He was serious. Grim. And for the first time Brooke thought there was a grain of truth to his words. "Your parents?"

"And brother."

"God, I'm sorry," she said automatically, though she still didn't trust him.

The corners of his mouth turned down. "Yeah. A Silverado's a great pickup. Turns out it's no match for a fully loaded log truck." His voice was flat. "Dad and my brother died at the scene. Mom a couple of days later. " His eyes had turned dark and she sensed a resentment that hadn't been there earlier. "Anything else you want to know?"

She felt a fleeting pang of regret but reminded herself that this man was an incredible liar, so she plowed on, ignoring the hard set of his jaw. "What about other siblings? I'd think they'd want to come to the wedding."

Something glittered in his eyes. Something dangerous. It came quickly but just as rapidly vanished. He gave his head a sharp shake. "Just Jake, and he's gone."

"When did it happen?" she asked.

He hesitated. Then lifted a shoulder. "A while. Goin' on twenty years or so."

"You were just a kid—teenager," she said, telling herself the story might not be true, not to fall for it, reminding herself this was the man who'd sworn he'd never let her go. And now he was back. Lying. Pretending to be someone else. All her defenses were up.

He shrugged at the mention of his age. "Doesn't matter. I got by."

"Hey!" Leah said, visible through the archway opening to the staircase. She was standing at the landing, where the stairs turned up-ward. She appeared to have calmed a bit, some of her inebriated anger having disappeared. And she'd changed clothes. Red lace peeked from beneath the thick collar of a fluffy white robe. "What is this? Twenty questions?"

"Fifty," he replied, looking up at her.

Leah glared down at her sister. "What're you doing, Brooke?"

"Just getting to know my new or soon-to-be brother-in-law."

"Sure." Leah let out a long sigh as she started down the steps. "See what I mean?" she said to Eli. "Impossible."

"What's impossible?" Brooke demanded.

"You, to begin with, and this entire hostile situation." She flung out an arm to dramatically encompass the entire house and every-one and everything in it. Then she gave Eli a pouting look. "I told you coming up here was a bad idea, that it wouldn't work."

"It would if you two wanted it to," he said and climbed the stairs. Leah stood on her tiptoes to kiss him on the lips. It was just too much.

Brooke needed time and space, some breathing room, so she found Shep's leash and threw on her jacket, then stepped into boots. As she did so, she felt the weight of Eli's wallet and knife in the pock-ets and smiled to herself. "I'm going to take Shep out for a walk," she said to the house as a whole as the dog trotted up and she snapped the leash to his collar.

"Now?" Neal asked as he deigned to come out of his makeshift of-fice. "It's really coming down outside. I saw on my phone it's gonna be bad, a blizzard."

"Short walk." She was desperate to get out of the house, to sort things out in her mind. "We'll be fine."

"If you say so." For a second she thought Neal might offer to join them, but he only said, "Just be careful."

"Always am," she lied and saw Eli raise a doubting eyebrow. Yeah, he knew way too much about her not to be Gideon. She just had to prove it, she told herself as she walked out the door, Shep pulling on the leash.

Outside the wind had died, at least temporarily. Her headache was lessening and she took in a deep breath of the ice-cold air. The street was quiet, a hush with the snow.

Huge flakes were falling rapidly, providing a veil and, in Brooke's case, a cover.

Her boots crunched, packing down the undisturbed snow as she passed a few houses, noting the winking lights and displays. She remembered that when Nana was alive, they too had strung colored lights over the eaves and at one point, long ago, displayed a wooden Santa with one mittened hand in the air and, over the opposite shoulder, a huge bag with a jack-in-the-box and a teddy bear spilling out of it.

But that had been years ago, when Brooke and Leah were children and life made sense. Now everything was upside down. She walked to the single streetlamp and stood just out of its glow. After checking to see that she was alone, she pulled Eli's wallet from her pocket and flipped it open. His driver's license was visible behind a plastic window. She squinted but saw Eli's picture on the card. His name, Eli John Stone, was legible and his birth date was listed, not the same as Gideon's, but she noted the California license was issued in the last year. . . . Height and weight, color of eyes and hair were meaningless; all could be altered with lifts, padding, contact lenses, and dye. She made note of his address . . . maybe a landlord could provide information. But behind the California license was an older one, this one issued by the State of Oregon, again to Eli John Stone. He appeared younger in this DMV picture, his hair darker, his eyes listed as hazel, his weight five pounds lighter.

Gideon!

"Got ya," she whispered.

She flipped through insurance and credit cards, then, with her back to the house, pulled off one glove for a steadier hand and took pictures of all of his ID with her cell phone. He had a little cash with him, under a hundred dollars, but there was no other clue within. *Who are you really?* She wondered if Eli Stone was his real name, if Gideon Ross was the alias.

If there was one.

But why would Gideon have lied on their first meeting?

Why would he get involved with Leah and insist on traveling here and meet her family? Just to taunt Brooke? After over a year? Nothing was making any sense. She stuffed the wallet back into her pocket. Lost in thought, she walked farther along the road that ran along the east side of the island. Across the dark water, blurred by the still-falling snow, the lights of Marwood were visible.

"It's beautiful, isn't it?" a voice said.

Brooke nearly jumped out of her skin.

Shep gave off a startled bark.

Turning, Brooke spied Gina Duquette as she approached. She was pulling a kid's sled filled with white sacks printed with the name, web address, and phone number of the bakery. In a separate box a scruffy black-and-white terrier was riding in the wagon, a Santa hat perched jauntily on his head.

"Didn't mean to creep up on you," she said. Bundled in a puffy coat, a knit cap, earmuffs and gloves, she dragged the sled into the circle of light cast by the streetlamp. "I just love the snow. It's so quiet out, you know. Peaceful. I love it almost as much as I love Christmas."

"What're you doing?" Brooke asked.

"It's a tradition I started about what—maybe eight, nine years ago. I make a few extra cookies, tarts, and rolls, whatever, but extra on Christmas Eve of course. And what we don't sell I donate, mostly to the church, but I always save some for the neighbors on the street. Jasper and I deliver them." She winked. "Goodwill, you know, and good for business. Look, I've got a bag for you and your family." She reached down, picked up a sack, and handed it to a stunned Brooke while Jasper stood and stretched, bright eyes on Shep.

"That's very nice," she said, restraining her dog from climbing aboard the sled to greet the little dog. "Are you sure?"

"Absolutely."

Shep, tail wagging as he strained on the leash, whined loudly.

"Brooke?" She heard Neal's voice.

"I guess I'd better get back."

"And I need to deliver the rest of these before the snow gets too deep," Gina said. "The Drummonds are here this year and they've got a new little granddaughter that I can't wait to meet."

"Brooke?" She heard her husband calling for her again, just as Neal's dark figure appeared and Shep, with an excited bark, ran up to greet him, nearly pulling Brooke's arm from its socket. "There you are!"

"Is something wrong?"

"No, no, the lights flickered again and I couldn't find the backup battery charger we brought, the one that you can plug your laptop into."

"It's in the bedroom, I think, the small overnight bag. Neal, this is Mrs. Duquette. She owns the bakery and is out playing Santa Claus to the neighborhood."

"Gina," the older woman corrected as the terrier made circles before settling back in his bed. "Mrs. Duquette was my mother-in-law, God rest her soul, and she was . . . I guess a woman who knew her own mind is the best way to say it. Glad to see you back here." She was smiling up at Neal.

"Back?" Brooke repeated.

"Yes, yes, I saw you at the house." She was still grinning at Neal. "When I was walking Jasper here. Late last summer, when the weather was a lot warmer than this."

"Last summer?" Brooke said and saw that Neal was standing stock-still.

"Yes, Labor Day, you were here with Leah!" She turned her eyes to Brooke. "Remember, I told you I saw her with a man. So how is she? I assume she's here with you."

"Leah's here," Brooke said, though her gaze was glued to her husband's face. "But this is Neal, *my* husband."

"You must be mistaken," Neal said to Gina. He was recovering a bit, but again Brooke noticed his telltale tic, pulsing at his temple.

He was lying.

Brooke knew it.

And if she remembered correctly, around Labor Day Neal had been in California, working with a client. . . . What the hell?

"Oh. Well." Gina frowned. "I must be slipping. I'm horrible with names and I admit it, but I never forget a face." Then, in the awkward silence that followed, she added, "Jasper and I'd better get running along." Wiggling her gloved fingers, she added, "Merry Christmas," then took up the handle of her sled again.

"What the hell was that all about?" Brooke said. "You were here in September? With Leah?"

Neal opened his mouth, about to lie, but thought better of it. "Okay, fine. Yes. You caught me." He let out a long sigh, his breath fogging. "It's about the money she owes us. You know money's been tight, what with Marilee's boarding school and college on the horizon. So Leah and I have been talking."

"About?"

"About selling the cabin," he admitted.

"What?" She couldn't believe what she was hearing. "Nana's cabin? My cabin? You're kidding, right?"

"No." He shook his head. "In September we met with a Realtor, over in Marwood." He motioned to the bay. "Thought we might put it on the market in the spring, when the market's good for vacation buyers. That's why I was so insistent that we come here," he admitted. "I thought it might be our last time."

"And you didn't think to talk to me about it. Your wife. The woman whose name is on the deed?" she said, stunned. "Instead, you went behind my back?"

"I knew—we knew you wouldn't go for it."

"Damn right I won't! This is my cabin, Neal, and someday it will be Marilee's! You and I—we agreed about that. Years ago. We wanted to keep it in the family."

"It's also half Leah's," he reminded her as the wind blew colder and the sound of the surf in the distance became louder.

"Not quite. Because of the loan you gave her."

"Yeah, yeah, I know, but that doesn't cover all of her interest. She still owns a portion."

"Nonetheless, you had no right—none—to talk to my sister without consulting me, no right to plot about selling the cabin." She stared up at him through the falling snow. "Neal, what the eff were you thinking?"

Before he could answer she was quickly putting two and two together. "You've been talking to Leah about this, haven't you? Oh—oh crap." It was hitting her like a ton of bricks. Neal and Leah—in this together. "I've seen you behind the woodshed door, and then again, I found out you lied about leaving your wallet at the store. Hank Thatcher told me you were on the phone the whole time."

"You've been checking up on me?" he asked, trying to look outraged.

"No! But I should have."

"You're a great one to talk, Brooke," he accused, but she wasn't going to listen to any outlandish lies or excuses he could come up with. She shoved Gina Duquette's sack of pastries into his arms, then slapped Shep's leash onto his palm. "The answer is no! I'm *not* selling. Ever. Got that?" So angry she was shaking, she added, "So go tell Leah and . . . and whatever his name is that the cabin stays in the family!"

With that, she took off at a jog, away from her lying husband, away from the cabin that he and her sister planned to sell, and away from Gideon-fucking-Ross.

She didn't look back, just felt the cold air fill her lungs as her blood began to pump through her veins. Her mind spun, the headache at bay now returning. How long had Neal and Leah been plotting to sell the cabin? How many times had they met? Was it all as Neal said, about money and selling Nana's cottage, or was there more to it? Gina Duquette had thought them husband and wife. In fact, she'd seemed certain they were a couple.

Were they?

No, that didn't make sense.

Leah was obviously over the moon in love with the man she believed was Eli Stone. Those emotions weren't faked. Brooke had witnessed her sister in love often enough to know.

But she hadn't met Eli until after Labor Day, sometime in September, so maybe Leah and Neal had been involved *before* Leah met Eli. Maybe they'd been having an affair for a long while. Maybe that was why Neal was so eager to lend Leah money, to keep her close and to keep her quiet.

Brooke kept running, filling her lungs, stretching her legs, and trying to keep control of her emotions. She needed a clear head no matter how heartsick she felt.

Don't jump to conclusions. Just figure out what's going on.

She reached the landing.

If the general store were open, she would have marched in, bought a pack of Marlboro Lights and a bottle of cheap wine with some of the money in Eli's wallet, and thrown herself a pity party. But the store was closed, and on second thought she didn't need a hit of nicotine or a slug of alcohol to settle her nerves. She needed to think and think clearly.

She felt as if she were a marionette in some dark scheme and her sister, husband, and Eli/Gideon were pulling the strings.

Well, no more.

It was time to turn the tables on them all.

God, she wished she had a cigarette.

No, no! Think, Brooke, think!

Brooke pushed herself and kept running down to the ferry landing and past the tall piers and boats rocking on the water. She felt snowflakes melting on her cheeks and smelled the salt from the sea, which of course reminded her of her struggle with Gideon under the water in Elliott Bay.

Unlike her sister, Brooke didn't like the role of victim; she refused to play it. No way. And she was tired of hiding and cowering and fearing her family would find out the truth. She'd never been a coward in her life, but ever since her affair with Gideon she'd let her own fears and the threats of others rule her life.

No more.

And an idea was coming to her mind, a plan beginning to form.

She made a big loop in the snow and started running toward the cabin.

The words of "Happy Xmas (War Is Over)" by John Lennon and Yoko Ono ran through her mind. She threw a question at herself. It wasn't "What have you done?" No, the question was, "What are you going to do?"

As the wind began to pick up, she knew the answer.

It was time to turn the damned tables.

CHAPTER 36

"Are you crazy? Brooke, it's Christmas Eve!" Caleb Reynolds said from the other end of the connection. Caleb, her coworker at Clayton Electronics, was a security expert—the best in the business, as far as she knew—and one of her closest friends at the company. He'd been in the military, working in army intelligence for nearly twenty years before being honorably discharged and hiring on at the company. Caleb had the ability not only to fix the bugs in their own products, but he was also at the cutting edge with tech security. For Caleb there was no dead end when it came to accessing information. Brooke suspected he was a hacker of the highest order, though he'd never copped to it, and if Bill Clayton or anyone at the company suspected him of it, they looked the other way. Somehow Caleb could access all kinds of corporate and/or government files. As far as she knew, he'd never crossed that invisible criminal line. But she wasn't sure. Tonight would be the test.

"Who asks someone to work on Christmas Eve?" She could almost see him shaking his head at her folly.

"I know, I know, but you're not celebrating with your kids until the day after tomorrow; you told me so at the office," Brooke whispered into the phone as the snow danced and swirled around her as she crouched in her neighbor's backyard. Thankfully, the Bennetts' house was dark and unoccupied, no lights burning. She'd found a thinning spot in the hedge separating the properties. From her position she was able to peek through the frozen branches to her own backyard, where lights glowed bright, reflecting in patches on the deepening snow. The woodshed obstructed part of her view, but she caught glimpses of everyone—Marilee, Neal, Leah, and Eli, even Shep. She reminded Caleb, "You said Tanisha had Kayla and Booker for Christmas. Isn't that right? You go over to her place to see what Santa brought, but you don't have them until the next time."

"But it's *still* Christmas Eve," he complained.

"Look, I'll owe you. Big-time. It's a lot to ask, but it's important. Really. Otherwise I wouldn't ask."

He hesitated.

"Please?"

He muttered something unintelligible, then sighed loudly. "Okay, I know I'm going to regret this, but lay it on me," Caleb said. "And I haven't promised to do anything yet." She heard a rattling of papers. "Wait a sec; let me turn on my computer so I can take some notes."

God, it was cold. She was shivering, the wind cutting through her jacket and jeans, her lips beginning to chap, her gloves unable to shield her from the freezing temperatures.

"Okay," he said, and she heard ice cubes clinking in a glass. "Ready."

"Good. I need information," she admitted. "Anything you can find on a guy."

"What guy?"

"That's just it. I'm not sure."

"Hold up a minute—"

"He's got several aliases, I think, and I'm not sure which one is his true identity. Maybe none of them. But the names I have are Gideon Ross, Eli John Stone," she said, then realized she had no idea how many names Gideon went by. "Also possibly Jake or Jason Ross or Stone, or any other amalgam of them. I've got two driver's licenses and some credit cards, and from the pictures on the licenses, you can probably do facial recognition, right?"

"Possibly," he said thoughtfully, the wheels seeming to already turn in his head. "But we're treading in dangerous legal waters here."

"I wouldn't ask if it wasn't important," she said again and heard a sound in the distance behind her. She stopped to listen, all her muscles tense, her heart racing. Had someone in the house seen her? Come outside in this storm? Eli? Neal?

From the corner of her eye she spied Gina Duquette pulling her sled in the opposite direction, vanishing behind the curtain of snow.

"Ask what?" Caleb said on the other end of the connection. "What is it you want exactly?"

Satisfied that she was still alone, she explained, "I just need a positive ID and a criminal background check on him. I want any accident reports, that sort of thing. Birth records, marriage licenses, divorce decrees, especially any arrest history or outstanding warrants. Anything you can dig up on this guy."

"With the double or triple or whatever identity."

"Yes!"

"I assume you have a reason for this?"

"God yes! My sister plans to marry this guy and we don't know anything about him. I have a feeling that he's conning her or worse. And now he's in our home and I'm scared to death. Seriously."

A pause. "I don't know . . ." More clinking, as if he were swirling a drink as he deliberated.

"Caleb, please." She heard the anxious tone in her voice. "I have a really bad feeling about him. I'm sure I've met him before and nothing about him is matching up, okay? The least he could be is a con artist."

"And the worst?" he asked, his voice low and sober. She heard the clicking of keys and imagined him, a balding man with smooth, dark skin, a tonsure of black hair, and a trim beard. She figured he was sitting at his desk, the square lenses of his glasses reflecting what he was seeing on his computer screen.

"I'm not sure," she admitted, remembering her near-death struggle with Gideon on the *Medusa*. She was suddenly as cold on the inside as she was on the outside. "I think he could be deadly."

"Then you should call the police."

"I will. But I need evidence. I don't have enough, nothing concrete. Just suspicions."

A pause.

She rubbed her free hand on her jeans for warmth. "Please, Caleb. Help me out here. This man, he's a predator. I know for a fact that he spied on my daughter."

"You know?" he said, and his voice was even more serious.

"Yes. I have no proof, but from what he's said, I know he's a voyeur. So I just need help to put him away."

"I could lose my job," he said, and she imagined him worriedly wiping his hand over his face before taking a sip of whatever he was drinking while he was alone on Christmas Eve.

"I'm desperate, Caleb," she admitted, her voice quivering, her teeth chattering.

She heard him expel a long breath. "Oh hell. Fine," he finally agreed. "I'll see what I can do, scratch the surface, and if I find anything suspicious or, you know, really bad, I'll send it to you."

Her shoulders sagged in relief. "Thanks," she said. "I'm not in the house right now, but as soon as I get back, I'll send the info to you from my personal email including the pictures and you can reply to the same."

"Not in the house? Where the hell are you? It's a damned blizzard outside here in Seattle. Streets frozen. Traffic a mess. I'm worried I won't be able to get to Tanisha's house in the morning, but the kids are all about it. A white Christmas, you know, and Santa will make it."

"I'm on the island—Piper Island. It's a little one off the Oregon coast, south of Cannon Beach; nearest town is Marwood.

"But listen, don't email me. I'll contact you first."

"How?" Her whole body was shaking.

"I'll email you first. You won't recognize the return address, so it might go to your spam account. Look for the word 'holiday' spelled backward, uh, with the 'Y' and 'H' capitalized and an extra capital letter 'L' in the word. 'Holliday' backward, got it? 'YadiLloH.' Separated by random numbers and symbols. It won't fool anyone who knows what they're doin', not for long, but it could slow 'em down for a while. And I'll destroy it . . . Holy God, I must be out of my mind."

"As I said, I owe you."

"And more than a bottle of that cheap-ass Scotch you gave at the Secret Santa Christmas party last week."

"There was a price limit," she said.

He snorted.

"Okay, okay. Top shelf. And I'll still owe you."

"You got it," he said. "For the rest of your damned life."

"You got it."

"All right, then," Caleb said in a little better mood. "I'll see what I can find." Then he disconnected.

Okay, that was a start.

She hoped Caleb could gather the evidence she needed.

If not, she'd have to goad Eli into a confession, and that would be tricky.

But maybe necessary.

She rubbed her hands together, trying to get the blood moving; her gloves just weren't cutting it.

Then, once she took another look inside and assured herself that everyone was still in the cabin, she slunk along the hedgerow to the front of the house and driveway. She slipped between the two vehicles, her SUV and Leah's Chevy Bolt. With one eye on the house, ensuring that no one was looking through the windows, she reached into the vehicle and under the seat to retrieve her sample case with all of the tiny spy equipment Clayton Electronics had to offer.

Two can play at this game, she thought, before going to work. Thankfully, all of her samples were wireless and already connected to her iPhone as well as her laptop for ease in showing potential customers the tiny microphones' and cameras' capabilities. Now all she had to do was strategically place the equipment. It wouldn't be easy with so many people in the house, but she considered it a last gasp effort to expose Eli as the fraud he was.

She pocketed the equipment and left the case and, with a prayer to a God she hadn't been tight with for years, slid Eli's knife from its sheath and, with an eye on the house, crouched between the two parked vehicles. Using all her strength, she plunged the blade deep into the side of one of the tires on Leah's car. She sliced as best she could, slipped the knife back into its sheath, and, silently praying that no one had seen her, walked inside.

Shep bounded to greet her and as she petted the dog, yanked off her boots, the sights, sounds, and smells of Christmas were overwhelming.

Once again the old turntable was spinning out Christmas tunes. Gina Duquette's decorated Christmas cookies had been spread on a platter and Neal had cracked out the eggnog and was pouring drinks. The fire was roaring, the tree lit, and while Neal tended bar, Leah set presents under the tree. Even Marilee had joined the group, her bad mood seemingly dispelled, a book open on her lap.

A happy family, to the untrained eye.

But Brooke knew better. Beneath the gaiety and visible Christmas spirit, something much darker lurked. Something evil. She thought about how innocent deception could appear. She was still wearing her jacket, nervously hoping no one noticed the bulge in its pockets or made the discovery of the knife and the wallet she'd stolen.

Where was Eli?

Missing, it seemed.

"Hey, there she is!" Neal said, finally noticing Brooke and offering her what seemed a sincere grin. "About time you showed up!" She forced a smile as she walked to the fire to warm the backs of her legs and remembered what the baker had said about seeing Neal with "his wife," who, in fact, had been Leah, the very person he was plotting with to sell this cabin. All behind her back. She wondered what else was going on between them.

As if he read her thoughts, Neal's expression tightened, but he held up a mug of eggnog. "How about some Christmas cheer?"

You lying son of a bitch!

"Sure," she forced out. "Just give me a minute or two. I need to get a sweater. Got a little cold out there."

Leah actually caught the tail end of the conversation. "A little cold? It's a damned blizzard! The lights keep going on and off and the wind is screaming. It's a miracle the ferry is still running, but it is. I called."

"Amazing. I'd better go warm up. Cold to the bone. Where's Eli?"

Leah rolled her eyes. "Outside." Her lips tightened. "I swear, it's like he has to smoke as much as he can before the wedding because he knows that after we say our vows . . ." She made an exaggerated slice of her hand across her throat. "No more." She glanced to the back windows. "I'm surprised you didn't see him . . . oh, there he is now." She grinned as Eli walked through the back door and stomped snow from his boots.

Brooke's heart nearly stopped.

Had he overheard her conversation on the phone?

Or had he seen her deliberately vandalize her sister's car?

He caught Brooke's eye for a second, then said to Leah, "Any chance of getting a drink here?"

"Absolutely," Leah said. "You?"

"In a few. Give me a sec." Without any further explanation or lies, she headed upstairs, still wearing her jacket. She went into the master bath and locked the door. After checking that the soap was still covering the camera's lens just in case the little bit of surveillance equipment had somehow been reconnected, she spread out the equipment she'd taken from her sample case. Within seconds she'd ensured the tiny cameras were wirelessly connected to her phone. They were activated by motion detection, which lengthened their battery life and kept the user from seeing hours of dead footage where nothing happened.

How many times had she explained the same to potential customers, never thinking for a minute that she would have to employ the very equipment she sold?

Quickly, she changed into a bulky sweater and boot-leg jeans. She slid Eli's wallet into a pocket and folded the hem of the sweater over the slight bulge. Then she strapped the knife to her leg, just inside the top of her boot, before sliding the flared leg of her jeans over her calf.

Nervously, she peeked into the hallway and ensured that she was still alone on the second floor.

The music had stopped, but no one appeared to be upstairs.

On silent feet she crept into the guest room and closed the door softly behind her. She noticed a picture Leah had obviously placed on the bureau that hadn't been there earlier. Eli was standing to one side, an arm looped over her shoulders, both in jackets and squinting, Leah's blond locks flying around her face, Eli's smile all too familiar as he held out the camera for the selfie. They appeared to be standing on a dock near a marina. Behind them, water stretched into the haze.

Brooke picked up the picture and squinted. Barely notable in the thin fog were the ghostly shapes of sailboats. If she wasn't mistaken, the prow of one of the boats looked exactly like that of the *Medusa*. She recognized the shape of the windows and a bit of rigging.

Was it possible?

Maybe, but there were thousands of boats that appeared the same.

With one ear to any noise in the hallway, she snapped a picture of the photo on her camera and would send it to Caleb. Maybe he could identify it. She considered stealing it so that she would have time to remove the picture from its bronze frame and mat, hoping for a bigger image of the boat, but she couldn't risk it now. She didn't have the time.

She felt in her gut that this sailboat was the *Medusa*.

You liar!

She wanted to take it downstairs and throw it in his face, to expose him for the fraud he was, but she couldn't. Not yet. Aware of time ticking by, she forced her temper to cool as she set the damning picture on the bureau again.

She had to keep working.

Fast, fast, fast.

Before anyone came upstairs.

Anxiously, she hid one of the tiny cameras on the ledge over the windowsill, which offered her a view of the entire room. After securing the camera with a bit of removable adhesive tape, she started to slip into the hallway when she heard footsteps on the other side of the door.

Crap!

Heart knocking, she slipped into the closet, the plastic hangers of Leah's clothes swooshing as she pulled the door shut. A second later someone came into the room.

She held her breath. The closet was small and tight. Brooke closed her eyes, her ears straining as she heard someone just inches away.

Rustling.

A soft thud. Something tossed onto the bed.

More rustling.

"What the fuck?"

Eli's voice. Only not quite so raspy. And angry.

"Where the hell?"

She heard him walk around the room.

Oh God. Oh God. Oh God.

She squeezed as far back as she could, felt nervous sweat break out on her forehead.

"I know it was here . . . shit!"

Please just leave!

He'd discovered that either his wallet or his knife was missing.

Now there would be hell to pay.

And she knew where his fury and frustration would be leveled. Well, so be it.

She heard the door open, then footsteps fading down the hall. "Leah!" he yelled, and then footsteps thumping double time down the stairs.

Silently, she opened the closet door a bit, saw no one in the room, and stepped out into the hallway. She was shaking inside, her heart beating as if it would fly out of her chest. She started to close the door to the guest room, then realized he hadn't shut it, so she hurried to the stairs.

She heard glasses clinking and muted conversation before Eli's now raspy voice demanded, "Have you seen my wallet?"

"No, babe," she said. "Isn't it in the bedroom?"

"No. I just checked."

"Your jacket, then? A pocket?"

"I already looked."

Leah sighed. "Sorry, I have no idea. It must be somewhere." Before he said another word, Leah said, "And why are we not hearing Christmas music?" Quick footsteps sounded, then, "How about this one? It was one of Nana's favorites."

A few heartbeats later Brooke heard the strains of "A Holly Jolly Christmas," a recording her mother and Brooke detested. But at least it provided noise and cover as Brooke affixed a second camera to the family portrait at the top of the stairs.

As she checked her phone to make sure the camera's eye took in the entire upper hallway and staircase to the entry below, she heard a rustling at the base of the stairs. She froze. Looked down the steps. Expected to have to explain herself. But the two interested eyes blinking up at her belonged to the dog.

Footsteps crossed the dining area and she straightened.

"Geez, Shep. Don't tell me you have to go out again?" Neal said, appearing at the foot of the stairs. "Oh." He caught a glimpse of Brooke on the upper floor. "I get it, he was looking for you."

"He found me," she said lightly and hurried down to the first floor, where she patted the dog on the head and changed the subject. "I think I was offered a drink earlier?"

"Just needs a finishing touch." Neal was already on his way to the kitchen and Shep trotted back to his bed.

Eli rounded the corner then, nearly running into her. His eyes narrowed a bit.

"I don't suppose you know where my wallet is?" he said, his lips blade thin, his gaze accusing.

She felt the slim leather in her pocket but drew her eyebrows together and slowly shook her head as if she were really thinking hard.

Then she smiled, met his gaze, and lied through her teeth. "I have no idea, Eli. No idea whatsoever."

CHAPTER 37

Obviously Eli didn't believe her.

He glared at her as she made her way into the kitchen and sat on one of the barstools at the peninsula. Her heart was hammering, but it slowed as she watched Neal concoct the frothy drink, adding whiskey from a bottle that was rapidly emptying, then the eggnog, a little powdered sugar, and a whisper of vanilla. "My own special recipe," he said with a smile that might have been disarming if she wasn't so pissed at him. He added a dash of nutmeg across the top and even went so far as to squirt a dollop of whipped cream across the top.

"That's decadent," she said.

"I know." He slid the drink to her. "Marilee's idea, and it's Christmas."

"Dad wouldn't let me have any booze," Marilee complained from her chair near the fire as the music died. "And he didn't have any cherries either."

"My bad," he said as Brooke took a taste of the drink and forced a smile. Meanwhile, Eli found his jacket, threw it on, and went outside. A few minutes later she heard the sound of an axe splitting wood.

Leah looked out the window and shook her head. "I guess someone's taking out his frustrations. He misplaced his wallet and is really pissed about it. So much for the Christmas spirit."

Brooke steered the conversation back to the drinks. "The whipped cream's a good idea," she told her daughter but let her eyes wander to the room, searching for the best place to hide a camera. She settled on the Christmas tree, where it would provide a panoramic view of the great room, the back door, and most of the kitchen. Once everyone went upstairs she could place it on an upper branch. Rather than Elf on a Shelf this Christmas, she decided, they would have Spy in the Sky.

How the Harmon family had evolved.

She took another sip and managed a smile, the wallet heavy in her pocket, the knife pressed hard to her calf.

Leah was fussing with the record player again, slipping an old LP onto the spindle, when she suddenly stopped. "Oh Lord, what's Shep got?"

"What?" Brooke saw that Shep had returned to his bed and was chewing on a toy. "It's just his crab," she said, seeing the toy she'd stuffed back into the closet when she'd found the bracelet Gideon had left wrapped around its claw.

"No," Leah said, her voice rising. "No, that's not it." Her eyes were rounding and she dropped the LP, letting out a small scream as she backed away from the dog and his bed. "Oh God, what kind of sick . . . ?"

"What?" Brooke was across the room in an instant. "Up," she said to the dog and he scrambled to his feet, dropping the toy on his cushion. Beside the crab, in two pieces, was the figurine of Joseph. His robed body in one spot, his bearded, severed head next to it. Red paint, made to look like blood, was visible on his short neck.

"Is that . . . is that blood?" Leah shrieked as she backed away.

"What the fu—?" Neal had run into the room and Marilee had joined them.

"Not blood," Marilee said and didn't seem disturbed at all. "It's nail polish." She picked up both pieces, her fingers near the jagged neck and severed head. Her nails were a perfect match to the stain on the tiny face. "Bloodie-Rosie," she said. "My favorite color."

"You did this?" Leah cried.

"What?" Marilee shook her head, her messy bun almost coming loose. "Of course not! Jes—"

Leah's face was a mask of horror. "I just can't even . . ." She shuddered visibly, her face pale as death. "How in the name of sweet heaven did it get on the statue?" She was asking the room at large, but her gaze had landed on Neal.

"Hey, don't look at me. I have no idea. None! The figurine was missing when we set up the crèche," Neal said, backing away, palms outward, as if he expected her to physically attack him.

"Well, it's not funny. It's not funny at all. It's sacrilegious and sick, sick, sick!" Her lips curled backward in disgust and she leveled her gaze at Brooke. "Is this your idea of a joke?"

"What? No! Like Neal said, it was missing from the rest of the set when we unpacked it. And why would I do that? And put it where Shep could choke on it?"

"You?" She turned her outraged gaze back to Marilee. "You're the one who owns and recognizes the nail polish."

"I already said I didn't!" Marilee pointed out, readjusting the band holding her hair away from her face. "Seriously? You think I would do that?" She pointed to the headless statue. "It was missing before I got here. And really, why would I?"

"Why would anyone?" Leah said, her eyes narrowing, and she rounded on Brooke again. "Why would anyone want to spoil Christmas?"

At that moment Eli, his arms laden with kindling, walked into the room, frigid air sweeping inside. "What's going on?" He kicked the door shut, then walked to the fire.

"It's horrible!" Leah said as he dropped the kindling onto the hearth and began stacking it. "Someone took one of Nana's figurines from the crèche and . . . and mutilated it."

"They did what?"

Was his concern real?

"See this!" Leah was suddenly bold enough to pick up the statue and march it back to the fireplace where Eli was still standing.

"Ooh." He turned away. "What happened?"

Eagerly, Leah filled him in on what she'd discovered. "It's someone's idea of a sick prank. Just awful."

"I wonder whose idea?" Brooke said as her gaze fell hard on Eli.

"For the love of—are you kidding me?" Leah let out a puff of disbelief.

Neal tried to be the voice of reason. "So let's just glue him back together, put a little nail polish remover on him, and set him up where he belongs."

"Like it never happened?" Leah said and sent Brooke a glare that was guaranteed to cut through the hardest of steel. "This is all part of a demented attempt to ruin Christmas. And we all know who's behind it!"

She obviously meant Brooke, but for once she didn't rise to the bait. She didn't have time. A beheaded statuette was one thing; child's play, she figured. She had to find a way to expose a con man—a dangerous man—and stop a wedding.

"It's Christmas, for God's sake!" Leah was visibly shaking. "I don't care who did this," she said, but they all knew it to be a lie. "Nothing's going to destroy this holiday or my—our wedding!" she declared. "And tonight we're going to midnight mass, and we're going to learn the true meaning of Christmas if it kills us!" When no one argued she lifted her chin. "And . . . and we might even join a caroling group or whatever, but this year, the year I'm getting married, it's going to be special!" She fought tears as she started for the stairs, then glanced over her shoulder, her eyebrows pinched together. "Coming?" she said to Eli, and it sounded more like a command than a question.

"In a sec," he promised. "Just got to get something out of the shed. I left my gloves out there."

"Fine." Leah didn't wait, just marched up the stairs.

Marilee's cell phone chirped and she, spying the incoming number on the phone's screen, answered it with a smile. "Hi . . . yeah, you too." Then, seeing that her mother was watching, she added, "Hold on a sec" as she hustled up the stairs. A pause and then, "Just the usual family drama," she said, her voice fading. A second later an upper door shut.

Eli walked outside again.

"I guess we should get ready for mass too," Neal said, reluctance heavy in his voice. "But first I'd better fix this guy." Neal carried the figurine of Joseph into the laundry area.

Brooke let out a breath. This was probably as alone as she was going to get, so she had to take a chance. Nerves strung tight, she carried a chair in from the dining room, climbed onto the seat, and pretended to mess with the Christmas lights. Instead, she slipped a tiny camera from her pocket and glued it quickly to one of the highest branches.

"Hey, what're you doing?" Neal asked, and her heart sank.

Had he seen what she was up to?

She started climbing off the chair.

"Careful!" he warned.

Too late! As she stepped off the chair, she tripped slightly, and down she went, the chair clattering loudly.

Shep, startled, scrambled to his feet, barking.

As Brooke landed, she saw Eli standing on the other side of the window, as if he'd been standing there for a while, as if he'd watched her plant the camera.

"Brooke! For the love of—" Neal knelt down next her. "Are you okay?" he asked, his forehead furrowed with worry.

"I—I think so." She stood with his help, then limped to the couch. "Nothing broken, pretty sure."

"But a sprain? Geez, I've heard those can be worse sometimes."

"I just twisted my ankle again, the same one as last year." The ankle that had been injured in her fight with Gideon on his boat and she'd lied that she'd tripped while running.

As if he read her mind, Eli smiled behind the cold glass.

Footsteps pounded from upstairs and Marilee rushed into the room. "What happened?"

Before she could explain Leah had hurried back to the living room. She was barefoot but already changed into a long tunic with gold threads through the creamy fabric. "Brooke," she said with some real empathy in her voice.

"Took a tumble," Brooke explained. "Just adjusting the lights." She hitched her chin toward the tree. "But . . . but I'll be fine."

"I hope so," Marilee said, her deftly plucked eyebrows drawn together in worry.

Neal scooted the offensive chair toward the couch where she was sitting and set a throw pillow on it. "Keep your ankle elevated. I'll get some ice." He set the repaired but still bloodied Joseph on the mantel and dashed to the kitchen.

As Leah surveyed the scene, Eli entered. She offered him a weak smile, then asked Brooke, "So . . . you can still go to midnight mass? Right?"

Of course not. Brooke shrugged, tried to appear disappointed. "Don't think so."

"A shame," Eli said, his brown eyes assessing, a hint of sarcasm in his words.

Neal returned with a Ziploc bag of ice and a kitchen towel. He helped her off with her boot and sock and she felt Eli's sheathed knife press against her opposite calf. "This Christmas has been a real comedy of errors," he remarked.

You don't know the half of it, Brooke thought, but just sucked in her breath as he pressed the makeshift ice bag to her ankle.

"Doesn't seem to be swelling," Neal observed.

"Not yet." Brooke adjusted the bag. "Maybe it won't if I elevate and ice."

"The RICE method," Eli said with a nod. Was that a reassuring smile? Or a smirk within his beard-shadowed jaw. "Rest. Ice. Compress. Elevate."

"I think I saw an ACE bandage upstairs." Marilee spun and flew up the stairs. Shep, still excited, chased after her. In less than a minute they both returned and she handed the elastic wrap to her father.

"Let me," Eli said and snagged the bandage from Neal's hand. "I do this for a living, you know."

Right. He was supposed to be some kind of athletic trainer.

As Leah watched her fiancé, Eli sat in the chair, lifting Brooke's leg gently and placing her heel over his thigh. He wrapped the bandage around her leg as if he'd done it a thousand times. Every time his fingertips touched her bare skin she forced herself not to react. Not to pull back. Not to show that she was repulsed. From the outside it seemed normal. Quick. Efficient. But she felt every brush of his skin on hers and once, when he glanced up at her to ask, "How's that?" she saw that his pupils had dilated slightly.

She held his gaze.

"Good. It's good."

"Then let's go," Leah said. "The ferry leaves in less than thirty minutes."

Brooke forced herself to her feet and sucked in her breath before crumpling back onto the couch. "I can't, Leah," she said as earnestly as she could.

"What? But this is important! I told you!"

Neal shook his head. "Maybe we should just—"

"No! No! We're going!" Leah was emphatic.

Neal argued, "But Brooke can't go and someone should stay with her."

"I will!" Marilee volunteered.

"No!" Leah cast a disparaging, almost disbelieving glare at her sister. "Midnight mass is what Nana would have wanted! And . . . and I need her blessing for this wedding, even if it's from the other side of the veil." Sniffing loudly, she said, "We're *all* going. Or the rest of us anyway. If Brooke can't make it, that's on her conscience." Leah motioned to the Nativity scene on the mantel with its injured Joseph, then to the cross mounted over the archway to the entry hall. "It's what Nana would have wanted."

Amen, sister, Brooke thought.

Everyone else went upstairs, ostensibly to get ready. She heard footsteps and bits of conversation. Marilee arguing that she didn't want to go. Neal placating her. Leah's higher-pitched insistence and Neal, again, this time calming his sister-in-law. Brooke thought about that, about how Neal and Leah had lied to her, had tried to manipulate her. She sensed there was a lot more going on there and wondered about all of Neal's business trips. Some to San Francisco. Some to LA. Once to Portland. As recently as September, and then he hadn't flown anywhere.

Not since Leah had met her latest soulmate in the form of Eli Stone or Gideon Ross.

Lord, what a mess.

The first person down was Eli.

"Sure you can't make it?" he asked, wandering into the living room and rubbing the back of his neck.

"Don't think so."

"Leah is disappointed."

"She'll get over it."

Marilee wandered downstairs. She glanced from Eli to her mother. "What's going on?"

"Just trying to talk your mom into joining us."

"She can't!" Marilee said almost angrily. "She's hurt."

"Yeah—I saw her fall," Eli said as he turned to Brooke. "So, what were you doing on the chair? Fiddling with the lights, is that what you said?"

Bastard. He knew! He'd seen!

"What does it matter? She fell. Probably sprained her ankle. She can't come." Rolling her eyes and shoving her hands through her hair, then adjusting her earring, Marilee said, "Can we just go already?" just as Neal and Leah returned.

"Yes, it's time. Come on, come on." Leah made a scooting motion with her fingers, and finally everyone bundled up in the front hall.

Even Eli.

Especially Eli.

Brooke waited as Neal opened the front door to the whistling wind and endless snow. "What a night," he muttered. "We'll be lucky if the ferry's running in this weather."

"It is. I checked," Leah assured him and marched into the elements.

Everyone else followed.

Eli stared through the archway at Brooke for a long moment, then pulled the door shut.

You damned psycho.

Brooke waited.

Within minutes she heard two engines starting.

Then, suddenly, right on cue, there was loud yelling, voices raised. A swear word or two audible. Car doors opening and shutting.

Neal returned and stalked into the living room. "One of the tires on Leah's car has been slashed, if you can believe that."

"What?" Brooke said, pushing herself upright, hoping to appear surprised. "Slashed? What do you mean?"

"I mean the goddamned tire's been intentionally sliced."

Leah swept in, boot heels clicking, her coat billowing behind her. "On Christmas Eve!"

Eli slid into the house as well, but he stayed in the entry hall, where he could survey the living room through the archway. Marilee skirted him, slipping through the dining area to the living room.

Leah was outraged, her cheeks burning bright. " Some little fu— jerkwad flattened my damned tire. And we don't have a spare! The car didn't come with one. Can you believe that? It's a new thing. And the company's supposed to come to your aid, like pronto, you know. You think we can get one tonight, on Christmas Eve, on this island? No!" She took a furious breath. "Or tomorrow? Do you think they'll come on Christmas Day? What are the chances? Holy fucking shit!"

She kicked at a throw pillow that had fallen to the floor. It slammed against the old rocker, setting it in motion.

"Maybe it's a sign," Marilee suggested.

"What? A *sign*?" Leah repeated, disbelieving. "Like from God? Like He's saying, 'Don't come to my house and celebrate my son's birth?' Sure! If it's a sign from anyone, it's from the devil! The same wacko who cut off Joseph's head and did God knows what else!" She threw up her arms theatrically, then slid down the edge of the fireplace to the hearth and buried her face in her hands. "I don't know what else could go wrong."

Oh, there's so much more, Brooke thought but didn't say a word. She noticed Eli's eyes narrow a bit as he stepped through the arch and into the living room.

"It'll be all right," Neal offered lamely. "We can still make the ferry if we hurry." That was true. Only twice a year, on Christmas Eve and New Year's Eve, did the ferry run this late, but they still had time.

When no one responded Neal added, "Look, we can all go in our SUV. But you," he said, looking at his wife, "you'll be stuck here without wheels."

"I think I'll survive." Would she? Not if Eli/Gideon had his way, she thought. Their last battle had been nearly to the death. And she had more she had to do. But of course, she couldn't admit to any of that, so instead she stroked the dog's head. "Shep and I will hold down the fort."

Leah drew in a long breath and found her feet again. "Okay. Fine. Let's do it!"

She was heading for the door, but as she swept out she glanced back at Brooke, her eyes clouding for a second; then she shook her head, as if dislodging a wayward thought before she marched outside. Everyone else followed and Neal shut the door behind them with a final, timber-shaking thud.

Once more Brooke waited.

Heard the SUV's engine roar to life and the crunch of tires in the driveway.

Shep looked expectantly at the door.

"Shh, boy, not yet," she said, stroking his scruffy head. Finally there was silence, and she swung her heel off the chair where it had rested and made her way to the front of the house. She peered out the window of the dining room and saw nothing but the steady falling snow.

Even the taillights of the SUV had disappeared.

"'I think we're alone now,'" she sang, but still waited, watching the Kit-Cat Klock tick off the seconds, its eyes moving back and forth, its tail swinging in rhythm.

Five minutes passed.

Then five more.

She glanced at her watch.

The ferry, if it was running, had left the island.

To be certain she slipped her phone out of her pocket and typed a group text to Neal and Marilee.

Did you make it?

A few seconds later bubbles appeared on the screen and then her husband sent back a thumbs-up emoji and Marilee replied:

Yeah. On the ferry. Brrr. Wish you were with us.

Marilee added a Mrs. Santa Claus emoji.

A blade of guilt sliced through Brooke's heart.

Had things been different she would have gone with them to the service.

Had things been different she would trust her husband and her sister.

Had things been different she never would have allowed Gideon Ross into her life.

Now it was time to get rid of him forever.

CHAPTER 38

Brooke kept the bandage on, just in case anyone returned. She hadn't really hurt herself seriously. Yeah, she'd bumped her shin and tweaked her ankle, but she knew it wasn't sprained. She'd staged the accident so she could skip mass and have time alone in the house.

With Shep curled on his bed and snoring softly, she went outside. Her fingers ached instantly from the freezing air, but she put up one last little camera, this one over the back door to take in the porch, yard, and door to the woodshed.

Once inside again she started up the stairs.

"Forgive me," she said to a picture of Nana on the landing. Her grandmother wouldn't have approved of her lying to get out of mass, especially at Christmas, but then, there were a lot of things Nana wouldn't have liked about Brooke. Maybe she'd work on all those supposed faults come the new year. That would be her resolution—if she survived.

Her leg ached a bit and her headache was threatening again, but she ignored the pain, made her way to her bedroom, and pulled out her laptop.

Hoping beyond hope that Caleb had gotten back to her, she checked her email.

She found nothing she didn't recognize.

"Come on, come on."

Time was ticking by.

She figured she had two and a half hours, maybe three at the most until the others returned.

With time ticking by she rapidly sifted through her spam folder.

Still nada.

Then she searched the guest room again, found nothing conse-quential, and left Eli's wallet under the bed, not far from where she'd found it. She decided not to tip him off yet, but deep down wished it was a dead rat. Wouldn't that be perfect? And Leah would have an ab-solute heart attack.

She kept the knife.

It had proved useful so far.

In the hallway she double-checked that her cameras were work-ing, and the images of the areas she was surveilling appeared on her phone when she accessed Clayton Electronics' security app.

All good.

Returning to her room, hearing the wind picking up and rattling the windows, she went through the footage the little spy cameras had taken and caught the fight downstairs, Leah stomping down the hallway and then, in the guest room, what appeared to be an argu-ment between her sister and Eli. There was no sound so she couldn't hear what they were discussing, but Leah was pouting. Again.

No surprise there.

But Eli looked straight into the camera's lens, as if he knew the tiny device was recording everything.

Brooke held her breath, thinking he would come over and pick up the picture frame, discover the camera, and remove it.

But he didn't.

She watched as they changed clothes.

All business, no lovey-dovey stuff. When he stripped off his shirt, then scratched the back of his neck, she saw it. The bit of ink, a tat-too covered by his longer hair. She zoomed in and the image was fuzzier, but it definitely could be the curled end of a tentacle from the octopus inked at the base of his skull. And as she zoomed in closer, she saw a scar she'd never noticed on Gideon, a small mar in the flesh of his back, where a bullet may have grazed him or gone through. Sure enough, he turned to say something to Leah and there it was. A small scar. Through and through, the bullet probably on the floor of Elliott Bay, the reason there'd been so much blood roiling in the water that horrid night.

"Gotcha." She should have felt satisfied. There was part of her proof. Instead, she was on edge, thinking of her family with him.

The rest of the footage was nonconsequential, but obviously an argument had been simmering between Eli and Leah, trouble in paradise.

Maybe she was getting wise to him.

"No way," she whispered to the empty house. Once Leah had decided on a mate she ignored every last warning sign that came her way.

The last images were of Leah and Neal in the hallway, after Marilee and Eli had gone downstairs. Again, the footage was silent, but their conversation appeared hushed, and whatever Leah said, Neal shook his head and wrapped his arms around her.

Brooke stared in stunned silence.

Neal kissed the top of Leah's head. Tenderly. His eyes closed, and when she turned and tilted her head up he kissed her on the lips.

"You damned . . ." Brooke let the sentence fade. She'd suspected Neal of cheating of course. There had been the Jennifer Adkins situation, and then he and Leah had always seemed to have some connection. She'd wondered about an affair when Marilee was very young, and although she'd thought there might be something going on, it wasn't until Gina Duquette had mentioned seeing them together that her mistrust had solidified. Still, she hadn't been really faced with proof until this tender scene.

Her stomach turned over and she told herself to let it pass for now.

"Bigger fish to fry," she said aloud, echoing her grandmother's words.

She checked the time. An hour had passed already, so she opened up her laptop, where she perused social media, first checking Leah's pages, then searching for Eli Stone and Gideon Ross, or Gideon John Ross or Eli John Stone or Gideon Eli Stone and on and on. She even added Jake to the mix; Eli had mentioned him as a brother.

Not that he couldn't have lied.

Not that none of those names, despite the information on his driver's license, might be his true identity. Fake ID's could be purchased if one had the right connections. However, in this case there were so many incarnations of the various common names that it was impossible to locate any person on the Internet that looked to be the man she knew as Gideon Ross.

A ghost.

If he'd ever existed.

"Who the hell are you?" she asked to the empty room.

The lights flickered again and she cursed her luck. She couldn't lose power now. She found her overnight bag and searched through it. No battery charger. Then she remembered Neal asking about it earlier, so he must've put it somewhere. She started to text him when the lights blinked again.

"No," she said. "No, no, no." Worse yet, her phone was about out of battery life. And where the hell was her charger? In her purse? Not by the bed. Downstairs in the kitchen?

She checked her email again, noting the time. The midnight service should be over, so they should be returning, back within a half hour or so. No new email had come in.

But when she looked into her spam folder she found a new message. The sender was a garbled mess of letters, numbers, and symbols, the letters that she nonetheless recognized as being sent from Caleb Reynolds.

Yes!

Quickly, she opened the email from Caleb Reynolds.

The message was direct:

GO TO THE POLICE!
You were right.
He's a scam artist with a complex background.
POSSIBLE MURDERER.
Call me.

An attachment was included.

She skimmed the documents he'd sent with the email and as she did, a cold fear washed over her. Not only was Eli Stone/Gideon Ross actually Elijah Jacob Rossario, known as "Ross," he was also involved in an accident near Estacada, Oregon, when he was a teenager. Everyone else in the pickup died at the scene, his parents and his brother, Gideon. However, it was suspected his parents and brother were murdered before the accident. Their wounds were more in line with a beating than with vehicle crash injuries. However, because of the mangled wreckage and bodies and ensuing fire, it was hard to determine the cause of death. Ross was the only survivor and wasn't unscathed. He'd ended up with a broken clavicle and bruised and broken ribs.

The cuts and contusions on his body were consistent with him being thrown from the vehicle, but there were questions about the rest of his family. Unfortunately, the driver of the other vehicle involved, the owner of a small logging business, died from injuries he sustained as his truck and load rolled down the same sharp ravine as did the Rossarios' extended cab pickup.

Did he slaughter his family and collect the insurance money and all their assets? Or was he a victim? Whatever the reason, no charges were ever brought against him. He lived with an aunt and uncle until he came of age and then he collected his inheritance and sailed the world on his boat, the *Medusa*.

According to records Caleb had plumbed from Las Vegas, Elijah Gideon Rossario was married to a woman named Emme Cosgrove, who supposedly traveled with him aboard his sailboat to French Polynesia. That's where her family lost touch with her.

"French Polynesia," Brooke whispered, fear sliding down her spine as she remembered the necklace she'd seen on his boat, the one she'd fingered with the fish hook made from bone. He'd seemed to tense when she touched it.

Now she knew why.

Oh. God.

Caleb included a few sparse links to news clippings about the accidents.

She skimmed them twice, then called the unfamiliar number, presumably Caleb's burner. He picked up on the first ring.

"This dude is bad news," he said before she could utter a word. "You see that, Brooke. This is serious stuff. He may have killed his entire family and his wife. He's certainly a person of interest. People around him either die or disappear, so my advice is to tell your sister to end it with him."

"What if he won't take no for an answer?"

"Then get the police involved. Hell, do it anyway. The guy's dangerous," Caleb said. "I just scratched the surface. I've only been at it a couple of hours, so who knows what more I might find? As far as I can tell he doesn't have a rap sheet, no charges have ever been filed, but that's only because he's slick. Got it?"

"Yeah." He was right.

She did get it.

Elijah Gideon Rossario, the man she'd known as Gideon Ross, the man Leah thought was Eli Stone, was deadly.

"Look, I'm sending you the only picture I could get of Emme Cosgrove."

A second later it arrived in the spam folder, again from the same garbled address.

"Got it," she said. Dreading what she'd find, she opened the attachment.

Then her heart stilled.

"Notice anything?"

She did. "Yeah," she admitted, her throat suddenly bone dry.

The woman in the photograph, a young, blond woman with bright eyes and an easy smile, looked exactly like Brooke.

"Oh my God."

In the picture Emme Cosgrove was younger than Brooke, her hair slightly darker, the wild curls the same, the high cheekbones, straight nose, and wide green eyes. And around Emme's slim neck? The very necklace Brooke had seen in the cabin of the *Medusa*. Across the bottom of the picture a single word was visible: MISSING.

Fear congealed inside her.

"I assume your sister resembles you."

"Aside from the coloring, our hair and eyes, yes," she admitted, thinking how often they'd been mistaken for each other growing up.

"I'm guessing she's in serious danger. Probably you too."

"You're right," she said to Caleb, suddenly frantic.

"So you're calling the police?"

And tell them what?

That she'd been snooping around about her sister's intended? That she'd called in a favor that could get a coworker fired? That she'd been involved with the same man and they'd had brutal, near-death struggles? That she had foolishly put everything she'd held dear at risk to have an affair with a man she'd barely known, a man who had been lying about his identity.

He's not who he says he is.

Someone else had known he was a con artist and tried to warn her when she was seeing him. Someone who knew her phone number and had access to her burner phone. That person might know more. But would they have proof?

"Did you hear me, Brooke? You're telling your sister to avoid him, right? You're going to the police."

"I think I need more evidence before I call in the authorities," she said, and she heard Caleb's unhappy sigh on the other end of the line. Just because she looked like Emme, the missing woman, wasn't enough. All her suspicions couldn't be backed up. If she had the necklace . . . maybe. But even then, she doubted there would be enough of a connection for the police to arrest him.

"Brooke, just stay away from him," Caleb insisted as the wind howled outside. "Have your sister break it off and change the locks. Who knows what he might do?"

Exactly, she thought, her blood turning to ice.

"I will."

"Promise."

"On my life."

"That's what I'm worried about, but I'm going to keep looking," Caleb said. "See what else I can find. I'll get back to you."

"Thanks," she whispered.

She thought of her family. All in one vehicle. With Elijah Rossario, suspected murderer. She had to warn them. She had to call the police. She glanced at the time. It was after one. The service was over.

She was about to text Neal when her screen lit up with a text from Marilee:

He disappeared.

Eli's not with us.

Mom, be careful.

He's not who he says he is.

CHAPTER 39

*M*arilee?

Marilee had sent the previous warning texts when she was seeing Gideon?

The messages were different, but just by a few words.

Or was it a coincidence?

Either way Brooke couldn't take a chance.

She wrote back:

I know. Stay with your dad. Go somewhere safe. Find a hotel somewhere in another town. Let me know. I love you!

She pushed send, hoping the message would go through, but her phone connection was failing. Dead. "Come on, come on," she said, shaking the thing, seeing a flicker of another message:

I told you I'd never let you go.

As soon as the words appeared they faded, the phone completely dead.

Her insides turned to jelly and she quickly used her laptop to skim through the cameras she'd set up in the house. The upper hallways and entry hall were clear. No one in the guest room. The living room camera had taken footage and her heart stopped for a beat before she realized that Shep had activated the recording.

All as it should be.

She turned to the outside camera, its tiny lens already starting to ice over. Snow distorted the view, but as she stared she thought she noticed a movement by the woodshed.

"No," she whispered as the figure appeared, dark and looming.

With a touch to the screen she enhanced the picture just as Elijah

Rossario moved to the doorway. He smiled into the camera's eye, snow collecting on his beard, his eyes dark with the night. And curled in the fingers of one gloved hand?

An axe.

Her grandfather's axe.

The one they used in the woodshed.

For a split second she couldn't move. Her breathing seemed to stop. The world spun slowly, as if off its axis. This couldn't be happening.

But it was.

She shot to her feet.

Just as the lights went out.

The rumble of the furnace died.

What?

No, no, no.

She couldn't lose power now.

But this wasn't just a blink or a flicker. This time everything went dead. Her computer was still glowing, its battery still viable, but when she tried to email, she discovered that her Wi-Fi was down.

She had no flashlight but thought it would be best if she didn't show herself. Elijah Rossario had already let her know that he was coming for her.

Were the doors locked?

So what?

He had a key. She knew that already.

She tried to dial 9-1-1, but her phone didn't respond.

You're on your own.

She couldn't stay upstairs or she'd be a sitting duck. No, she had to get out, get help, run to the nearest house, anything.

The house wasn't in total darkness; the computer screen still glowed and the dying fire downstairs illuminated the stairs and the dark hallway somewhat, casting a dim orange illumination.

Just what she needed.

Click.

Creeaak.

A downstairs door opened.

Whoosh. The wind blew inside.

The fire burned bright for a second, fed with fresh air.

Frantically, she thought. She couldn't be trapped up here. There was nowhere to hide. Even if she locked herself in the bathroom, he could break down the door.

He had an axe.

She had a knife.

Not good odds.

Shep let out a sharp bark.

What?

Then the dog started growling, and the thought of Gideon attacking Shep with the axe was too much. She ran down the stairs as she heard a yelp, then whimpering and the scrape of claws scrambling on hardwood.

"Stop!" she yelled over the whimpering. "Don't you do anything to that dog!"

And she flung herself into the living room.

Which was empty, the coals of the dying fire casting a bloodred glow.

"Shep?" she said, then more loudly, "Shep!"

She spun around, bracing herself. Where was Gideon? Where was Shep?

Her pulse was pounding, adrenaline racing through her blood.

"Shep. Come!"

At the open back door she shouted into the night, "Shep, come!" Before she noticed the impressions in the snow. Not only paw prints running off the deck and into the surrounding forest, but fresh footprints in a direct path from the woodshed to the house.

She didn't move a muscle

Shep's name froze in her throat.

No human footprints were visible.

He hadn't chased the dog.

Where was he?

Panic coursed through her.

She thought she heard the scrape of a footstep somewhere in the house behind her.

Muscles tensed, ready to spring, she slowly turned, her eyes searching the house with its eerie reddish glow. Was he standing in the umbra near the staircase? By the hutch in the dining room? In the darkness that was the kitchen?

Somewhere.

She couldn't see.

But he was here.

She knew it.

Could feel him.

She inched toward the door.

Reached down, slid the knife from its sheath.

Every nerve-ending stretched to the breaking point, she peered into the weird orange shadows.

And then she heard his voice. No longer raspy, it was as recognizable as her own.

With clarity, Gideon said, "I want my knife back."

She froze. From the corner of her eye, she saw movement in the kitchen.

"Did you hear me?" he said, leaping onto the counter, standing high above her, the axe in his hand. "I said, I want my knife back."

"And I want my life back," she said, her gaze focused on him, on the axe. His face was cast in an eerie orange glow, the blade of the axe glinting. "Leave me alone."

"Too late."

The front door was close. She just had to sprint to it, but how far could she get in this blizzard? If she screamed would anyone hear her?

"I told you I would never let you go," he warned.

"But you were going to marry Leah."

"A means to an end."

The fire popped loudly and she jumped.

Get to the door. Somehow you have to get out of here. In the house you have no chance. Get the hell out!

"So why marry her?"

"To be close to you."

"After all this time?"

"Patience," he said. "I told you once I was a patient man."

"You're a sick man," she countered, her mind spinning with ways to escape. In the meantime, though, she would keep him talking, knowing that the tiny camera in the Christmas tree was recording it all. As long as there was movement in the room. She inched closer to the door and he shifted. In one leap he could land in front of her. There wasn't time to unlatch the door and run into the night.

"How did you get here?"

"A lie about needing to go to the restroom at the church and a few dollars in the right pocket of the owner of a boat who didn't have anything better to do on Christmas Eve than ferry someone to the island. It's convenient that the church doesn't allow cell phones to be active during mass, so Leah couldn't call." Then he looked around. "And just so you know, the island isn't out of power. Just this place."

She felt sick inside. "You cut the wires?"

"Nothing so dramatic. Just threw the main power switch." He grinned, and it was pure evil.

Keep him talking. By now Neal has probably called the police. They could be on their way. Or not. She blurted out, "I found the bracelet."

"I know."

"Why? Why would you leave it here?"

If not the front door then the back. It's not locked. Get him to commit to jump one way, then feint and run out the other.

"So you wouldn't forget me."

"As if I could," she said, her fingers sweating on the knife. If she could just get close enough to him, to strip away the damned axe. "And it's more than that, Elijah," she said and saw his eyes narrow at the use of his real name. "You want to terrorize me. Just like you terrorized Emme," she threw out.

Again he flinched, this time his lips flattening against his teeth.

"I know about her, and I'm not the only one. So no matter what happens tonight, no matter what you do to me, you're already found out. It's just a matter of time. Good thing you're a patient man."

He warned, "You leave Emme out of this."

"Why, because you killed her?"

Get out. Don't goad him! Appeal to his obsession for you. Pretend that you still care for him, that breaking up with him was a mistake.

But she couldn't.

The man repulsed her.

And he wouldn't believe it anyway.

She had to find some way to escape.

After she got his confession, the proof she needed to expose him. To stop him. Her heart thundered, her neck taut, every muscle tense.

"Kill Emme?" he repeated. "Is that what you think?"

"That's what happened."

He was shaking his head. "Emme fell overboard."

"And you didn't save her? Didn't go to the police?" she challenged, so close to the fireplace that she felt the heat radiating from the coals. From the corner of her eye she saw the poker.

"No one would believe me."

"Because you murdered your family? Because the police are still trying to figure out how to prove that you killed them and staged the accident? Killing them along with the driver of the log truck, a completely innocent man?"

Brooke, why the hell are you incensing him? Why? Run! He's said enough for the police. Get out and run! Now!

"You've got it all wrong," he said, his lips barely moving, "All wrong."

"I don't think so," she said. "You already tried to kill me. I remember."

"You're the one who brought the gun," he reminded her. "I found it, you know," he said as she kept slowly moving toward the fireplace.

"I've got it."

"On your boat? Where the hell is the *Medusa?*"

"Dry dock," he said. "I'd hoped you and I would sail off on it."

"Are you kidding? After what you've done to me, to my family?" He was so nuts. And so dangerous.

"It was all a game."

"Not a game, Elijah," she said, her pulse pounding in her eardrums.

"Gideon. Call me Gideon."

"Murder is *not* a game." She reached the firebox and his eyes had followed her every move. "You're a murderer and you've been living a lie all your adult life. And the walls are closing in. And just for the record, I *never* loved you. Never. I was just unhappy and you came along and I made the worst mistake of my life. I didn't even *want* you. I was just using you to fill a void, to get back at my cheating husband," she said, realizing the truth. "I despise you." She flung herself toward the poker.

"You bitch!" He leaped, the axe raised.

Hand on the poker, she whirled, ducking his blow and slamming the iron poker over the back of his head.

Stunned, he swung wildly.

She hit him again; then, using his knife, she slashed.

The sharp blade sliced across his chest.

He roared in pain and fell backward, still clutching the axe.

Stumbling up, he swung again, but she was already out the back door and into the blizzard.

Across the deck, slipping and sliding, plowing through the snow, she headed for the forest. Her phone, deep in her pocket, was useless to call or text, but she hoped that someone could find her through the location device.

And she still had the knife and the poker.

If she could use them.

The wind was brutal, screaming through the trees and rattling the branches. Frozen limbs slapped at her or broke off, scraping at her arms and legs as she plowed on, along the narrow path, snow falling from the sky and falling from the laden branches.

He was behind her.

And he had a light.

From the corner of her eye she saw the beam bouncing along the trail she'd broken through the snow.

But he was wounded.

How severely she didn't know, but it was enough to slow him down. And she knew the island so much better than he. If she could circle around to the landing and the houses that were occupied, she might have a chance. Someone might help her. But he was close.

She heard him crashing through the undergrowth.

Run, run, run.

Up through the trees to the dunes, where frozen blades of dune grass shivered and the sea stretched out endlessly. White caps showed on the rolling dark water and the roar of the ocean pounding the shore thundered over the howling wind.

She'd lost track of Shep.

She'd seen his paw prints entering the woods, but then they'd disappeared. She couldn't think about what might have happened to him, her loyal dog. Even he was a victim to this madness, she thought

as she took note that she was leaving her own footprints. Even if she could outrun this monster, he would track her down relentlessly.

Relentless.

Obsessed.

He would follow her to the ends of the earth.

Until her fate was the same as that of Emme Cosgrove, whose body was, Brooke believed, lost somewhere in the deep sea among the islands of Polynesia.

On the beach she realized her mistake. She'd been so freaked out that she'd run out here by instinct. But on the unbroken shoreline she was an open target. Out here there was no hiding.

Except . . .

There was a place she'd gone as a child, a spot in the beach grass and brush on a dune that she and Leah had called the cave. It wasn't a cave at all but an opening in the thick Scotch broom that grew on the dunes.

Would it still be here?

Would it provide cover?

Even if she did find it, would it be a dead end where she'd be trapped?

If it worked she might be able to get away and back to the houses that were occupied. If not . . .

She wouldn't think that way.

She just had to keep running along the shoreline, her frantic mind whirling as she raced toward the northern point where the ocean crept into the bay.

"Brooke!" he yelled and she glanced back once to see him, not fifty feet behind, lagging, hauling the heavy axe with him.

Not since their last struggle on the deck of the *Medusa* had she wanted a gun, but now she would give anything for Neal's little pistol that, according to Elijah, he still had hidden on his boat.

Keep running, she told herself, angling back toward the dunes, searching for a light, any sign of life. But the few houses on this side of the island were dark. Unoccupied. Of no help.

Where was the break in the vegetation of the dunes? Where?

Did it even exist any longer?

She was breathing hard, her lungs tight from the cold.

Her blood was pumping fast.

She felt the area where she'd tweaked her ankle, but it was solid, holding her up, the pain minimal compared to the harsh, gut-wrenching fear curdling through her blood.

Run, run, run.

"Brooke!" he yelled again. "Stop!"

No way. No effin' way.

The lack of visibility made finding anything impossible, but she cut up to the dunes again and ran through the grass and clumps of Scotch broom, all covered in ice and snow. If she could outrun him and get to the main road . . .

"Brooke!"

He was so close.

She couldn't see him in the whiteout but kept running inland . . . and noticed the house. Dark and uninhabited, it rose on the dunes, a large deck stretched from sliding doors facing the ocean.

She took a chance, running across the deck, her tracks leading to the front of the house and the road, and then she slid behind a hedgerow and waited. Shivering. Squinting. Freezing. She slid the knife into the waistband of her jeans and held the poker like a base-ball bat. When he rounded the corner—

A sharp bark threw her off.

Shep?

The dog dashed toward her.

No!

With a roar, Elijah appeared, springing from the curtain of snow, the axe high over his head, blood pouring from his soaked sweater.

Brooke didn't think twice.

She rounded on him, both hands on the poker, and he went down with a thud.

The axe fell away, buried in the deep snow.

Shuddering, Brooke watched as the life slowly seeped out of him.

"You—you're mine," he whispered hoarsely, blood bubbling from his lips.

"Never," she vowed. "Never. You asked me once how far I'd go for something I wanted. Now you know."

EPILOGUE

With Shep following, Brooke finished her run through the park, crossed the street, and walked into her quiet house. She was breathless from the run, her clothes damp from the predawn fog. "Fun, huh?" she said to the dog before drying his rough coat with a towel.

As Shep drank from his water bowl, she stretched, rotated her neck, and didn't like hearing the pops as she tilted her head. She filled the coffee maker with ground beans and water, hit the Start button, and climbed the stairs to her bedroom. Hers alone.

Neal had moved out months ago. Even his office was hers now.

She ran through the shower, shampooed her hair, and rinsed her body, then pulled on a sweatshirt and yoga pants and let her hair dry naturally.

The smell of fresh-brewed coffee called to her as she headed downstairs and poured herself a cup. Cradling the warm mug, she stared at the gray dawn, the lights of Seattle visible through the rising fog, the broken fountain still a lonely sentinel in the backyard.

She hit a switch on the wall and the Christmas tree, not as tall as in previous years, sparkled with its tiny, twinkling lights glowing, the bright star on the top a shining beacon.

For better days.

For better weeks.

For better years.

The past twelve months had been a roller coaster. Neal had moved out in January, after the horrid debacle over Gideon/Eli had been put to rest. But at least the truth had come out.

Neal had confessed that he and Leah had never stopped loving each other, and the "star-crossed" aspect of the relationship had played to her sister's theatrical side. For months, even years, they would stop seeing each other, but eventually they couldn't fight their attraction or some such nonsense and would spend a hot weekend together.

Disgusting.

But she couldn't complain too much; she too had stepped out of her marriage and she'd taken up with a murderer who had died on the beach of Piper Island. At her hand. A lot had come out about the man she'd met in Pike Place Market, none of it good. The police, using the information she'd gathered while squaring off with him last Christmas along with their own investigation, assured her that most likely he'd killed his family and Emme Cosgrove, whose body had yet to be found. The authorities, both in Polynesia and the United States, were working on it, information and logs found on the *Medusa*, which had been stored in a barn in North Bend, on the Oregon coast, adding to their case.

Marilee had opted to come home.

The trauma at the cabin last Christmas had convinced her that she wanted to be close to family, so she'd returned to Allsworth, a bit of a heroine, a girl with a fascinating if horrifying story to tell. She wasn't happy that her parents were split, on the road to divorce, but she was handling it. And she wasn't exactly innocent. Marilee, always into all things technical, had admitted that she'd made the anonymous calls and texts, sending them from a burner phone Nick Paszek had helped her procure. She'd known "Gideon" wasn't on the up and up. She'd cut school on the very day Brooke met him. She'd happened on her mother at Pike Place Market and had hidden behind a fish stand because she didn't want to be caught. Then she'd seen the exchange between Gideon and Brooke and followed them. While Brooke had ignored the warning signs and done little research on him, Marilee had dug as deep as she could. Though she hadn't known him to be a murderer, she'd found out he had another identity that was soon scrubbed from the Internet, at least as far as she could check.

Marilee had discovered Brooke's burner phone in the Explorer. Rebelling, she thought she would pay her too-strict mother back with her pranking texts rather than confront Brooke face-to-face. Marilee had come to regret it.

Now, Brooke walked into the living room where she saw a picture of Nana and her mother on the back deck of the cabin. Taken years before, they were both wearing sunglasses, seated in deck chairs.

The island property was not up for sale.

Leah, Neal, and Brooke had come to an uneasy agreement. Brooke had made the decision that the place would be put into Marilee's name when she turned twenty-five. Legally, Neal had no say in what would happen to the cabin, and Leah had eagerly taken Brooke's cash offer to sell what little interest she had left in it. If the island cabin held too many traumatic memories or if she just wanted the cash, Marilee would be free to sell it.

Brooke had decided to let go.

She heard footsteps on the floor above and Marilee, in pajamas, her hair falling out of a loose ponytail, yawned on the upper landing. "Merry Christmas," she called down as Shep hurried up the steps to greet her.

"Merry Christmas."

"Dad coming over?" Marilee asked hopefully.

"Of course. In a couple of hours."

"Good."

Was it? Brooke didn't know, but she and Neal were trying to be civil to each other, even kind. They had a daughter to think of, and though it was difficult they had to tamp down their egos, frustrations, and fears and try to work things out. If it was possible. She wasn't sure.

As for his affair with Leah? It seemed to be on the rocks. Because of the lack of drama, Brooke figured. As long as Leah could play the tragic, wounded figure and hers was a star-crossed love, she was into it. When it was real life and *she* was the other woman? Not so much.

Marilee stretched. "I'll be down in a sec."

"Good."

Taking a sip of her now tepid coffee, Brooke looked at the Christmas tree with its softly twinkling lights and touched a favorite ornament, a rocking horse engraved with *Baby's First Christmas* and the year of Marilee's birth. Her heart twisted a little. There were other ornaments as well, some with pictures of their family or just Marilee or even Shep. Others had been created by Marilee's little hands in preschool and elementary school. A Styrofoam eggshell in the shape of a bell, a wooden clothespin with tiny wings to look like an angel.

Could she really let it all go?

Neal wanted a second . . . or was it third . . . or maybe thirtieth chance, but she wasn't ready.

Let him deal with Leah.

Her phone buzzed in her pocket and she saw Austin Keller's face on the screen. Then came a simple text message: **Merry Christmas.**

Her stupid heart fluttered. This hadn't been the first time they'd texted and they'd seen each other at the school. She'd felt a bit of attraction to him and told herself to forget it. A high school crush should be kept locked away in the pages of the school yearbook. And truthfully, she had so many other issues to deal with. Yet she liked his rugged good looks, his easy smile, the fact that she'd known him forever, and, most importantly, how dedicated he was to his daughter. . . .

No, she told herself. *No, no, no.* She bit her lip and stared at the screen, then wrote:

Backatcha. Merry Christmas.

Bubbles appeared, then a new message.

I was thinking? How about a drink on New Year's Eve?

Oh. Wow. It didn't seem like the smartest move.

Yet what would it hurt? Would a simple drink cause any more damage?

Impossible.

She couldn't help herself and wrote back:

Why not? How 'bout it?